# Sweet Pea
## and the
# Three Days of Darkness

DUSTIN M HESS

## Clever
# Sparrow
### PRESS

Clever Sparrow Press is the self-publishing
imprint of independent author Dustin M. Hess.
*cleversparrowpress.com*

*Cover illustration and design by Kate Lozovska*

ISBN: 9798999823007

Sometimes it may seem dark, but the absence of the light is a necessary part.

— J. Mraz
*"93 Million Miles"*

# PROLOGUE

THERE IT WAS AGAIN. Turning off her flashlight, everything went pitch black as Sweet Pea focused her almost-fifteen-year-old senses on a faint light across the swamp. Glowing at the base of a tree cluster, it flickered like a soft white fire — too fuzzy to be a flashlight, too big to be a firefly. Staring harder, her stomach lurched as the blurry dot moved quickly right to left, disappearing into the trees.

*Oh my God, someone's over there.*

Just when she was close to retaking control of this place, of maybe her life, her brain snagged a thread and started unraveling. Who in their right mind would be out here at this hour? Of all places. It didn't make sense. The safest, smartest thing to do right now was to leave — fast — go back to the road and flag down a car just like they did last time. But she couldn't let the swamp win again.

Sweet Pea whispered to herself. "As long as this pond's between us, I'm safe." Training her beam across the water one more time, she caught a face peeking out from between two trees. It jerked back into its hiding place before she got a good look.

"Looks like you're just as scared of me," she said, trying to comfort herself. "Kinda like Dad always said about spiders."

Sweet Pea turned off her light and crept around for a better angle, feeling the slightest bit less likely to be murdered than she did a few minutes ago. Pushing the boundaries of her own personal safety net — again — she snuck further along the bank, cutting the distance in half. Blasting her beam back on the tree line, she tried to catch her target in the act of repositioning, but nothing was there. She scanned left and right along the trees, up one and down another, but whoever was there must have taken cover.

Her pulse spiked. "Unless they're on the move, too — *shit!*"

Breathing heavier, she fumbled with her flashlight, firing it in every direction, desperately trying to locate the figure. She sidestepped her way back toward the fallen tree, head on a swivel, checking her back, then her front, then her back. Leaning against the upended clump of earth and mangled roots, she killed the light again and listened for any sound that wasn't made by her own self.

After a full minute of begging her lungs to relax, a splash broke the tension on the other side of the pond, drawing Sweet Pea to peek around from her hiding place. A second splash dotted the silence, followed by the loud croaking of a bullfrog.

"Dumb frogs," she muttered, turning back around — but she wasn't alone any more.

*AAAAAAAAAGH!*

Two screams erupted simultaneously, triggering a family of muskrats to run from their nest and dive into the pond. The first scream came from Sweet Pea, startled by the dark figure in front of her. The second belonged to the dark figure, who mirrored her surprise with a matching howl.

Scrambling from the scare, they collided and went down, climbing over each other in the darkness. Sweet Pea's flashlight never left her trembling hand, as she struggled to find the switch, finally lighting the chaos with a *click*.

She gasped. "What are you doing here?"

"I came over to ask you the same thing."

# 1

*Summer 1985*

---

A BEAM OF SUNLIGHT traveled ninety-three million miles just to shine on Sweet Pea Beverly. She liked how it felt on her shoulders, but she never wondered what would happen if the sun burned out someday. To a seven-year-old girl, the sun was just a big yellow circle that you drew in the top corner of your picture, right above the cotton-ball clouds and jaggy grass lines. Sometimes it wore sunglasses, but it never, ever burned out.

As a wave of summer rays drenched the Beverly's backyard, Sweet Pea ran like a hot, sweaty roller coaster, laughing with every step. You couldn't tell if it was one big, long, twenty-syllable laugh or twenty rapid-fire mini-laughs. Her big brother, Gus, was in hot pursuit, toting a pair of squirt guns and a pretty obnoxious nine-year-old smirk. He was faster — and dryer — than his little sister, staying far enough behind to give her hope, but close enough to keep her in range.

*Squirt-squirt*

The chase rumbled past a pair of rocking chairs on their back porch, where Gus and Sweet Pea's mom and dad relaxed with a front-row view. Hanging fuchsia baskets dangled overhead and potted azaleas dotted the corners of the porch — happy bursts of purples and reds to offset the white siding and black shutters. Lattice guarded the western end of the house, casting a checkerboard of shade across their laps.

Phil Beverly watched over the railing with a look of approval as his kids flew by. His thirties had been kind to him so far, still showing no signs of a beer gut or male-pattern baldness. His head moved from right to left as he followed the action, brown bottle in-hand, three swigs from empty.

*Squirt-squirt-squirt*

Liz Beverly sat at her husband's side, gabbing away on their new cordless phone. She was less interested in the squirt gun chase, giving her undivided attention to her best friend Julia's juicy story about their new jazzercise instructor. She studied her nails and played with her frayed denim shorts while they talked, only peeking up for a nanosecond when a butterfly flew past her nose. If zombies were eating her children and building towers from their bones, she wouldn't have noticed.

*Squirt-squirt-squirt-squirt*

By now, Sweet Pea was soaked. Her sopping wet ponytail had lost its bounce, with a few stray hairs stuck to her wispy cheeks. And since she was unarmed, Gus was dry as a bone, his dirty-dishwater blonde hair flopping just above his blue eyes.

"Daddy, make him stop!" she wailed from the far corner of the yard. But even as she begged for mercy, she giggled and kept running, looking over her shoulder to invite more.

"Hey Gus," called her dad, "that's enough, you win, buddy." Gus took one look at his parents, paused at the garden hose to refill his water weapons, then took off running. His father's third-party negotiations only turbocharged his primal hunger for sibling domination.

Sweet Pea took advantage of the ten precious seconds that Gus lost when he stopped to reload. She snuck around to the opposite side of the porch and nestled herself into the tall zebra grass at the base of their house. It was her go-to hiding spot, and even though she felt as invisible as Harry Houdini, it wouldn't take Sherlock Holmes to figure out where she'd disappeared to.

Gus played along, slowly circling the porch, scanning the yard for signs of prey. Guns drawn and fully loaded, he crept with a smile toward her hiding place, stopping a few steps shy of the tall grass.

"Show yourself, Pea Brain," he warned, looking for a foot, finger or strand of hair that didn't belong in the landscaping. Sweet Pea's entire butt inadvertently waved hello.

"Prepare to be exterminated," said Gus, raising both barrels of his super-soakers. "And hide somewhere better next time."

Before he could squeeze a trigger, a force hit him square in the chest, knocking him backwards and catching him so off-guard that he went down. He could barely see through the thrust of water that continued to blast him, but he was pretty sure he saw his dad standing over him, beer bottle replaced by garden hose.

The watery assault finally ended. "The young lady would like for you to stop," he said with a drawl, half-father, half-sheriff. He kept the hose trained on his son, ready to fire again like Gus had done to his sister all afternoon. Sweet Pea ran from her hiding place, dashing around her puddled brother to her statuesque father's leg.

*Wooooooo!* she celebrated, swinging her arms and basking in the thrill of being rescued from her trigger-happy sibling. Phil smiled, patting her head with one hand and protecting his mid-section with his other. He took a step toward Gus, who was still crumpled on the ground, rubbing water from his eyes.

"Sorry about that Gus, I thought you were a forest fire." Gus wasn't amused.

"I mean, sorry pal, thought I saw a scorpion crawling on your chest," he continued, drawing a gurgle from Sweet Pea, who was half-afraid to laugh at her brother's demise.

Gus was now visualizing which one of them he would pummel first.

"Okay, okay, I'll tell you why I did it." Phil leaned over, whispering just above Gus's ear. "Your mother told me to."

Gus finally looked up, *are you serious* written across his face. His dad nodded convincingly, prompting him to stand and glare in his mother's direction. She sat at the opposite end of the porch, seemingly unaware, playing the innocent bystander role to perfection. Gus processed the possibility for a few more seconds.

"Mom!" he screeched.

Liz stirred ever so slightly in her rocking chair, her big green eyes finally engaging with the family. Her natural blond hair followed the movement of her neck before stopping perfectly just above her shoulders.

"What is it, Gussy, do you have to go potty?" She had a hard time accepting that her little ones weren't little any more.

"Nope, I'm good," conceded Gus with a sideways look, realizing there was a hook inside the worm he just swallowed. "Very funny," he muttered to his dad, throwing a fake left jab at his stomach. Phil flinched a little, but in the same motion applied a friendly headlock to his son. He stopped short of giving him a noogie, but they wrestled around until nobody was angry.

"Did I miss something?" Liz asked, realizing that she, in fact, must have missed something.

"Never mind, Mom," Sweet Pea said playfully, making their way back to the porch. They were usually the players on the field, and their mom was usually the one asking *did I miss something* from the bleachers. But even though she was rarely at the center of the action, Liz always had her head in the game.

"Well, since nobody's going to share what happened with me, I guess I won't be sharing any of the ice cream sandwiches I bought this morning," she bluffed. Gus and Sweet Pea rushed inside and swung open the freezer door. Their parents followed close behind, his still-muscular arms reaching around her still-small waistline. As they all worked at opening their wrappers, Hubbard, the family dog, made his full-speed entrance.

The eighty pound Yellow Lab spun out on the kitchen tile, gathered himself, and jumped toward the open freezer door. His body slammed into the refrigerator and knocked it back a few inches. The deep *thud* was followed by wild sounds of hyperventilating and unclipped nails. He flailed around for a few seconds, legs spinning in place, then shot out of the room like his tail was on fire.

"And that's why we call him Fridge," said Gus. Sweet Pea laughed at her brother's comedic timing, which wasn't really a joke at all. Even two rounds of obedience class couldn't tame his refrigerator crashing, so the name just stuck. It was like an alarm went off in his head every time the door was opened, and the only way to turn it off was to hurtle himself into the stainless-steel appliance. They eventually got used to it, and their refrigerator had the scratches and dents to prove it.

"Finish up your snacks," Liz said, "then I want you two up to your rooms for a little bit." Sweet Pea walked to the sink to clean ice cream sandwich goo from her lips. She made a quick pass with a paper towel but missed ninety percent of it.

Gus wiped his chocolaty hands on his shirt tail. "Race you upstairs," he said, taking off around the corner. A grin swept across Sweet Pea's face as she ran after her brother. He easily reached the top first, thanks to his unsanctioned head start, then pivoted right in her face and stuck out his tongue.

"Loser!"

Sweet Pea returned the favor, sticking her black tongue out at Gus.

"Winner!"

"Ew, your tongue is disgusting," he snarled, slinking off to his room. "Go away, I'm watching Raiders."

Sweet Pea tried to think of something to one-up him before the door closed.

"You think you're Indian Joe, but you're not," she blurted.

"Wow, nice try, but the correct name would be *Indiana Jones*," smirked Gus. "J-O-N-E-S," he repeated. "We've got some lovely parting gifts for you..." Gus squinted as he spoke, making his righteousness even more nauseating.

Sweet Pea accepted her defeat with a smile. "Whatever, Pea Brain," she said, whipping her shoulder and walking to her room.

Gus laughed. "You can't call *me* Pea Brain. I call you that because of your name. Sweet *Pea*. *Pea* Brain. Get it?"

"Don't care," she said, reapproaching the conversation. "Wanna play school?" And just like that she was over it. Erased from her memory banks. Scratched from the record books. She reached for his hand but Gus pulled away.

"I'm not holding your dumb hand." His brain time-traveled to when they were younger. Helping her up the sliding board ladder.

Crossing streets on trick-or-treat night. Walking down the hall to preschool. But now, fourth graders don't hold hands with second graders.

"I guess I'll come over after the snake scene," he said, disappearing behind his bedroom door. A tiny fire warmed Sweet Pea from the inside out, as she danced to her room and plopped down on her bed with a happy sigh.

ONCE GUS REACHED HIS STOPPING POINT, he wandered over to Sweet Pea's room. They took turns saying the Pledge of Allegiance, teaching lessons to the imaginary class, and being the bad kid that got sent to the principal's office. Then they played restaurant, followed by mad scientists, and finally Barbies. Gus usually ended up playing the boy doll that kissed Barbie, but also kissed Barbie's sister when Barbie went for a drive in her convertible. Innocently enough, Sweet Pea called this game "Love Triangle," a term she learned when Julia would visit and tell her mom funny stories.

After the games wound down, Gus made his way downstairs to the spare room where Hubbard slept. He laid down beside the big fluffy dog bed, reminding him that he was a good boy with a few good pets on the head.

After Sweet Pea put her toys away, she floated down to the living room, still flying high from her afternoon dose of brotherly love.

"Hey, Pea, how was playtime?" her mom asked from the couch.

She hesitated. "Good," uttering one word when so many others were trying to come out.

Her mom pried for more. "I heard you guys doing school, did you get sent to the principal's office again?"

"Mom," started Sweet Pea, ignoring the question, "I really love Gus." She had exchanged love you's with her mom and dad every night before bed, but saying this out loud about her brother was a first.

"And I'm sure he loves you back," Liz replied, as much surprise in her voice as there was pride. "Your father and I are so glad you two have each other — even if you don't get along *all* the time." She beamed a sheepish smile and put her arm around Sweet Pea. "I love days like this when we can all just be together. You know what they say — the family that plays together, stays together."

Phil appeared out of thin air, planting a corny kiss on Liz's cheek. "Especially if you have a really pretty mom," he explained to Sweet Pea.

"Oh, Phillip," she gushed, flashing her hubby a flirty look as Sweet Pea marveled at their sappy exchange.

"So … who wants some pizza?" he proposed, instantly dissolving his romantic gesture and forfeiting any points he might have earned.

*Oh, Phillip*, she deflated.

"Pizza Hut!" begged Sweet Pea, as Liz nodded with a shrug.

"Only if it's pan," Gus interjected from a few rooms away. "I refuse to eat thin crust. It's barely pizza." He swaggered past them toward the front door. "I'll ride with Dad to pick it up." Eavesdropping was his specialty.


THE BEVERLYS SAT AROUND THE DINING ROOM TABLE, devouring pizza and breadsticks, not caring that their paper plates were drenched in grease. They laughed and ate and laughed some more until nothing was left but crust and crumbs. The day was winding down, but the summer sun wasn't ready for bed yet.

"Whoa, look outside," said Gus, staring out the front window. Phil opened the front door and everyone stepped onto the covered porch, their eyes glued to the sky.

"That's so pretty," whispered Sweet Pea to nobody in particular. Her mother and father stood in silence, taking it all in. The pale blue Pennsylvania sky jumped into deep purple on the western horizon. Cloud beds glowed hot pink, lined up in rows like a neon cornfield hanging over the valley. And sitting on the distant ridge line was a simple circle, deep orange, proud of its colorful canvas.

They felt their way to the wicker furniture without looking down. Sweet Pea sat on her dad's lap and leaned back, sprawling out her wiry arms and legs. Gus matched her position on his mom's lap as she wrapped her arms around him and hypnotized herself in the glowing sky. Nobody said a word as they drank the last drops of the setting sun. In a few minutes, the big fireball was gone, and the evening sky slowly spilled black ink over the beautiful artwork.

It was the perfect ending to a perfect day for the Beverly family. Maybe they were feeling the warmth of love and togetherness, or maybe it was just the sun drugging them with Vitamin D. Either way, Sweet Pea was convinced that Mother Nature had painted that sky just for her. Like it was the sun's way of saying *thanks for playing in my rays, today*.

Mother, father, sister and brother fell asleep with happy thoughts padding their pillows. Unfortunately, it would be a long time before any of them went to bed feeling this good again.

# 2

———

GUS WAS THE FIRST ONE UP, as usual, enjoying the solitude of the quiet house from his spot on the couch. But it wasn't long before signs of life echoed from upstairs, as a few heavy footsteps signaled his dad's imminent arrival. Phil trudged down the steps and into the kitchen on a mission for orange juice.

"Good morning, Guster," he grinned with too much energy, peeking into the living room before looking in the cupboard for his favorite glass.

"Morning," Gus mumbled, staring out the window at a robin tugging a worm from the solitude of its hole in the ground.

Phil moved his search to the dishwasher, finding his glass on the back of the top rack and holding it to the light for further inspection.

"Is the dishwasher clean? I can't tell if that's dried juice or if the glass is just cloudy."

"Don't know," said Gus, flipping on the television. It wasn't his job to know stuff like that.

After deeming the glass to be clean and ready for service, Gus's dad poured his morning OJ and walked into the living room. "Ready to help me with some work today?"

"Maybe," Gus replied, his eyes fixed on the television, a little distraught that Smurfette was trapped in Gargamel's cottage again. "What kind of work?" He was hoping for something that wouldn't make him sweaty.

"Pressure washing," said his dad, gulping down some Tropicana and releasing a loud *aaahhhhh*. "Nothing like pounding some C to get your blood jumpin'." Phil took pride in his unique ways of saying things, but no one else in the house shared his enthusiasm.

"Why can't you just say, 'Mmmm, this orange juice is good'?" reprimanded Gus. "Or maybe just drink it without making weird sounds and don't say anything at all."

"Let me explain. Pounding some C, like Vitamin C, really pounding it down, drinking it hard." Already, it was a stupid argument. "And blood jumpin' sounds like blood pumpin', but it's like a cooler way to say it." Whether or not Phil believed his own words, he took pleasure in pushing Gus's buttons.

"Freak," said Gus, having enough of the conversation. "So what are you pressure washing?"

Phil deflected the insults like a pro. "*I'm* not pressure washing anything, but *we* are doing the front siding. I just need your help with the hose and ladder." He put the juice carton back in the fridge. "I want to get out there before it gets hot, so get dressed and be ready in ten minutes." Phil waited for the complaints to ensue.

"Okay," said Gus without a fight, sending a shockwave of disbelief throughout his dad's receptors. "But when Sweet Pea gets up, I might want to play instead."

"We'll see about that," his dad said, "but you have to put in some good work first."

"Okay," replied Gus, "we'll see about that."

Father and son headed outside to get started. In order to remove anything from the garage, Phil first had to clear a path to it. Between his collection of ladders on the wall, a fleet of half-broken-down mowers and wheeled equipment at the back, and piles of junk everywhere else, it was a miracle that their two vehicles could even be parked inside.

He moved a few rakes and slid a bucket of short-handled tools out of the way to unbury the pressure washer. Reminding Gus to stay put until he moved the SUV, Phil climbed into their white Chevy Suburban, backed out of the garage and parked in the driveway.

"Can I check if Sweet Pea's up yet," Gus whined as he dragged the pressure washer from its hiding place. He'd been on the job a grand total of three minutes.

His dad ignored the request, lifting the tallest ladder from the wall and carrying it to the front yard. "I'm going to be up pretty high, so I need you to hold the ladder." He could tell that Gus wasn't listening. "Hey, this is important — I need you to pay attention."

"You know I'm only nine, right?"

Tiny pulses of agitation shot through Phil's nerves. "Gus —" he snapped, shaking his head and searching for the right words to perform an attitude adjustment. They never came, so he kept working, extending the ladder and leaning it against the house. He plugged in the pressure washer while Gus made the hose connections. "Go ahead, turn it on."

Gus pushed the power button and a loud hum sent a chip-munk scurrying.

"Alright, I'm going up," said Phil. "While I'm on the ladder, I need you to put your foot right here and keep your weight on it." He demonstrated exactly what to do. "Got it?"

Nodding up at his father, he watched him climb with spray wand in his left hand as he gripped rungs with his right. Gus kept his foot right where he was told to. Within seconds, he heard the trigger engage, saw the pressurized hose twitch, and felt a cool mist raining down as their two-story house was methodically blasted clean.

While he steadied the ladder, his mind was busy conjuring up things to do once his sister was awake. Interrupting his daydream, Phil came down the ladder, moved it over about ten feet and went up again. Lather, rinse, repeat.

"Hang in there, buddy, we're almost to the porch roof," said Phil, happy that he'd found a groove and was getting his work done. "Once I get on the roof, you can go inside for a break. I won't need you until I'm ready to climb back down."

Gus could barely hear him over the sound of the pressure washer. A nice breeze blew through the trees as Phil leaned the ladder against the porch roof, climbed up and stepped off at the top. He looked down and gave Gus a thumbs up.

Excited to be temporarily relieved of duty, Gus turned to go inside, but Sweet Pea was already coming out the front door. Her *My Little Pony* pajamas were a match to her wild mane of hair.

"Well, well, well, look what the cat dragged in," mocked Gus. "Or out, I guess."

Sweet Pea wrinkled at the greeting, failing to imagine how a cat could have pulled her around. "Let's play something," she said.

"Okay, but nothing stupid," qualified Gus, open to suggestions but only if they suited his mood.

Sweet Pea sat on the wicker chair as they went over their options. No hide-and-seek. No scooters. No freeze tag. No sidewalk chalk.

"I know," Gus said with an inventive look on his brow. "Let's play covered wagon."

Sweet Pea was always up for a new Gus game.

"I just made it up," he said, "follow me."

Gus explained the rules as he led Sweet Pea to their long, white SUV, which kind of resembled a nineteenth-century covered wagon. They opened the rear driver-side door and stepped inside, closing it behind them before climbing over the second row seat and into the back to watch for Indians. Their imaginations took over from there as they crossed rushing rivers, dodged flaming arrows, fired their guns and rolled along the plains.

"Looks like we're safe," said Sweet Pea, laying low on the carpeted floor of the cargo area, reloading her imaginary musket.

"Check again," Gus whispered.

"I just checked. It's your turn." Both kids crouched down, waiting for the other one to volunteer when they heard the driver's door open. The vehicle bounced with the weight of a new passenger, as the door slammed shut and the engine roared to life before they could blink.

The Suburban jolted backwards, launching recklessly out of the driveway then braking hard and screeching violently forward. Gus and Sweet Pea were thrown around like groceries that spilled from their bag, banging off the back cargo door with a *thump* that went unnoticed in the commotion. As the SUV sped away, the man at the wheel never looked back.

A small cloud of smoke from the spinning tires wafted toward the Beverly house. Floating up and fading into the morning sky, it drifted past Phil on the edge of the porch roof. His mouth hung open and the wand drooped at his side, standing perplexed as the tail lights of his vehicle disappeared down the road. In nine seconds flat, his Suburban had been snatched right from under his nose.

PHIL SCRAMBLED DOWN THE LADDER as fast as he could, convinced that one of two things had just happened. Either his wife had just left the house in the biggest pissed-off hurry of her life, or someone had just stolen their Suburban. He wasn't sure which scenario was worse.

Walking through the front door, he would have his answer in a matter of seconds. "Liz, you there?"

"What was that noise?" she said, a little uneasy as she entered the foyer.

"I think someone just stole the Suburban," he said in disbelief, not sure of what to do next. "Broad daylight, I can't believe it. Who steals a car at eight o'clock in the morning?" He looked out the window, then at the floor.

"What do you mean, someone stole the Suburban. Our Suburban?" Liz fretted, heading to the front window to look outside. "Have you been making the payments?"

"Yes, our Suburban, and yes, the payments are fine," he snapped, rushing to the back of the house. "Where are the kids? Let's keep them right here until we know what's going on."

Liz looked like she was trying to do long division in her head.

"The kids were with you, Phil," she said, unsure of her words. "Sweet Pea went out to play with Gus." Her voice was sharper now, spiked by an anxious rush. "They were both with you." Pace and panic were taking over.

Phil went into denial mode, storming outside to prove her wrong, almost jarring the screen door off its hinges. "Gus went inside ten minutes ago —" he yelled on his way to the garage. "They were with you!" As the words left his mouth, he realized that he never actually saw him go inside.

Spilling onto the front porch, Liz frantically pursued her husband. "I watched Sweet Pea walk out the front door, so you're telling me you never saw her?" Her eyes swept desperately left to right as she continued to blast him. "How could you not know they were out here?"

Phil rushed around the garage. "Gus! Sweet Pea!" He ran to the back yard, then back inside the house, calling their names again. It was becoming evident that something was wrong, as his brain replayed every second from every angle. How long was his back turned? Did he leave the keys in the Suburban? Why would his kids have been inside it?

Liz rushed outside, phone in hand, walking circles in the driveway, trying to calm herself enough to make the call. She fumbled it to the ground and struggled to pick it up as her brain started misfiring.

Phil stormed to his wife's side, grabbing the phone and pressing it into her open hand. Neither of them said a word as her fingers found the numbers.

"911, what's your emergency?"

She looked to her husband, waiting for him to stop the spinning of the Earth. He gazed back, helpless, motioning for her to say something. Liz formed words without realizing she was speaking. "Oh my God … oh my God…"

"Hello, Ma'am? What's your emergency?" The operator's voice pinged around her ears like she was trapped underwater.

Liz managed a deep breath. "Someone just took my children…" Her body trembled, slumping forward like a knife had plunged into her stomach.

Phil steadied his fading wife, leaning on her as much as she leaned on him, clutching hard as reality walloped them both.

# 3

—

THE WHITE SUV sped down the curvy two-lane road, rushed through an intersection and veered up the on-ramp to the interstate. Gus and Sweet Pea lay crumpled on the floor behind the second row of seats, as the speakers pumped the soft melodies of their dad's Air Supply cassette. Nobody had said a word in the few minutes since the Suburban's unauthorized transfer of ownership. Not the driver, who was sweating and nervously watching his mirrors. Not Sweet Pea, who was clutching Gus's arm so tight it left fingernail tracks. And not Gus, who was busy thinking of an escape plan.

"Exit thirty-two," the driver muttered as he passed a road marker. He drove just over the speed limit, and even signaled as he changed lanes. From the floor of the vehicle, Sweet Pea looked at Gus with wide eyes. Putting a hand on her shoulder, he gave her a reassuring nod that would have been more convincing if they hadn't just been carjacked. He noticed her quivering lip and figured tears weren't far behind, threatening the one advantage they held in their current predicament — the driver didn't know they were there.

A few miles down the road, the blinker signaled right as they left the highway and approached the bottom of the off ramp. Gus had been thinking: Politely ask the man to drop them off at the nearest Walmart? Open a door, jump out and run? Find something heavy and hit him from behind? Maybe they could just lay low, wait him out and sneak away when he got to where he was going.

Sweet Pea's thoughts were of a different variety: What if she never saw her parents again? What if she never saw Hubbard again? What was the man going to do to them?

The vehicle came to a stop at a cluster of signs. Before Gus did anything, he needed to see where they were and what he was dealing with in the driver's seat. He crawled to the window and raised his head enough to see their surroundings. Exxon station to the right. Hampton Inn to the left. He recognized the area.

The seat in front of him still blocked his view of the driver, so he squirmed a few more inches and stretched his neck out a little farther. Gus was still hidden from view, but he could finally see the man at the wheel. He was a pretty big guy, wearing a gray t-shirt and a dirty baseball hat that used to be white. Curly black hair spilled out the back of his cap and covered his neck. Gus noticed a small tattoo on his right arm — it looked like cursive writing, only a few letters, maybe somebody's name. He tried to see the guy's face, but the angle of the mirror was no help.

While Gus made strides playing detective, Sweet Pea wasn't doing so well playing the victim. She tried to signal Gus, but he was oblivious, his eyes fixed on the driver. Her muscles seized as she tried to crawl towards him. A desperate scream bubbled up in her throat, but she kept it in. The vehicle was moving again, and Sweet Pea really needed Gus — he was only three feet away, but she never felt farther from her brother.

"Gus!" she said in a loud whisper. He whipped his head and looked into his little sister's eyes. He knew instantly that she was on the verge of losing it. He mouthed the words *it's okay* but it didn't matter.

"GUS!" she said again, louder this time. She started sobbing, just a whimper, but was slowly losing control of all the little things she'd done to stay quiet. Gus scampered over to her side and pulled her face toward his chest.

"Shhhh, it's okay, it's okay," he whispered. "We have to be quiet."

The sound of a crying seven-year-old girl filled the stolen SUV. The Suburban swerved as the man in the dirty hat whipped halfway around in his seat, not seeing anybody but realizing that his clean getaway just got more complicated.

"Sonuvabitch!" He slammed his hands on the wheel and kept driving.

Gus rose from his hiding place, helping Sweet Pea off the floor so they were visible now over the second row seatback. All eyes met in the rearview mirror, and it was impossible to tell which one of them was more terrified than the others.


THREE NOTES INTO ANOTHER LOVE BALLAD, the annoyed driver switched from tape to radio, scanning the dial for something more befitting of grand theft auto. Stopping at the first sound of hard rock — and cranking the volume — the lyrics reminded him repeatedly that he was, in fact, breaking the law.

The Suburban eventually rerouted and turned onto a road

with less traffic. Driver and passengers exchanged high-strung glances every now and then, but still nobody talked. Police sirens cried in the distance, but grew quieter as they continued driving south.

The vehicle slowed as they approached a dirt road on the left, almost hidden by the remnants of an old iron furnace. It was a massive tapered structure of stone and clay, standing twenty feet high — Sweet Pea thought it looked like a pyramid with its top chopped off. A cloud of dust kicked up from the tires as they turned onto the rougher terrain, and the further they drove, Gus didn't recognize things any more.

The Suburban lurched over deep ruts, while its dirty windows offered a glimpse of a small pond on the right. Beyond a cluster of trees, it seemed to stretch into the distance. Tall reeds fringed the shore, and a massive, dead tree lay on its side, a ball of gnarled roots erupting from the ground. More than half its trunk jutted over the water, partially submerged, its skeletal branches trying to resist being pulled under. Sweet Pea took it all in, her fingers tracing invisible patterns on the glass.

Gus's brain went back into survival mode, flying through their dwindling options and desperately trying to figure something out.

"I'm scared," Sweet Pea whispered to her brother, breathing heavier.

"Don't worry, we'll be alright. He didn't know we were in the car, he's probably just going to take us to a Walmart or something now and let us go." The vehicle came to a stop at the far side of the swamp.

"This doesn't look like Walmart," Sweet Pea said as the driver got out, slamming his door and locking them inside.

He looked off in every direction, then back at the white Chevy that didn't belong to him. He stared through the glass at the two children who didn't belong to him, either. Unleashing a tirade of violent words, several of them beginning with the letter F, the man in the dirty hat stormed off to the water's edge, then back to the SUV, then over to the pond again.

"I think we should make a run for it," Gus proposed. He wanted to believe they were going to be okay, but a TV show kept creeping into his mind. One night when he was little, he had gotten out of bed and spied on his parents watching television in the living room. From his hiding place behind the couch, he learned the true story of an Ohio man who strangled his wife, drove their kids to a swamp and drowned them before setting their car on fire.

Gus was hoping for a much better outcome.

"Ready to run?" he said again, but she didn't answer.

The blank look on her face showed little faith in Gus's plan, picking up on the fear he was trying to hide from her. She was the second-fastest kid in her class, but this was no playground. She just wanted her mom and dad to show up and save the day. Or the police, or the fire department, or the army. At the very least, she wanted Gus to come up with something better than *run for it*. Then again, he was always right, so maybe he was right about this, too.

"Sweet Pea," said Gus in an effort to break his sister's trance. "PEA!" he urged, putting his hands on her shoulders, trying to unlock her brain. "Paisley, I need you to listen." Gus hadn't called his sister by her real name in years.

Her eyes darted to his.

"Nobody's gonna help us, we have to go now," he said, finally having her attention as she nodded along. Brother and sister climbed into the second row, eying the door as their hearts pounded. "I'm gonna unlock it, and when he's not looking, we're gonna run. Together."

"You have to hold my hand," her voice cracked.

Gus locked his fingers around hers. She squeezed hard, watching his eyes follow the man's movements outside, as he eventually wandered to the other side of the Suburban.

"Okay, on the count of three —" He swallowed hard. "One... Two..."

The door locks clicked open — but Gus hadn't gotten to three. The driver whipped open the opposite door, thrusting his head inside as Gus and Sweet Pea flinched away from the terrifying whites of his eyes and sharp black whiskers covering his chin and throat. Hot breath rasped through his nostrils as he pinned them with a narrow, menacing glare.

"Get out," he said firmly.

The petrified kids couldn't budge.

He opened the door the entire way and stepped back from the vehicle. "Get the hell out!" he yelled in a scarier voice. Obeying out of fear, they stepped out of the SUV and shuffled to where he pointed.

Sister and brother stood facing the swamp, no more than three feet from its edge. The driver approached, stood in front of them like he was going to say something, then walked behind them, out of sight.

"Don't turn around," he ordered.

Gus waited to feel a tire iron strike the back of his head, wondering if it would hurt or if he would just wake up somewhere else. Sweet Pea hadn't seen the scary show that Gus had seen, but her mind was conjuring its own horrifying version of what might happen next. Looking over the murky water, their backs to their SUV and the stranger who kidnapped them, they stood motionless except for the heaving of Sweat Pea's tiny shoulders. Gus was all out of plans.

Out of nowhere, a low voice materialized behind them, inches from their ears. "If either of you tell anyone about me … your parents, your friends, the cops … someone's gonna get hurt … and I know where you live."

Fear had them by the throat, now.

Then, like the part of a nightmare where you start to realize you might not die after all, they heard footsteps rushing away, followed by the opening and closing of a car door. The engine came alive and the Suburban dropped into gear, shattering the silence.

Right on cue, a large bird stirred from the rushes, half-running and half-flying from her hiding spot, quickly going airborne over the still water. Spinning tires threw dirt and stones at the backs of their legs, but they were fixated on the gorgeous blue heron soaring in front of them. Its graceful legs trailed behind, gliding past their wide eyes, skimming the surface in slow motion.

Sweet Pea marveled at the heron's effortless flight, imagining that she, too, could run to the water's edge and take off. The fear that had gripped her so tightly was loosening its hold. Taking her first real breath since their game of covered wagon was interrupted, she slowly turned around to see their SUV disappearing down the lane. She prayed she wouldn't see brake lights or a sudden U-turn, but it kept going. He wasn't coming back.

"I think we're gonna be okay," said Gus. She kept squeezing his hand, and he didn't even mind.

BROTHER AND SISTER SCANNED their desolate surroundings, trying to process what had just happened. It was like they were on another planet, stranded without a rocket ship to get them back to Earth.

"You okay?" Gus asked, noticing her pupils were still dilated.

Sweet Pea nodded, barely, staring at the dead tree in the water.

"C'mon," he said, walking back the way they came in, "let's go home."

They walked slowly along the bank, leaving the swamp behind them after a few hundred feet as the lane twisted. Gray skies and a thin fog refused to budge, and the air smelled musty and gassy like something had died. Sweet Pea waited for the sun to peek through the clouds, but it never came.

Both kids watched their feet as they walked, kicking stones that got in their path. After a few more minutes of silently pretending that everything was fine, they heard the sound of traffic up ahead.

"Almost to the road," Gus muttered, breathing a little heavier now. Finally, the dirt lane emptied onto pavement, where Gus readied himself to wave down the first passing car. Standing on the shoulder, it came and went with a blast of air that sent him backpedaling.

"Don't get hit," blurted Sweet Pea, pulling on his arm, keeping him closer to where she stood.

More than a few cars ignored them before a gold minivan finally pulled over and turned on its four-ways. Gus noticed two young kids in the back, as a woman rolled down her window. She looked like a mom.

"Do y'all need help?" she asked. "Are you lost?"

They nodded, while Gus read her face and looked over the van for any red flags. It felt safe, so he took the next step.

"Can you please give us a ride to a pay phone? We need to call our parents."

"Sure I can, sure I can," she replied, getting out to open the sliding door. "Whatever you need, don't you worry."

"I'll need a quarter, too."

She smiled. "I got you a quarter."

Gus and Sweet Pea maneuvered around two toddler seats, smiling at their binky-stuffed faces as they buckled their seatbelts in the back row. Gus thought about all the times his mother had warned him not to ride with strangers, but he was pretty sure she wouldn't mind just this once.

A few miles down the road, the woman pulled into a gas station and dug into her purse for change as Gus and Sweet Pea made their way to the phone along the side of the building.

"Let me know if y'all need help," she offered from her seat.

Gus slid the coin into the slot and dialed their home phone number. It rang once.

"Hello?!" Their dad answered like he was expecting a ransom call.

"Hey Dad," Gus said nonchalantly. Yelling and commotion erupted on the other end of the line. "Yeah, we're okay, the guy let us go…" More chatter poured through the phone. "I'm not sure where we are, though, is it okay if this lady gives us a ride home?"

Liz burst onto the call. "Gussy? Where are you! Are you okay? Is your sister with you?"

"Yep, she's with me, we're good, Mom," said Gus, motioning to the woman in the car. "Here's the lady I was telling you about. Can you give her directions to our house?" He passed the phone to the woman, who wiped a tear from her cheek and filled in the Beverlys on how she ended up with their kids.

Gus and Sweet Pea climbed back inside the van, relieved to be heading home. He sat with his shoulders back and chin up, realizing how close they were to becoming permanent fixtures at the bottom of the swamp. Sweet Pea rested her head on the side window, tapping a finger repeatedly on her knee, staring at the gray sky, hoping for one more glance of the blue heron.

# 4

*Seven years later*

---

PHIL BEVERLY DRAGGED HIS RAKE from the garage to the front yard where piled rows of grass clippings littered the lawn. He'd waited too long to mow again, so it looked like a farmer's field at harvest. For the past hour and a half, his weak little mower choked through clump after clump of too-tall grass, spewing out more work at every turn.

He stood there, surveying the land, leaning on his rake handle as he went through his cleanup options: divide the yard into four equal parts, raking the grass into the center of each quadrant to be bagged; or do it olympic swimming pool style, going one lane at a time and building up piles at the end of each column. In his mind, this was a very important decision, so he would stand here and think about it as long as he needed to.

Phil's grass raking conundrum was interrupted by a blaring car horn. He looked up to see a beat-up Honda Civic speeding past, its occupants pointing and laughing. "Rake it up!" one of them shouted as they disappeared down the road.

He turned back to the yard, ready to rake, when Liz walked out the front door. Maybe she had an opinion on which way he should do it? She walked briskly down the driveway and crossed the road to their mailbox, as Phil admired every step she took.

Leaning into his work, he tried to pop his biceps a little as he started raking one corner of the yard into a pile. He moved diligently in a circle, adding more grass to the center until the area was clear. His wife crossed the road again, up the steps of the porch, opened the door and disappeared without uttering a word or offering a glance. Phil looked up, paused for a few seconds, then kept raking.

From the second-story bedroom window overlooking the front yard, Sweet Pea watched her father, noticing everything he had stopped noticing about himself. When he stared at the ground, she counted the minutes that he lost track of. When the kids in the car mocked him, she felt the humiliation that he was oblivious to. And when her mother walked right past him, making no eye contact and saying nothing at all, she sensed the stony rejection of his sad attempts to impress her.

Sweet Pea moved away from the window and slouched onto her bed. She opened the drawer of her nightstand and pulled out a small photo album with her best mandala drawing on the cover. She couldn't remember the last time her parents had film developed, so her book of memories stopped short at age seven. But that didn't stop her from immersing herself in every photo — navigating the glare of the glossy prints, smelling the faint trace of developing chemicals, and feeling the weight of the heavy paper as she flipped through its pages.

As the sounds of yard work trickled through her window, she nestled into her pillow and opened the album. Birthday parties, trips to the zoo, Christmas mornings, beach vacations. She couldn't believe how young Gus looked in some of the photos, and how happy he was being her brother.

One page away from the last sleeve of pictures, she hesitated — knowing what lurked behind the door, but knowing she would open it anyway. There she was, standing in their backyard, clothes soaking wet, a big summer grin on her face. Gus stood behind her with squirt guns pointed to the sky, shining with invincibility.

Fourteen-year-old Sweet Pea stared into the eyes of her younger self. "Gus really got you good," she laughed, pulling the album closer, her lips almost touching it. "Whatever you do, don't play covered wagon tomorrow, okay?" She removed the picture from its sleeve and sat up, tears from both eyes landing on her pillow.

Walking to the window, she stared aimlessly at their big oak tree, its huge shadow swallowing her father. She clutched the photo and watched him finish his work: raking, piling and bagging, over and over again until their yard was back to normal. Sweet Pea slid the picture back in its sleeve and put the album back in its drawer, then rolled back onto her bed.

Staring at the swirly patterns on her ceiling, just like her dad stared at his grass piles, she thought about what could have happened that day if the man hadn't let them go. She could still see his black whiskers and smell his breath like he was right there in her room. If it weren't for Gus, it might have all gone so differently. Snapping out of her trance, she snuck across the hall to her dad's office, peeking out the window to make sure he was still outside.

The leather office chair was cold on her legs, sitting and spinning until a smile whirled across her face. After a few rotations, she grabbed the face of his desk and came to a stop, checking again to make sure the coast was clear. The contents of his desk were strictly off-limits, but she pulled out the bottom left drawer, grabbed a blue folder and opened it on her lap. "Might wanna get a lock on there," she mused.

Inside the folder hid a collection of newspaper articles, police reports, and pictures of their old Suburban crashed on its roof. Headlines strutted across the pages, dancing in front of her eyes:

**KIDNAPPING SUSPECT IN CUSTODY**
**CHILDREN UNHARMED**

**CITY MAN GUILTY: GRAND THEFT AUTO**
**FALSE IMPRISONMENT**

**HICKS SENTENCED TO 10-15 YEARS IN PRISON**

She had read them a hundred times before, hoping that one day the little girl in the articles wouldn't be her. "*Unharmed*," she scoffed. But the story never changed.

Closing the blue folder, she opened a yellow one and flipped through her drawings that her parents kept hidden away. Page after page she admired the somber lines of the dead tree in the swamp, a heron flying over water, and white vehicle with a dark figure at the wheel. There were easily a hundred pictures there, getting progressively better from front to back, starting with rough seven-year-old scenes and ending with beautiful pencil sketches of herons that could almost pass for photographs.

Before Sweet Pea could dig any deeper, a floorboard creaked and she whipped her head to the door. Her pulse jumped, but no one was there, as she hurriedly stuffed folders back into the drawer and speed-tiptoed out of the room.

From the opposite end of the hall, around the corner and out of sight, Gus stood pressed against the wall, holding his breath. The sound of Sweet Pea plopping down on her bed triggered a sigh of relief that quickly turned into a sly grin.

A FEW SPARE SLICES OF MEATLOAF slumped on the serving plate in the middle of the dining room table. The scattered remains of green beans and mashed potatoes dotted Sweet Pea's plate, but her mother was already auctioning off leftovers.

"Who wants a few more beans? I don't want to throw them away," she advertised. "Lots of vitamins and minerals here." Neither Sweet Pea or her father looked up. "How about the last scoop of potatoes?" She pushed a heaping spoonful toward Sweet Pea. "C'mon young woman, more potatoes."

Sweet Pea couldn't eat another bite. "Maybe when Gus gets back he'll want it."

Gus was at his friend Austin's house for dinner, again. When he wasn't invited, he invited himself.

"Yeah, save it for Gus," said Phil, pushing back his chair and taking his plate to the sink. "He'll wolf it down for breakfast tomorrow." He walked out of the kitchen, retired to the couch and turned on the TV.

Liz scraped plates while Sweet Pea put away the milk carton and finished clearing off the table. "Why can't Gus eat with us more," she said, returning the salt and pepper to the cupboard. "It's no fair that he always eats at Austin's. They have tacos like every night."

Her mother rinsed a large bowl and stuffed a few glasses into the top rack of the dishwasher. "He's getting older. Gus is sixteen, he likes to hang out with his friends." She squirted dish detergent into the door, latched it shut and pressed a few buttons. "You know, it might be kind of fun if you had a friend over for dinner sometime?" Sweet Pea's face flushed red. "What about Claire, she seems like a nice girl?"

Sweet Pea paused long enough to make her mother think she was actually considering it. "Yeah, maybe — I don't know."

"You can invite a friend over any time you want. You know that, right?" Liz was painfully aware that Sweet Pea didn't really have a group of friends yet. Or even one good friend, for that matter. A few kids had come and gone over the years, but nobody had ever stuck. "If you want me to call Claire's parents for you, I'd be happy to do the talking."

"No, maybe I'll just ask her in school tomorrow," Sweet Pea said, wiping the table with a wet cloth. She had no intention of asking Claire or anyone else to come over, but at least her mother would stop asking her about it.

Liz turned off the overhead light and retreated to her after-dinner spot on the couch. Sweet Pea sat at the empty table, barely noticeable in the dimly lit space, taking in the sounds of channel surfing one room over.

She heard a baseball game, somebody was trailing by two runs in the bottom of the seventh. The channel changed and she heard a woman singing a long, powerful high note, followed by wild applause from a studio audience. It changed again and she heard a man delivering news: *Scientists are calling it a solar phenomenon with the potential to darken the sky for days.* The television kept talking, but Sweet Pea stopped listening.

Hubbard, the refrigerator-obsessed dog, perked up and trotted to the front door, perking up Sweet Pea as well. "What is it, boy? Is Gussy home? Uh huh!"

The doorknob turned and in walked Gus, a big red salsa stain down the front of his shirt. "Gus!" yelled Sweet Pea, smothering him with a hug before he could take off his shoes. He quickly escaped, recoiled and rolled his eyes, but Sweet Pea persisted. "How was Austin's? What'd you guys do? Mario?"

"Holy hell, get outta my face," he said with no eye contact. Sweet Pea just smiled.

"Hey Gus," his mom called from the living room, "do you want some mashed potatoes? We have some beans here, too."

"No thanks, I had tacos." She offered him leftovers every time he missed the family meal. "Just put it in the fridge and I'll eat it for breakfast tomorrow."

Phil smirked from the couch, "Told you so." He only seemed to use his smug tone on Liz. She shot him a cold glare and stormed out of the room, leaving him to be right all by himself.

Gus popped his head into the living room just long enough to see what his parents were watching, then made a beeline for his bedroom. Sweet Pea followed, trying to get his attention before he could disappear behind his door.

"Wanna play Mario? I mean, if you didn't already with —"

"Nope, I'm good," said Gus, grabbing his Nintendo controller and powering on the game.

Sweet Pea was confused. "Thought you weren't playing?"

"I am, but not with you."

She stared at her brother through the open door, trying to figure out what she did wrong.

"I don't even have to play, I can just watch and —"

Gus slammed the door in Sweet Pea's face, pinning her nose two inches from his black and yellow DO NOT ENTER sign.

She didn't flinch a muscle, blinking back tears as the theme song played in his room. Eyes closed, she hummed along to the tune, picturing the opening sequence that she wasn't a part of. Wiping away a tear that escaped, she trudged down the stairs,

poured herself a glass of milk and joined her mother at the kitch-
en table.

Liz looked up from her magazine. "What's with the door?"
she asked. "Is he mad about something?"

"No, I was closing it and my hand slipped. I didn't feel like
hanging out." She took a swig, staring into the bottom of her glass.

"You sure you two aren't fighting again?"

"Nope. Gus loves me."

# 5

A MORNING FOG BLINDFOLDED THE SUN and put a gray filter on what everyone had hoped would be a summery day at Family Castle Amusement Park. The Beverly family had planned all week long that Saturday was park day — not that a trip to Family Castle was all that special any more. It was less than two miles from their house, so it was way more exciting for first-timers and out-of-towners.

Season passes were always on Santa's list, and just about every kid in school grew up there when they were little, and worked there when they were old enough. The Beverlys were trying to milk every last drop of the good old days, but the rides were less amusing, the food was more expensive, and the whole place was losing its magic. If you asked the park, maybe it was the Beverlys who had changed.

Arriving through the castle gate, they were greeted by the crackly sound of trumpets bellowing from aging loudspeakers.

Not so long ago, the kids would have rushed to the roller coaster line or dragged their dad to the drop tower. But Gus flew solo now, leaving Sweet Pea's fate in the hands of their parents. It's not that they didn't want to ride rides any more, but motion sickness had forced their green faces into early retirement. They approached the fountain at the center of the park and stopped to make plans.

"Okay, it's almost noon," said Phil, turning his attention to Gus. "Before you run off, this is our meeting place. No later than three o'clock."

"Yep, Austin should be here any minute."

Sweet Pea solicited her brother for the umpteenth time. "Can I hang out with you guys today?"

Gus ignored the question like a politician, then shuffled off to the other side of the fountain. "There he is, I'm outta here."

Liz shot Gus a parting scowl, then sidled up to Sweet Pea for damage control. "I've got a little surprise for you," she whispered, hoping to offset the latest in a seven-year string of letdowns.

"What kind of surprise?" Her eyes changed from a dark shade of disappointment to a lighter shade of curious.

"Well, I called Claire's mom yesterday, and they're going to meet us here."

No response. She kept up the sales pitch.

"I thought it might be fun for you to spend the day with a friend, like Gus does with Austin."

Silence. She poured it on thicker, trying some humor.

"You know, since me and your dad are *sooooo* boring."

"But I'm not really friends with her," Sweet Pea cut in. "She's in my class, but we don't really talk that much."

"I know, but this is a good way to get to know each other a little better. They're a really nice family, and she said Claire talks about you all the time." Liz wasn't above fibbing.

It wasn't that Sweet Pea didn't like Claire, she just didn't like the queasy tummy and never-ending what-ifs that took over when she met new people. What if Claire didn't even want to do this? What if they liked different rides? What if she was allergic to funnel cakes? Sweet Pea had to have a funnel cake. This whole Claire thing just wasn't a good idea.

Her mother went for the close. "So what do you think about my surprise? Awesome, right?"

"I guess," Sweet Pea bluffed, "I thought you were gonna tell me you were pregnant."

AUSTIN AND GUS MADE THEIR WAY THROUGH THE PARK, looking for kids they knew, or girls they might like to know. It wasn't very crowded, so it didn't take long to cross the midway to the games, where they sat on their favorite people-watching bench.

"So what's new Guster? Let's find you a girlfriend today."

Gus squinted, annoyed. "Dude, I don't even care."

"And that's why you don't have one, because they see *I don't care* written on your forehead. In a really bad font." Austin imagined laughter from a studio audience. "Like Papyrus. Nobody's gonna take you seriously if you write your thoughts in Papyrus."

Gus nudged Austin with an elbow aimed at ending his comedy routine.

"Ha! Burned you." Austin shifted gears. "Speaking of burns, guess what won't be burning much longer?" He didn't wait for an answer. "The freaking sun. I heard my parents talking about it yesterday. It's going to burn out or something next week."

Gus was used to Austin's exaggerations and claims that the sky was falling, so he had good reason not to think the world was ending.

"If the sun was burning out next week, I don't think people would be playing ring toss." Gus watched as a young family stepped up to the game worker just across from their bench. The parents handed over money in exchange for three red rings.

"I'm serious, Guster Ulysses Beverly," Austin babbled. "I don't remember all the details and scientific stuff, but this is for real, it's supposed to happen next week. My dad heard about it at work, then he told my mom about it when they thought I was in my room. But I wasn't — I was like five feet behind them in stealth mode, but they were like 'where is he, I think he's upstairs.' My aunt was even talking about it when she picked up her bowling ball at our house later on. Then I found some nerd's message board on our computer that explains everything."

"One question," Gus said, processing Austin's verbal hyperdrive. "Why does your aunt keep her bowling ball at your house?"

"Funny story. My uncle won't let her go bowling any more because of the guy that gives out shoes. He used to like her in high school, and now he's divorced, so he's always flirtin' around with her. You know, giving her free games and extra cheese for her soft pretzel. So she keeps her ball at our house and tells Uncle Ralph she's going to choir practice. Totally diabolical." Austin watched a cluster of ants working on a dropped ice cream cone, waiting for Gus's reaction.

"What's her average?"

"Huh?"

"Your Aunt's bowling average?"

"I don't know, she probably sucks — like a ninety-eight?" Austin slouched, realizing Gus's diversion. "Seriously man, the sun. My parents are totally freaking out, but they don't know that I know. I actually saw my mom rubbing my dad's back, telling him everything would be okay. I was thinking like, wow Dad, you're kinda wussing out. And then I was like, whoa Mom, you're kinda manning up."

As they talked, the ring toss family threw their first ring. The dad clanged one off the top of a colored glass bottle, a little too hard. Back at the bench, Austin was determined to make Gus believe him.

"Anyway, they're calling it some kind of 'solar phenomenon.' I must have heard the word *phenomenon* fifty times in the past twenty-four hours."

"Phenomenon," said Gus. "Fifty-one."

Gus joked, but this was starting to feel different than Austin's usual running of the mouth. "I'm sure it's nothing. If it were anything serious, we'd all be lining up at Cape Canaveral to catch a shuttle."

Over at the ring toss table, the mom threw their second ring. It sailed over all the bottle tops and knocked over a cup of soda that belonged to the game attendant. Gus looked on as the family shared a laugh over her bad throw.

"Alright, enough doom and gloom," Austin transitioned, "what's up with your sister?"

"Huh?"

"I don't know, you always seem like you're ready to throw her down a well if she looks at you the wrong way." Austin had best-friend rights to make brutally honest observations.

"Don't even ask." Gus's eyes were fixed on the ring toss table, where the father handed the third and final ring to his son. The boy scanned the bottles, then the prizes, then looked down at his wide-eyed little sister. He passed the ring to her outstretched hand, smiled and gave her a few pointers on how to throw it. Her tiny hand gave it a fling but it barely cleared the counter they leaned against. Clapping encouragingly, he held up his hand and gave her a big high five.

Gus stood up and walked away, turning back to Austin. "C'mon, let's go to a different bench."

Sweet Pea's mom was first to spot Claire and her parents. "Yoo hoo!" she yelled, loud enough for half the park to hear. Phil rolled his eyes while Sweet Pea's face crumpled. Liz was way more excited than they were about this rendezvous with the Wexlers. The grownups made their introductions as the girls wandered to the same general vicinity.

"Hey," said Sweet Pea.

"Hey," replied Claire, fidgeting with a Band Aid on her forearm.

After a few minutes of parent chatter, Phil handed Sweet Pea a ten from his wallet. "Why don't you and Claire go do your own thing and meet back here in an hour or two? Get some food, ride some rides, spy on some boys." He waited for laughter that never came.

As if her mom's *yoo hoo* wasn't embarrassing enough, *spying on boys* conjured a deeper shade of red. "C'mon Claire, let's go hide in the bushes and stalk some children," she quipped. "Got your binoculars?"

Phil covered his tracks. "You know what I mean. Boys your own age. And then you can talk about which ones are cute, or hot, or —"

"Phillip, please stop talking about teenage boys," Liz said, trying to restore normalcy. "Bye girls, back here by three."

Sweet Pea and Claire jaunted off, leaving four smiling parents behind. Two of them were faking smiles so their daughter saw a united front. The other two were faking smiles to hide their reactions to the teenage boy comments.

It took all the strength in Liz's body not to yell "I love you Sweetie! Have fun with your new friend!" — but she managed to control herself. She wanted so desperately for her daughter to have a good friend. Someone to be fourteen with. But ever since Covered Wagon Day, Sweet Pea only wanted to be with Gus.

The girls strolled through the half-empty park, doing their best to make conversation. "So, what do you want to ride first?" asked Sweet Pea.

"I don't care."

Sweet Pea had already been thinking. "Let's just do the Pirate Ship."

Claire gave a deferring nod as they walked in silence to the ride entrance and made their way to the back row of the ship. Neither of them said much as the ride eased into motion, barely moving at first, then quickly gaining momentum. The ship swung high, dipped low and tickled their stomachs on every pass. Sweet Pea glanced over at Claire, who looked like she was about to scream or cry or vomit — or any combination of the three. At the top of the ship's backswing, Sweet Pea looked out across the park and noticed Gus and Austin sitting on a bench way over by the ice cream stand.

"Guuuuuussss!" she yelled at the top of her lungs. The pirate ship swooped for another pass — down, up and back — as Sweet Pea waved her arms at her brother. He was deep in conversation with Austin and didn't notice.

"There's my brother!" she boomed in Claire's ear, but she was focused on the distant horizon, trying to ignore the gut-wrenching forces that pushed and pulled on her well-being.

"Guuuuuussssss!" Sweet Pea screamed again. Claire stared at a piece of gum stuck to the floor, dizzy and defeated by the mighty ship. Finally, the vessel took smaller strides as the motor wound down and the brakes brought it back to port.

The girls exited the ride and walked down the ramp. "That was so wicked," said Sweet Pea, "did you like it?"

Claire's face was slowly regaining color as she straightened her glasses. "I guess," she mumbled, desperately hoping it was their one and only voyage of the day.

"I was trying to yell at my brother. Way over on the ice cream bench, but I don't think he heard me." Sweet Pea led Claire past the carousel and flying swings as they approached the place where she had just seen Gus. The bench was empty.

"Darnit, he's gone already." They migrated toward some food booths. "You know, Gus never really hears me."

Claire twirled a lock of red hair, mustering her longest sentence of the day. "Well, he was really far away and the ride was pretty loud."

"Yeah, but I mean — not just like that. Half the time I talk to him, it's like he's not even listening. Or he is listening but doesn't care what I say." Claire got in line for a soft pretzel. "We used to do everything together, but now, he's just ... ugh. Sometimes I think he wishes he didn't have a sister. Know what I mean?"

"Uh huh," replied Claire as she licked the salt off her pretzel and coughed. The girls kept walking as the conversation moved throughout the park.

"This is so cool that we can talk about this," said Sweet Pea. "I never really get to talk to anyone about Gus. He makes me so mad sometimes."

Claire ripped off a piece and stuffed it in her mouth. "Yeah," she mumbled in between bites.

They made their way back to the bench where Gus and Austin had been. As they sat, Sweet Pea talked and Claire listened. Half an hour passed as she emptied her head about brothers who grow up, parents who argue, and what it's like to be taken by a stranger. It was a one-way conversation, but both girls were content in their roles.

"Thanks," Sweet Pea finally said.

Claire smiled, revealing a glob of chewed dough sticking to her top teeth. "For what?" she replied, trying to clean it with her tongue, not noticing Sweet Pea wiping a quick tear.

"I think you just helped me make a decision." Sweet Pea stood up and took her new friend's hand. "If Gus doesn't care about me anymore, I'll just have to *make* him care."

They walked hand-in-hand back through the park, as Claire pulled toward the food stands again. "Wanna share a funnel cake?"

Sweet Pea's brow went up just a smidge. "I thought you'd never ask."

# 6

―――

PHIL AND LIZ BEVERLY SPENT THE PAST HOUR getting to know Tom and Bonnie Wexler. They had all agreed not to follow their kids around, so they loitered near the gift shop at the park entrance. A security guard well past his prime eyed them up a few times during his rounds, but deemed them to be no threat to the public. After downing two souvenir cups each of fresh-squeezed lemonade, the Wexlers needed a restroom break, giving the Beverlys a moment alone.

"So, what do you think?" Liz asked, loaded question. She had noticed him drifting off from their conversations half a dozen times.

"What do you think I think?"

"I asked you first."

"Well, he talked about lentils for twenty minutes straight. No, Tom, I didn't know lentils were a legume." Phil cringed. "Let's just tell them we have to go let our dog out or something and sneak back at three."

"Oh, that would be great," she scoffed. "They were shooting each other looks every time you tuned out. It was so obvious. You're gonna blow this for Pea."

Phil sensed an argument brewing, and knew he could either bail out or dig in. He reached for his shovel.

"That's right, all my fault," he vented. "You invited them."

Liz pretended to read a sign on the wall, disguising their argument. "Yeah, I forgot, nothing's ever your fault."

"What do you mean by that?"

"You know."

"No, I don't." *She better not be going where I think she's going.*

Liz kept a full case of bottled up emotions from the past seven years. She reached for her bottle opener.

"Leaving keys in the ignition?"

He stormed away but came back hard like a pass rusher. "Seven years, for God's sake let it go —"

"They could've been killed, Phil, and I'm just supposed to let it go?" She was whisper-shouting, but it still came off louder than they realized. "Not one sorry from you. Ever." Her eyes glowed red. "And you wonder why I don't want to be with you any more."

"They were fine, he let them go. You're just as guilty for sending her outside behind my back. So I'll apologize when you apologize."

Their seething back-and-forth was picking up steam, each trying to out-hurt the other.

Liz elevated again. "They were *not* fine." She glanced at a group of onlookers who quickly minded their own business, then refocused on her husband. "A father is supposed to protect his children. *You* let it happen —"

"Shut the hell up," he sneered, triggering a brooding silence. It was the meanest thing he had ever said to his wife, and they both knew it.

They glowered so terribly at each other, like two married people never should. Before anything worse could happen, the Wexlers emerged from around the corner.

"Hey Beverlys ... *we're baa-aack!*"

Liz turned away, hiding tears. Phil faked some small talk, trying to hide the eight-hundred-pound gorilla that had just trampled them. But the damage was already done.

SWEET PEA WIPED POWDERED SUGAR from her mouth as the girls circled the park. Claire walked with powdered sugar all over her face, which Sweet Pea would have pointed out if she weren't busy devising a plan. She stopped and stared at each ride they passed, looking them up and down, then moving on to the next one.

"Wanna ride the Castle Cars?" Claire asked. No reply. A few minutes of awkward silence followed. "Do you wanna ride something?" she tried again, her voice inflecting more with each unanswered question.

"Hold on, I'm thinkin' about stuff."

They made three laps around the park like this — Sweet Pea deep in thought, and Claire deeply confused over her oddball behavior. As they rounded the corner into Castle Cove, Claire had had enough.

"How much longer do we have to —"

"This is it," Sweet Pea interrupted. Both girls stood in the shadow of the Turret of Terror, the park's crown jewel hundred-and-forty-foot drop tower. She whipped her head to Claire. "Okay, I need your help for this to work."

"For what to work?"

"Just do what I say, okay?" Claire was clueless. "Don't worry, it's just a little joke on Gus."

They moved closer to the safety railing at the base of the ride for a front-row view of the action. A loud *clang* startled them as the ride came alive. The drop platform lifted into a slow climb, gently hoisting a handful of riders up-up-and-away. The smiling faces had survived it before; the talking faces were convincing themselves they were going to be okay; and the blank faces were pretty sure they might die. Sweet Pea had a different look on her face.

"When I give you the signal, I want you to go find Gus and tell him that I need him right away."

"I don't understand, what are you doing?" Claire's voice quivered as her heart pumped a little faster.

The Turret of Terror climbed higher, halfway up its journey to the top. From the ground, Sweet Pea and Claire could only see dangling feet above them, as a few of the poor saps kicked nervously at the air. The platform crept closer to its peak, disappearing into the gray clouds, moments from its breakneck descent.

Sweet Pea was taking deep breaths now, like she did in gym class when they had to jump off the high dive. "On my signal ..."

"Wait, tell me what you're doing!" Claire panicked. "I don't like this."

A metallic *crunch* echoed above their heads as the release mechanism disengaged. Screams shot in all directions as weightless riders plummeted to the earth, holding their harnesses for dear life. In three seconds flat, the free fall halted like the tugging of a leash. Smiles returned as riders unstrapped, climbed out of their seats and ran down the exit ramp.

Sweet Pea grabbed Claire by the arm. "Now! GO!" She ran up the ramp, leaving Claire frozen in place.

"Wait!" Her pulse quickened but she didn't know what to do. Claire's brain thawed just enough to let her turn and run for help. At first it was a falling-forward jog, like she was afraid to get in trouble for running in the park, but a rush of adrenaline turned off the outside world. She didn't want to be part of Sweet Pea's game any more. Shaky breathing muffled her pounding heart as she picked up speed, her heavy strides slapping pavement as she scanned the crowd for her parents. Turning half around, still in a full sprint, she thought she caught a glimpse of her mom.

*Slam!*

*Whack!*

*Thud.*

Claire was flat on her back, with no idea how she got there. Her hand went to her temple as a blast of pain shot from the left side of her skull. She lifted her head just enough to survey the damage, spying red across her shirt and down her right leg. French fries were scattered everywhere, and more red caught her eye, splattered on the ground. For a nanosecond she thought it was blood, but even in her slightly concussed state, she realized it was only ketchup. Her eyes followed the trail of fries to another girl on the ground, a few feet away, holding her nose and writhing around.

A small crowd assembled as the two crash victims gathered their surroundings. Both girls sat up slowly with the help of a man in a navy blue park shirt, and just when Claire thought her day couldn't get any worse, her stomach lurched. The human bowling pin that she had just plowed over had an unfortunately familiar face.

Dawn Booker used to go to their school, a grade or two ahead of Claire and Sweet Pea, but she was shipped off to be someone else's problem a few years ago. That was around the same time she earned the nickname *Feral Dawn*, as her legend was made by attacking anyone who looked at her the wrong way — jocks, nerds, teachers, janitors, lunch ladies — even the librarian one time for shushing her. And now her bloodied face and professional wrestler physique were drawing a bead on Claire.

"Claire!" yelled an approaching voice from the crowd. Her frenzied mother rushed to her side, taking in the situation. "Honey, what happened? Are you okay?" Mr. Wexler and the Beverlys were close behind.

Feral Dawn cut their moment short. "Hey you dumb piece of shit, watch where you're going." She stood up and brushed herself off, looming over Claire like Godzilla over Tokyo. Part of a french fry hung from her eyebrow piercing, but nobody said a word.

Claire's dad stepped forward to save the day. "Whoa, young lady, you need to watch your mouth. Where are your parents?"

Emitting a non-human growl, Feral Dawn lunged at Tom Wexler, dislodging the fry from her eyebrow and drawing a gasp from the crowd. He retreated behind his wife's shoulder, an act of cowardice which seemed to satisfy his attacker for the moment.

Phil and Liz had been so concerned with Claire's condition that they forgot about their own daughter. "Claire, honey, where's Sweet Pea?" asked Liz.

A switch flipped in Claire's head and her mouth fell open. "*Sweet Pea's in trouble,*" she mumbled. "I was coming to tell you."

Liz reacted. "What do you mean? Where is she?" Flashbacks flooded her brain.

"She was getting on the drop tower, but she was acting really weird." Before she finished her sentence, Phil was sprinting across the park.

As soon as Claire had run off, Sweet Pea hurried up the Tower ramp. The worker checked her wristband and motioned her to the base of the ride, where she climbed into an empty seat. Looking straight up, she took in the view of steel beams, braces and cross-braces with an access ladder running right up the middle. *Wow, looks taller from here*, she thought.

She glanced over at the ride worker, whose back was turned, waiting for more riders. Then, just like she had practiced in her mind for the past hour, Sweet Pea made her move. Climbing up onto the safety harness, she pulled herself onto a small ledge, stepping through an opening into the shaft of the tower. Her right foot found the bottom rung of the ladder.

*Hurry-hurry-hurry — don't look over here, Mr. Ride Operator.* She climbed straight up without thinking about how many rungs she left in her wake. *Alright Gus, let's see what you think of me now.* That's all the longer it took for someone to spot her.

"Hey! Look!" A man on the ground pointed up to Sweet Pea. The tower operator spun around to see his rider climbing rung after rung, getting further and further out of reach. He ran to the controls and hit the kill switch to lock it down, radioing for help on his walkie.

*Don't look down, just get up there and Gus will do the rest.* Hand over hand she went up with the agility of a trapeze artist. *Almost there, almost there.* Sweet Pea was about seventy feet off the ground when a group of park officials arrived, calling for her to stop, barking at each other about what to do next. The higher she went, the more she started to realize that this kind of act didn't have a safety net. The adrenaline that fueled her little stunt was running on fumes.

As the rungs started looking farther apart, she was scared to let go of one to grab the next. Her left foot took a few empty lunges at a higher step, then quickly returned to its perch. She looked out across the park, searching the ground for her brother, waiting for him to save her like he did in the Suburban. And just like that day, her muscles froze and her system shut down. But this time she was clinging to a piece of steel a hundred feet above the ground.

As the shape of a fourteen-year-old girl dotted the tower's silhouette, a few guys in park shirts were ready to climb after her, but a group of managers insisted they wait for the fire company to arrive. A commanding voice broke through the bureaucracy.

"Move!" Phil ordered, pushing his way past bystanders, security guards and park workers, barely breaking stride as he reached the base of the tower. A few sets of arms held him back, as he looked up and strained to see his daughter. His eyes locked in on her body, curled up like a baby in a crib, her arms wrapped around the ladder like her favorite blanket. He ripped free from the two well-intentioned workers and jumped onto the platform of the paralyzed ride. In one swift motion, he pulled himself onto the ledge above the harnesses and swung up into the shaft.

"Hold on, Pea!" he bellowed like a man standing on the edge of the world. "I'm coming up!"

# 7

---

EYES CLOSED TIGHT, Sweet Pea wasn't sure if the tower was swaying or her head was teetering on the inside. Either way, this wasn't turning out the way she had planned. She wanted to climb back down, but her brain wasn't delivering the message to her arms and legs. Peeking down past her feet, it felt like she was dangling from a cliff in a bad dream. She heard people calling to her from the ground, their voices floating by like lost balloons. Her arms were getting shaky and muscles all over her body were starting to burn as she started to question it.

*What am I doing up here?*

Somewhere in the daze a familiar sound snuck into her head, and she tuned to the incoming frequency. It was her dad's voice, but firm and new like an action hero was playing the role of her father. Through her watery, wind-blown eyes, she looked down the ladder again and saw a shape moving in her direction.

"Keep holding on!" yelled her dad from what seemed like a

mile away. Sweet Pea's eyes glazed and her lungs forgot to breathe as everything was hitting her now.

Distant sirens carried through the air, intensifying as red lights bounced off food stand windows and electrified the shiny metal rides. A ladder truck drove through the midway, followed by a smaller firetruck, an ambulance and a news van. A long, gritty *honnnnnnk!* parted the crowd, but a cluster of trees and a few small structures blocked the rescue parade from reaching the tower. From fifty yards away, its ladder was useless. Four firemen jumped out and grabbed their gear, hustling toward the scene. "Got ourselves a jumper," one muttered to another.

Gus, Austin, Claire and the Wexlers were front row now, craning their necks like everyone else. Liz had drifted to the back of the crowd, fidgeting with the strap on her watch, unable to look. All other eyes were fixed on the two shapes that interrupted the straight lines of the tower — one stationary and one moving steadily upward.

Inside the tower shaft, Phil was twenty rungs away and closing. "I'm almost there —"

"Daddy, I feel weird."

Her left hand dropped to her side as the fingers on her right hand peeled off the ladder, loosening her bear hug. Screams shot up from the ground as her body wobbled and waned.

Ten rungs away, Phil rocketed faster toward her, oblivious to the hundred-foot height.

Sweet Pea's knees buckled, crumpling her into a crooked ball and triggering a flailing panic that somehow left her upside down and clinging to the ladder again.

Phil braced himself against a crossbeam and reached up. "Gotcha!" He grabbed her arm and climbed one more rung to support her weight, carefully turning her around and wrapping her arms around his neck.

Sweet Pea whimpered into her dad's chest, giving way to full-blown sobbing as he held her. Not one thought of Gus or Claire or the Suburban or anything from the last seven years crossed her mind as she succumbed to the relief of being rescued.

"It's okay ... you're okay," he said, starting the long climb down. After several rungs of serious silence, he went for a laugh. "You know, if you wanted to see where our car was parked, you could have just asked."

Sweet Pea didn't say anything, but a few quick snorts interrupted her sobs, just enough to let him know she was laughing on the inside.

The crowd below cheered on the heroic rescue, as father and daughter slowly descended back to earth. Firefighters and medics made sure everyone was alright, strangers gave each other high fives, the local news reporter checked her makeup, and park management slowly exhaled. Smiles were everywhere — everywhere except the pale white face of Liz Beverly.

GUS AND AUSTIN JOCKEYED FOR POSITION, waiting for Sweet Pea to make it through the crowd. "Whoa, that was intense," said Austin. "Your dad's awesome."

"Yeah," realized Gus, "and I can't believe my crazy sister just climbed the Turret of Terror."

"Maybe she took the name of the ride literally and wanted to terrify everyone."

Gus tuned out Austin and made eye contact with Sweet Pea as she approached with their dad. He wasn't sure if he should give her space, give her a lecture, or give her a hug. But all he got to give her was a passing glance as she bustled to the outstretched arms of their mother.

"*Oh, sweetie,*" said Liz, smothering her daughter with a suffocating bear hug. Phil joined in, putting one arm around his wife and pulling Gus in with his other arm. Everything had happened so fast, but it was starting to sink in, as a rush of redemption slowly poured over him.

Sweet Pea looked up and locked eyes with Gus. He felt like the kid who didn't know the answer, about to be called on by the teacher. What do you say to someone who just did something so random and reckless that you couldn't tell if it was psychotic, suicidal or just plain stupid? He should have said something nice, like *I'm so glad you're safe, or we should all hug like this more often.* But he didn't.

Feeling her stare, like she was blaming him somehow, he lashed out. "What the hell's wrong with you?"

Sweet Pea's skin bristled as his words crumpled her like a piece of paper. She ended the group hug, squaring up speechless to her brother's scowling face.

Their parents were shocked, even by his standards. "Gus!"

"It's okay, guys, he doesn't care about me." She glared harder. "Do you? Probably hoped I fell."

"Whatever, psycho, get your own life and leave me alone."

"You knew I needed you up there!"

"Whoa, hold on," said Gus, sensing a crack in her argument. "No idea what you're talking about. I didn't know you were playing King Kong until I saw everyone else running over here."

"Nice lie," mocked Sweet Pea, "Claire told you I needed you, but you never came."

"She never said a word," Gus said believably, "so you're the liar."

The crowd of nosy onlookers that had gathered and dispersed

once already, was slowly gathering again. Phil finally stepped in to break up the sibling melee. "Okay, you two, that's more than enough." He put his hands on Sweet Pea's shoulders and escorted her away from Gus, over to where Claire was standing with her parents.

Fuming mad, Sweet Pea approached her funnel-cake friend, ready to put Gus in his place. "Tell them, Claire. You told Gus to come before I even climbed up. It was all part of our plan." Sweet Pea's eyes pulsated like a possessed doll. Claire's eyebrows sunk down, realizing just how much her blown assignment had actually meant.

"Claire?" she repeated, moving in for the kill.

"We need to be going," Mrs. Wexler intervened, taking her daughter's hand and briskly walking away. Mr. Wexler scurried behind them.

Gus launched another grenade. "Well, well, well … looks like I'm right again … and you're back to zero friends."

"I HATE YOU!" erupted Sweet Pea, tears welling up again that she couldn't dare let him see right now. Whatever the level above fuming mad is, she was there. As Gus slinked away, her eyes focused on Claire, who was being hurried off like a secret service detail.

"Thanks for nothing!" she screamed across the park, her voice cracking apart. The Wexlers walked faster. "I thought you were my friend!" she wailed, her words hitting Claire's ears like long-range missiles. The Wexler family was almost running now, trying to escape the chaos behind them, already suffering a few direct hits.

Gus wandered over to his hunched over sister, his forked tongue ready for more. "Aww, poor little Pea Brain."

"Lighten up, man," said Austin, cantering in on his white horse, "that's enough." Sweet Pea looked up, completely unfamiliar with the bright light that was shining in her direction.

Gus scowled at his best friend. "Mind your own business," he said instead of punching him, brushing Austin's shoulder as he stormed off.

Phil and Liz took Sweet Pea under their wing one more time, walking her in Gus's direction but in no hurry to catch up. They all knew that another group hug was highly unlikely to occur any time soon.

Sweet Pea looked back, gave Austin a peace sign and mouthed the words *thank you*. Standing alone in the tower's long shadow, he smiled and dipped his chin in a subtle Hollywood nod. It was his first time putting Gus in his place, and he couldn't have been happier with the results.

A WOMAN WITH A *GUEST RELATIONS* BADGE approached the Beverly family, who had quietly migrated to a corner of the park where they wouldn't bother anyone.

"Hi, we're very sorry for everything that happened today, but we think it's for the best if you all just leave the park now." She spoke like the smile was painted on her face. "Okay then, follow me."

Mother, father, sister and brother were escorted to the castle gate in a walk of shame. As if their near-death experience and domestic disputes weren't enough, now they were banished from the kingdom. They trudged through the parking lot, got into their car, buckled their seatbelts and stared out their windows. The three-minute ride home loomed like a three-hour road trip, as the four occupants desperately needed some downtime.

Their vehicle rolled toward the exit, past an energetic teen in the parking booth. "Have a royal good day!" Phil resisted the urge to flip him off.

Sitting at the stop light, Liz turned on the radio to make the awkward silence less awkward. Flipping from commercial to commercial she landed on the news.

*Local officials are urging all residents to take necessary precautions for next week's impending darkness.* The light turned green but Phil didn't go. *Some experts say it's still too early to predict exactly when daylight will return.* Horns honked as their car sat still, the grownups passing worried looks back and forth. *Stay tuned to HOT97 for the latest updates on this unprecedented solar phenomenon.*

More horns blared as the light changed to yellow then red. Phil punched the gas and they lurched forward, cutting through the intersection just before the cross-traffic pulled out. As they drove the familiar stretch of road from Family Castle Amusement Park to their house, they each imagined their own version of what an "impending darkness" was.

Liz changed the station to avoid piling more drama on top of their already dramatic day. Going through the presets, she stopped when she finally heard music. Elton John took over the airwaves with a reminder that losing everything can feel like the sun's going down on you. And nobody in the car seemed to disagree.

# 8

*Arco, Idaho, 24 miles west of National Laboratory*

---

A MIDDLE-AGED MAN IN A CHECKERED SHIRT and sweater vest ordered food for his family at a burger joint on the edge of the Idaho desert. Two Atomic Burgers, one fish and chips and a chicken finger platter. Their waitress scribbled on her pad and wandered back to the kitchen.

One hour earlier, the man was wrapping up another long day at the Idaho National Lab, where he studied next generation nuclear power. Twenty-four hours before that he was explaining, for the tenth time, to another roomful of high-ranking government officials and nuclear scientists, what he discovered and how he discovered it. And one week before that, he was watching the instruments in his lab spit out some impossible but irrefutable numbers from his solar disturbance watchdog project.

The waitress returned with drinks and an inquisitive look. She talked with a New Jersey accent, but she was from Idaho. "Two iced teas and two Mello Yellos. Hey, aren't you the guy from the news?"

The man smiled politely as his wife and kids tried not to laugh. "Yep, that's me — Artie, the guy from the news." He pushed his black-frame glasses up his nose, picked up a straw and tapped it on the table a few times until the wrapper started to come off.

"So is the sun really gonna burn out?"

"Well, Cheyenne," he said, looking up from her name tag, "you're in luck, the sun is not going to burn out." He dropped his straw into his iced tea and took a big drink. "Let me try to say this in a way that won't be too confusing."

Cheyenne already looked confused.

"The sun is basically a big nuclear reactor, right, that's how it burns all the time. Well, evidently there's something passing through our part of the universe right now that's messing up the nuclear fusion reactions. Some kind of electromagnetic cloud that's throwing off the fundamental forces of physics a little bit. A weak force hiccup." Artie passed out straws to his wife and kids, while Cheyenne scribbled on her pad again. "The disturbance is low right now, but we're pretty sure it will peak next week. Then it should just move along on its happy way. But for a few days, the sun won't be able to do what it usually does. It's like it will be on low-energy mode. Do any of your lights at home have a dimmer switch?"

"Um, yeah," she said, nodding aggressively to the first thing she understood.

"Well, it's just like that. It will be like someone's dimming down the sun for a few days. It will still be burning, but not strong enough for its light to make the ninety-three-million-mile journey to Earth. Then, when the disturbance is gone, the sun can do its thing again. The dimmer switch will go back up, and day and night will be back to normal." He bypassed his straw this time and took three big gulps. "Any questions?"

Cheyenne looked at her notes:

CLOUD MAGNET

HICCUPS

DIMMER SWITCH

"Nope, got it." She gave a quick closed-lip nod and snapped back into waitress mode. "Thanks everyone, your meals will be right up." Up until now, the only thing she knew about nuclear physics was which toppings came on an Atomic Burger. For Cheyenne, and the rest of the world, that was about to change.

THE SLAMMING OF GUS'S BEDROOM DOOR announced that he wasn't in the mood to talk about his feelings. He crashed on his bed and fired up his Nintendo, still brooding from the big fight at the park. He could have punched a wall, or listened to news about solar phenomena, or plotted revenge on Austin, but his coping mechanism right now was defeating Bowser and his Koopalings.

*Slam!*

Sweet Pea's bedroom door seconded the motion. Still coming down from the day's events, she felt like a concrete helmet was strapped on her head. She sprawled on her bed and covered her face with her hair, but it couldn't mask the reality of what she had done. Her stomach had finally just settled, as she narrowly avoided her body's attempts to vomit itself back to normalcy. Nonetheless, she was left with a pounding headache as a souvenir from their trip to the park.

*I can't believe I did that.* She thought about how high the tower was. How brave her dad was. How scared her mom was. How innocent Claire was. How sweet Austin was. And how terrible her brother was. *Did I really think Gus was going to climb up the tower and rescue me? I really am a pea brain.*

Maybe it was her second brush with death or the voice she found in the aftermath — or both — but the walls in her room looked different now. Her dad had always told her that greige was a mixture of gray and beige, but she only ever saw them as gray. Now they were putting off a nice, warm beige color all around her.

She rolled over and grabbed the photo album from her drawer, flipping to the back and removing the squirt gun picture. Setting the warped, tear-stained photo on her desk, she grabbed a handful of magazines from her shelf and started flipping through the pages. Stockpiling her mom's old issues of Good Housekeeping always made her feel like a grownup, but right now she was fully embracing her adolescence. She found the ad she was looking for and cut out the face of a crying baby, just the right size. Adding a dab of glue, she plastered it right over Gus's face, laughing out loud at the finished product: Invincible Gus was reduced to a beet-faced cry-baby. Sweet Pea reveled in her creative bliss, distracting the other side of her brain that desperately wanted to know what would happen when the sun went out.

LIZ AND PHIL DIDN'T SLAM ANY DOORS, but they were both nursing open wounds from the knives they had thrown a few hours earlier. Sitting at opposite ends of the couch, they scanned all the news channels, studying the TV screen one update after another.

*Darkness is expected to cover the planet ... The solar disturbance will blacken the skies beginning Wednesday ... How long can we be without sunlight? Here's what the experts are saying...*

Phil picked at the upholstery on the cushion he sat on. "They're just saying three days, right? Not really a big deal."

"No, they said it starts Wednesday night and we won't see the sun again until Sunday morning." She pushed her eyebrows into a peak, counting on her fingers. "That's five days."

"You don't count the days on the ends, it would only be three days of darkness —"

"What if they're wrong and it doesn't come back for a few weeks? Or a month? Do you think a tsunami could reach us here?"

He rolled his eyes at the thought of a wave destroying central Pennsylvania. "People in Alaska do this all the time. They go for months without sunlight, so I think we can all handle a few days." More threads pulled away from the spot that Hubbard used to chew.

"Great, let's just build igloos and we'll all be fine," she scoffed.

He dismissed her as usual. "It's the sun. We have another five billion years before it burns out. I'm not rushing out for lamp oil and astronaut food yet. Besides, you don't want to be with me any more, so why do you care what I think?"

"True, I guess I should just *shut the hell up*," she quoted him.

The spat lumbered on for a few more minutes, as both adults continued to show off their lack of emotional intelligence. At some point, they remembered that their children's needs right now were probably more important than their own.

"So what should we do about Pea?" said Liz. "I've been telling you she's not okay, she's not okay, but you always insist she's fine." He continued obsessing over the couch cushion. "She basically tried to kill herself, Phil. We have to help her."

"So I guess me climbing up that ladder doesn't count as helping her?"

"Wow. You actually stepped up for once in your life, but now you're mad because nobody thanked you?" She stood up and walked to the edge of the room. "My hero."

"Let's just get the kids down here and talk about next week." He knew they needed to talk about more than that. "And she wasn't trying to hurt herself. She just wanted attention."

"Oh, good, you're a psychologist, too, I feel so much —"

"Gus! Sweet Pea! Get down here!" He was done with that conversation.

Brother and sister emerged from their caves, avoiding each other like two magnets facing the same direction. They occupied opposite ends of the living room and made zero eye contact as their mom and dad brought them up to speed on the latest news. New vocabulary words filled the room, like "electromagnetic cloud" and "weak force disturbance," and they learned there's more to Idaho than just potatoes. Their dad even used the dining room dimmer switch as a visual aid to his storytelling. It was Sunday evening, and starting Wednesday night, the world would experience complete darkness that would last for three days. Maybe longer. Gus looked calm. Sweet Pea not so much.

"So what if it's not back to normal when they think it will be?" she asked her dad.

"That's exactly what I said," Liz chimed in, joining sides.

"Yeah, what if they're just saying that so people don't freak out?" Sweet Pea dialed in on her dad. "What if this is, like, the end of the world or something?"

Phil turned to bad humor. "What if all the what-ifs had a what-if parade and what if nobody watched it?" Crickets. "Fine, I know it's a little scary, but it's not the end of the world. Actually, it might be kinda fun."

Gus couldn't resist. "Yeah, almost as fun as climbing a hundred-foot ladder."

Liz jumped up before another shot could be fired, grabbing her purse. "C'mon Pea, I have to run to the store. You can be my helper."

Sweet Pea hustled out the door behind her mother. "Where

are we going?"

"Just taking a little break from Gus," she said, whipping open her car door. "And your father." They buckled their belts and backed down the driveway.

Sweet Pea leaned back in her seat. "You know ... I don't even care what Gus does any more." The more she said it, the more she actually believed it.

As mother and daughter drove around town, they talked about Brenda and Dylan's breakup on Beverly Hills 90210, the jean jacket at the mall that cost too much, and taking Hubbard on more walks because he was starting to look a little plump. Eventually, the conversation turned to carjackers, amusement park rides and the end of the world. Neither of them had all the answers, and Sweet Pea couldn't articulate exactly why she did what she did at the park, but the more they talked, they both understood each other a little more.

Seven years ago, they had taken Sweet Pea to see a therapist, and then a psychiatrist, but it didn't last long. She barely talked to either of them, mostly because one of them had a "weird nose" and the other one's office "smelled like old chicken." That's all it took to derail the focus of a seven-year-old.

Liz felt guilty about not sticking with it, but she was afraid to give her tiny daughter the medications they prescribed — the list of side effects was scarier than being kidnapped again. She'd always planned to try again when Sweet Pea was older, but their car talk right now was the closest thing to therapy she'd ever had.

"Hubbard needs food, let's hit Pet Depot real quick." Liz pulled into the plaza and parked the car, putting her hand on Sweet Pea's shoulder before they got out. "One more thing — I'm sorry it didn't work out with Claire." She fumbled with the car keys, looking for the right words. "It was probably my fault, you know, for setting it up and not even telling you about it. From now on, I'll let you make your own friends. At your own speed."

"Whatever, it's fine," said Sweet Pea, briefly flashing back to her ugly goodbye at the park. "Claire's nice and everything, but she's just not my kind of girl."

# 9

---

SWEET PEA AND HER MOM walked into Pet Depot just as the manager — who had the face of a chinchilla — was locking the doors. He told them to take their time, but they still hurried toward the dog food aisle, as teenagers in untucked Pet Depot shirts rushed about their closing duties. A few puddles of urine dotted the landscape as a handful of customers browsed around for last-minute purchases.

"Darnit, they don't have it," Liz uttered at the empty space on the shelf. "I'll have to find a worker and see if they have any in the back."

"Can I go pet the kittens?"

"Sure, just don't talk to strangers, don't leave the store, and don't make eye contact with boys who are older than you." Sweet Pea's mom smiled, but she was only half joking. "Go ahead, I'll be right over."

Sweet Pea disappeared around the corner while her mom

found a worker — who strongly resembled an English Sheepdog — and sent him to look for Hubbard's food. She wandered over to the chew toys while she waited, but quickly ducked behind a turtle tank. One aisle over was Mandy Jo Dipetto, her old friend from high school who lost that title when she stole her homecoming date in tenth grade, her prom date junior year, and then tried moving in on Phil their senior year. These days, her face was plastered in makeup, her hair color wasn't fooling anyone, her jeans were too tight in the back and her shirt was too loose in the front. When she walked by the snake cages, they hid behind their rocks.

*Heaven help the poor animal that relies on her for food and water*, thought Liz, peeking around an end display of collars and leashes. She played hide and seek for a few minutes, successfully avoiding an awkward conversation or a forced hello. They hadn't spoken since high school, and she desperately wanted to keep that streak alive.

Finally, the shaggy-haired boy came walking toward her with a big bag of dog food slung over his shoulder. "Here you go, ma'am. Found one." Catching a glimpse of Mandy Jo, he threw it to the floor and bolted off in her direction, his teen-aged tongue dragging behind him.

"Gee, thanks," she said, struggling to hoist it onto her own shoulder, chalking up yet another defeat at the hands of her nemesis.

Sweet Pea never missed a chance to visit the kitten cages. They were up for adoption through the local shelter, and she always begged her mom to take one home, even though her dad was allergic. Today's tenants were two black-and-white males and one gray striped female. They slept all over each other with their faces mushed against the wall of the cage, heaving in unison. She was pretty sure the gray one was cooing.

"You guys are the sweetest," she whispered, reaching her finger in, barely grazing the top of the striped kitten's head. It twisted on its back, which led the other two to reposition their pile. Sweet Pea smiled as the black-and-white ones were closer now, scratching both their chins at once and rubbing behind their ears.

"Can I pet one?" A girl's voice interrupted her out-of-body experience. She turned around to see a girl, about her own age, with green eyes, straight black bangs and an abundance of purple eye shadow.

"Yeah, sure." As the girl tickled the gray kitten's belly, Sweet Pea noticed her combat boots, black leggings, cheetah print skirt and denim jacket. She looked down at her own t-shirt, gym shorts and sneakers and instantly felt like a kindergartner.

"I love animals," the girl said solemnly, staring at the closed eyes of the striped kitten. "Like, when I'm petting a ferret, nothing else matters."

Sweet Pea debated speaking up or staying quiet.

"It's a cat."

"I know."

"You said ferret."

"No, I said you smell like a ferret."

Sweet Pea slowly processed the joke. Or was it an insult? Maybe a threat? She worried that she was about to get shoved into the cat litter display. Trying to read the expression on the girl's face, she came up empty. Then, slow as a sloth, the green eyes turned toward her and a grin split her glossy lips.

"Just messin' with ya," she chuckled. Sweet Pea still wasn't sure. "I actually do have a ferret, but I one-hundred-percent agree with you that this thing right here is a cat. Totally messin' with you, dude."

Sweet Pea's bully alarm stopped beeping and her heartbeat went from allegro back to adagio. Her only knowledge of ferrets, according to her dad, was that they sucked the breath from little girls while they were sleeping. "What's your ferret's name?"

"Chupacabra."

"Oh," she paused, expecting her to say Gabby or Sophie or Daisy. "My dog's name is Fridge. Well, actually it's Hubbard, but we call him Fridge, too."

"My ferret's name is actually Chupacabra."

"That's different."

"Well, I asked for a pet chupacabra for Christmas one year, but my mom got me a ferret instead. Had to do it."

Sweet Pea's fascination shifted from the cats to her visitor.

The girls traded positions a few times to reach the other kittens, sharing a few *ooh's* and *aah's* when the gray one batted one of the black-and-whites in a very gentle boxing match. It tumbled backwards into the food and water dishes before springing to its paws. The kittens played in their spilled food, fighting over the water that hadn't left the bowl. Spending all their energy on a few minutes of showing off, one of the kittens stretched and yawned.

Sweet Pea pretended to yawn back at him, triggering a real yawn from the cheetah skirt girl.

"Hey, no fair," she said, catching her breath, "you triggered my yawn cortex."

"That's not even a thing," argued Sweet Pea.

"Dude, it's real."

They shared a laugh and teased the gray cat some more when a thought shot into Sweet Pea's brain: *Oh my God, I think I'm making a friend.*

The girl interrupted. "Hey, I gotta run, my mom's gonna kill me. She's about to go all '*Get your ass over here, Mindy Lou*,' you just watch." Then she called her mother a name that was strictly forbidden in the Beverly household.

"Okay, Mindy Lou."

"Ew, drop the Lou."

"Okay, just-Mindy … I'm Sweet Pea. Not my actual name, but —"

"What's your actual name?"

She cocked an eyebrow. "Chupacabra."

Mindy's laugh echoed throughout the store, as she took off running. "Later, Sweet Tea!"

Before Sweet Pea could digest her encounter, her mom came around the other end of the aisle, struggling to walk with the giant sack of kibble yoked around her neck.

"C'mon, tell the kitties goodbye." They made their way to the checkout as Sweet Pea scanned the store for Mindy but didn't see her anywhere.

"Mom, guess what I did? You'll be proud of me." She couldn't wait to brag up the new, better version of herself. She was an independent, friend-making machine. Sweet Pea 2.0.

"Hold that thought," her mother said, only half listening while they approached the cashier.

"Thirty-two ninety-nine is your total," mumbled the worker — a round-faced young woman with the likeness of a Persian cat. While Liz paid, Sweet Pea noticed a stack of flyers on the counter.

She grabbed a copy as her mom took the receipt and suplexed the dog food over her shoulder one more time. The manager unlocked the doors as they made their way to the car. Liz vented about unstocked shelves while Sweet Pea read the flyer:

## FUN-WITHOUT-THE-SUN
# PITCH-BLACK PALOOZA

**WHAT:** LIVE MUSIC, FOOD, GAMES, KIDS' AREA, PETTING ZOO & MORE!

**WHERE:** DOWNTOWN CULVER, MARKET STREET TO LINCOLN AVENUE

**WHEN:** BEGINS WEDNESDAY @ SUNSET, ENDS SATURDAY NIGHT

**WHY:** BECAUSE THE WORLD'S NOT ENDING...OR IS IT?

Climbing into their vehicle, Liz checked her makeup and re-applied some lipstick in the rearview mirror.

"So what did you want to tell me?" But before Sweet Pea could answer, her mom snapped her head to the window. "Hold that thought —" She glared across the lot, where Mandy Jo emerged from between a row of cars.

"Who's that?"

"Mandy Jo Dipetto. We went to school together." The stake-out continued. "God sakes, you're not twenty any more." They watched her strut across the parking lot. "And locking your baby in the car while you hit the bars doesn't count as parenting."

Mandy Jo got closer to their car but veered off to a different row. "And would you look at that … looks like her baby's not a baby any more." Rushing behind her to catch up was her teenage daughter, wearing a cheetah skirt, too much eye shadow and a denim jacket. "Apple doesn't fall far," said Liz, shaking her head with some twisted sense of enjoyment. "So help me Sweet Pea, you'd better never think of going down that path, young lady."

Sweet Pea didn't say anything, not knowing which path was which any more. The Dipetto ladies got into their car and disappeared out of sight.

"Anyway, what did you want to tell me?" She shifted the car into reverse. "What's gonna make me proud?"

Sweet Pea called an audible. "Oh yeah. I let one of the kittens chew on my finger tonight. You know how I always used to be afraid it would hurt? Welp, not any more." The lie came out easier than she thought it would. But compared to the truth — I just made friends with the daughter of your sleazy arch enemy — there were far less consequences.

As they drove home, Sweet Pea stared out her window at storefronts and passing cars. For someone who just lied to her mother's face, she didn't feel guilty at all. She was way more bothered that she had just pretended not to know Mindy.

# 10

---

G US AND HIS DAD SAT IN SILENCE after the girls left. Neither of them wanted to talk about the park, and their brains were too fried to care about the darkness right now. Gus stared at the television for twenty minutes without realizing it was the shopping channel's Sunday evening special on ladies' watches.

Phil was no better. He was lost in a crossword puzzle, struggling to think of a nine-letter word for *not dealing with things*. Father and son were running out of ways to avoid the real topics much longer, but Gus was determined to keep the nothingness going.

He raised his left eyebrow. "Wanna go for a hundred?" His dad looked up from the newspaper, calmly folded it and placed it on an end table.

"I absolutely do," he said with a rise, realizing that his son's idea was exactly what they needed. "We have enough daylight if we go now."

They emptied into their backyard along with Hubbard, taking a quick detour through the garage to grab a frisbee. They weren't big on sports that ended in the word *ball*, but the challenge of catching one hundred frisbee throws without a drop got their blood pumping.

Their yard was perfect for frisbee. Long and straight on one side, with a pair of young trees on the other side as obstacles for angled throws. The only problem was the family's lack of dedication to pooper scooper duties. As a result, a dozen or so organic landmines were half-buried in the tall grass on any given day. One wrong step and you wouldn't care whether you caught the frisbee or not.

"You need to stretch first?" asked Gus, walking off enough distance between them to make it interesting.

"I'm good. You act like I'm ninety."

"Well it's been a while since we did the hundred."

He gave his hamstrings a secret stretching when Gus wasn't looking. "Fire when ready, grasshopper."

Gus flung the disc straight as an arrow, perfectly level to the ground, right into his dad's waiting hand. "One."

"I remember teaching you how to throw when you were five," said Phil, sailing it back across the yard. "The good old days."

"Back when you and Mom still liked each other." There was no filter between his brain and mouth. Gus tossed the frisbee back at a high angle, throwing it far right and watching it drift left, landing precisely in his dad's waiting hand.

"We still love each other, Gus." He was defensive but not angry.

"Yeah, but you don't seem to *like* each other very much." The frisbee came back at Gus like a laser, his right hand shooting up to make a clean catch in front of his face.

"You know, I really just wanted to throw the frisbee with you.

Just frisbee." It flew at a pretty good pace while each player pondered what to say next. Their serious faces looked like they were tossing a hand grenade back and forth. Thirty-five. Thirty-six. Thirty-seven.

Gus broke the silence, digging in deeper and still refusing to take the high road. "Maybe that's part of the problem," he said, reaching high for catch number thirty-eight. "You always avoid stuff." He flung the frisbee high and straight so it peaked about twenty feet above his dad's head, before floating slowly back down like a U.F.O. into an easy two-handed catch.

"Great, my sixteen-year-old son thinks he's my therapist." Phil whipped the disc back hard. "Maybe you should work on your own mouth … and being kinder to your sister."

Forty. Back again for forty-one. Forty-two.

The frisbee kept flying, barely pausing in between catches before launching on returns. Neither of them wanted to push the envelope much further, content with the stopping place of their brief but poignant exchange. Dropping the frisbee would be like losing the argument.

Had there been a camera crew in the yard, they would have captured some amazing footage for the highlight reel. Jumping catches. Running saves. High archers that looked like they'd never come down. Father and son were focused on the hundred, but the longer they said nothing, the more Gus's accusations were eating away at his dad.

*If I would've said anything like that to my dad, I would've been tarred and feathered.* But what bothered him even more was that Gus was right.

"Eighty-eight!" Gus announced with spunk. The late summer sun had already sunk behind the tree line, so the last dozen throws would be made in the yellowing leftovers of the day. Hubbard snoozed on the porch, having long since given up any hope of snatching a dropped frisbee.

Phil racked his brain, thinking about all the things he'd been avoiding in his life. He barely noticed number eighty-nine leaving Gus's hand, but he nabbed it a few inches from the ground. Flinging it back half-heartedly, the frisbee barely stayed airborne. Gus charged the short throw and snagged it just before it caught dirt.

"What was that?!" he blurted out, questioning his dad's distracted toss. Turning around and walking back, he flicked his wrist in frustration, putting some extra mustard on a line-drive return. Phil backpedaled to haul it in, sidestepping a small pile of brown stuff. More frisbees flew as he reached a point in his mind — he was ready to answer the bell that Gus had rung fifty throws earlier.

"Okay, here's something I've been avoiding," he said, releasing a perfect curve around the nearest tree. Gus trotted to his left, safely cradling number ninety-seven. "There's something I need to tell you."

They stared at each other from across the yard, both realizing that the other was serious. "I got a letter from the courthouse last week."

Gus was caught off-guard, his mind instantly filling in blanks. Had to be a divorce, it wouldn't really shock him, this must be "the talk." What else could it be — didn't pay their taxes? He threw the frisbee back without realizing it left his hand. Ninety-eight.

"I don't want your mother and sister to know about this," Phil deadpanned. "Can you keep a secret?" His question floated across the yard along with frisbee number ninety-nine.

It came in waist-high, no wobble, and Gus clamped down with both hands as it hit his palms. So much for his divorce theory — whatever this was it required a pact of secrecy.

"Okay, yeah, what'd it say?"

Phil finally spit it out, his words piercing the dusk. "Hicks is getting out of prison tomorrow."

Gus's heart catapulted into his throat. He whipped the frisbee — the one hundredth frisbee — in a wounded duck delivery that crash-landed nowhere near its intended receiver. A clump of dirt and a few blades of grass flew up from the wreckage.

Phil walked toward his son, stepping over the frisbee like it wasn't even there. Gus wasn't there either, flashing back to 1985 — the whiskery throat, his hot breath, the threat he'd made if they told. In a split second, Bruce Hicks was back like it was yesterday.

"What happened to ten to fifteen?"

"Sorry, Gus, he went informant, ratted out his old boss and got some kind of deal. You okay?"

Gus knew exactly why his dad didn't want the girls to know. The Beverly family didn't need any more hurt or hysterics right now, especially Sweet Pea. That's "what the hell was wrong with her," even though he never cut her any slack for it. Keeping this quiet right now was for everyone's own good.

Father and son stood three feet apart, surrounded by a yard full of dog shit and a belly-up frisbee. Gus looked up at his dad with newfound respect. "I won't tell Mom if you don't tell Sweet Pea."


THE FIRST STARS PEEKED OUT from their hiding places, helping the night sky change into its pajamas. The moon hadn't shown its face yet, but when it did, it would carry a quizzical look above the Beverly house tonight. The evening appeared calm and quiet, but a blanket of anxiety was settling over Culver.

The garage door opener sprang to life, vibrating the art on the adjoining living room wall as the door hummed along its tracks.

From opposite ends of the couch, Gus and his dad sent and received gestures to keep their backyard pact under wraps until the time was right. They had spent the last twenty minutes convincing each other they were doing the right thing, and now that the girls were home, it was time to act like everything was fine. Hubbard met them at the front door, drawn by the rustling of the dog food bag.

"Hey Liz, hey Pea," said Phil from the couch, trying a little too hard to sound normal.

"Hey," said Sweet Pea, representing the only reply from around the corner.

As soon as their shoes were off, they went straight upstairs without a word. Sweet Pea immediately started her bedtime routine, happy to avoid her brother. Her mom followed suit, happy to avoid her husband. The men stayed put, happy to avoid any potential situation where they might have to cover up their clandestine conversation.

They turned their ears to the ceiling, surveilling the soundscape of the nightly bedtime routines. Running water. Flushing toilets. Footsteps. Light switches, and eventually, bedsprings. Once the coast was clear, they tiptoed upstairs, taking their turns in the house's only bathroom and getting themselves ready for bed.

Phil poked his head into Gus's room. "Night, buddy."

"Night."

He checked to make sure Liz's door was closed across the hall, then whispered to Gus. "Secret mission tomorrow."

"Yeah, shouldn't we have code names or something?"

"*Shhhh…*"

"You brought it up."

"Whatever. Goodnight." Phil closed his door and took ten steps down the hall to Sweet Pea's room. He tiptoed inside, making his way to her bedside where the nightlight's glow fell on her closed eyelids.

"Goodnight, honey," he whispered, softly kissing the top of her head.

"Goodnight," she whispered back, "I'm not sleepin' yet."

He wanted to comfort his daughter, but he didn't want to re-hash all the bad parts of their day right before bed. Maybe she had a good evening with her mother and wasn't even worrying about things right now.

"Love you," he said, "we'll have a good day tomorrow." He rubbed her shoulder and slowly backed out of her room, happy with his choice of words.

Sweet Pea kept her eyes closed, trying to think about having a good day, but all she could think of was the dying sun and the view from the tower she'd climbed. She wanted to picture some-thing happy to help her fall asleep, but Gus's face kept popping up and ruining it. Her consciousness finally drifted and started telling her a story, unfolding a surreal landscape behind her eyes.

Mallory Park, her favorite playground when she was little, was transformed into a desolate, frozen wasteland. A thick, oppressive fog hung low, casting an eerie blue pall over the scene. The green grass had withered into a dull, gray dust, and the once rippling pond was iced over like shiny black glass. Leafless, colorless trees with bare, brittle branches hung over park benches and swingsets, their cold steel masked in frost.

A small group of people huddled at the water's edge, looking all around the park for something that wasn't there. The group kept multiplying, spawning more people, shoulder to shoulder as far as she could see. Among them, a girl ventured onto the frozen pond, her footsteps echoing in the chilling silence. Carefully nav-igating cracks in the ice, she reached the center, where a cast iron hand pump jutted up through the surface.

Grasping its long, frozen handle, determined to thaw the park's frozen heart, she could barely move it. Repositioning her weight to try again, a resounding crack shattered the ice beneath her feet. She plunged into the manhole-sized opening, thrusting her arms out and clinging to the edge to avoid going under.

A man rushed to her aid, running onto the ice as their eyes met. "Keep holding on! I'm almost there!" he yelled, but another crack gave way, plunging him into the icy depths as he disappeared from sight. A guy that looked like Gus watched with a cruel smirk from the edge of the lake, a bag of popcorn clutched in his hand.

The trapped girl sank deeper every time she moved. From above the dream, Sweet Pea closed her eyes tighter, wishing the girl to safety, but when she opened them, she found herself immersed in the nightmare — literally — as she was the one stuck in the lake, now. The chilling cold was paralyzing her limbs, slowing her breathing, consuming her thoughts. Everything was more real now as the line blurred between dream and reality.

*It's just a dream ... I know it is ... c'mon, wake up...*

A sudden burst of color entered her vision, as a gorgeous cheetah emerged from the fog, sauntering through the crowd with its golden coat and piercing black spots. Mesmerizing green eyes scanned the frozen world, as the big cat glided over the lake like a hovercraft, barely touching the surface as it approached Sweet Pea.

She started to panic as it prowled, toying with her hope of being rescued and her fear of being eaten. Face to face, the cheetah stared her down while curling its tail around her arms, pulling tight like a lasso. Whisking her up and out, shards of ice flew across the lake as it drew her closer and parted its lips. She waited to feel the snap of its jaws, but when it opened its mouth, words came out.

"I'm totally messin' with you, dude."

Placing her down on a safe patch of ice, the cheetah felt a little more human, and Sweet Pea felt a little more animal. It slinked toward the frozen handle, coiled its tail again and started pumping. Golden sparks shot out like Sweet Pea's favorite "glowing spaghetti" fireworks, as energy surged from the center of the lake. It kept working the handle, building more power, lifting the thinning fog with each motion. From the east, faint colors of a summer sunrise crept into the park, breathing a warm new gradient into the sky.

A sudden blast of heat went off like a bomb, its shockwave knocking Sweet Pea backwards as she shielded her face. When she opened her eyes, she was standing ankle deep in crystal clear water, not far from the man who had tried to save her. He was soaked from head to toe, sitting upright, locked in a staring contest with Gus on the bank.

Grass sprouted from the park grounds and leaves grew on the naked trees like a time-lapse video. The lush park was back in seconds, birds were chirping, and the people went about their business like nothing had ever happened. Gus turned and walked away, head hung low, tossing his empty box onto the ground and spilling the last few kernels.

The green-eyed cheetah pounced through the shallow pond, splashing around like an untamed beast, before circling its wild rumpus back in Sweet Pea's direction. She watched in slow motion as it flew low like a heron, legs extended back, right past her gaping mouth.

"Later, Sweet Tea," it purred over its shoulder, disappearing from sight as quickly as it had crashed her dream to begin with.

# 11

BACON SIZZLED OVER THE FRONT LEFT BURNER as Liz cracked eggs into a skillet on the front right. They hissed as they hit the hot surface, bubbling to life in what was about to become a Monday morning omelet. Phil worked the cutting board beside her, exerting his knife skills on a small pile of peppers and onions.

Putting their grudges on pause, they had spent the early morning hours negotiating a cease-fire and trying to figure out a plan of attack for the rest of the week. First up was a family meal for the family that desperately needed one.

The smell waltzed through the downstairs, pirouetting around the corner, leaping up to the second floor in search of a dance partner. Gus's door opened first as he stumbled into the hallway, eyes still closed, following the scent back downstairs to the frying pan where it originated.

"Bacon," he said to no one, having made it all the way to the kitchen table without opening an eyelid. He couldn't remember the last time his parents cooked breakfast, so he knew it was a trap, but he was more than willing to fall for it.

"And the first omelet goes to Gus," said Liz, shuffling it onto his plate as Phil delivered a few strips of bacon. She pivoted to the toaster and grabbed two hot slices as they popped. "Don't forget your whole grains," she added with an other-motherly smile, giving it a quick diagonal cut.

Gus looked at his mom, then his dad, then back to his mom. "If this is a dream, don't wake me up til I've had seconds."

More signs of life echoed down the stairwell as Sweet Pea made her approach, sliding her shoulder along the wall as she descended into Bacon Land. The plan was working to perfection, as all four Beverlys sat in the same room, at the same table, about to share the same meal.

"Your mother and I have been talking," Phil started, "and we have a plan for the rest of the week." The kids barely looked up from their plates. "Obviously, a lot happened yesterday, but … yesterday's the past, tomorrow's the future, and today is —"

"A gift," said Gus through a mouthful of eggs. "That's on a poster at school."

Liz whispered to Phil without moving her lips. "I thought you were using the other one."

He gave her a quick nod. "Remember kids, today is the tomorrow you — "

"Worried about yesterday!" Gus was thoroughly enjoying himself.

"The *other* one," she directed.

Phil regrouped. "Let's all learn from yesterday, live for today and hope for tomorrow."

"Thank you, Albert Einstein," Gus noted. "Got anything from your own brain?"

"Anyway," his dad conceded, miffed but impressed by his son's knowledge of life quotes. He regained the momentum of the meal and delivered a short talk about sticking together no matter what. Sweet Pea and Gus ate while they listened to their parents' plan for the week — supply shopping, meal prepping, emergency planning, and most importantly, spending Thursday through Saturday at the downtown Pitch-Black Palooza.

Sweet Pea watched her dad taking control of the room, fending off Gus's glancing blows, unafraid of what dragons might lie ahead. One of those dragons stood at the stovetop, ready to singe his eyebrows at his slightest misstep, but he didn't look scared. He was still feeling the swell of his tower-climbing, daughter-saving heroics, and Sweet Pea could tell. The little bit of glow coming off him was enough to lighten up the dark corners of her mind that were under attack from dying suns, falling stars and jet-black skies.

"Ready for more?" her mom asked, hovering a pan of food over her plate.

"Nope, I'm full."

"Maybe next week, after things are back to normal, we can do more meals like this. More bacon. Unless you'd rather keep eating Pop-Tarts and frozen waffles," she bluffed.

"No —" Gus and Sweet Pea said accidentally together, causing them to snap their heads and make eye contact for the first time since their clash at the park.

"Bacon," Phil agreed, maneuvering behind Liz. Sensing an opportunity, however futile it might have actually been, he placed his hands on her shoulders, intending a nice little massage. She squirmed away, clearly not in the mood for physical contact. His glow diminished as he took plates to the sink and started cleaning up. He muttered something that nobody heard, causing Liz to mutter something they all heard.

Gus got up and made his way to the living room. "Thanks for the grub."

"Yeah, thanks," seconded Sweet Pea, wandering over to the front window, gazing out and up. She was half-expecting to see a gigantic crack in the sky, or a bandage around the sun's forehead. But it looked just like every other Monday morning.

"Sky's still blue, sun's still shinin'," she said to herself. It was somewhere square in the middle between an optimistic observation and a good attempt at convincing herself that everything was fine.

LATER THAT AFTERNOON, Gus and his dad loitered just outside the laundry room, waiting for Liz to emerge from her cave of lint balls and humming appliances. Every secret mission starts with a good lie, but the most they could muster today was a mediocre one. Footsteps got closer, setting their plan into motion.

"Gus and I are running to check out some generators, I heard McCartney's got some in."

She whisked past them both, trying to keep the overloaded basket from spilling socks and underwear, barely even registering his words.

Gus took his turn. "We'll be back in a couple hours," he said as she started sorting lefts and rights on the couch, determined to find a matching pair for every sock. On a thirty second delay, she finally realized they were talking to her.

"Where are you going?" she inflected, somewhat engaged now.

"McCartney's then maybe up the road if they're out," said Phil.

"Out of what?"

"Generators, I just told you that."

"Yeah, we need a generator," Gus added, sending his dad's face into a wince, followed by clenched teeth and eye signals directed at his son's bad acting.

"You guys help me finish laundry first, then we can all go together. See if Sweet Pea wants to go."

Phil was prepared for the counteroffer. "If they have the one I want, I might need to put the seats down, and all Hubbard's stuff is in the back and I don't want to move all that crap right now. So this has to be a two-man trip." He didn't wait for approval, heading swiftly to the door and sliding on his shoes. Gus trailed close behind, more nervous than he thought he would be.

"Fine, but don't be gone all day," she conceded from the other room.

Safely out of view, father and son gave each other a quick nod, acknowledging the successful completion of Phase One. Phil rustled through a crowded drawer for his keys and wallet as Gus finished tying his shoes.

"Wait for me!" called Sweet Pea, bounding in from the back porch, unaware that she was jeopardizing their getaway. "Where are you going?"

There was a good chance that Sweet Pea's interjection could bring her mom back into the mix, so they had to act fast.

"This is just a me and Gus trip — you stay home." He shuffled Gus out the door before Sweet Pea had a chance to think. They opened the garage door, climbed into the Subaru and backed down the driveway. Spies aren't supposed to have emotions, but a bolt of guilt hit him right in the chest. He threw the car into park.

"Hold on, I forgot to tell your sister something." Walking around to the front porch window, he peeked through the screen, watching her play with a crab-shaped magnet on their fridge. He got it for her at the beach when she was little — it had googly eyes and its claws wiggled when you tapped it. To make up for his rude departure, he wanted to cheer her up before he left. His voice jumped through the window.

"Sorry I was so crabby!"

Sweet Pea flinched, yelping like a startled dog. Her arms spazzed out and the crab shot across the room, breaking into pieces on impact.

"Dad!" she cried. "You broke Mr. Crabster!"

Liz flew into the room, evaluating the commotion and gathering shell fragments. She looked the length of the house and saw her husband's blank face staring through the window screen. "Just go, Phil," she huffed, "you're not funny."

Feeling ten times worse now, he offered a fleeting "sorry" and retreated to the Subaru, hanging his head as he pulled on the locked door handle. Gus wore a disapproving look in the passenger seat. Without breaking eye contact he unlocked the driver's door, shaking his head as his dad climbed in.

"I wasn't gonna say anything, but you really shouldn't leave your children in a running vehicle with the doors unlocked. I've heard it's not safe."

Phil fought fire with fire. "If anyone kidnapped you again, they'd bring you back after two minutes." Reaching for the gearshift, he realized he just told a kidnapping joke to someone who had actually been kidnapped. "Sorry, strike that from the record." He put it in reverse and left the driveway, checking his mirrors and taking a quick look back at their house as he drove away.

"Alright Guster, our secret mission is officially underway."

A FEW MINUTES DOWN THE ROAD, they flew past Family Castle, as father and son both pretended it wasn't there. Gus fiddled with his seatbelt while Phil pointed at something on the opposite side of the road. "Is that a beaver? Maybe a groundhog…" It was too soon for either of them to take in the sight of the tower.

As they drove north out of town, Gus was ready to review the prison release objectives. "So how's this gonna work?"

"I told you, you didn't have to come," his dad offered sincerely, accelerating up the on-ramp. "If you want out, that's one hundred percent no prob-lem-o, I'll turn around right —"

"I'm good." After their frisbee talk, Gus spent a lot of time thinking about that day in the swamp. What bothered him more than the man's threats and the dead smell of the marsh gas, was the look on Sweet Pea's face. She was so scared, more than any seven-year-old deserves to be, and she was too young to realize that a nine-year-old wasn't really going to be able to save her. He felt her eyes pouring every drop of hope and desperation into his, begging for a sign that they would be okay. His own fear had sunken down somewhere in his ribcage to make room for hers, and he felt an overpowering rush to protect her. She was his mission that day, and seven years later, he couldn't let it go.

"Okay," his dad consented. "His release is set for three, so we should get there about ten till. It took longer than I planned to leave the house, but we should be good."

"And we're just spying, right? Not talking to him or anything. I don't want him to see me."

"We're staying way back, trust me, I just want to see where he goes when he leaves." They passed a sign:

ROCKHILL STATE CORRECTIONAL INSTITUTION

24 MILES

"He probably wouldn't even recognize you now, Gus. I'm

hoping he gets on a bus and heads to Albuquerque or somewhere halfway across the country. He's got no family, no reason to stick around here."

Gus stared out his window at trees flying by, shifting his thoughts to what awaited them at Rockhill. The words from the swamp were buried in the back of his mind, but always ready to replay: *Someone's gonna get hurt ... and I know where you live.* He always wondered if the man thought they told the police about him, if he thought they were the reason he was caught. Because if he did, then he might have a pretty good reason to stick around.

"Do you think he's going to come after us?"

The car radio played softly as they banked around a left turn, then emptied into a stretch of open road. It was bad timing on her part, but Blondie sang about finding someone, one way or another, and getting them.

"Honestly, Gus, no, I don't. He's getting out of prison, do you really think he wants to go right back in?"

"Then why are we doing this?"

"Because, I need to see it with my own eyes. I don't know if he's staying two blocks from us, or at some halfway house two hours away. We're just going to keep tabs on him, then once it's all clear and I know he's not a problem, we'll tell the girls."

The next twenty minutes were dead silent as they approached their destination. The wooded surroundings were beautiful and creepy at the same time, a product of the mass misery that was caged just around the bend. Gus swallowed harder reading the sign to his right:

PRISON AREA
DO NOT PICK UP HITCHHIKERS

"Almost there," his dad said. "Keep your hands, arms and feet inside the vehicle at all times and please do not feed the bears. Or the prisoners."

Gus didn't have a comeback. He just wanted to get the secret mission over with.

# 12

---

M R. CRABSTER WAS IN CRITICAL but stable condition, lying on a paper towel with super glue seeping from every crack of his freshly mended body. He was a shell of his former self, but thanks to Sweet Pea and her mom, there was a good chance he could be hanging around again really soon.

"Laundry's done and your crab guy is fixed," Liz said. "I need a chore break — let's take Hubbard on a walk." She got out her good running shoes and started lacing them up. "We can drive him over to Thistlewood and pretend we live in the fancy neighborhood?"

"Okay, I guess." Sweet Pea was still a little sour from being left out of wherever her dad and brother had gone.

"C'mon, it's really nice out. We don't need the boys."

Sweet Pea grabbed the leash from its hook and threw on her ballcap. She wanted to agree with her mom's "girls rule boys drool" sentiment, but it wasn't happening. She did need her dad right now, but the closest thing she had to a significant male role model this afternoon would have to be Hubbard.

The Thistlewood development was about two miles away, so they skipped the forty-minute foot commute in favor of a three-minute drive. Hubbard favored this decision too, hanging his head out the backseat window as they rolled along. Much to his delight, the flaps of his snout rippled with moving air and his eyes were blown shut like a skydiver who forgot his goggles.

Their car stopped at an intersection, with the main road crossing in front of them. Across that road was the entrance to Thistlewood Estates, marked by a country-clubbish sign with natural stone pillars and hardscaping that probably cost more than the Beverly's entire house.

"I'm gonna park on that street with the empty lots," her mom said, navigating Oxford Lane to Cambridge. "Then we can walk a few loops and wonder what all these people do for a living." She pulled along an empty stretch of curb where no homes had been built yet, staring across the street at the stately structures and their three-car garages. "Sorry we don't live somewhere nice like this."

"I think our house is nice," Sweet Pea said innocently, exiting the car and following Hubbard's lead. Her mom jogged a few steps to catch up.

"Maybe someday, if the school triples our salaries."

"Yeah, and if we're not sucked into a black hole this weekend," Sweet Pea added. Hubbard tilted his head and gave her a sideways look as he trotted along.

Her mom laughed it off. "I have to admit, of all the crazy conspiracies going around, that might be my favorite one yet." Breathing a little heavier from their aggressive stride, they made a left at the next corner. "I could see locusts or aliens ending the world — maybe — but I'm not buying a black hole." This coming from the same person who twenty-four hours earlier feared a tsunami was going to strike Pennsylvania. At least in front of Sweet Pea she was putting on a brave face.

"Honey, the sun's just going down for a few days then coming right back up. I promise."

"I don't know," Sweet Pea replied, pulling on the leash to keep Hubbard away from an out-of-nowhere Great Dane that was quickly approaching. It got a few steps closer, then stopped short, obeying a signal from an underground fence.

"Your dad doesn't think it's anything to worry about, either." She didn't really care what her husband thought right now, but she knew it would ease her daughter's mind. Sweet Pea nodded her head as they approached the next street, walking up a slight slope toward a row of homes with larger lots, longer driveways and more peaks on their roofs.

"Wow, these must be doctors up here," her mom said.

"I thought the other street was doctors," Sweet Pea wondered out loud.

"True. These must be surgeons."

They kept walking as the sound of a lawn mower got louder. Hubbard heard a few muffled woofs from somewhere on the opposite side of the street, to which he politely woofed back.

"You know who lives a few houses down that way," Liz asked rhetorically. "Austin's family."

"Oh," mused Sweet Pea, "I didn't know they were Thistle-wooders. I was only in the car once when we dropped off Gus and it was dark. That was here?"

"Yeah, they're in that one," she said, stopping to point way down the street at a brick house with a black metal roof and black shutters. It wasn't a mansion like the rest on Surgeon Row, but it was still twice the size of Sweet Pea's house. They had to almost yell at each other to be heard now, as a bright orange riding mower approached from the lawn on their right, driven by a shirtless teenager wearing a hat and sunglasses. They moved further into the street to avoid him, but he steered a little closer to their path and accelerated.

Now he was waving to them, as he cut the engine and parked the machine at the edge of the lawn he had just mowed. Stepping down, he removed his hat and glasses and flashed a familiar smile. Sweet Pea had never seen Austin with his shirt off, but she was looking now.

"Well hello there, what brings you lovely ladies to the Thistle-hood?"

"Hey Austin," said Liz as Sweet Pea gave him a salute. "We just wanted somewhere different to walk the dog — you know, before the sun dies." Austin was her favorite friend of all Gus's friends over the years. He was always a gracious guest at their house, stayed out of trouble, made Gus laugh a lot, and to meet him you'd never know his family had money.

"Cool, cool, for sure," he said. Sweet Pea tried not to notice that he had muscles now — she failed — as they were actually glistening in the sun.

"So why are you mowing here, mom said you live down there," Sweet Pea gestured.

"Excellent question, Miss Paisley, if I might call you that." She blushed. "Because, Dr. Antonelli pays me a hundred bucks to mow it. And he wants it done twice a week." He wiped some sweat that was running down his pecs. "I've made like a million dollars this summer, it's totally dialed. And speak of the devil —"

A well-dressed, well-built, well-to-do man approached their group across his lawn, carrying three waters. You knew you were in Thistlewood because it was the name-brand water like celebrities drink.

"Who would like a bottle of southern France's finest," he asked with the slightest hint of an accent, extending the offer as they instantly obliged. Sweet Pea took the green bottle in her hand, marveling at its teardrop shape, half-afraid to open it and spill a drop. Liz pushed a few strands of hair behind her left ear and accepted hers, performing a strange attempt at a curtsy.

"Chuck it here, Dr. Seb," blurted Austin, making a target with his hands and hauling in the pass. "So … introductions … this is my friend's sister and her mom, Sweet Pea and Mrs. Beverly."

"Hi, I'm Liz," she corrected. "Mrs. Beverly lives in a retirement home near Philly."

"Pleased to meet you both," he laughed, tossing Hubbard a tiny milkbone from his pocket. "I'm Dr. Antonelli, or Dr. Seb, or just Sebastian." The girls smiled harder than was required, as he handed Austin a small wad of bills. "I heard the mower stop and was coming out to pay this fine young man, when I saw that he had company." His words sounded like they were meant for all three of them, but his eyes only talked to Liz.

"Well thank you, Sebastian," she said before taking a tiny sip. "That was very nice of you, we love Perrier."

"We've never had —" Sweet Pea stopped herself, realizing her mother was fibbing to impress the rich guy.

Liz quickly changed the subject. "Well, we won't keep you, I'm sure you have a lot going on," she said, taking Hubbard's leash from Sweet Pea. "Thanks again for the water, it's very" — she blanked on how to finish her sentence — "very, um, delicious." *Oh my God, I'm an idiot.*

"You're quite welcome. Come back for more delicious water anytime." He laughed without breaking his infatuated stare. "And actually, I've got nothing at all going on. It's the one day this week I'm not removing someone's appendix." The girls secretly made eye contact and stifled their grins.

The grownups started talking about jobs, neighborhoods, running shoes and dog leashes before inevitably spinning theories about solar phenomena and how long the darkness would last. As they delved deeper into their conversation, Austin and Sweet Pea drifted down the street toward his house, engaged in their own chat session.

"Let me guess, Gus wants to kill me," said Austin, counting his mowing money.

"I don't think so, with everything else goin' on he probably doesn't care any more."

"What did I even say to him anyway, I don't remember."

Sweet Pea acted it out, giving her best Austin impression. "*Yo lighten up man, that's enough.*"

Austin's hand flew to his forehead, laughing and stumbling like someone shot him. "Whoa! Yes! That was totally me!" He regained his balance as they kept walking, realizing they were almost down to his house now.

Sweet Pea looked back up the street and saw her mom and Hubbard still visiting their new friend, the laparoscopic surgeon. "We should do something tomorrow. You, me and Gus. Don't tell him it was my idea, but if I'm there, then he'll team up with you to pick on me, then you and him will be friends again."

He thought through the scenarios. "I'm liking that. My parents are doing a bunch of crap anyway to get ready for Wednesday night, so we should definitely do something. Family Castle?"

Her eyes shot lasers. "Very funny. I don't think so." She softened quickly. "I wonder if mini-golf is open?"

"Valley Putt? Yeah, good call little sis. I'll make it happen." As they stood outside his house finalizing their plans, Sweet Pea realized her excitement for tomorrow's outing was eking out her anxiety for the rest of the week. She couldn't wait to get home so she could go to bed and fast-forward to the first hole.

Austin interrupted her thinking. "Wanna know the best news ever that will make tomorrow even more awesome?" She nodded, expecting him to crack another joke or pull a rabbit out of his hat. "I got my license!" He extended his own half of a high-five that was quickly completed by Sweet Pea. "I can pick you guys up in my Jeep as long as it's cool with your parents. You'll know it's me when you see the banana split."

"Huh?"

Austin pointed to the back of his yellow Jeep sticking out of his garage, sporting a BNA SPLT license plate below the left tail light.

"Ohhhh, I get it, bananas are yellow, too," she groaned. "We'll also know it's you because we'll see you driving."

"Good point."

"Tomorrow will be good. I better go rescue my mom now, she's still talking to Dr. Seb."

"Yeah, I think your dad would appreciate that," Austin said coyly. "Okay, later, I'll get a hold of Gus," he trailed off as he jogged across his driveway. "This is happening!"

Sweet Pea made her way back up the hill, where she saw Hubbard fast asleep on the sidewalk, sprawled out like he owned the place. Her mom saw her coming and wrapped up their conversation.

"Ready Pea? Let's wake this dog up and get moving."

"It was so nice to meet you both," Sebastian said, "and you too, Mr. Hubbard." He rustled another milkbone from his pocket that got him on all four paws in half a second. "Sweet Pea, take care of your mother once that sun goes down."

She nodded convincingly and picked up Hubbard's leash.

"Liz, if your family needs anything during this ordeal, please don't hesitate to ask. I can lend a helping hand."

"Well, my husband is buying a generator as we speak, so we should be good if the power goes out. But if we get thirsty, I know where the good water's at." She beamed at her own joke, but most of the smile was carrying over from the past ten minutes of talking to someone who actually listened to her. She forgot how good that felt.

"Take care," he said, holding a long gaze as they disappeared down the street.


GUS AND HIS DAD SAT IN THE SUBARU, parked across the street and down about fifty yards from a set of prison doors where a cab was waiting. It was almost three o'clock.

"Shit, remind me to buy a generator before we go home," said Phil, frantically preparing his mental checklist of things that had to go right in the next hour.

"Oh, I thought that was just part of our cover."

"No, I pulled an eighty/twenty. I tell your mother mostly something real, but some of it's not entirely true, so then it doesn't really feel like a full lie. It's actually a pretty good way to — wait, there he is."

They froze as Bruce Hicks emerged from the building. It lacked all the drama of the prison movies where a small battalion of guards walk the ex-con through giant cast-iron gates, some giving him a push in the back, others tipping their caps. Here and now, he just walked out all by himself and stepped to the cab like someone who had visited his uncle for an hour. His curly black hair was gone, there was no dirty ballcap on his head, but even from a distance it was unmistakably him.

Gus processed the moment as the cab pulled forward, putting even more distance between their vehicles. He looked at his dad, who was motionless and staring blankly ahead, erasing any doubts that this was indeed his first stakeout.

He gave his dad a loud nudge. "Go!"

Phil popped the clutch too hard and stalled the engine with a couple jerking lunges. "Sonuvabitch," he hissed, now having uttered two cuss words in front of Gus in the past five minutes. He turned the key and squealed away from the curb, progressing through gears now like a Formula One driver.

"Easy, don't make a scene, oh my God," said Gus, also escalating his vocabulary in the heat of the moment.

They made up the ground quickly, as the cab came into view just ahead of them, approaching a stop sign that would give their first indication of where he was going.

"Left is south to Culver. Right is north to good riddance," said Phil, watching like he had a stack of chips on red at the roulette table. The cab's left turn signal blinked as its wheels rolled, heading south. "That's okay, he could still be going anywhere. Doesn't mean a thing."

Gus was silent, leaving the speculation and false confidence to his dad. They followed the cab closer and closer to Culver, letting another car get between them as a shield, as neither one of them said much at all. With each passing mile, their stomachs started to ache in more places, and Albuquerque was looking more and more like a bad bet.

The cab's tail light blinked again, signaling the Culver exit. "Great," said Phil, realizing they wouldn't be getting the easy way out of this.

"You watch," said Gus, "he probably gave the driver our address." As terrifying as that thought was, it didn't last long as the cab made a right before they even got to Family Castle. They stayed back and kept following, breathing a little easier now, as every minute they drove put more distance between their home and wherever he was heading.

"Maybe Piedmont, that's out this way," Phil said, trying to connect the dots. Another ten minutes down the road, the cab turned onto a street that used to have some nice shopping plazas and a few places to eat, but almost all of them had shut down over the years. Gus noticed the trash-filled parking lots, the tall clumps of weeds growing up through crumbled asphalt, and curbs and sign posts that were missing most of their paint. The cab drove slower onto Pennsylvania Avenue, a main drag in its heyday, passing one empty storefront after another. Signs for cigarettes and lottery games dotted a few windows, singing their siren songs to anyone who hadn't gotten out yet.

"Look, he's pulling over," said Gus. Their car was pretty far back, but they kept their distance and pulled into a spot that wouldn't blow their cover. They had a good visual on the cab as it entered the parking lot of the Thunderbird Motel.

"Welcome to the Thunderbird, Mr. Hicks," mocked Gus's dad. "Will that be oceanfront or courtyard view?"

Gus was puzzled. "So he's staying at a motel in Piedmont?"

"Well, it's not really a motel any more," his dad explained. "It's kind of like a half-way house, it's all section eight or something. If you're getting out of jail or getting off drugs, they say the T-bird will take you in."

The back door of the cab opened and Hicks got out, presumably the first time in seven years that he set foot on ground not belonging to the state correctional system. He looked around, briefly in the Beverly's direction, but Gus and his dad felt safe in their spot without even ducking. They watched him wave to the cab driver before walking to the office and going inside.

"So," asked Gus, "is this good or bad? That he's here?"

"I don't know."

"What's the next part of your plan?"

"I'm not sure."

"So your whole plan was just to follow him and stare at him?"

"No, now I'm going to monitor him, I want to get a read on him." Phil was struggling to sound confident.

"What does that even mean?" Before Gus could roll his eyes any harder, a door to one of the motel rooms opened and a skinny man walked out wearing a sweaty wife-beater and carrying something long and shiny in his right hand.

"Pretty sure that's a machete," said Gus, focusing on the scene as the man sat on a plastic lawn chair and proceeded to sharpen the long blade on a rusty file. In twenty-four hours, Gus had gone from looking for girls on a bench in the park, to looking at guys with machetes in a motel parking lot.

The office door opened and Hicks walked out, followed by the front desk attendant, directing him to a unit at the back of the lot. Hicks passed the machete man on the way to his room, and to the Beverlys' dread, the two men greeted each other with a handshake and a bro hug. They exchanged a few words, nodded very seriously about something and bro hugged again before Hicks trudged off to his room.

Gus felt a cold dread wash over him, that seemed to start in his head and spread to his chest. He looked to his dad, hoping for some sign of calm or comfort or understanding.

"C'mon Guster, let's go find ourselves a generator."

# 13

—

TUESDAY'S SUNRISE OVER CULVER started out as the kind you would see painted and framed in a hotel lobby or a dentist's office: unremarkable. But just as the predictable pinks, reds and purples did their usual thing, a very unusual color entered the mix. Slicing right down the middle of the pastels was a glowing stripe of emerald green, bleeding outward and gaining clarity as the sun climbed over the ridge. The swatch weaved through billow clouds, hanging like a sash across the sky's shoulder, putting its spunky attitude on display. This was no *Ghostbusters* or *Wizard of Oz* sky, swirling with doom or signaling a lurking evil — it just looked like a toddler took a green crayon and scribbled across someone's nice painting.

Had anyone still thought the sun's upcoming disappearing act was a government hoax or just plain malarkey, this was the first real sign that something was going on up there. But the early morning light show had washed back to pale blue by the time the

Beverlys, and most of Culver, were awake. As the family of four crawled around their morning routines, none of them realized what they had just missed. Even if they had been up, they might not have noticed the sci-fi sky due to Phil's obsession with his new thirteen-thousand watt power generator. He insisted on educating his family on every feature from the manual, rattling off fuel options and running watts of every appliance in their house.

"Okay, the fridge takes two thousand to start but only seven hundred to run. We can still run the TV and the AC, plus all the lights. This thing is awesome."

"It better be, you were gone long enough yesterday," said Liz. "And how did we pay for it? That's bigger than the one we talked about."

"I told you, we went to half a dozen stores, everyone was sold out, I had to shop around." He knew she would never set foot in McCartney's and see the fully stocked shelves. She stared him down, waiting for the rest of his answer.

"I put it on the card, had to." A trend that happened more often than it should.

"Which card?"

"Eh, it's all Monopoly money."

She amplified so Gus and Sweet Pea could hear her in the other room. "Kids, please don't follow in your father's financial footsteps."

"I choose not to follow any of his footsteps," Gus said matter-of-factly.

"You say that now, son," he said, opening the refrigerator door, "but someday you'll be poundin' the C just like me." He chugged down half the carton of orange juice as if drinkware had never been invented.

The back and forth eventually fizzled out as they migrated toward the television, drawn by the voice on the news.

*A developing story out of Idaho this morning, as officials at the National Laboratory now say the solar phenomenon could extend beyond initial projections...*

Sweet Pea looked to her dad. "More than three days?!"

The broadcast jumped to a big room with a dozen people behind a podium, half of them in suits and the other half in military uniforms. A man in a sweater-vest and black glasses stepped to the mic and responded to questions from the crowd.

*Yes, we initially calculated seventy-two hours and we still believe that is the most likely scenario. ... Some new findings by Dr. Bryant are causing us to re-evaluate those projections, based on several factors. ... Yes, the electromagnetic cloud has increased in size, but this is not — I repeat, not — a reason to panic. ... Sunday still carries a strong possibility for daylight, and we're proceeding as such...*

Phil addressed the worried looks in the room. "Sounds like a nothing-burger, my money's still on three days. Everything's fine, it's not the end of the world."

The news anchor chimed in ... *And now a live look at Manhattan, as a growing number of people have taken to the streets, calling themselves 'The Sundowners'...*

Sweet Pea's eyes locked on the screen, fascinated by the scene of demonstrators in Times Square, as people of all ages, races and religions loitered about. Some were setting up tents on sidewalks, others were waving homemade signs, and all of them looked like they fully believed the end of the world was coming. As the camera panned past the crowd, Sweet Pea digested a few of their messages.

A long-bearded man touted a black sign with white spray-painted lettering:

SINNERS REPENT / MATTHEW 4:17

Across the street, a handful of people dressed in all white paraded with a banner:

END OF DAYS / ARE YOU READY?

And a woman leaning against a bus stop shelter held a cigarette in one hand and a poster in the other:

THE SUN'S DONE / AIN'T COMIN' BACK

Their chants interrupted her brain for a minute, infiltrating her headspace as they repeated over and over again: "No More Light! No More Life!" They were answering the question that Sweet Pea had been asking herself since the news broke: *Won't things start dying if there's no sunlight?*

She had thought about it a lot the last couple nights lying in bed, thanks in part to the cover of her fifth grade science book, featuring an image of sunlight illuminating a water droplet on the edge of a leaf. She remembered it clearly, because she ran out of book covers that year, so the title, "Photosynthesis: Key to Life" was ingrained in her mind from early September through late May.

Her brain took the journey. *If there's no sun, the plants will die, and then animals that eat plants will die, or they'll eat other animals. And if that happens, then people won't have plants or animals to eat, and they'll die, too, unless people eat each other. But that only happens in zombie movies, and those aren't real, but none of this feels real any more, so who knows? And won't it get really cold without the sun? What if it gets so cold that even my heavy winter coat doesn't help, or building a fire doesn't work because there's no oxygen from photosynthesis? How long would it really take before everyone freezes to death or the Earth turns into ice and cracks apart?*

Noticing the hypnotized look on Sweet Pea's face, her mom grabbed the remote and turned off the television. "Aren't you guys going with Austin? You better get ready."

"Yeah, I know, relax," said Gus, shuffling off to watch for the Jeep.

"That's nice that he invited Pea."

"I guess. His cousin Michelle really wanted to go, and she's the same age, so they can hang out. Whatever."

Sweet Pea was impressed by Austin's trickery, trying not to laugh at how hard Gus fell for the made-up-cousin line. And she couldn't wait to see how he explained her back into non-existence. But her excitement was already giving way to the jitters in her stomach, and the Sundowners' voices in her head — just loud enough to remind her that maybe everything wasn't going to be alright.

A FLASH OF YELLOW SWERVED into the Beverly's driveway, accompanied by the thumping bass of rap music. As the Jeep came to a hasty stop two feet from their garage door, Austin shifted to park and adjusted his hat, backwards and crooked. A subwoofer rumbled in the back as lyrics threatened to knock someone out, apparently because his mother told him to, which launched Austin into a shadow boxing routine of epic proportions.

Brother and sister approached the hundred-decibel concert on wheels, as Sweet Pea motioned Gus to check out the license plate. He wasn't amused. Maybe it was some jealousy kicking in because he didn't get a new Jeep for *his* sixteenth birthday, and knew he'd be lucky just to inherit his pap's rusty old truck. Or maybe he still wasn't over their encounter at the park. Either way, if neither were the case, just the sight of Austin boxing in the mirror with his crooked hat was enough to get his goat.

"What's up, fools, ready to golf?"

"Hey," said Gus, stepping into the passenger seat. "Nice Jeep."
Sweet Pea climbed in the back. "Yeah, nice banana split."

Austin turned toward his passengers and threw a few fake jabs in their direction as the song still rattled the vehicle. Gus didn't flinch, but Sweet Pea put her hands up in sparring position and played along, even taking a pretend knockout blow and splaying out on the back seat. Austin started blurting out a ten count, but Gus cut him off after three.

"Okay, we get it, you knocked her out."

Austin turned down the stereo and straightened his hat. "Geez, this is gonna be a fun day," he said, shifting into reverse and backing onto the road. Their parents yelled goodbye and waved from the front window, as Austin hit the horn in a pattern of *honk honks* that continued down the road.

"Where's your cousin?" asked Gus, finally realizing that their foursome was one short.

"They said she got sick last-minute, but I think it was just shark week and they didn't want to embarrass her."

"Shark week?"

"Crimson tide … Code Red … Aunt Flo…"

"*Ohhhhh…*"

Sweet Pea didn't mind the spin of Austin's lie, because it laid the perfect alibi that Gus would never challenge or follow up on.

"You should have said something," countered Gus, "now we're stuck with crazy climber all day." He wasn't planning the unprovoked attack on his sister, but it just came naturally when Austin was around.

"Dude, what if she climbs up the windmill on the back nine." Austin piled on just enough to sell it, but made eye contact in the rearview to signal Sweet Pea that her plan was off to a good start.

Gus snorted. "I guess she can come, maybe she'll accidentally fall in the water hazard."

"*Kerplunk!*" Austin cackled and checked the mirror again as Sweet Pea raised her left brow. She was glad that they seemed to be over their fight already, even if it meant she was in for a long afternoon of being their punching bag.

VALLEY PUTT WAS BUSIER than anyone would have expected on a late-summer Tuesday afternoon, just a day before the skies were supposed to go dark. The crowd was primarily teenagers, as kids from just about every school in the county were spread across the course. Apparently Gus and crew weren't the only ones itching for a last gasp of normalcy that also doubled as time away from their stressed-out parents. The sign out front might have had something to do with it, too:

END OF THE WORLD SPECIAL

$1 PER ROUND

GOLF TIL THE SKY FALLS!

Gus, Austin and Sweet Pea made their way to the end of the line, which was only about five or six people long. The three of them had never really done anything together before, not without the company of parents, even though Sweet Pea had begged for years to join Gus and his friends. But after Austin stood up to Gus at the park, she had a tiny bout of survivor's guilt, worried that their friendship was ruined because of her. Playing the sacrificial lamb was her way of making things right, even if she had to endure a barrage of insults and unpleasantries to get there.

But she also realized she could salvage a half-decent time with her brother's funny best friend, who also happened to be a little ripped. Even with all that in the works, Gus might never have agreed to it if he hadn't started feeling a little sorry for his sister's plight in life, coupled with the mystery of Bruce Hicks and his machete-wielding acquaintance. The closer Gus kept her, the easier she was to protect.

Sweet Pea interrupted their conversation about golf ball colors. "Aren't you guys worried about the sun?"

"What about it?" said Gus.

"The thing on the news. Longer than three days now."

"Nope."

"Me neither," added Austin, paying the guy at the counter three dollars and grabbing a putter and purple ball. "I'm bettin' my bottom dollar that the sun'll come out, just like Dorothy said."

Gus picked a green ball and tried to find a putter with a grip that wasn't unraveling. "That was Annie."

"Annie who?"

"The orphan."

Austin pointed quizzically at the girl in front of them. "How do you know she's an orphan," he whispered.

"Not her, dunce. The song's from *Annie*, not *Wizard of Oz*."

Sweet Pea took her putter from the rack and held it like a microphone, busting into song with all the theatrics of a high school musical. "*The sun'll come ouuuuuuut … to-mor-row … Bet your bottom dol-lar that … to-mor-rowww … there'll be suuuunnnn.*"

Austin gave a small round of applause, and Gus accidentally allowed the far left corner of his mouth to pinch upwards.

They moved onto the practice green and waited their turn for the first hole to open up. Gus sank just about every shot that left his putter, calculating angles off the brick edging, tapping in three-footers and dropping back to twenty just to show off. Austin launched more than a few balls off the green and out of the practice area, with one narrowly missing a lady's head and another rolling all the way to the parking lot under a truck. Sweet Pea's stroke looked more like a hockey slapshot or a shuffleboard push, but she was enjoying herself nonetheless.

The group ahead of them finally finished the first hole, as Austin took his position on the tee. "Hey, before we start, there's something I need to tell you," he said, ushering to Sweet Pea. "Gus, tune out, this is just between me and her."

Gus shrugged as Sweet Pea walked over and leaned in for her update on their secret plans.

*BLUUUUUURRURP!!*

Sweet Pea recoiled so hard she almost fell backwards over a fake rock. Austin's ginormous belch nearly took her head off, sending the boys into a state of pandemonium. Gus launched the hardest, cleanest high-five she had ever seen. The slap was so loud it had to hurt, as Austin followed up with a leaping chest bump and double finger guns, clicking away like Wyatt Earp.

"Sorry, little sis," laughed Austin, "that was all Doritos and Dr. Pepper."

Sweet Pea gathered herself and tried to laugh it off like it wasn't completely disgusting and embarrassing. "Cool Ranch by the smell of it."

They snaked through the front nine, navigating waterfalls, abandoned mines and a pirate ship, while picking on each other every step of the way. The kids in the group ahead of them were from Culver, and the group behind them had a couple girls wearing Lady Comets Basketball t-shirts, their rival school here in Valley. A few holes over was a crew from Piedmont that looked a little rough around the edges. Sweet Pea saw them uprooting a shrub on Number Five when they thought nobody was looking.

After a few more holes, they approached the box for hole thirteen with Austin and Gus deep in a Super Mario World conversation.

"Hey guys, who's up first?" Sweet Pea asked, but both were preoccupied with their Mario and Luigi impressions. "This is the windmill hole, whose turn is it?"

"Just hit your ball," said Gus impatiently.

"Crazy climber," muttered Austin with a wink.

Sweet Pea placed her ball and took her best golfer's stance, staring at the windmill that towered in front of her. In the real world it was about as high as a basketball hoop, but the longer she stared at it, the larger it loomed. For a split second, she saw the Turret of Terror, then it blinked back to the windmill. She watched its outstretched blades turning methodically clockwise, chopping up shadows across the green with each rotation. Her shot had to go through a small opening in the base, which was blocked every few seconds, mesmerizing her mind as she timed one rotation after another.

Her eyes started going cloudy, like someone turned on a fog machine and blasted the thirteenth hole. The windmill kept stretching higher and higher upwards, and even though her feet were on solid ground, it was making her head spin like it did on the tower a few days ago.

A faint voice floated behind her eyes, "*Dude, she's gonna climb it...*" but she kept dodging the wreckage that her mind threw at her. Another voice passed through, "*Hey, Pea Brain...*" but she didn't budge. A hand grabbed her shoulder, jarring her back into reality with a gasp and triggering a wild swing of her club. Her yellow ball blasted off like a PGA tee shot, smashing into the windmill and ricocheting two holes over, splashing down into a rocky canal of rushing blue water.

Within seconds, Gus, Austin and Sweet Pea were in pursuit, jumping over boxwoods and boulders while trying not to step on anyone's putting lines. They dodged a small group of people that looked like they were getting yelled at by the manager, and made their way to the fake lagoon where the canal emptied.

"I see it," shouted Austin, pointing at a yellow dot floating in the foamy water. Gus handed Sweet Pea the ball-fetching pole from a nearby gazebo, and she extended it a few more feet to try to reach her ball. Behind them, the commotion was getting louder, as the manager was escorting three kids off the property. Gus saw him trying to take a flask from the girl, but she was putting up a good fight.

Sweet Pea leaned a little further over the edge of the lagoon, extending as far as her arm could go, but she was still a foot short.

"Austin, hold my hand, I'm gonna lean out."

They locked hands as he steadied himself, easily anchoring the added weight as she planted one foot and extended like a ballerina. As the pole scooped up the bobbing yellow ball, Austin turned to Gus, who was still watching the girl with the flask.

"Yo Gus!"

Gus turned just in time to see him drop her hand, releasing a battle cry.

"*Ker-pluuuu-uuunk!*"

Sweet Pea fell in slow motion, ignoring the reflex to flail as her body went horizontal over the water. Her eyes found Austin's a split second before splashdown.

Totally underwater, she closed her eyes and felt the shock of the temperature change. The lagoon was only two feet deep, so it wasn't hard to resurface, but when she did there were tears in her eyes. It was her own plan to get picked on all day in the name of rekindled friendships, but as she sat there in the water, rubbing her eyes, something wasn't sitting right with her. Before she could lift a finger or say a word to Austin, someone else beat her to it — a voice shot through the air.

"Hey douchebag!"

The girl with the flask shoved the manager out of her way and pounced down the sloping hill to the lagoon. She stormed past Austin, hitting him with a piercing glare that only a Dipetto could unleash, before extending a hand to Sweet Pea.

She wanted to yell Mindy's name and do a triple backflip, but she just sat there, soaked and staring dumbstruck at her pet store pal.

"C'mon, I don't have all day," said Mindy, sly as a fox, pulling her out and checking on the manager's position who was making his way down the hill.

"Where did you —"

"Can't talk Sweetie, gotta bolt." She took a swig from her hip flask. "Find me downtown on Thursday, let's have some fun."

Mindy hurried away in the opposite direction, eluding the manager who had almost caught up but was now trying to catch his breath. She passed Gus and Austin, who had been keeping their distance, crossed a few holes and ran up the ramp of the pirate ship on her way out. Grabbing the hat and sword off a Blackbeard statue, she climbed onto a wooden deck at the ship's bow, turned and faced the crowd.

Hugging the mast with one arm and looking all the part, she belted out a half-drunk chantey. "*Yo Ho! Yo Ho! A pirate's life for me!*" Tipping back her flask, she slashed her sword three times at the air and abandoned ship.

# 14

WITH THE KIDS OUT OF THE HOUSE, Liz and Phil had some time to themselves. Alone-time brings out the best in people who like each other, and the worst in people who don't, so they bickered and squabbled about every little decision they tried to make. With the darkness on the horizon, they needed to be on the same page, but when he zigged, she kept zagging. It didn't help that Bruce Hicks and the Thunderbird Motel occupied a corner of Phil's brain.

His plan to "keep tabs on him" was amplified when Hicks befriended the seedy-looking guy with the big knife, all just a fifteen-minute drive from his family. For all he knew, they were discussing new recipes or puppy training techniques, but Phil feared the worst. Like waking in the middle of the night to the gleam of a machete in their bedroom.

He needed to know that Hicks wasn't planning a visit any time soon, but he still wasn't ready to tell Liz. The first time he snuck out for a drive-by, he told her he was fueling up the vehicle and filling a few extra gas cans for the weekend. His second run at surveillance featured a lie about helping a friend from work move a refrigerator up from his basement. And his third jaunt of the day was sponsored by a quick fib about running for sandwiches from "that really good place across town."

In his trips to and from the Thunderbird, Phil puzzled over how to keep Hicks away, but the whole thing was outside his comfort zone. He had never threatened anyone, never been in a fistfight, never even held a gun in his hand. If his tower climb last week was the bravest act in his forty years, stalking an ex-con was easily his most brainless.

During his third trip to the T-Bird, he parked in his normal spot and geared up with his trusty Bushnells. After a few minutes, the door to room 106 opened and Hicks wandered outside for a smoke. Three drags into his Camel, the door to 110 opened and his buddy in the wife-beater joined him, sans machete.

"What are you two slimeballs up to," Phil muttered to himself, contemplating his next move. "I can't just sit here forever ... How bad can it be if I just go over and ask him a couple questions ... What are they gonna do, shoot me?"

He psyched himself up with a few air-guitar riffs and reached for his coffee cup to get a quick swig of confidence. Looking back into his binoculars, his chest surged with a jump-scare as he saw both men staring at him. "Shit! They see me ... they see me," he said as the color left his face.

The men approached as Phil squirmed in his seat, trying to look nonchalantly tough while playing the innocent bystander at the same time. He bent his mouth into a shape that was supposed to be convincing, but it looked like he just ate a pack of Sour Patch Kids. From across the vehicle, Hicks put a knuckle to the front passenger door window.

*Tap-tap-tap*

Phil pressed the button to put it down, but the ignition was off so nothing happened. He fumbled around with his keys, trying to power the window, holding up a finger to let his visitors know it would just be a minute.

"Hello?" said Hicks through the glass, right before it went down, leaving nothing between the men but a thick line of tension.

"Hey there fellas, how can I help you?"

"You can start by telling me why you've been watching me," he said with a drawl. Not a southern drawl, it was a slow-burning, intimidating hit-man drawl.

"Watching us," his cohort added from behind his shoulder.

"Watching you?" protested Phil.

"Yeah. This ain't the first time you've been here."

"Well, I was actually just getting ready to —"

"You think I don't know who you are?" said Hicks, dead serious but a little bit playful, like he was enjoying it. Phil was caught off-guard and missed his turn at a reply. Machete man paced.

"You're Mr. Suburban." The name drew a laugh from his sidekick, which in turn drew a cocky smile from Hicks.

Phil realized very quickly that Bruce Hicks didn't forget a face. He had hoped that seven years of prison would have clouded his memory banks, or that maybe he wasn't paying attention at the hearings or sentencing when Phil and Liz shook their heads and shot their looks. But here they were, having a chat in a car on a Tuesday in Piedmont.

"So, Mr. Suburban, why are you watching me and my friend, Rotty? What's so interesting about us to you?"

"Well, I'm a big fan of undershirts and I was wondering where your friend got that nice wife-beater he's wearing?"

"It's an A-shirt, man!" blurted Rotty, pushing his face through the open window like a Rottweiler. Hicks pulled him back and refocused on his stalker.

"So, you're a funny guy, huh?" He wiped his nose with the side of his hand and smeared it on the car door. "That's really good, really good."

Phil wasn't laughing, but his ill-advised humor was the only thing keeping him together. His knees were bouncing up and down in tiny tremors but he couldn't get them to stop. He tried to swallow but gagged on what little saliva was there.

"Okay, listen — *cough-cough* — I don't want any trouble, I just need to know that you're going to leave us alone." There was a long pause as the three men watched a car approach, slow down, accelerate and drive off.

Hicks opened the passenger door and hunched down on the curb, facing inside the car at eye level. "You think I should leave you alone?"

"Look, the kids never said a word to the police, I promise. None of us did. You got caught because you stopped for ice cream in a stolen vehicle *during* the pursuit."

"And how the hell do you know that?"

"It was in the police report, I swear. A couple off-duties were there and saw your car. I mean, my car. They chased, you fled, crashed on two-nineteen."

"I thought I was in the clear, I needed a fix." Hicks explained. "Mint chip relaxes me."

"Yeah, he likes mint chip!" Rotty flexed, scolding him for not knowing.

"So," Phil kept the momentum going, "sounds like it's all in the rearview mirror now — no pun intended," he chuckled into their blank faces. "Since we obviously didn't rat you out or anything, we're all good, then. No snitches, no stitches … right compadres?"

"Not so fast." Hicks leaned in, his eyes turning a more menacing shade of whatever color they were. "I saw you at the courthouse when they walked me out. I heard what your pretty little wife said about me."

"I don't know what you're talking about," Phil said unconvincingly. He never thought it would come back on him like this, but Liz had gone full mama bear at the sight of the man who took her cubs. He didn't know which part Hicks actually heard that day, but on the menu were: "I hope he rots in jail", "I can't even look at that animal", and "you know what happens in prison to people who mess with kids."

"How about I help you remember," said Hicks, sliding into the passenger seat and upping the ante.

Phil scrambled, desperate to regain control, and went for the one card he had up his sleeve. "How about this instead." He reached slowly past his unwelcome passenger and put his hand on the glovebox latch, maintaining eye contact with a reassuring look that said *don't worry, I'm not reaching for a gun.* Hicks didn't look very worried anyway, as Phil opened the glovebox, pulled out an envelope and placed it beside him. It was a pretty smooth move, but the fact that it took place just a few inches from the man's crotch made it a little awkward.

Hicks was amused, opening the envelope and counting the bills. When he got through the stack, he counted it again before turning to Rotty.

"Five hundred dollars."

Nobody said a word. The standoff had now become a poker game.

"Mr. Suburban thinks five hundred dollars is something. Rotty, do you think that's enough to get us that nice pontoon boat?"

"Naw, man, definitely not enough," laughed Rotty, adding a tiny dance step to his reply.

Hicks locked eyes with Phil. "Three thousand and you'll never see me again."

"Or me," touted Rotty.

"Consider it reparations for my lovely stay at Rockhill."

The Beverlys lived paycheck to paycheck, so coming up with three grand would require moving money they didn't really have — and hoping Liz didn't notice.

"It's not my fault you got —" Phil reconsidered his words. "Two thousand, I'll bring it tomorrow," he said, about to add contract negotiations with criminals to his résumé.

"This ain't a used car lot. Three."

Phil nodded like a bobblehead, frantically going through every credit card balance in his head and plotting multiple cash advances. "Okay, three thousand, I'll have it tomorrow."

Hicks confirmed with his own nod. "Be here at noon tomorrow. I'm in —"

"Room 106, yeah, I kind of know where you live," crowed Phil.

"That's nice, Suburban, I know where you live, too. Tell your wife and kids I said hello."


THE BANANA SPLIT, A.K.A. AUSTIN'S JEEP, left the Valley Putt parking lot blaring more bass-heavy beats from its Kicker subwoofers. The three golfers had made their exit without saying much to each other, still walking on eggshells from the lagoon splashdown and Sweet Pea's surprise visit from the drunk pirate. As the boys rapped along with the Fresh Prince's ode to summertime, Sweet Pea was having a hard time sitting back and unwinding.

"Dude — I'm hungry," Austin yelled across the stereo and road noise.

"Taco Tuesday!" hollered Gus triumphantly before turning the volume down a notch.

"Let's do that place past the quarry, at the old flea market."

"If they're open," added Gus. "They're not there half the time."

"Hey backseat, you hungry?" Austin gave Sweet Pea a look in the mirror, but she was staring out her side of the vehicle and putting off *do not disturb* signals. He gave a shrug.

"I need a rap break," said Gus. "Play something else."

Austin dug through his CD collection to find something more chill. Before long, the boys were trading verses and butchering harmony on the love theme from *Footloose*.

Despite finding it funny — okay, maybe adorable — that Austin knew every word to "Almost Paradise," Sweet Pea wasn't showing it.

A few songs later, they came to a remote intersection with a blinking yellow light. If there were tumbleweeds in Pennsylvania, this would be their favorite place to roll around. On the other side of the road was an old outdoor flea market that had shut down years ago. It currently resembled a miniature shanty town, rows and rows of long roofs over abandoned stands, tables and rudimentary storefronts that used to bustle on weekends. A taco stand still operated there, keeping its doors open even when everything else stopped. (Borough officials turned a blind eye to minor details like food inspections, taxes and labor laws because the burritos were to die for.)

Gus spotted smoke coming from a vent on their roof. "Looks like we're in business," he said, finally allowing his brain to fantasize about tender barbacoa drizzled in homemade tomatillo salsa. They parked the Jeep and got out, admiring the hand-painted lettering on the front awning:

CHOZA DE TACOS

"I thought it was called La Choza?" asked Austin.

"Me too, they must have changed it. I'd ask them, but no hablo español."

"Welcome to Taco Hut," said the man behind the counter, as proud of his broken English as he was of his authentic Mexican cuisine.

"Pea, get over here, we're ordering," Gus called back to his sister.

"Not hungry," she said, still buckled in, lying her head on her arm like it was a pillow.

Gus interrupted Austin's studying of the menu board. "Go see what she wants."

"She just said she's not hungry. You deaf?"

"She's obviously pissed about the golf course. Just go over and say you're sorry or something so she eats."

"Nah, she's good. It's all good," said Austin, returning to the menu. "She actually wanted me to push her in. Don't sweat the technique, Guster."

"Welcome to Taco Hut," the man said again. They started to think those were the only four words he knew in English. As Austin and Gus placed their orders, Sweet Pea climbed out of the Jeep to stretch her legs. What started as brooding had slowly reduced to sulking, but now she was content with just pouting around until she felt better.

She looked up at the big blue sky, squinting as the sun poked holes through the thin end of a puffy cloud. Walking around the empty parking lot, Sweet Pea headed to the far end of the front row and disappeared behind it to keep exploring. The old flea market structures reminded her of long, skinny garages with no front walls, each row about five school buses long. Her stomach growled, but she ignored it, refusing to eat with *them*. Walking past booth after booth of dusty, empty stalls, she wondered how long it had been since this place was a thriving flea market. When she was little, she thought flea markets sold fleas, which she now knew wasn't true, but she still felt itchy as she wandered.

Stumbling onto the third row, something caught her eye halfway down the line. Making her way to investigate, she wrinkled her face at the sight of an old woman sitting behind a table, flanked by a faded sign draped over the front:

MISS AURORA'S SOAPERY & APOTHECARY

A warm orange tapestry dressed the rear wall, pulling her in and funneling her eyes to the table of soaps — dozens of bars stacked high and wide, sorted in columns of matching colors. The white-haired soapmaker sat in a green suede recliner with bronze nailhead trim. Everything on her table looked ancient, but not in a dirty or decrepit way — ancient like a lost civilization had teleported it there. Sweet Pea looked around, expecting to see other customers or signs of life in adjacent booths, but it was a ghost town.

She approached as the woman stared down at a knitting project on her lap, acting invisible to her customer. The curious fourteen-year-old had only known soaps named Dove, Dial or Irish Spring, so she was fascinated by the swirly patterns and rough, wavy edges of the hand-cut bars in front of her. This was her first soapery, and she had no clue what an apothecary was, let alone how to pronounce it.

"You lookin' for soap?" the woman asked, still not making eye contact, lacking any hint of salesmanship. Sweet Pea was taken aback by her groggy voice, still trying to make sense of the odd business location.

"No, ma'am."

*"Mmmm-hmm."*

Picking up a purplish bar and giving it a sniff, Sweet Pea wondered if the guys had gotten their food yet. With the current state of affairs, she wouldn't be surprised if they drove off without her. She browsed a little longer, running her fingers over the rough textured ends, but she didn't want to give the impression that she was going to buy something.

"Welp, I have to get goin'," she said, putting it down and backing away. "Have a nice day."

"Them boys ain't left yet." The woman seemed to know things. "Tell Miss Aurora what's troublin' you."

Sweet Pea paused and processed the possibility that Miss Aurora was reading her mind. Or more realistically, she had heard three car doors closing and no sound yet of a vehicle driving away. But nothing was troubling her — at least nothing she wanted to discuss with a person she just met behind a taco stand.

"Nothin'," she replied, looking sideways. "Sorry ma'am, I have to go."

"Not everyone lookin' for soap," Miss Aurora said as her customer turned to walk away, "but everyone hopin' to get a little cleaner."

Sweet Pea stopped and thought about the words that just flew into her head, as the smell of barbacoa clashed mid-air with the soapy fragrances. Did she mean clean like washing up after playing outside, or clean in the way they used to talk about in Sunday school?

"Let's find you a soap that'll get you right."

Her brain was working a little harder now, wondering if it was okay to be interested in Miss Aurora's offer, or if these were the types of situations her mother had warned her about. She turned back around and stared, letting her eyes space out into a blur while she thought about all the things she had been worrying about this week, and last month, and the past seven years. The wall of soaps ran together like a rainbow as she fazed in and out.

"These here are my soaps from the sky," pointing to the stacks on the left. "And these here are my soaps from the field," pointing to the piles on the right.

Now totally intrigued, Sweet Pea reapproached the table and checked out the soaps on the left side. The deep orange-purple bar was labeled *Dawn*, a golden-yellow one, *Daylight*, and a darker reddish soap read *Dusk*.

"The sky's always makin' hope, no matter how dark a night try 'n steal it away." Still knitting, Miss Aurora didn't look up.

Sweet Pea hadn't noticed before, but the scent of each bar was painting a picture behind her eyes now. The purples, yellows, reds and oranges were washing out the dark canvas that too often appeared when she wasn't distracted.

Moving over to the stacks on the right, she led with her nose this time, pulling in the sweet, fruity aromas of a flower patch. She picked up a pink-to-red bar, *Hibiscus*, and next to it were bluish-purple soaps labeled *Lilac*. On the end of the table was one that spoke to her the most — a wild spiraling pattern of crimson reds, navy blues, pastel lavenders, hot pinks and the purest whites. She took a bar in her hand and read the elegant cursive writing on the label: *Sweet Pea*.

Her body, mind and soul froze for two seconds. *What the actual heck*, she thought, shivering out a tiny chill and quickly putting the soap down like it was a voodoo doll.

Miss Aurora placed her knitting aside, and Sweet Pea could see a flower pattern on whatever it was she was working on. "The fields keep growin' their love, even when you too blind to see it."

Getting up from her recliner, she moved in slow motion, grabbing a cane and trying to stand up. She opened and closed her mouth a few times, like a cat trying to swallow medicine, and slowly lifted her hand to push a few strands of white hair out of her face. She looked toward Sweet Pea with milky eyes that tried to meet hers but couldn't find them.

"Ma'am, I don't have any money with —"

"It's Miss Aurora," she offered.

"Miss Aurora, I didn't bring any money." Sweet Pea was trying not to stare at her blank white eyes, and wanted to ask about the soap with her name on it, but she wasn't sure what to say. Before she could formulate a plan, Gus's voice called out from the other side of the roof, sounding almost serious like a parent looking for a lost child.

"Now them boys are ready," Miss Aurora laughed, also at half-speed. "Here," she said, taking two bars of soap and wrapping them in brown paper. "These are yours, child."

Sweet Pea took the package and put her hand on the woman's shoulder, silently thanking her for the gift.

The woman cleared her throat. "Now you remember — to fix up somethin' right, you gotta go back to where it got broke."

Sweet Pea appreciated her random musings and sage advice, nodding politely at the old lady before realizing it fell on blind eyes.

"Sweet Pea!" came Austin's voice this time, sending her sprinting down the row and back toward the taco stand. Rounding the corner, she was met by Gus's worried face, which he quickly tried to hide.

"Let's go, where were you?"

"Nowhere," she said, climbing into the Jeep with her package tucked under her arm.

THE RIDE HOME WAS FILLED WITH SOUNDS of chewing, swallowing and occasional belching, but otherwise an awkward silence still permeated between the front and back seats. The Jeep flew into the Beverly's driveway with the same reckless abandon as its earlier arrival, this time stopping only eighteen inches short of the garage door. Gus and Sweet Pea thanked Austin and waved as he backed out, then headed inside for the evening.

Their mom was reading on the couch while their dad was reading in the kitchen, a surefire sign that they were fighting again or in the process of avoiding one.

"How was your day," asked Liz. "Any hole in ones?"

"She means any holes in one," chirped Phil.

"No, *hole in ones* is plural of *hole in one*," she retorted.

"Welcome home, kids, to the land of Your Mother's Always Right."

Gus and Sweet Pea rolled their eyes at each other before entering the mix.

"It was good," said Gus. "I had a couple but we didn't really keep score." He scanned the room and noticed lots of food and supplies that weren't there when they left, so he figured they were all prepped and ready for Thursday.

"Anyone hungry?" asked their mom.

"No, we had tacos at La Choza."

"I heard they changed their name," said their dad. "Tacos De Choza or Choza De Tacos. I don't know, same thing."

"Wow, Pea, you finally got to eat tacos with the boys," said her mom. "Awesome."

"Yeah, it was good," she lied, not interested in a major discussion about her not-so-great day.

"What's in the package?" her mom asked.

"Soap."

"Oh, where'd you get that?"

"Yeah, where'd you get that?" seconded Gus, clearly not having paid much attention to her earlier.

"I found a little soap stand," she said, offering no details and causing one of Gus's brows to raise. He looked to his mom and shrugged.

"I think I'm gonna crash in my room," Sweet Pea muttered. "I'm tired."

Both kids grabbed a quick drink before heading up. Gus trailed behind her on the stairs and followed her to her room, tossing a smuggled granola bar onto her bed and rushing off before she could turn around and acknowledge it. She unwrapped it in two seconds and devoured it in five bites, wearing an oat-covered grin as she ate. Just as the last bite was gone, her dad popped his head into her room.

"Hey, just wanted to check in." He sensed that she was a little down, but he also felt guilty for not spending much time with her the past few days. He was so consumed with his secret missions that he almost forgot to be a dad for his oft-traumatized daughter. So they talked about reading the break on putting greens and what it feels like to ride in an open-top Jeep, before hitting more serious things like the Sundowners and what to expect over the next few days.

"I know the whole dark sky thing is scary, but I'll protect you. Promise." He put a hand on her shoulder and looked in her eyes until she nodded. "Brand new generator in case the power goes out," he said with a smile.

"Right, I know, you told me," rolling her eyes. "And if yours isn't good enough we can borrow one from Sebastian."

"Who?"

"A guy we met on our walk yesterday. Doctor, actually. He

told mom he would help her if she needed anything like that. He was really nice."

Phil tried to hide his jealous curiosity. "Okay, okay, that's good then. All good in that department," he babbled while his imagination revved its engine. "Anyway, just making sure you had a good day." They fist-bumped. "Get some rest, I'm heading down to watch the game."

Just down the hall, Liz was having a one-on-one with Gus.

"Knock, knock, knock, it's mom-o'clock," she said entering his room. He didn't mind a short conversation as long as she didn't mind him playing Nintendo. So he nodded along and mumbled "uh huh" at all the right moments while she emptied her head. He could tell she hadn't talked to anyone all day, so he kind of felt bad for her.

"So, you and your dad got that generator yesterday. It's really nice." Gus had a feeling he was about to be interrogated. "That's cool. You guys were gone a long time, what took so long?"

"Yeah, we went to like half a dozen stores, everyone was sold out," he said, reciting his rehearsed line to perfection. "They had to get one from the back, so —" He was pushing it now. "Then the guy who brought it up couldn't find us and we had to get in line twice." Cherry on top.

Having spent most of the day by herself, Liz had time to ponder her husband's activities from the past twenty-four hours. It wasn't like him to run that many errands and be that helpful, to the point of suspicion. Was he secretly drinking? Smoking? Was there another woman? And why would he drag Gus along for any of it. It didn't make sense. Maybe he was just stressed out like everyone else and going for long drives, scream-singing his Guns 'N Roses albums.

"Alright, buddy, glad it worked out." She didn't believe a word

he said, but knew that whatever they were hiding, it was probably Phil's plan and Gus was just following orders. So she held her
cards and kept her leverage.

"I'm heading down for a cookie, want one?"

"No thanks, I'm good." He was relieved that she didn't question him further, but he was fully prepared to keep it going. He
thought about just telling her where they were and who they saw,
but he didn't want to start World War III between his parents.
Besides, he was getting closer to rescuing Princess Toadstool from
Bowser's castle, and that felt more important right now.

# 15

---

THE NIGHT SKY WAS HAVING AN IDENTITY CRISIS. It typically played the perfect backdrop for stargazers, wishmakers and wide-eyed wonderers, but the electromagnetic cloud was messing with its mojo and convincing it to bend some rules, wreak a little havoc and play the villain. For the past four-and-a-half billion years, day followed night, and night followed day — but that was about to change.

As midnight pushed into the early morning hours, the moon glowed with a hint of emerald, in a prelude to the last sunrise before the dimmer switch. The Beverlys were sound asleep, missing out again on the colorful tricks played by the cloud as it flitted on the outskirts of the sun's orbit.

Through Sweet Pea's blinds, a cast of greenish moonlight tiptoed over her pillow, kissing her on the cheek before washing over the plush giraffe wrapped in her arms. Across the hall in her parents' room, their white duvet cover lit up with enough greenery to see two shapes facing opposite directions. And one door down, Gus slept in pitch-black ignorant bliss behind extra-heavy-duty blackout shades. All under the same roof, but each on their own wavelength, they dreamed of soapmakers, money-stuffed envelopes, cheating husbands, and tacos. The morning sun would wake them up in a few hours, but after that they would be on their own for a few days.

WEDNESDAY'S GREEN SUNRISE was more aggressive than the spiny crack of color that pierced the sky a day ago. As every newscast and headline reminded the good people of Culver, and Planet Earth, this would be the last day of sunlight until Sunday, if not longer. Most folks planned a day of last-minute prepping, some planned parties, some planned a day of prayer, and others looked to cross a few things off their bucket lists, just in case. The Beverlys were as ready as they could be for the darkness, so they were looking forward to a day of rest to build up some mental health points. All of them except Phil, whose mental and physical health hinged on a successful delivery of three thousand dollars to the Thunderbird Motel.

Sweet Pea sat on the upper deck of their backyard swingset structure, taking in a mid-morning summer breeze. She spent a lot of time there when she was younger, and even though she was a little too big for it now, it still made a nice getaway to hang out in the shade of the blue and yellow striped canopy. From her perch near the back of their half acre, she stared toward the only house she'd ever known, picturing little Sweet Pea running from Gus's squirt guns. She traced the exact path with her eyes, remembering every step she took that day. She could see her hiding place along the foundation, imagining Gus ready to douse her, reliving her dad's garden hose rescue.

Her heart started pumping faster at the thought of her dad saving the day. As his other rescue flooded her head, Sweet Pea pounded her fist against the railing, trying to rattle her brain so it stopped playing the movie of her tower climb, but it kept rolling. The swingset deck was only five feet high, but it started swaying like the Turret of Terror, feeding the dizzying scene in her head.

What bothered her most about that day were the questions she kept asking herself afterwards. *Am I crazy? Like really crazy, the kind that ruins peoples' lives and they don't even realize it's happening … Why didn't my brain stop me from climbing up there? … Gus was right — what's wrong with me?* It made her wonder what she might do next, or if this was her wakeup call and she was back to normal. She sniffled and dabbed at a tear to hold it back.

Out of the corner of her eye she noticed her dad coming across the yard. Hiding her quivery face, she looked into the toy telescope and gave the fake steering wheel a turn.

"So, what are we doing first tomorrow morning," he called out, "at the palooza thing." He looked puzzled. "Is it still called morning if the sun doesn't come up?"

As he got closer, she was able to minimize the pictures of the hundred-foot ladder, hoping that her pulse would follow suit.

"I don't know." She fidgeted with the wheel. "Why do they call it a palooza, anyway?"

"Beats me," said her dad. "I would have named it the Pitch-Black Block Party, but I'm not on Borough Council."

Sweet Pea nodded, staring off into the distance, following the flight of a circling hawk. Her dad looked to see what she was looking at, and he locked in on the hawk, too, swirling a couple hundred feet up and over. He wished he could fly like that, gliding over everything below, higher and higher until it all got smaller and smaller. He could swoop down, drop the cash at the Thunderbird and launch back into the sky before Hicks could blink. He could fly over Culver the next time Liz went for a walk, scanning the ground below for doctors and watching their moves. Maybe he could fly high enough, far enough and fast enough to blast a hole in the electromagnetic cloud so the sun could fire up its nuclear reactor again.

"Funnel cake."

The words interrupted his hawk fantasy.

"What?"

"I want a funnel cake tomorrow," she said. "That's what we should do first."

"A breakfast funnel cake it is," he nodded, "you got it."

"Is it still called breakfast if it's not called morning?"

He loved it when she made the exact joke that he would have made. Plopping his butt down in a swing that was sized for kids, he squished his legs underneath him and awkwardly pushed just enough to create a back and forth motion.

Sweet Pea ducked under a beam and slid down the sliding board, almost smacking her forehead at the top. She climbed into a swing beside her dad and pushed off the ground with a two-foot spring that sent her sailing. They swung side by side for a while, enjoying the comfort of each other's company. Neither one of them was in a hurry to leave the mindless monotony of their pendulum-like state. Being next to her dad made the impending darkness less gloomy for Sweet Pea. And being next to his daughter eased Phil's mind just enough to let him think about what he had to do next.

HUNCHED IN THE CORNER of their upstairs spare room with a cordless phone, Phil put the finishing touches on his top-secret transfer of funds. The total was coming from three different accounts and two different credit cards, applying the same strategy that Gus used as a toddler who didn't want to clean his plate — the old "Spread It Around Trick."

If the pile of lima beans was dispersed randomly to five or six areas of the plate, with no pile having more than two or three beans each, along with one or two bites of meatloaf and a puddle of sauce left behind as a diversion, it becomes hard to tell at a glance that Gus didn't eat his beans. Same goes for the three grand.

Now he just needed to get out of the house, drive to the bank branch past Piedmont that they never go to, get the cash, go to the T-Bird, make the drop and get home without raising any suspicions. He knew it was too risky to make up another fake errand — Liz was smarter than that — so he enlisted his partner in crime to pave the way.

Liz hollered from another room. "Phil, we're making an ice cream run. And before you blame me, it was Gus's idea this time."

"Okay, just you and Gus?"

"Pea's coming too, care to join us?"

"No thanks, I have a few things I need to do here." *Nice job, son.* "Bring me some Moose Tracks?"

"Fine, don't join your family on the last day before the sun dies," she said while grabbing her keys and purse. "That's great."

It was eleven thirty-five, a little later than their plan called for, but once they were gone, he could still make his stops and get there by noon. He spied out the front window, watching their Camry back out, when it stopped suddenly and pulled back into the driveway. Sweet Pea got out and headed for the front door.

Looking hard at the clock on the wall, Phil tried to mask his impatience as she stepped inside.

"Hey, what'd you forget?"

"Nothin', just have to pee," she said casually, stopping to untie her shoes, place them on the shoe mat, mess with her bangs in the hall mirror and slowly walk upstairs to the bathroom.

Sweat was burrowing up through Phil's skin, wetting his armpits and dotting his brow. Pacing like a father-to-be in the maternity ward, he checked the time again and wondered how much longer he could wait. After what seemed like an hour — it was only two minutes — he heard the toilet flush and the sink run. Much to his dismay, Sweet Pea washed her hands very thoroughly, which was pushing the limits of this pitstop even further.

Traipsing down the stairs, she eventually made her way back to the shoe mat, tying each one in a double knot, even readjusting the laces on each side to be the same length. Phil's eyes bulged as he tensed up like a racehorse behind the starting gate, waiting to bolt.

"Moose Tracks, huh," she said stopping halfway through the door and turning back around. "How come —"

"You better get out there, your mom's waiting."

"Do you think they named it that because the chunks of fudge are like moose poop?"

"Wow, that's a great question," he said, now physically shuffling her out the door. "Go ask your mother and let me know when you get back."

He watched their car leave for real this time, safely vanishing down the road. Making up for lost time, he grabbed his things, darted to the Subaru and sped off to complete his first-ever payoff at a shady motel.

It took a lot longer than expected at the bank, but Phil hurried out the door with thirty crisp one-hundred dollar bills in an envelope. He'd never held that much cash in his hands before, and knowing how he was about to spend it made him sick in the gut. *I thought he'd take the five hundred, but if it keeps him away, I guess it's worth it.* His blood pressure was no-doubt spiked and he really needed to find a restroom, but it was already past noon and he still had a five-minute drive to the motel.

Speeding down the empty streets of Piedmont, he flew past the ugly remains of what used to be a happy slice of smalltown America. The old movie theater marquee still displayed most of the letters in R_SKY BUSIN_SS from the last time it operated in the early eighties, and the gas station on the opposite corner still hung rusty numbers from its dilapidated signboard, a dollar twenty-two per gallon. The only signs of life here right now were a pair of young women pushing a stroller and passing a cigarette, an elderly man sitting on a bench, and a car sitting at the intersection ahead. Running right through the four-way stop in an anxiety-ridden blur, Phil didn't notice the Camry on his right, its three passengers licking ice cream cones.

"Hey, that's Dad," said Sweet Pea from the back seat. All three heads followed the shape of the black family Subaru and Phil's clueless profile, driving left to right in front of them on his way to God knows where.

## TWENTY MINUTES EARLIER

Sweet Pea lollygagged out the front door and got in the car, as Gus fumed in the front passenger seat.

"About time — seriously, why didn't you go earlier."

"What's the rush, Gus," said his mom, backing out and heading down the road, "they're not gonna run out of ice cream."

Gus was on the clock, and his dad was counting on him to get them out of the house and be gone long enough for him to go and get back.

"Ugh, she's just annoying," he mumbled, using his well-documented annoyance as cover for his new role as undercover accomplice.

"Anyway," their mom said, "since this is the last normal day for a little while, let's make it extra special and go out to Markle Dairy."

A mini panic attack seized Gus, realizing that their normal ice cream stop out past the school was in jeopardy of being replaced by the one on the other side of Piedmont — a stone's throw from the Thunderbird Motel.

"Yes, I love it there!" said Sweet Pea.

"Ew," stalled Gus, trying to think of anything, "I heard they use unpasteurized milk."

"Did Austin tell you that?" his mom said. "You can't believe anything he says."

Gus countered. "Let's just go to Scoops, we all like it and we won't be eating bacteria."

"I want Markle," voted Sweet Pea, "we always do Scoops."

Gus kept trying. "They don't even have Moose Tracks, Dad wanted Moose Tracks."

"Okay, okay," their mom ruled, "sorry Gus, but this is a Markle Dairy day. I don't really care what your father ordered — I'll say they were out and get him butter pecan. Our secret."

As they drove the winding road into the countryside, Gus knew his dad would soon be on the same road, or at least one parallel to theirs. The degree of difficulty on Gus's assignment just went up a few points, as he had to keep their two vehicles away from each other without knowing exactly where his dad's car would be at any given time, and without being in control of the car they were riding in.

Pulling into Markle Dairy, Gus felt safe for the time being. Unless Hicks and Phil went for ice cream after their meeting to celebrate, there was zero chance of a run-in here. The three Beverlys ordered and sat at a table outside, as Gus tried a few more tactics to extend the visit and buy some time. It worked for a little while, but when their cones were half gone, his mom made the next move.

"Let's eat the rest in the car — I want to take you guys over through Piedmont to that cool road that goes along the stream."

Gus knew that road would be a close call, cutting through town just a few blocks up from the motel and the possible sight of their Subaru.

"Or —" Gus grasped at straws for a viable Plan B, "we could drive up that mountain road past that goat farm that Sweet Pea likes." His dad would have been proud. "Remember all those cute baby goats?"

"Goats sound fun, but I don't have enough gas to run all the way up there and back." Mom three, Gus zero.

So they drove back toward Piedmont, as Gus obsessed over the time and tortured himself with the probabilities of their cars crossing paths. Sweating it out, he twisted in his seat as they approached town. Piedmont basically had one main street, so once they crossed the intersection they would be safe.

Their car approached the stop sign, as the Beverlys took in the sights. Sweet Pea stared at an old man on a bench and wondered what he was thinking about. Did he even know about the sun? What if he didn't have anyone, no wife or family or friends, and he had no idea what was going on. She pictured him waking up tomorrow, trying to find his bench in the dark and then after a day or two, thinking that the sun isn't coming back and the world must be ending.

"Kids, roll up your windows — smokers." Liz shook her head as two girls shared second-hand smoke with the baby in their stroller. Before she could fully judge them, a car approached the intersection from their left. "This guy's not stopping." It blew right through the stop sign.

"Hey, that's Dad," said Sweet Pea.

In a frozen moment of surprise, their heads stared at the passing vehicle in slow motion. Liz didn't speak, but her brain was generating all kinds of answers to the questions she'd been asking herself. Adrenaline ran from her toes to her fingertips, dulling her senses and boiling her blood, trying hard not to believe there was another woman. She slowly pulled out and turned the wheel to follow her husband, keeping a safe distance back to maintain the high ground in whatever kind of lie he was about to be caught in.

# 16

WITHOUT BRAKING, THE SUBARU took a hard left into the motel parking lot, squealing to a stop a few doors down from room 106. Phil stared at his reflection in the rearview mirror, telling himself this was the right thing to do, convincing himself it was the easiest way out. Counting the money one more time, he closed the envelope, closed his eyes and inhaled — the deep breath before the plunge — then slowly let it out.

Slamming his car door shut, he hustled down the exterior walkway to Hicks' door.

*Knock-knock*

He took a few steps back and scanned his surroundings. A small common area led to the motel office, dotted with a few cheap plastic tables and chairs and a landscaping bed that was just weeds and dirt. He'd seen too many shows where the guy went into a hotel room to make a deal and never came back out, so he wanted Hicks to come out to him. For some reason, he was more nervous now than he was when confronting him the day before.

*Knock-knock-knock*


WATCHING HER HUSBAND WAIT OUTSIDE a motel room for his mistress to let him in was not what Liz thought it would be. Not that she ever really expected it to happen to her, but over the past few years as they drifted apart, she imagined what she would do if she ever caught him cheating. And her and Julia would joke about what body part they would chop off first. (His ring finger.)

But now that she was watching it unfold from the cover of her car across the street, the fury she expected to flood her veins wasn't there. She just went sad and numb, giving in to the fate of whatever was about to happen.

"Mom, what are we doing?" asked Sweet Pea from the back seat.

"Spying on Dad," answered Gus flippantly, having given up on weaving more lies into their web. The gig was up.

Staring helplessly at the distant door to room 106, Liz felt like she was falling from a rooftop, waiting for the thud. At any second, she fully expected to see some nameless bimbo, or one of the new teachers at school, or — more likely — Mandy Jo Dipetto. *So help me God, if it's Mandy Jo…*

But as the door finally opened after five knocks, every emotion in her being pulled a u-turn as Bruce Hicks stepped into the light. The first wave was pure shock at the sight of the man who wrecked her family. That was followed by a wave of mass confusion as to why he was out of prison — and meeting Phil at a cheap motel. And the third wave was sheer relief that it wasn't a woman.

"You're late."

Phil checked his watch, not realizing he was almost a full fifteen minutes late. "Sorry, man, traffic was a — "

"What happened to noon?" said Hicks, stepping toward Phil.

"It's basically noon, I didn't know you had me on a timer."

Hicks looked him up and down, wincing like he was in some kind of pain, shaking his head in a slow, deliberate, disapproving back and forth.

"You know, Suburban, it doesn't really sound like you're sorry."

"No, I am, really, I literally just told you I was sorry. In fact —"

"Shut up," Hicks interrupted. He reached into his pocket, pulled out a lighter and sparked the wheel, lighting a flame a few times while he thought. "You're fifteen minutes late, so the price just went up fifteen hundred."

Phil pulled out the envelope and frantically started flipping through bills. "Look, here's the money we agreed on, that's all I have, just take it."

Hicks, master of the dramatic pause, did nothing and said nothing for sixty seconds. It wasn't really a staredown, because neither man was looking at the other one. Phil stared at the ground, waiting for the verdict, as his tormentor looked at the sky, then a beer bottle near the curb, then a length of broken spouting on the roof, before pocketing his lighter and walking back toward his room.

"Hey!" Phil's voice lurched. "We had a deal!"

"Come back when you have all forty-five. Maybe I'll see you guys around," he called over his shoulder.

It's not that Phil couldn't drum up the money if he really had to, but he was tired of being the mouse to Hicks' cat paw. He knew the three thousand was ridiculous to begin with, and he knew that Hicks was toying with him. But the way he looked right past him, not taking him seriously, barely acknowledging him as any kind of threat made Phil feel the same way he did around Liz. The energy of those worlds colliding somewhere inside his shrunken state launched a chemical reaction that spilled over.

Picking up a cantaloupe-sized chunk of concrete from a nearby pile of rubble, he threw it as hard as he could at one of the tables, unleashing a primal scream as it left his hand. Hicks snapped his head to full attention. Unfortunately, his feat of masculinity drew more attention than he intended, as the cannonball skipped off the tabletop, careening up and over, smashing right through the office's picture window. The impact blasted a huge hole in the center of the glass, triggering a waterfall of splintered shards as the shockwave spread out, leaving only a few jagged edges around the frame by the time gravity was finished.

Phil looked at the window, then at Hicks, then back to the window, which now featured an angry man sticking his head through the frame.

"That didn't sound good," said Gus, not realizing his mom had already jumped out and hit the ground running.

"Stay in the car!" she yelled back.

In the fifteen strides it took her to reach the parking lot, Liz didn't have time to process whether she was running to help Phil or hurt Hicks — she just needed to get there. She'd never heard a roar like that come from her husband, so she knew that whatever was going on was serious. Arriving on the scene, she tried to catch her breath as she took in the spectacle around her: the motel manager stood in the remains of the shattered window frame, waving his hands as he barked into a telephone; Hicks stood by his door, looking like he'd been knocked down a peg or two; another man in a sleeveless shirt emerged from his room carrying a big knife; and her husband stood at the center of it all.

"Phil!" she snapped, causing his head to whip and his jaw to drop.

But the manager interrupted their moment. "Alright, who broke my window?"

"That was me, sir, it was an accident," Phil confessed. "I was just trying to scare your guest over there. Not the one with the machete, the other one."

As the men talked, Liz honed in on Hicks, shifting her concern for Phil to a new rush of adrenaline aimed at the criminal just a few steps away. She flashed back to the trauma of that summer, and the fifty-two agonizing minutes waiting for the phone to ring that day, not knowing if she would ever see her kids again. It changed her, and she tried not to let it make her a hateful person, but she blamed him every day for their family's problems.

"You again," she said to Hicks. "Can't you just leave us alone?"

"Maybe you should tell your husband to leave *me* alone," came the voice she hadn't heard since the courtroom.

"Honey, go to the car," Phil cut in, taking her arm and trying to move her along. "I'll handle this."

"I'm just trying to live my best life, ma'am, but he keeps pokin' around my front yard here."

"Yeah, he keeps pokin' around!" Rotty accentuated from somewhere behind them.

"This is all you —" Liz said with more conviction than she'd felt in years. "If you hadn't decided to steal our car, none of this would be happening." Her brain fired up pictures of young Sweet Pea and Gus.

"Let's go —" Phil tried again, but she yanked her arm free of his grip.

"Nobody's leaving 'til the cops get here," the manager said, stepping between the Beverlys and the exit. Rotty quietly returned the machete to his room.

Hicks wasn't done. "Look lady, I get it, I get it — but I didn't just *decide* to steal your car."

Liz and her furrowed brow paused. Phil felt his entire body temperature jump ten degrees as his head swelled like a steam engine, followed by a mass exodus of color that left him bone white.

Hicks smelled blood in the water. "Aw, Suburban, she doesn't know. That's cute. You never told her?"

Liz darted her eyes to Phil's, his words sinking in.

"Never told me what?" she asked.

"It's nothing," he stammered.

Red and blue lights shot across the windows of the Thunderbird, as Culver's finest pulled up to the curb. A police officer walked past Sweet Pea and Gus, who were loitering near the curb for a better view. The manager met him immediately, talking fast, pointing to his window, then pointing to Phil.

Hicks leaned in to Liz, unsheathing the missing pieces of her story. "Hubby had a little gamblin' problem. I was just doin' my job."

She might not have believed someone like Hicks, but Phil's petrified stance, saucer eyes, and gaping mouth were a dead giveaway. Standing in the center of the commotion, she tuned out the world as her brain put it all together. *Just doing his job.* The car was taken because of Phil. Their kids were taken because of Phil. Seven years of arguments, fights and accusations were all because of Phil. He didn't just hide his gambling from her, he watched what it did to his marriage, his family, especially his daughter, and still didn't have the decency to come clean. The betrayal pushed on her chest, cutting her breaths short. She couldn't look at him. Phil put his hand on her shoulder, where it was summarily dismissed.

"Sir, I need to ask you a few questions," the officer said, but Phil wasn't there. He was standing right in front of him with both feet on the ground, but he was flying a hundred miles an hour on the inside, scrambling to come up with one more lie to convince Liz it wasn't true.

"Sir, I'm talking to you —"

"I'll tell you what happened," interjected Hicks, "this guy comes outta nowhere, threatens me and my friend, then throws a block of concrete at us."

"Tried to kill us, your honor," Rotty added for good measure.

Bits and pieces of the conversation started to register in Phil's conscious mind, which was preoccupied with his other predicament.

"That's not true," he finally caught up, "I can explain everything."

Hicks sensed an opportunity. "Check his pockets, officer, he was waving around a big wad of money, too, maybe he stole it from the office, or he's some drug dealer or — I dunno."

"That's ridiculous, I never —"

"Sir, can you empty your pockets?"

"You can't be serious, I'm a school teacher, they're lying to —"

"Sir, I have three witnesses all putting you in some trouble right now." He turned to Liz, who had faded a few steps into the distance. "Ma'am, do you know this man?"

She glared at her husband's guilty face, contemplating the power of her next words.

"No, officer, I just stopped to see if anyone needed help." She held her stare to drive the knife a little deeper. "I need to be on my way."

Phil had never truly been hurt before by anything she had

said during their fights. Words of anger, insult, and resentment were a dime a dozen, but this was new. He felt it right in the center of his heart, causing the air to leave his lungs in a low whimper as she left him there.

Liz walked away from the broken window, the broken trust, and the broken pieces of their marriage. She approached Gus and Sweet Pea with welled up eyes, shepherding them across the street and back into the car without answering their frantic questions.

"That's him, isn't it —" Sweet Pea said, her stomach lurching harder with every second of silence. "How can he be out? What's Dad doing over there?!"

As their mother continued to float above them in a state of disconnect, Gus tried to comfort his sister. But aside from confirming that she did, in fact, just lay eyes on their infamous childhood carjacker, he didn't know why they were just leaving their dad.

Looking back across the street, Sweet Pea was the first one to notice her dad walking toward them. She was also the first to notice his hands were behind his back, and the police officer was holding his arm. None of it looked real to her, like they were just acting out a play, or filming a TV show. The man in blue turned her dad's body toward the patrol car, as the sun reflected off the handcuffs around his wrists. Just like a movie, she thought. Then, like every bad guy who gets cuffed and stuffed, his head was ducked into the back seat and the door was slammed shut.

# 17

---

HOURS CAN FEEL LIKE DAYS when you're slowly losing control of all the little things that are keeping you together. Sweet Pea spent the car ride home spiraling in the fleeting hours of Wednesday's last light. She needed answers and explanations, but her mother's silence forced her to make up conveniently desperate, or desperately convenient, scenarios to help her brain pull up on the yoke.

*Maybe Dad was driving around looking for us because he changed his mind about ice cream, but then he got lost and turned into that motel? Or maybe he went there to check about getting rooms for us if the power goes out in our neighborhood? Or maybe he's an undercover agent and he went there to put Hicks back in jail and this is all part of his cover?*

As the day wore on, Liz stuck to her one and only story, no matter how many times Sweet Pea or Gus asked what happened: "Your father was trying to protect us, and the police took him away to keep him safe." No amount of tears or begging or panic would pry another word from her lips. "End of story," she parried every time.

She was only able to be so callous because her heart was lying on the ground somewhere back in Piedmont. The Liz that drove them home and wandered aimlessly around their house was just a shell, still picking shrapnel from learning Phil's big secret. Her empty answers were partly due to shock, but also because she wasn't ready to tell her kids the truth. *Hey kids, funny story ... seven years ago, your dad lost so much money gambling that his bookie sent a goon to repo our car — and you were in it!*

As Liz grappled with her new reality, Sweet Pea slipped a little closer toward the darkness that was literally on her doorstep now. From her bedroom window she watched it sucking the last drops of light from the sun in an eerie display of colors that had no business calling itself a sunset.

It made her think about an elderly neighbor of hers when she was little, Mr. Barkman. She was walking to school with Gus one winter day, when they saw him lying on the sidewalk, flat on his back with a snow shovel still clutched in his hand. He had suffered a heart attack and died right then and there, undiscovered for an hour or so before they arrived. His colors were all wrong, and even at her young age, she knew that life had left his body. She remembered staring at his still eyes and blue lips, leaning over his gray skin, trying to make any sense of it. She had managed to stifle those images of her first dead body, until tonight's dying sun brought them shivering back to life.

As darkness finally set in, *the* darkness, Sweet Pea was fully prepared to lie awake until two a.m., consumed by anxious energy and half-asleep nightmares. Most likely her dreams would be of Hicks pushing her into the black swamp waters, or her dad rotting in a jail cell at the end of the world. She always used the morning sun as a reset button for whatever she was dealing with, turning her life off and on again so the anxiety wouldn't pile up too high.

But if tomorrow morning was just a continuation of the previous night and all its baggage, she wondered if her body could handle the mass of worries stacked on worries stacked on worries. Before she could torment herself any longer, sheer exhaustion kicked in, sending her snoring in the face of all her troubles.

Down the hall, Gus immersed himself in more Super Mario before powering down for the evening. He had already come to terms with the day's events, and knew that tomorrow would probably be an interesting one for the Beverly family.

Further down the hall, Liz was alone in their bed for the first time in their eighteen years of marriage. Phil's pillow had been thrown to the floor as she staked claim to the entire queen-size mattress. Just her and a thousand thoughts circling her head, no matter how hard she tried to make them stop.

And down the road, all the way to the county sheriff's department, Phil sat on the edge of his cot, trying to convince the deputy to let him make another phone call.

"You already had your calls. Lights out."

"But nobody answered. I need to try her again, this is all —"

"Buddy, you're stuck here til you get your arraignment, and God knows when that will be with everything going on."

Phil's silence begged for more information as the man paced.

"They said the judge probably won't be seeing anyone for a few days, so you might as well get comfortable." Phil stood up, then sat right back down. "He's up in Warren County taking care of his parents or something. Robinson was supposed to fill in but nobody's seen her."

"Please sir, I have kids at home. My wife didn't answer, just let me try her one more time."

The deputy approached the cell door, motioning for him to come over. "Hate to tell you this … but maybe she doesn't wanna talk to you." Phil deflated. "I see it all the time, man. While you're here in this bed, someone else is there in your bed."

"Sebastian," he muttered to himself, staring at the floor.

"What's that?"

"Nothing."

The deputy turned to walk away. "Get some rest, tomorrow's a new day." He thought about what he said, then shrugged. "Actually, I guess it's not."

JUST AS THE SCIENTIFIC WORLD HAD PREDICTED, beginning with Artie in Idaho, Thursday morning arrived without a single sunbeam. No faint glow on the eastern horizon, no gradual changing of the guard from dark to light. The night sky waited for the next shift to relieve it of duty, but nobody showed up, so it just kept doing its thing.

The weak force hiccup, as the nuclear physicists called it, was right on schedule, weakening the sun's nuclear reactions to the point that its light and heat were percolating but going nowhere. The sun's dimmer switch was officially turned down to low, leaving Earth and most of her solar system fumbling around in the dark.

Sweet Pea and Gus rolled out of bed and downstairs around the same time, while their mom slept in.

"This is weird," she said, staring out their front window beside her brother.

"Yeah, it's even weirder than you," said Gus.

She liked that he was still picking on her. It made her feel like she was normal, because if something really was wrong with her, and she really was crazy, he would have been more sensitive and careful not to hurt her feelings. Or would he? Maybe her theory had holes.

"Whoa, look —"

Gus followed her pointer finger to a caravan of possums hiking the road in front of their house. It was almost nine a.m. and they were still out wandering around like it was midnight.

"I guess they didn't get the memo," he said.

Sweet Pea opened the front door and Gus followed her onto the porch.

"Hey little dudes," she whisper-yelled, before realizing it was daytime and she didn't have to whisper. "Attention possum family — go to bed!"

Gus shined a flashlight on them, lighting their eyes and drawing their attention. They changed direction and never broke stride (albeit very small strides), turning up their driveway and heading right for the porch. It took a few seconds for the humans to realize they were about to be invaded by their new nocturnal friends, eliciting a yelp from Sweet Pea as brother and sister hurried back inside and slammed the door.

"Attack of the possums," Gus laughed, "that's messed up."

"Almost as messed up as you," she jabbed, heading to the fridge in search of breakfast. That's all it took to trigger it. *Is it still called breakfast if it's not called morning?* Thoughts about her dad cut in on the few minutes of fun that she had allowed herself to enjoy.

"Wonder if Dad's coming home today?"

"I don't know," Gus said, "he knew that Hicks was out. We

went spying on him a few days ago."

"For real?" she said, picking a few grapes off the bunch.

"He didn't want to tell you or mom. Said you guys had enough to worry about."

"But why won't Mom tell us now. I don't get it." She offered a few ripe ones to Gus.

"Something must have happened. She doesn't seem to give a shit that he's in jail."

"You're right, I don't," their mom's voice crashed the party from around the corner of the stairwell. "And whatever happened yesterday is between me and your father."

Caught in the act, neither kid challenged their mother's stance, as she cut through them for a look out the window. She took in the scene, scanning the dark, distant sky and the faint shapes of trees past their neighbor's house. It was just three days, she told herself. She didn't need Phil whether it was dark or light, night or day. He got himself into this mess, so he could get himself out of it, and she wasn't going to sit around waiting for him to save the day.

"Aw, the cute little possum family is on our porch," Sweet Pea motioned. The Beverlys gathered themselves and stared at the mother and her seven babies, noticing their slightly confused circadian timing as they made themselves at home next to a large planter, under the cover of some long fern leaves.

"Where's your papa?" Sweet Pea rhetorically asked the babies as they nestled in.

"Their dad must be out hunting for food," said Liz. Whether or not she knew that mother possums drive away the father possum soon after mating, she tried to cover for him so Sweet Pea didn't think all families were like hers.

Gus nodded. "Yeah, or maybe he's in possum jail."

THE FLYER FOR THE PITCH-BLACK PALOOZA had been hanging on their fridge for a few days, so before things went south in Piedmont, they had all been looking forward to some "fun without the sun." For Sweet Pea it was a structured distraction so her mind didn't dwell on dying plants, plunging surface temperatures and prison sentences. It allowed her to think about happier things like which food trucks might be there, and how many songs her favorite garage band, The Hemlocks, would play when it was their turn on main stage.

Once the novelty of daytime looking like nighttime wore off, Sweet Pea and Gus spent the middle part of Thursday keeping to themselves and not doing much of anything. Their mom had the news playing in the living room, but there was enough tension in the house over their absent father and Liz's gag order, that nobody really wanted to be around each other at the moment.

Staring at the scenes from New York and L.A. on her TV, Liz had almost forgotten that this wasn't just a Culver thing. She was living through a global scale phenomenon, something that people would talk about for centuries, and as she sat there alone listening to reporters spewing their stories, everything started feeling bigger. One of her least-favorite news anchors caught her attention as she channel surfed.

*I'm serious, Tom. We should all be praying that it doesn't go past three days. The feds aren't telling you this, but it's going to get very cold, very fast here on Planet Earth. You want to run around like this is some kind of party, go ahead, but let's all hope that massive electromagnetic cloud that's big enough and bad enough to shut down the freaking sun doesn't mess with our power plants back home here and black out our grid. Do they even know that it won't affect the sun's gravitational pull on Earth? Can you imagine if that's off by even just a little bit, we're talking about changing the orbit of not just our planet, our whole solar system, and I don't know about you, but I don't like our chances as a civilization if we crash into Mercury or Venus a couple months from now...*

*Click*

Liz turned off the television. She waited in vain for Phil to blast holes in every conspiracy theory the talking heads threw out, but his words never came. It always annoyed her how quickly he dismissed the shock and awe of whatever was worrying her, but now without his skepticism front and center, the fears rang louder and truer inside her head, giving them more life whether she believed them or not.

Her brain changed channels to the Thunderbird Motel, jumping back to a rerun of yesterday's calamity.

*Maybe he had a good reason to keep secrets about Hicks. And what if the whole gambling thing was some kind of addiction and he couldn't help it? Maybe this whole thing is my fault now for getting him sent to jail.* She quickly course-corrected. *No ... he lied to me, he lied to Gus, he lied to Sweet Pea ... all these years. And here I go again trying to find a way to blame myself.*

She popped up off the couch. "Hey kids, get down here!"

Two bedroom doors opened and cautious footsteps made their approach.

"Get your shoes on — it's time for a funnel cake."

# 18

THE LONGER IT TOOK THEM TO DRIVE DOWNTOWN, the more it bothered Sweet Pea that her dad wasn't behind the steering wheel. This was supposed to be a family activity — the whole family, not just three-fourths — so no matter how hard her mom tried to act like everything was normal, it wasn't.

Windows down and elbows out, they passed under a massive PITCH-BLACK PALOOZA banner that marked the entrance to the festivities, as the streets of Culver were crawling with revelers. Concrete barriers blocked the road ahead of them, as traffic slowly funneled into an alley running behind the storefronts. Liz hit the brakes as a group of kids ran across the path of their vehicle, barely looking back as the last one mouthed *sorry* in an attempt to apologize for his friends.

They rolled along with the line of cars, passing parking lots on their left that were overtaken by tents and tables of vendors selling their handiwork. Up ahead they could see a row of food trucks, but a pair of roadblocks routed them down another alley to the right. Jutting into the sky were giant spotlights on extended ladder trucks, doing their best to make everyone forget the skies were black.

Based on the sights, sounds and smells that were hitting the Beverlys' senses, this was already bigger than most of the downtown festivals they'd been to. Sweet Pea was pretty sure she saw a petting zoo around the corner, which at this point in time was about the only thing she was looking forward to. She definitely was not in the mood for forced family fun, but if there was a baby goat in need of petting, she was in.

Traffic finally emptied into an area north of the six-block Palooza zone, as Liz struggled to find a parking spot. Gus moaned as she drove right past two open spaces, before pulling into a lot that was clearly marked NO PARKING. She performed a clumsy nine-point turn, barely avoiding the rear fender of a pickup truck, before finally getting pointed in the right direction.

"Where the hell are we supposed to park," she uttered as a burst of wrinkles shot across her forehead.

"Dad would have found a spot by now," said Sweet Pea, sounding more like her brother than she ever thought possible.

Liz let it slide, not even bothering to shoot a scowl in the rearview mirror.

"Here's one," she said, regaining control as she eyed up a curbside opening.

"Yeah right," snorted Gus, "when's the last time you parallel parked — nineteen twenty?"

Ignoring her carful of critics, she pulled mirror-to-mirror with the SUV ahead of the empty space, threw it into reverse and stuck the landing, three inches from the curb.

"How's it look on your side, Gus?" she taunted.

"Fine, I guess."

"Good, let's go have some fun."

They got out of the car and looked around, gawking at the late-afternoon sky as they kept trying to come to grips with the absence of natural light. They each had their own way of dealing with the solar phenomenon, in all its spectacle and great unknown.

"I know this is a little weird without your dad here," their mom attested, "but there's nothing we can do right now to help him, so let's just —"

"Did you even try?" huffed Sweet Pea. "Just bail him out or whatever, this is ridiculous."

"We are *not* doing this," her mom argued, side-stepping a large man devouring a plate of monkey bread, as the three of them anger-walked through the crowd.

"Yeah, you're not doing anything," she barked at her mom before turning to Gus. "Any idea why Dad's in jail? Or when he's getting out? Didn't think so, me neither." She directed her laser eyes back at Liz. "Real normal, mom."

Liz took the high road again, trying to ignore the cattle prod that Sweet Pea was rattling at her.

"Oh my God," fumed Sweet Pea, releasing a disrespectful puff of air from her lungs.

Liz stopped walking and faced her, hackles raised. "Sorry I'm not *normal*," she retaliated. "Like the sky, is that normal? Sneaking off to hotels? Climbing up a drop tower? What's normal, Pea, tell me, I'm dying to know."

Sweet Pea gave the telltale signs of a direct emotional hit. First her chin, then her bottom lip, followed by her eyes filling with tears that in no way could she let her mom see running down her face right now.

Gus sputtered to the rescue. "Hey look, I see funnel cakes," he said, going for the save before one of them said something even more regrettable.

The neon glow of the funnel cake sign cast a pinkish glaze over their faces as they waited in line. The smell of frying batter induced a brief powder-sugar-covered getaway from life's troubles, as they took a minute to gather themselves.

Liz knew she crossed a line and genuinely wanted to make things right, but she had a hundred emotions firing on overdrive, and it was hard to pull out an instant apology.

Sweet Pea couldn't believe that her own mother brought up the tower, calling her out just like Gus had done that day, tearing down what tiny shred of self-confidence she was clinging to.

And Gus stood right between them as a human buffer, thinking about how differently things would be right now if their dad hadn't gone to the Thunderbird yesterday.

THE HOURS THAT FOLLOWED THEIR DUST-UP found everyone minding their manners and going through the motions as they searched unsuccessfully for some fun without the sun. An unspoken truce settled over them as they eventually made their way to Lincoln Square, the central hub of their tiny downtown business district, nestled in the shadow (if there were such a thing) of the Culver water tower. The intersecting streets widened into a roundabout with a large historic street clock in the center, surrounded by shops with awnings, steel benches, hanging planters and all the picturesque makings of small-town America.

For the next three days, it would also be home to the main stage for the scheduled entertainment, which at the moment was the Culver Junior High Marching Band. The Beverlys were glued to a bench, suffering through a medley of barely recognizable movie themes, when Gus perked up like a prairie dog.

"Austin!" he boomed, startling everyone in a twenty-foot radius, including his best friend who looked just as thrilled to be hanging out with his parents.

"Beverlys!" shouted Austin, making his way through the crowd and dishing out a line of fist bumps.

"Where's the esteemed Phillip Beverly, I owe that man a fist bump."

"Oh, he'll probably catch up with us later," hesitated Liz, "but I'll give him a special fist bump just for you."

Sweet Pea rolled her eyes, but she wasn't in a hurry to tell him that her dad was in jail, either. Austin's arrival was the only bright spot to this dark day, and she was curious to see if any awkward vibes were lingering from the golf course.

Liz eavesdropped while the kids made plans, realizing she was about to be abandoned.

"Guys, don't go running off without me, this was supposed to be family time. You can hang out with Austin tomorrow, okay?"

Before Gus or Sweet Pea could raise their objections, a voice interrupted from behind them.

"Oh my God … Lizard!" bubbled Julia, wrapping her arms around their mom in a sneak-attack super-hug so tight they waited for her head to pop off. The two thirty-somethings bobbed up and down, still embracing, gushing over how long it had been since they'd seen each other. A few people stared at the boisterous reunion, until a loud smack of Liz's hand on her best-friend's butt made even more people rubberneck.

"So embarrassing," cringed Gus.

"Fine, you three go do whatever," shot Liz. "Meet back here at ten."

Gus, Austin and Sweet Pea didn't give her a chance to rescind her offer, springing out of sight before she finished her sentence.

Sitting back down on the bench, Liz and Julia chatted about life while an out-of-tune trumpet section annihilated selections from *Dirty Dancing*.

"It's so good to see you," said Liz. "I mean it, you don't understand."

They did everything together before Gus was born, and then less, and then to an even lesser degree when Sweet Pea came along. But Julia never had kids of her own, so even when they did hang out, their plans usually competed with naps, babysitters, and early bedtimes. As the kids grew older, they still tried to do things, but Julia's eternally single outlook started to clash more and more with Liz's family life. So the last few years had been reduced to saying hello here and there, occasional jazzercize sessions, or randomly running into each other at the grocery store.

"Just you and the kids? Where's Mr. Perfect?" gagged Julia. It was no secret that she wasn't a fan of Phil. Most of it stemmed from the way he handled everything after the kids were taken, but even before that, Julia pegged him as the guy who stole her best friend.

"He's not here. Not coming, either."

"Oh my God — you two are separated! I knew it."

"No, it's not like that." She paused. "I don't think."

"I'm calling it right now — you're separated, you're single," she chirped, as if her word was final.

"No, trust me, it's complicated. Ugh."

Julia stood up and pulled Liz by the hand. "Nothing's complicated unless you make it complicated. You just need to —"

"No, this is actually complicated."

"How complicated?"

"Like, jail complicated."

Julia's eyes grew a few sizes and her mouth dropped. Liz grabbed her hand and dragged her old friend down the street, half a spring in her step.

"No more Phil talk."

"Okay, promise," said Julia. "But you owe me a story."

Liz smiled and gave three big exaggerated nods. "Let's just go have some fun like the good old days. Well, maybe not *that* much fun."


Gus, Austin and Sweet Pea made a lap around the whole Palooza, scoping the scene, trying to decide what to do. The whole place took a good twenty minutes to walk from end to end. Sweet Pea begged for a stop at the petting zoo, but the boys overruled her and insisted on carnival games, feeding Austin's newfound obsession with winning a prize.

"That rim is like half the diameter of a real basketball hoop," Gus said, analyzing the hoop shoot game with Austin. "And it's gotta be eleven feet high."

"Doesn't matter. I'm money all day."

"You know it's all rigged. You just blew ten bucks on stupid Skee-Ball," noted Gus. "Stop the bleeding, man."

"Don't tell me how to spend my grass-mowin' money," Austin said, stretching his arms, doing shoulder circles and twisting his torso as he prepared to dust off his jumpshot. "Austin wants a prize," he insisted, randomly going third-person.

"Hey Pea, think I can hit two outta three?"

Sweet Pea stood a few feet away, but her mind was on the other side of the solar system, so she never heard his question. *I really wanted to pet that baby goat. And I shouldn't have eaten that funnel cake without Dad. That was supposed to be us. He always did stuff like that for me when — wait, I'm talking about him like he's dead. He's not dead, he's just in jail.*

Austin was dealing with his own bout of paranoia. *Great, she's still mad about the kerplunk, she won't even answer my dumb question. Maybe I went too far, I probably could have just faked letting her hand go, or caught her right before she hit the water. I wonder if she thinks I'm a dick?*

"Hey Gus, here's a dollar, you go first," proposed Austin.

He approached Sweet Pea as her brother stepped up to the hoop shoot counter.

"Sorry about the other day," he said, soft enough that Gus couldn't hear.

"It's okay," she murmured, minus her usual spunk.

"I can tell you're kinda mad still."

"No, it's not that —"

Austin thought for a few seconds without saying anything, then tried to dig a little deeper.

"What is it, do you — "

"I don't want to talk about it."

"Guys, I'm up," Gus called. "Watch me burn these nets."

Austin put a pin in their conversation, one that Sweet Pea was happy to avoid revisiting any time soon. They pivoted to watch Gus fire away.

"*Kareem — sky hook!*" yelled Austin, nudging Sweet Pea to join in, but now she was staring at her feet and rubbing the side of her head.

Three airballs later, Austin took over.

"Here's how it's done, son," he boasted, trading places with Gus.

Sweet Pea drifted a few steps back, still not entirely present or accounted for. The more she thought about things, the more she didn't even want to be there. The sound of the boys celebrating snuck into her ears, but she didn't want anything to do with anything happy right now. Her dad was probably sitting in his cell with nothing but bread and water, or maybe some gruel, while her mom was gallivanting around with Julia.

Another celebration erupted behind her, as she kept her back turned to the hoop shoot game, trying to clear her head and get back to reality. Finally, she heard Gus and Austin approaching, but before she could turn around, something soft touched her cheek. The head of a huge stuffed giraffe slowly crept into her peripheral vision, greeting her with Austin's best pretend giraffe voice.

"Will you be my *fwend*?" it asked, bringing the rest of its giant body into view.

She looked confused. "Since when do you like giraffes?"

"I don't. I mean they're alright, I guess."

"Then why'd you pick that?" puzzled Sweet Pea.

"It's for you," shrugged Austin, holding out the plush animal. "Here."

A little slow to the party, Sweet Pea's eyebrows lifted and she took a quick breath as she finally realized what was happening. She pulled in her long-necked friend for a tight hug, nestling her chin into its fur until she forgot where she was. She wanted to say thank you, but she could tell her voice would be all quivery, so she just kept her eyes closed and hoped he would know that she really, really liked it.

A FEW STREETS OVER, JULIA AND LIZ found a booth selling wine slushies and sampled a few flavors before going with blackberry sangria. For the past hour, Liz avoided the subject of Phil, but as her plastic cup got closer to empty, she started spilling the beans. First just a little bit, then a little bit more, but when she realized how good it felt to keep talking about it and give her misery some company, she just kept going. The lies. The gambling. Everything.

"You said you didn't know him? To the police!" marveled Julia, busting into a laugh that mocked Phil and praised Liz at the same time. The ladies raised their cups and toasted the night.

"Here's to freedom," declared Julia.

"Freedom," Liz repeated, but even as she said the word, an image of her husband and his current lack of freedom popped into her head, as they tipped back their cups one more time.

"Liz, Liz, don't whip your head or anything, but look over there — tall, dark and handsome coming our way."

Peeking sideways in a thinly veiled attempt at subtlety, she spied Sebastian about ten steps away and closing. Their eyes met, or at least the one she was using to sneak a look at him did.

"Oh my God, I know him," she said through her teeth.

"Perfect," grinned Julia.

He approached them with a smile. "I'm dying to know what two lovely ladies are toasting on this perfectly enchanting evening?" He just had lines like that on standby.

"Sebastian?" inflected Liz. "Fancy meeting you here," she said innocently, but ignoring his question all the same.

"Liz, I was beginning to wonder if our paths would cross tonight."

"Looks like they did," giggled Liz. "X marks the spot."

Julia cleared her throat. "Freedom," she proclaimed, drawing their attention. "We were toasting freedom. With sangria."

"Sorry," Liz quickly apologized, "this is my friend, Julia. Julia, Sebastian."

"Freedom of speech? Freedom of assembly? Freedom of religion? Which was it?" he bantered.

Julia answered. "Let's call it freedom from husband —"

"Hey," panicked Liz, "let's change the subject, here. How about that sky today? Dark, huh?"

The group survived their first wave of icebreakers and introductions, moving into a second round of stories and smalltalk. Eventually, Sebastian told them that he came with his teenage daughter, who ran off with her friends an hour ago, too. He conveniently mentioned "ex-wife" at least three times.

That's all it took for Julia to invite him to join their slushie party. "The three of us are sticking together, then, since it seems like children and spouses are horrible creatures. You guys need a slushie … so I guess I'll get another one too."

"Okay, but only if you allow me to treat," he offered.

"I guess I can allow it," flirted Liz, without realizing she was flirting. "Just one more."

Sebastian paid for three wine slushies and they wandered off together, in search of anything to do until their kids needed them for more money or a ride home. The first day of darkness was winding down, but the night was just getting started.

Liz had zero experience in the past eighteen years with anything remotely resembling a first date, so she was entering uncharted territory. *Not that this was a date,* she told herself, *I'm just walking around a carnival at night with a new friend who happens to be interesting. And funny. And attractive. And a surgeon.* Lucky for her, she had plenty of help available from Julia and slushie number two.

# 19

---

IN HER ENTIRE LIFE, SWEET PEA had never won a big prize, and nobody had won a big prize for her, so the joy of receiving her new giraffe was closely followed by the realization that she had to carry it around the rest of the day. They only had about an hour left until their ten o'clock rendezvous, and as much as she had enjoyed snuggling him from street to street, her hands were getting sweaty and she needed a break.

"Guys, let's just camp here for a while, I'm tired."

She took a seat on a wide set of concrete steps in front of the post office, a little off the main thoroughfare where the crowds of people were still bustling around.

"I could chill here," said Austin, "my dogs are killin' me."

Gus followed suit, heading to the top step and sprawling out where he had a good view of the sky.

"Did you guys notice yet?" he said, looking up at the stars.

Sweet Pea and Austin stared up, trying to match his line of

sight, but they had no clue what he was talking about.

Gus turned to Austin. "All those stars — but something's missing."

"The sun's always missing at night, dipshit."

*"Ohhhhhh wait,"* realized Sweet Pea, "I just got it."

Gus mouthed a word to his sister, cupping his hand so Austin couldn't read his lips. Sweet Pea smiled and nodded on the receiving end.

"I give up, Galileo, what is it?"

The Beverly siblings toyed with him for a few minutes, dangling their carrot of knowledge until he threatened to take back the giraffe.

"Okay, okay," said Sweet Pea, "I'll tell you." She strung him along a little more before finally informing him that the moon was nowhere to be seen, even though it was almost full last night.

Austin checked all one-hundred-eighty degrees of the horizon, confirming its absence.

"Dude, the freaking moon burned out, too?"

Gus and Sweet Pea valiantly kept straight faces, but the first hint of her smile sent a laugh spitting out of Gus's mouth. They tried very hard not to insult his intelligence, but by the time they explained to him that the moon only reflects sunlight and can't make its own, he had taken the giraffe hostage, dangling him over a railing above some shrubbery.

"I'll drop him, I swear," he said, trying not to smile. As he paused to come up with a clever line about hostage negotiations, he noticed a face in the distant crowd from his perch. He stared long enough that it drew Gus's attention.

"What are you looking at?"

"Where'd you say your dad was?" asked Austin.

"I didn't. Why?"

Austin pointed across the street and half a block down to the trio of Julia, Liz and Sebastian, raising their plastic cups and chugging their drinks before high-fiving and letting out a celebratory *"Wooooooo!"*

"He might want to get here. I think Dr. Seb's on the prowl."

JULIA WALTZED UP TO THE TEENAGER who was working the Rootin' Tootin' Shootin' Gallery, asking him if it was easy to win a prize. He shrugged and uttered an inaudible word or two, before she pulled out a dollar and ponied up.

"Hold my drink, kid. You can take a sip if you're thirsty."

"Ma'am, I'm only sixteen," he lectured. "Even if I were old enough, I wouldn't drink while I was working. And I wouldn't drink after a stranger. How do I know you didn't —"

"Good lord, shut up and let me shoot," said Julia, grabbing the electronic rifle and eying up targets across the decorated homestead scene, complete with cowboy boots, a barrel of dynamite, and a cuckoo clock.

Liz and Sebastian chatted while she had her way with a few bull's eyes.

"I notice your ring finger is being weighed down by that diamond —"

She gulped.

"But the man who put it there, I presume, doesn't seem interested in spending time with you."

"Jules, go for the rattlesnake!" she blurted, not ready to entertain his assertion.

Sebastian's eyes looked away, then down at the ground as he regrouped.

"How many shots you have left?" Liz asked Julia.

"Two. Wait, three."

"And how many shots do I need to take?" whispered Sebastian, leaning closer to Liz's ear.

"Well, you're o-for-one," she said, stepping up and slapping a dollar bill in front of the attendant. Her cheeks were getting warmer, no doubt from the alcohol, but also because it was starting to sink in that maybe she was sending signals that she didn't really want to be sending. Or did she? Phil deserved this, she told herself over and over for the past twenty-four hours. He earned it fair and square for the past seven years, and she had nothing to feel guilty about.

Julia handed over the rifle, brooding a little because she didn't win a prize.

"Okay, so how do you hold this thing," wondered Liz, figuring it out on the fly as her first two shots missed everything.

"Darnit — I'm no good."

Sebastian stood right beside her now, acting like he was holding an invisible rifle to demonstrate a proper grip and stance.

"Like this."

"Let me guess, you hunt elephants on safari in your free time."

"Lions, actually."

She adjusted her grip and squeezed off three more shots, all sailing high over grandma's rocker.

"Here, let me show you."

Sebastian put one hand on the barrel of the rifle and his other hand on the small of her back. He moved his fingers gently up and down in a way that no shooting instructor was ever trained to do.

Alarm bells wailed inside her head, sending a shiver across all two hundred and six bones in her body. A hand was touching her back — caressing, more like it — and that hand did not belong to her husband. Her pulse pushed into her temples, pounding with guilt, louder and faster. She closed her eyes, hoping for divine intervention, but all that came to her was a picture of Phil's pitiful face.

"I'm sorry," she said in a breathless whirl, dropping the rifle and stumbling away, losing herself in the crowd. Sebastian watched her go, not feeling so rootin' tootin' himself, either.

WHEN GUS AND SWEET PEA FINALLY TOLD AUSTIN that their dad was in jail, his usual slick banter went missing. His brain went right to jokes about prison food, getting shanked in the yard, and their mom playing doctor, but his mouth safely filtered them all. Still on their post office perch, they game-planned what to do next, keeping a distant eye on the trio at the shooting gallery.

"Let's follow them, she's on the move," said Gus.

As they hustled down the steps, Sweet Pea questioned Austin.

"What did you mean, 'he's on the prowl?'"

"Nothing."

"Austin —"

"I'm just saying, he lives on my street, and I see lots of people coming and going from the Antonelli residence. And by people, I mean women."

"And?"

"And he was eying her up the other day, I saw it, now they're here, I'm just sayin'."

Sweet Pea's angry thoughts were multiplying. *So Dad's in jail but she won't say why. And instead of going there to get him out, or even visit him, she comes here like everything's fine. And now she's running around with Thistlewood's most eligible bachelor. Dad would never do this if she were the one in jail. She can think whatever she wants about him, but at least he always puts us first.*

"I see her up ahead, she's by herself, coming our way," said Gus, leading their pack in her general direction.

"Nobody say anything, just play dumb —"

They walked around a big group of people, timing it just right so they crossed paths with their mom.

"Hey, guys," she said enthusiastically, overcompensating for her welled up eyes and shaky voice.

Austin was emotionally uninvolved, so he took the lead while Gus and Sweet Pea took notes.

"What's up, Mrs. B, how's your evening going?"

"I'm ready to go, actually. Gus, Pea, say goodbye, let's head to the car."

"You said ten," Gus stated. "It's like nine-fifteen."

"I know, but I'm tired. Slight change of plans."

Sweet Pea stared but said nothing. *Mmmhmm. Tired.*

"I can take them home," said Austin. "We were just getting ready to head over to the stage and watch this band from Piedmont. They're not as good as The Hemlocks, but I might grab some merch."

Liz didn't want to deal with another argument.

"Fine, but home by ten."

"They don't play til nine-thirty. How about eleven," bartered Gus.

"Ten-thirty. And watch your sister." She walked off in a hurry, barely remembering to thank Austin from twenty feet away.

When she was out of earshot, Sweet Pea grilled Gus.

"Are you as mad as I am right now?"

"Nope."

"So you're okay with all this?"

"Nope."

"Gus —"

"They'll work it out. Everything will be alright in the end."

She stared at him, not sure how a human being could be so robotic. As they walked toward the main stage, she noticed that her teeth were clenched, so she made a few chewing motions to try and relax. Still not satisfied with Gus's lackluster take on their current situation, she glared at Austin, signaling him to chime in, but he held up both hands in the "I'm staying out of it" pose.

"You guys want a t-shirt? I'm buyin'."

"Who are they again?" asked Gus.

"Bon Jovi cover band — Bad Medicine — they kinda suck, but their logo's alright."

"Pass," Gus said.

"Pea, want one?"

She was distracted again and staring off. "Hold on, I think I see Claire — I'm gonna say hi and I'll be right back."

Gus nodded as she scurried off into the crowd. It was starting to thin out, but still pretty impressive for the streets of Culver on a Thursday night.

Sweet Pea made her approach, sneaking up behind her unsuspecting friend and giving her a *Rah!* as she grabbed her shoulders. Mindy jumped hard and screeched, pivoting in half a second with her fist raised, then melting into a smile when she saw who it was.

"Whoa! You actually found me —"

"Yeah, I thought that was you."

Sweet Pea knew that telling Gus she was "going to see Claire" was a green light, and "going to see Mindy" was a red light, or yellow light at best. Mostly because Mindy drank, their mothers were enemies, and she loudly called Austin a douchebag the last time they all saw each other.

"So what's up? Who are you here with?" Mindy asked.

"My brother and his friend. I just came over to say hi, I can't really hang out."

"Dude, you have to —"

"They're my ride home, and I have to leave in an hour, anyway."

"I'll get my friend to drive you home. He's over there, trust me, no problem at all. He does everything I tell him to," she said with an evil grin.

A week ago, Sweet Pea would have politely said no and been on her way.

"Hold on," she said, "I'll be right back."

Shuffling back through the crowd, she approached the sound of overpowering drums, clunky riffs and drowned out vocals pouring from the speakers. She recognized the song from the radio, but their cover was even worse. Gus and Austin lingered near the back of the crowd, so they were easy to get to.

"I'm going to hang out with Claire til it's time to go. Her parents said they can take me home."

"What?" he yelled over the noise.

She repeated herself louder until he confirmed with a nod.

"Yeah, okay, I guess that's okay," he shouted. "Don't be late."

She flicked a look at him, then ran off as the song ended to lukewarm applause.

*"Thank you, Culver! We are Bad Medicine!"*

Sweet Pea was happy to miss the rest of their set, as she left the boys behind and ran head-first toward Mindy and whatever she meant by "let's have some fun."

# 20

---

HEADING AWAY FROM LINCOLN SQUARE, Sweet Pea and Mindy were both happy to find a quieter street to get away from things where they could actually hear each other talk. They noticed a lot of the vendors were putting their stuff away, but some stayed open, hoping for another sale or two from the late night crowd. The girls bought sodas and decided to split an order of cheese fries, parking their butts on a plastic picnic table in a makeshift dining area near the food trucks. Their table had a full day's worth of ketchup, cheese and sauces smeared on it, but they found a clean spot for their elbows.

"I'm so glad you came over, I needed to get away from those losers," said Mindy. "I can only take so much."

Sweet Pea barely knew Mindy, but she didn't get that anxious first-impression feeling that seemed to doom her other attempts at friendships. Her dad always told her you can learn a lot about someone in the first two minutes you meet them. And based on their brief encounters at the pet store and golf course, they just seemed to get each other. There was a calm to their conversations, like neither person had to try.

"So which loser is driving me home?"

"That would be Stache, and he's here with Rosie, so she'll probably be in the car, too. Don't worry, they're good dudes. Just annoying the hell out of me tonight."

Sweet Pea dipped a fry into a cup of cheese, while Mindy unzipped her backpack pouch and pulled out a flask.

"Ignore the pour," she said, dumping a few ounces into her own soda cup. "I'm sure a girl like you doesn't need Jack in your coke, but try not to judge."

"What do you mean, girl like me?"

"Well, I'm guessing you come from a nice home, with nice parents, and you get good grades and all that stuff."

"If you only knew."

Mindy swirled her cup and took a sip. "Nah, you're good, all you Culver kids are. Your dad probably still tucks you in at night."

"Yeah, I mean he would, if he weren't in prison." *Wow, that's a sentence I never thought I'd say. I wonder if this is how the bad kids at school feel, like the ones whose parents aren't around and get in trouble all the time. Now it's like I'm bragging about it to make her like me.*

Mindy's eyes lit up as she realized the pages of Sweet Pea's book were about to get more interesting than her cover.

"No way."

"Yup," she laughed, "maybe not prison, but definitely jail. I don't really know the difference. Which one is worse?"

"Um, trust me, prison is worse, that's where my dad's at," said Mindy without batting a mascara-caked eye.

They ate the last of the fries and shook their heads, laughing at the cheerful tone of their serious conversation.

Mindy jumped up. "Okay, let's go do something fun before it gets too late." She rushed away with an ear to ear smile. "Follow me!"

Sweet Pea dodged a few people, kept pace and caught up to her, just as she turned the corner and came to a stop.

"Ta-daaa!" announced Mindy, arms outstretched in front of the petting zoo gate. "I wanted to do this earlier, but nobody else wanted to."

"Me too! I'm starting to think we're sisters. For real."

They each dropped a dollar in the money box and were greeted by the sniffing snout of a potbelly pig.

"I begged my brother to stop here earlier," said Sweet Pea, stroking its head. "All I wanted today was to pet a goat, is that too much to ask."

"I don't know, maybe you should ask *him*," said Mindy, pointing behind Sweet Pea to an incoming goat. He was a speckled mess of browns, golds and creams, not quite waist high.

She turned just in time to avoid a headbutting, hunching down to the perfect petting level, creating an instant bond with her square-eyed friend. For at least the next five minutes, she had a full-blown conversation with him, asking how his day was, complimenting his little horns and trying to stroke his goatee.

Some people would have rolled their eyes or thought she was strange for talking to animals, but Mindy was in the middle of her own encounter with a light fawn-colored alpaca. Theirs was more like a staring contest, all eye contact and mind reading, sending each other signals about the cosmos and the meaning of life.

Eventually they moved on to other parts of the pen, buying tiny bags of corn and feeding anything with an open mouth. It was a nice little getaway from the rest of the world, and it was even nicer to be able to share it with someone.

"Hey, this reminds me, how's your ferret?" asked Sweet Pea.

"Chup is awesome. He stinks a little, but he's my bud. Kinda like you."

Sweet Pea chuckled, but on the inside she was feeling more and more like Mindy was the friend she never had. Her newfound contentment was short lived, when a random brain cell reminded her to check the time. Ten twenty-four. Her heart sank.

"We have to go!"

"Shit —" realized Mindy, heading for the gate with Sweet Pea close behind.

As fast as her flustered body and mind were flying, everything went slow motion as she watched Mindy's hand slip into the unattended cash box and swipe a stack of bills. It was a move so smooth it couldn't have been her first time, as she barely broke stride and didn't even look to see if anyone had noticed.

The girls were flat-out running down the street, heading back to the main stage area. Mindy stayed in front while Sweet Pea tried to keep pace — her heart rate was managing the shock of what she just witnessed, while her stomach was dealing with the cheese fries. She could see Mindy's friends up ahead on a bench.

"Stache! Let's roll, pronto!"

A tall kid in an army jacket whipped his head, decorated with a thin black mustache that was so perfectly manicured it almost looked fake. He motioned to a girl in a Phillies hat and they all made their way to the parking lot behind Mindy's lead.

Nobody said much as they rushed past car after car, before Stache and Rosie finally approached a black Camaro. Sweet Pea and Mindy flew into the backseat, as the doors slammed shut and it roared to life. She told them how to get to her house, which was just a five-minute drive, then sunk back into the seat and thought about what might happen when she got home. If Gus was also a little late, they might get there at the same time. If he left on time, there could be a gap. And if they had left early, they'd be way ahead of her. No matter what, if her mom happened to look out the window and see a Camaro instead of the Wexler's minivan, she was busted.

As the V8 engine thundered along, she leaned her head against the passenger-side window, playing out the scenarios and staring up at the moonless night sky. Knowing it was up there, hiding in the pitch blackness, was freaking her out. She had seen hundreds of night skies with no moon before, but this felt different, like a big shadowy figure was holding its hand over the glow so nobody could see it.

"Here," said Mindy, poking her hand at Sweet Pea in the darkness of the back seat. "Present for you."

Sweet Pea opened her hand, knowing it was about to be filled with stolen treasure, but her brain hadn't come up with a good way to say no without making her cool friend think she was just that dork from the pet store. She felt a small wad of bills hit her palm, as Mindy closed her hand around the money.

"Don't worry, nobody's gonna miss it." She sensed her hesitation. "It's not like I stole it from the goat — he would want us to have it."

"You're just saying that."

"Think about it. They use the money to keep their little petting zoo going, which is cute and all, but you think that goat likes being caged up and trucked around all the time? He should just be livin' his best goat life on a goat farm somewhere."

"Foraging," Sweet Pea mused.

"Yes, foraging."

"Turn right at the stop sign," Sweet Pea said to the front seat, thinking about Mindy's theories. She knew it was wrong to steal, but maybe if there was a good reason to do it, then it wasn't such a bad thing to do? She flipped through the money, trying to count it in what little light there was. *Wow, twenty-five bucks.*

"I guess you're right, but I can't take it. You keep it," she said, trying in vain to stuff it back in Mindy's hand.

"Dude," she laughed, "that's your cut. I got mine."

Before Sweet Pea could muster another argument, she realized they were on her street and almost home.

"Just pull along the road, down here, don't go in the driveway," she told Stache as the car slowed to a stop.

"Good luck, Sweets — find me tomorrow," smiled Mindy as if nothing criminal had just happened.

She climbed out and rushed to her porch as the Camaro disappeared, frantic now as she realized she would know her fate in a matter of seconds.

The fact that her mother wasn't waiting on the porch or staring out the window were very good signs. She took a deep breath, closed her eyes, then exhaled before calmly opening the front door. She could hear her mother's semi-panicked voice in the back room, questioning Gus.

"Mom, I'm home," she called out, closing the door louder than usual to signal her arrival. Liz was there in two seconds, staring her up and down.

"Sorry I'm late — Claire's dad had a bathroom emergency right when we were leaving."

Her mother was more relieved than suspicious, and if she was mad at anyone, it was Gus for allowing her to go off with someone else, even if they were adults. He didn't realize how big of a deal that was to a parent who had a child go missing.

"That's okay, honey, I was just worried when I didn't see you."

She temporarily forgot that she was mad at her. "Next time, and I just told your brother this, no riding with friends' parents unless we — I — know about it first."

"Okay, sorry."

Sweet Pea would have felt a whole lot guiltier about her string of lies if she hadn't spent most of the day hating on her mother.

Liz gave her an accepting nod, and that was the end of it, as the three Beverlys dispersed to their rooms and turned in for the night.

Sweet Pea sat on her bed, brushing her teeth and reflecting on the day's events. She placed a big imaginary X on a big imaginary calendar, marking off the first day of darkness. *One down, two to go,* she thought, finishing up in the bathroom and crawling under her covers. She grabbed her trusty old giraffe to help her nestle in and get sleepy.

*Darnit, I forgot my new giraffe — I don't even remember where I left him.* She traced her steps in her mind, replaying everything, narrowing it down to the post office steps or the bench behind the stage. *Oh well, if I can't find him tomorrow, I can just buy a new one with my half of the treasure.*

# 21

WADDLING DOWN A WIDE, EMPTY SIDEWALK late Friday morning, when the sun should have been up hours ago, a dazed and confused raccoon didn't know whether it should keep hunting for food or go to sleep. He'd been out all night and didn't have much to show for it, as the goldmine of littered scraps and overfilled trash cans he craved was miles away in downtown Culver.

Here in the neighboring town where he did his scavenging, it was unusually quiet, since most of the humans had migrated to the Pitch-Black Palooza a day earlier. He was about to take his empty stomach and go home, when a bite-size mouse scuttled across his path and accelerated into its highest gear. Hot on its trail, he passed the courthouse and town hall before cornering him near the foundation of another large building.

A series of evasive maneuvers led the pair running up stairs, over walls and along railings before spilling into a window well at the rear of the block. With a twitch of his whiskers, the mouse wedged its helpless body between a metal bar and a small pane of thick glass, as the raccoon closed in for the kill. The masked marauder suddenly froze, shooting up on his hind legs as he realized he was being watched.

Meeting his gaze on the other side of the window was Phil Beverly, standing on his cot in the holding cell at the sheriff's office. The mouse stared at the raccoon, who stared at Phil, who stared back and forth at the two animals. He could scare away the raccoon and save the mouse, or he could let nature take its course and feed a hungry stomach.

He pictured Hicks as the raccoon and himself as the mouse. Then Sebastian was the raccoon and Liz was the mouse. Then Phil was the raccoon and Sweet Pea was the mouse. All his thoughts from the past day and a half collided.

*AAAAAAAAGH!*

He pounded his fists on the glass until the raccoon bolted away, abandoning his prey. The mouse put two paws on the glass and blinked at Phil before scampering off.

"Hey, keep it down in there," yelled the deputy. "What the hell's your problem."

"My problem? Seriously?" said Phil. "I'm literally in jail."

"Magistrate will be in tomorrow, tell it to the judge. Relax, it's not the end of the world." He thought about what he said. "Actually, maybe it is," he said with a shrug and walked away.


UNFORTUNATELY FOR SWEET PEA, her mother was the kind of person who couldn't let a good deed go unthanked. And she was already feeling badly about their last encounter with the Wexlers — the one that ended with Sweet Pea's meltdown as Claire was hurried away. So, the fact that they were kind enough to bring her home last night inspired her to pick up the phone.

That phone call did not go the way Liz thought it would.

Storming upstairs with a fire in her stomach, she swung open Sweet Pea's door and flipped on the light switch. Still asleep, her unsuspecting daughter stirred and sat straight up, thinking their house was burning down or a burglar was ransacking the place.

"Where were you last night?"

"Huh?"

"I just got off the phone with Claire's mom," she said, tensions already rising, "so let's try this again. Where were you and who were you with?"

Sweet Pea had told very few lies in her fourteen years, so the feeling of getting caught was new territory. But her defense mechanisms came alive, right on cue.

"I should ask you the same thing."

Liz's eyebrows briefly raised in surprise, but came back down twice as hard.

"I suggest you give me an answer in the next ten seconds or —"

"Or what —"

"Or you're grounded, for starters."

Sweet Pea had only been awake for thirty seconds, but she hit the ground running, uncorking all her bottled up frustrations.

"Why were you with Dr. Seb last night? Why's Dad in jail? Why aren't you helping him get out?" As each question left her lips, her voice grew stronger, but the last one was a full-on demand. "WHY WON'T YOU TELL US?!"

Liz stood shocked, unprepared for the brutal cross-examination.

"I wanna go see him," said Sweet Pea, her voice shaking for the first time. "Now."

"Oh, you're not going anywhere," her mom snapped. "You're grounded and when you decide to tell me who you were with, we can talk about how long your —"

"Mindy Dipetto," she passive-aggressively confessed.

"Dipetto?"

The exchange lingered in the air as they paused to assess damages. Liz slowly shook her head, connecting the dots.

"Unbelievable," she huffed. "Do you know what her mother —"

"And this is exactly why I didn't tell you —"

"You didn't just 'not tell me' — you *lied* to me. Let's get that straight."

Liz went on a minutes-long lambasting of Mandy Jo, drudging up their high school rivalry, her drinking while she was pregnant, her D.U.I.s, the time she left her toddler (Mindy) at the grocery store, her drug-dealer boyfriends, her bar fights, her eviction notices, and the list went on.

"Mindy's not like that," fired Sweet Pea.

"You have no clue what she's like, she's not even your friend, you don't know her! You're not capable of making good decisions, so I'm making them for you from now on."

Sweet Pea's eyes squinted, absorbing another blow from the person who was supposed to love her most. *Not capable of making good decisions.* She knew what that was referring to. Climbing off her bed, she stood and reloaded.

"If Dad were here, he wouldn't care. He would actually listen to me," she said, half yelling and half sobbing. "He would do anything for us, but you're just — you only care about yourself."

The sensible side of Liz knew this wasn't true, that a teenage girl is going to say anything to hurt her mom in the heat of battle. But her vulnerable side had slowly been poked, prodded and pulled apart for the past two days while she covered for Phil. She knew how much Sweet Pea looked up to him, depended on him, and how much it would hurt her if she learned the truth. She's a mom, and moms protect their kids.

"You WILL NOT be spending time with Mindy Dipetto. I'm the parent here, and —"

"Are you? You don't act like one."

Liz's yarn finally unraveled.

"Fine — you wanna know?" she barked.

Sweet Pea nodded, shedding her snarky expression and stuffing her hands in her pajama pockets, bracing for impact.

Liz took her time, staring at the floor while her brain sifted through piles of words, trying to find the right ones.

"Sweet Pea — your dad wasn't being honest with us about some things."

It didn't get any easier from there, as she talked about his gambling, colored in the details of the day their car was stolen, and explained his current situation with Hicks and the police. All those days in between were Sweet Pea's life, forever changed by one man's actions. But it was a different man than she had always thought it was.


IT WAS AROUND NOON WHEN GUS decided to leave his bedroom and attempt a food run to the fridge. A couple hours ago he had overheard every word of the latest family shouting match in his sister's room, coming to three realizations: Sweet Pea lied to *his* face, too; his straight-laced little sister has friends that are more badass than his; and, apparently he wasn't in on *all* of his dad's secrets.

Creeping downstairs, he could hear the television and see its flickering light on the walls, but otherwise the house was quiet. He tiptoed into the kitchen, peeking around the corner for a glimpse at his mother on the couch. She was either sleeping or meditating, but her eyes were definitely closed, so the coast was clear. He was in no mood for another round of questioning, or a lecturing, or even a guilt-ridden apology or serious heart-to-heart. He just wanted a sandwich.

*I'm sneaking around my house in the dark at noon. This is weird.* He opened the refrigerator and gently slid out the lunch-meat drawer, going stealth mode as he picked up the bags of Lebanon bologna and muenster cheese. Reaching for spicy mustard with his other hand, the bags rustled again, triggering a noise from the other room.

In two seconds, Hubbard charged in like he had a running start from down the street. Gus tried every hand signal imaginable, whispering *whoa-whoa-whoa* and trying to hide the lunch-meat, but it was too late. All four paws left the floor as Hubbard launched his body at the fridge, slamming into Gus, tumbling both of them into the refrigerator. He let out an *oof!* and tried to get to his feet, but his butt was wedged onto the middle shelf and Hubbard was piled on his lap.

"Gus?" came his mom's voice from the other room.

Climbing out of the wreckage, he tossed a slice of meat toward Hubbard's drooling jaws, slammed the door shut and ran back upstairs without saying anything.

Gus sat in the middle of his bedroom floor, rolling meat and cheese by the light of his TV screen. He thought about his mom and tried to make sense of why she didn't tell them sooner. And that made him think about his dad, who he hadn't really pictured in jail up to this point, but now he wondered what he ate for lunch, what kind of bed he'd been sleeping on, and whether or not he had a TV to watch.

After his third bologna rollup, he tried to wrap his brain around one more thing: why did Sweet Pea tell him she saw Claire last night? As much as they'd been through together the past seven years, he thought this week had really brought them closer for the first time in a long time. He actually didn't mind her hanging around with him and Austin. So for her to not trust him or ask him to cover for her — which he would have — was somewhat of a gut punch.

His advice to his sister that "everything will be alright in the end" had already aged significantly over the past twelve hours.

IN THE TIME SINCE THE MORNING SCRAP with her mother, Sweet Pea memorized every line on her ceiling. The light on her nightstand cast upwards through the lampshade, highlighting the textured swirls, spinning her head along with them as she processed the aftermath.

As if the sting of being told you can't make good decisions — or basically, you suck at life — wasn't enough, she also had to swallow the pill that her dad wasn't everything she thought he was. Thinking back, she remembered countless talks they had about who the man was, why he took their car, why bad things happen to good people. He had so many chances to tell her the truth, even if it were just a watered-down version of it, but he always had someone or something else to blame.

And maybe some of that was her fault for putting him on a pedestal, but the more she thought about him being involved and hiding it from her all those years, the deeper she sunk into her bed. She went back and forth from angry, to confused, to disappointed, and it all sat squarely on her chest. It wasn't suffocating her or making it hard to breathe, it just pinned her down so she couldn't move, and she didn't even want to try.

It was different from the feeling she had when she finally re-alized Gus wasn't her world. She knew he wasn't the world's best brother, but she told herself that to get through some hard times in the years after the Suburban. When she was ten, there was a particularly bad three-day stretch.

Every time she closed her eyes to sleep, she pictured Hicks holding her down in the swamp water — it was horribly real and she couldn't make it stop. She felt the water going up her nose, swallowing it and choking for air, like when she got pulled under by a breaking wave at Cape May one summer. And then those same thoughts started coming to her when she wasn't even trying to sleep. Like in school, or at the dinner table, or sitting on their back porch.

By the third day of not sleeping, she stopped eating, too, and started seeing Hicks everywhere. He was driving her school bus, teaching her English class, standing in the corner of their dining room in the evening. And when bedtime finally came, and every-one else turned out their lights, she told her parents she was fine so they didn't worry about her, and faced her dark room alone.

She knew if she just laid there, he would come. And if she closed her eyes, he would be waiting in her dreams. Whichever one came first she didn't remember, but that night, something dif-ferent happened when Hicks had her in the water. Before he could do his thing, Gus literally flew down from the sky, swooping low over the water, grabbing her hand and pulling her to safety. All in slow motion, of course. He wasn't wearing a cape or superhero tights, he was just regular Gus, but he could fly.

To this day, she doesn't know if she dreamed him into the scene, if the universe decided she'd had enough, or if God himself put Gus there. It didn't matter, because from then on, she had her magic amulet to ward off the next round of monsters, Hicks or otherwise. That is, until she realized real-world Gus was not the same as dream-world Gus. Which is exactly what just happened again with her ladder-climbing, hero-turned-villain dad.

She wondered what the swamp was like now, if anyone else had been there since then and thought the tree branches looked like deathly fingers. Or if the heron — her guardian heron — still lived there, waiting to help other kids in trouble. She didn't know how long herons lived, but she wanted to thank it someday, in this world or the next, her feathered savior of the swamp. Maybe none of it was there any more, dried up and grown over, or bulldozed and developed into rows of little pink houses.

So here she was, lying on her bed for the past three hours, staring at her ceiling, contemplating life and trying to figure out what was next. These were the kinds of days she relied on a beautiful sunrise or crisp blue sky to convince her everything would be okay. But it was Friday afternoon and she hadn't seen the bright side of anything since Wednesday.

Desperate for a sign, and bored already with her grounding, she flipped through a few of her old books and magazines, but they read like empty pages. She rummaged around her dresser top, which was cluttered with hair accessories, bracelets, birthday money she forgot to spend, and a few pairs of balled up socks. A brown paper package caught her eye — she knew it hadn't been there long, but she forgot what was in it.

*Ohhhhh, my soaps!* She dumped them onto her bed, realizing she never even opened it that night after Miss Aurora was nice enough to give them to her. She smiled at the sight of the Sweet Pea bar.

*Wait, did I tell her my name? I don't think I did. She must've heard Gus calling for me. Okay, that would've been freaky.*

The other bar lying right beside it was orange and purple like a cloudy morning sunrise. She picked it up and studied its colors, trying to make a connection of some kind. Maybe she was looking for something that wasn't there. But then the patterns of the soap started taking shape — staring at the orange, a cheetah ran through her mind. And she'd seen that purple somewhere, too — eye shadow.

Maybe the same universe — or God — that was turning off the sun knew she needed a helper to get through another three days of darkness, so it sent her a friend. Did it matter if that swashbuckling friend came with a drinking problem, a trainwreck of a mother, and a propensity for theft? Mindy wasn't perfect, but maybe she was exactly what Sweet Pea needed right now.

She laid with her soaps, holding one in each hand, thinking about their hour-long adventure last night. It ultimately got her grounded, but if it hadn't been for Mindy, she wouldn't have learned the truth about her dad. It was a hard truth to hear, but now that the initial shock was over, she was glad she knew. It wasn't fair to her, or anyone in their house, to keep it secret any longer.

For a split second earlier this morning, Sweet Pea actually felt bad for her mom. He lied to her, too. But any shred of empathy was destroyed in the fire of their exchange. It still echoed in her head: *You WILL NOT be spending time with Mindy Dipetto.* For as long as she could remember, her mother just wanted her to have a friend. And now that she finally found one — after all these years — she said no.

Staring out her bedroom window into the black afternoon sky, Sweet Pea continued fixating on her mother's words of forbidden friendship.

"Yeah, we'll see about that."

# 22

LIZ NEVER REALLY HAD TO DISH OUT a tough punishment in her sixteen years of parenthood. There were a few blips on the radar, usually handled by Phil, but for the most part, Gus and Sweet Pea were good kids who didn't get into trouble.

So she spent the first half of the day second-guessing everything she had said, wallowing on the couch, rewinding and playing back her confrontation with Sweet Pea a dozen times.

*I can't believe she lied to me. And the mouth on that girl —*
*she's never talked back like that. Damn right you're grounded ... but*
*maybe I was too hard on the Mindy thing. Her mom's a loser but*
*what if she's a decent kid? ... And I don't feel bad for telling her about*
*Phil. He had seven years to do it himself, so guess what — you don't*
*get to tell me how to do it.*

The day crawled along aimlessly without a sun in the sky to pace her brain. After a few naps and half-awake daydreams, Liz wandered around the kitchen, picking at food she wasn't hungry for and rearranging the magnets on their fridge. Anything to avoid a potential Round Two with her grounded teenager. She stared out the window above the sink, looking at the dark outline of their swingset, remembering the first time Sweet Pea went down the slide like it was yesterday.

Back when the kids were little, they had bought a new play structure one spring, spending a little more than they had planned to, but super excited to do it for the family. Phil spent a whole week assembling it, going through box after box of beams and bolts, declaring every day that he was "almost done." By the time it was actually finished, they couldn't wait to replace their rusty old tetanus-shot swingset and have something nice.

Seven-year-old Gus went first, climbing up and sliding down in seconds, but Sweet Pea got scared and froze at the top of the slide. Liz assumed Phil would take the hero position at the bottom, coaxing her to safety and getting the big hug when she landed, but he passed the baton to his wife. She still remembers what he said to her, and how much it meant at the time: "I think she needs her Mommy for this one."

Her mind had gotten the best of her a lot during the first years after they were born, always wondering if she was doing things right, giving the kids what they needed, or being a good enough mother. So hearing the words out loud, that her daughter needed her, resonated like a tuning fork for her soul. And now she could still tap into the rush of pure love that slid into her arms that day. It was a defining mother/daughter moment in her life, one that she unburied sometimes when she needed a lift.

*But look at us now.* She wondered what Sweet Pea was thinking about in her bedroom, now that some time had passed, and if this would leave a mark. The news about her dad must have crushed her, as if she wasn't already having a doozy of a week.

It would have been so much easier if Phil were here, sending in the other parent so she could keep her distance and recharge her emotional batteries.

"Good lord, it's almost four o'clock," she said out loud, checking her watch. "They're probably starving."

Walking upstairs, she started mentally preparing for the knock on Sweet Pea's door. *Poor kid, I actually feel sorry for her.* Liz was hoping for a teary-eyed apology, but she knew it would probably be the silent treatment or more fire and brimstone. Approaching Gus's room, she knocked and made her first contact since morning.

"Hey, you hungry?"

"I could eat."

"Okay, let me see what your sister wants."

Continuing down the hall, she approached Sweet Pea's room and lightly rapped her knuckles. She waited a second then slowly turned the knob.

The room was empty.

Their house wasn't the kind that someone could be in another room and you wouldn't know it, and her door was always open when she wasn't there. Liz gave a quick look into the office across the hall, then walked back to Gus's room.

"Have you seen your sister?"

He returned a blank stare to his mother and followed her back to Sweet Pea's room, looking under her bed and flinging open a closet door.

"Well she didn't just up and vanish," she blurted.

Then her heart stopped.

"Oh my God."

Sweet Pea's bedroom window was open a few inches, drawing a cooler than usual summer breeze into the room. Turning on the overhead light, Liz rushed to the window and opened it the rest of the way. The screen was gone, tossed aside on the shingles of their front porch roof, lying in the wake of her great escape.

"Whoa," said Gus, standing in the doorway. "Looks like she flew the coop."

## ONE HOUR AND FIFTY MINUTES EARLIER

STARING OUT HER WINDOW, still reeling over the slugfest with her mom, Sweet Pea turned her thoughts to her dad. One second she pictured him catching her fall on the tower, but the next she saw him making deals with the devil — and losing them all. Why now? Maybe the sun going dark wasn't a coincidence. What if everything good in the world was going away, and this was how it begins?

A few cars passed by, interrupting her counting of the stars, but their street was mostly quiet since the whole town was at the Pitch-Black Palooza. *This sucks. If she thinks I'm staying in my room for more than a day she's crazy.* Before she had a chance to feel any worse about her life, the deep sound of a big engine approached and slowed down, but didn't go away.

Opening her window for a better look, she heard the low rumbling of a vehicle, but there were no headlights or taillights anywhere. Finally she caught a glimpse of metal down the road where a dark-colored car had pulled off. Two big oak trees were blocking her view, but she heard a car door close as her eyes strained to see two people running toward her house.

*Crack!*

An acorn pinged off the siding, just missing her window. Sweet Pea stared harder, with no help at all coming from the sun or moon.

"Sweetie Pie!" came a voice from the dark.

"Hey!" whispered Sweet Pea, recognizing the creative one-off name more so than the voice that said it. She could see shapes now hiding at the corner of her foundation — one was Mindy and the other was wearing a ballcap with a ponytail. "Must be Rosie," she said to herself.

"C'mon, let's go, get your butt down here," muttered Mindy.

"Can't, I'm grounded."

"Let me guess, you told your mom you were hanging out with me last night."

Rosie laughed, prompting Mindy's fiendish giggle.

Sweet Pea had spent too much time lately thinking about people that had let her down or didn't understand her. The one person who did was standing right below her.

"Hold on —" she said, fidgeting with the screen in her window until one of the corners popped out. The other three released much easier, as she leaned half her body through the opening and gently lowered the frame onto the roof.

"Need help?" Mindy called up, still keeping the volume of their conversation on low.

"We'll find out in a minute," she said, stepping all the way onto the roof. She tried to close her window but it got stuck near the bottom. *Close enough.* It was the same roof that her father stood on seven years ago, oblivious to the world behind him. Sweet Pea wasn't going to be like her dad.

Climbing down a porch roof was nothing compared to scaling a hundred-foot ladder. She hunched low and inched her feet down the slope, all the way to the edge, carefully peeking over the side. Mindy's face beamed up at her like a child watching for the first firework to burst in the sky.

"Yes! Step onto this, it'll hold," Mindy said, giving the trellis a firm shake before climbing up the first few rows of slatted wood. Sweet Pea backed into position, swung her foot over and made contact on her first try. As her other foot dangled, stabbing at a landing place, Mindy's outstretched hand guided it onto the trellis, and the hard part was over. The girls scampered down pretty easily from there, celebrating with a quick hug and muted squeal before bolting to the getaway car.

"Shotgun!" called Rosie, climbing into the front seat.

"Hey, Stache," Sweet Pea greeted her driver, as if she'd known him for years, taking her spot in the back with Mindy. "Don't peel out or anything — I'm grounded but I just snuck out my window."

"You got it, boss," he replied, shifting into drive and slowly pulling away.

It only took a few minutes for Sweet Pea to realize that joyriding in the back of a Camaro with your friends was a much better way to spend an evening than being stuck in your room with nothing to do.

GUS AND LIZ DIDN'T KNOW if Sweet Pea ran off five minutes ago or five hours ago, but most likely she had a pretty good head start. He sensed his mother's anxiety levels rising past her eyeballs, so he did his best to take command of the search efforts and keep her engaged.

"Okay, let's go over what we know. She snuck out her window and now she's gone."

Liz rolled her eyes, expecting more.

"Actually," Gus continued, "we don't even know that she's gone. What if she fell off the roof and she's laying in the front yard with a broken leg? Or collarbone?" He kept thinking. "Or spine?"

"Gus —" she stopped him. "Can you please just try to help me without making things worse."

He agreed with a smirk. "Let's check the front bushes just to be safe."

The duo was off to a rocky start, but as they walked the yard with their flashlights, Gus was already thinking about calling for backup.

"You probably don't want to hear this, but maybe Dad could help?"

Liz didn't answer.

"That way it's not all on you. I don't know how bail would work or anything, but we could probably just talk to —"

"No," she cut him off, "we don't need him."

"C'mon, he's not —"

"Gus, enough. Not going there."

Now Gus took his turn at eye rolling, as they walked back in the front door.

"Fine, if you won't let Dad help, then I'm going to the bullpen," he said, picking up the phone. "Don't worry, it's not *Sebastian*," he said, applying an airy, upscale accent to his name.

Liz turned red in the face, a blend of anger and embarrassment, while she listened to Gus call Austin and fill him in on the latest Beverly crisis. By the time they hung up, Austin was officially on board and thrilled to be joining their search party.

"Okay, he'll be here in ten minutes. Let's think about this," he deliberated, stroking his beardless chin. "Unless she actually ran away, like jumped on a train, she's probably just downtown, and we both know who she's with."

"Yeah, I already figured that." Liz thought for a few seconds. "What if we find her and she won't come with us? Can you guys help me pick her up and stuff her in the car?"

Gus put his hand to his head and groaned. "If that's your best plan, then we're getting Dad.'"

"Never mind, we'll figure it out," said Liz.

After a few minutes of anxious pacing and awkward silence, Austin's Jeep pulled into the driveway and they were on their way. The group discussed their loosely knit plans to find their daughter/sister/friend, trying to think how she would think. The wildcard in the deck was Mindy — she went to school at Piedmont so they didn't know much about her. Gus knew she was still fifteen, not old enough to drive yet, so they were probably on foot. Unless Mindy had older friends, which meant they could be anywhere.

"Let's head downtown and check the food trucks," said Gus. "She's probably eating a stack of funnel cakes."

Parking was even harder to find on Friday than it was the night before, so they settled for a space a few blocks away. On the long walk over, Austin cracked a few jokes to lighten the mood.

"Hey Mrs. B — why didn't the sun go back to college?"

"Austin, please not now —"

"Because it already had a million degrees!" He nudged her shoulder without breaking stride. "Am I right?"

He laughed hard enough for the three of them, but he wasn't finished.

"Okay, I heard that one somewhere, but here's one I totally made up. Ready?"

"She's ready," injected Gus.

"Okay, okay, let me think how it goes — where does the sun stay when it's on vacation?"

They turned the street corner and entered the south end of the Palooza, just below the bouncy houses and kids play area.

"Mom —" implored Gus.

"I don't know Austin, where," she halfheartedly played along.

"At the Four Seasons!" he gushed.

Gus and his mom looked at each other, cringing in unison, before speed-walking ahead of Austin with smiles on their faces.

"You bring up the rear and keep your eyes peeled," said Liz.

"Ten four, I've got your six."

Arriving downtown, there was street lighting on the corners and the main activity areas had spotlights, but a lot of the stretches in between were dark. None of this made it easier to find someone in the crowd, assuming she was here at all. They made their way to the food trucks, scanning the lines at each window and checking all the faces eating at the picnic tables. Gus even described Sweet Pea to the lady working the funnel cake stand, but they came up empty at every turn.

"Let's check the stage, or that dumb petting zoo, I know she wanted to do that yesterday," said Gus.

"Good idea," Liz said, starting to get a little more worried as they journeyed to the opposite side of the Palooza. Halfway there, they heard a distant commotion coming from the next intersection, rippling back to where they were. They could see a throng of people pushing through the crowd, followed by another rush of more people, crossing the intersection and disappearing around the corner. People were yelling from all directions now, realizing that something was happening, but nobody seemed to know what it was.

By the time they reached the corner, the pandemonium was over already. A group of kids in Culver football t-shirts were talking to a security guard, pointing down an alley past the barricades at the edge of the festival. One of the kids was sitting on a curb, holding the side of his head as blood trickled down his jaw line.

"Looks like we missed the action," said Austin. "Musta been a jock fight."

Screeching tires interrupted the murmur that had settled over the masses, as the sound of a fast-approaching vehicle got louder. Liz turned to see headlights speeding toward them, still on the other side of the barricade but picking up speed and getting dangerously close. It lurched into a hard left, drifting sideways as it laid on the horn, executing a perfect power-slide that rounded out a few feet from the blockades, spitting gravel at the crowd. The black Camaro gathered itself, tires spinning, correcting down the straightaway as its passengers leaned out the window, flipping the bird at the shell-shocked football players.

Even more shell-shocked was Liz, realizing that one of those middle fingers belonged to Sweet Pea. Her mouth dropped to the sidewalk.

"Found her," said Gus.

# 23

SWEET PEA DIDN'T KNOW ANY OF THE SONGS that blared from the door speakers as they sped further away from downtown. Their Led Zeppelin-fueled getaway safely reached the outskirts, as the Camaro climbed a twisty up-and-over mountain road and slinked back down through a farm-lined valley on the other side. The classic rock soundtrack made her feel about fifty times cooler than any other point in her life, so she wasn't about to tell her fellow passengers that she had a New Kids On The Block poster on her bedroom wall.

"Dude, he never saw it coming," Mindy said to Stache from the back seat. "That was classic."

Rosie re-enacted the scene that had just taken place back at the Palooza, fake-punching Stache in slow motion as he followed his high beams on the road ahead. Mindy took a sip from her flask before passing it up to the front seat.

"Classic," repeated Sweet Pea. She had only seen one fight

in school before, and that was just two girls in sixth grade who scratched and clawed on the playground. So witnessing a hit-and-run suckerpunch to the side of the head that dropped Culver's star running back was a pretty big deal. She kind of felt bad for the kid, seeing him crumple to the ground, but her adrenaline had kicked in the second she heard the crack of the fist — and then all that mattered was running fast and not getting caught.

"Where did you land it?" asked Mindy. "Ear, jaw or temple?"

"I dunno," Stache said, "I just threw hard and hoped for damage. Definitely some good skull, I'd give it an eight point five."

Rosie weighed in. "I had a good view, that was a nine. Easily. Thistlewood prick..." she scoffed, chasing her statement with a hit from Mindy's flask. "I'm sure his mommy will put a Band-Aid on it tonight."

"Just like your mommy would," Mindy teased Rosie.

"Well she'd probably be drunk so it would go across my eye."

They laughed as a pounding riff led into a new song that all of them apparently loved, triggering massive air-guitaring and air-drumming as the car accelerated. Sweet Pea laughed along and pretended to know the song as she double-checked her seatbelt, making sure it was clicked in the whole way.

"So what's up with your madre?" Mindy asked Sweet Pea. "I mean, you snuck out your window, so she must be in the Shitty Mom Club, too."

"Yeah, pretty much. Freaking grounded me for nothing. I don't even care any more."

"Well at least she still grounds you," said Mindy, "my mom doesn't give two shits what I do. I'd almost rather be in trouble when I got home, just so, you know —"

Sweet Pea nodded across the backseat, sensing that Mindy was opening up to her. Even though her own parents had been her world up until a couple days ago, the last forty-eight hours were casting long shadows on her memory banks.

They kept driving along the dark country roads, passing a few homes and farms that Sweet Pea recognized from their family drives. Stache knew the area, too, as he turned onto a few connector roads that seemed to go nowhere, but eventually emptied onto a section that was familiar again. Only a few stars dotted the night sky, but Sweet Pea thought they made a beautiful backdrop to the passing barns, silos and fence lines as the Camaro crested hills and glided around curves.

The painting in her mind was erased as their car jostled onto a rocky, uneven dirt road, slowing down to a crawl so they didn't bust an axle. The girls in the back leaned in so they could see between the front headrests, as the road eventually evened out and disappeared into a thicket of trees. Driving under the canopy, Sweet Pea noticed a wide stream running parallel on their left, reflecting their headlights whenever they turned the wheel to avoid another pothole or downed limb.

"Where are we going?" she whispered to Mindy.

She shrugged. "Stache, what evil comes our way?"

"Cool little place up ahead my brother showed me," he said, turning around in his seat so they could hear him. "Perfect spot to wait for the end of the world."

"I know!" blurted Sweet Pea. "I'm so glad someone else thinks it, too. Like how do they know the sun's coming back. They can't even predict when it's gonna rain."

The Camaro veered into a small pull-off and parked, while Rosie handed flashlights from the glovebox to everyone as they got out.

"This way," Stache said, taking Rosie's hand and leading the pack down a path toward the sound of water.

"*This way,*" echoed Mindy, grabbing Sweet Pea's hand and mimicking their steps, mocking his attempt at a romantic gesture.

"So, are you guys worried about the sun?" continued Sweet Pea. "I mean, what if we never have another blue sky ever again as long as we live?"

Rosie and Mindy laughed it off, but Stache connected.

"I don't think it's coming back. Seriously. And it's gonna get cold as hell in a few days."

"Hell is literally made from fire and lava," said Rosie.

"And sin," added Mindy.

"Okay then, cold as North Dakota," Stache conceded.

"It's just a dumb cloud passing between Earth and sun," argued Mindy. "No big deal."

The group walked another fifty yards, sloping down a hill as the path emptied into a clearing next to the bank. Their flashlights illuminated a footbridge over a series of small falls, cascading over long, flat rocks, feeding a deep plunge pool at the bottom. The rushing water created white noise that momentarily canceled out the rest of world. As for the bridge, it was probably a nice little structure back in its day, but even in the dark they could tell it was rotting out in places.

"Watch your step," said Stache, focusing his beam on a board that was only half there. He stepped over it and walked out to the midpoint, calling attention to a few more places not to plant your feet. The girls followed him, managing to stay on solid wood, as they all sat down and faced the falls, dangling their feet, which is the best and only thing to do on a footbridge.

"Yo, pass me some Jack," said Rosie. Sweet Pea was sitting in the middle, so Mindy handed the flask to her on the way down the line. Not counting the times her dad made her fetch a beer from the fridge when he was doing yardwork, this was the first time she was up close and personal with alcohol, holding it in her very own hand.

*Yep, I'm really sitting on a bridge over a waterfall in the middle of nowhere holding a bottle of "Jack." I hope they don't ask me to try it. I'm sure Mindy wouldn't care, but I don't know about Rosie. Stache seems okay, but he did just punch some guy in the head for no reason.*

"C'mon, pass," said Rosie, prompting Sweet Pea to quickly hand it over.

"We have about an hour to kill," Mindy said, "I'm good right here for a while, but I'm running on empty."

"What's in an hour?" asked Sweet Pea. Stache and Rosie looked at each other, surprised that Mindy hadn't told her.

"Oh, nothing much, just a little ol' barn party," she said, turning the flashlight up under her chin before cackling like a vampire.

"What barn? Whose party?"

"Don't worry, it's nothing too crazy, just people hanging out. We won't stay too late."

Sweet Pea hadn't thought through any type of plan yet that involved how, why or when she would go home. In the back of her mind she had pictured herself sneaking back up onto her porch roof in the middle of the night and climbing through her window undetected. Which made no sense at all, now that she stopped to think about it.

Surely her mom knew she was gone by now, and was probably looking everywhere and worried sick. *Welp, that's what you get. I don't feel bad.* The universe had sent her to Mindy, or Mindy to her, just like two soaps in a bag from a blind lady at a flea market. She finally had a friend, so going home would have to wait. *I guess I'll cross that bridge when I get to it. Not the one I'm sitting on. She laughed to herself. Austin would've loved that one.*

WITHOUT THE HELP OF THE SUN OR MOON giving clues to the hour of the day, Friday night looked and felt no different from Friday morning or afternoon. The hour on the bridge went fast, as the soothing sound of splashes and gurgling water rolled over rocks and put half of them to sleep. The excitement of Sweet Pea's day had drained her mind, body and soul, so she didn't stand a chance against the babbling hypnotist in her ears.

"Hey, Sweet Potato," a voice interrupted her nap. "Wake up, time to go," said Mindy, nudging her shoulder. Opening her eyes, she heard laughing and made out the shapes of three people in the dark. It took a few seconds to remember why it wasn't morning and what she was doing on a bridge, but she was quick to her feet.

"Barn party — reservation for four, please," she declared, strutting past them and leading the hike off the bridge and up the trail.

Mindy celebrated — *Wooooooooo!* — springing along like a cartoon character, happily losing the bet she made to herself that Sweet Pea wouldn't want to go.

The Camaro and its passengers left the grove and found the main road, driving the opposite direction from Culver. The head-splitting music from their earlier ride was back to normal volume, as the group seemed a little less hellbent right now. Sweet Pea didn't have much time to get comfortable, as they turned onto a long driveway, not more than a few miles from their last stop. She expected to see a barn up ahead, but the only thing in their headlights was a double-wide trailer.

"Is this it?" she asked.

"No, we have to get JP first," said Mindy. "He should be watching for us, let's just sit here."

"And who's JP?" asked Sweet Pea.

"He knows some of the guys having the party, and we kinda

know him, so it's just easier if we show up with him."

Stache chimed in, "Yeah, and also — he's a dickhead."

"Very true," said Mindy, "but he's a dickhead who has beer."

Sweet Pea was feeling more comfortable around her new friends, so she tested the waters.

"Just letting you guys know … I don't drink."

"Dude, you're fine," Mindy reassured her. "Stache doesn't drink either. He just smokes."

Hearing that she had an alcohol-free ally made her feel better.

"Okay, maybe I'll try one of your cigarettes later on." She had no intention of smoking, but it felt like the right thing to say.

Snickering filled the car as Rosie repeated *"cigarettes"* in air quotes. Sweet Pea watched them all trade sly looks that made her feel like she wasn't in on the joke.

"Here he comes," said Mindy, opening her door and climbing out to make room. Stache popped the trunk as JP approached, dragging a gigantic cooler behind him.

"Cold beer, here!" he yelled, imitating a stadium hot dog vendor, making his way to the back of the car. Mindy helped him load the trunk, then the two of them climbed into the back seat. Sweet Pea was afraid she would have to sit right against him in the middle, but to her relief, Mindy got in first, giving her a quick wink like she read her mind.

"JP, you know Stache and Rosie, and this is Sweet Pea."

"What's up, y'all," he said, landing his gaze on Sweet Pea like a hyena spotting a gazelle. She felt her skin change temperatures.

"Hands off, you're like nineteen," warned Mindy.

JP heeded the threat, looking down into his lap where he had piled a few cans of beer. He cracked one open and passed it to Rosie, then opened another one for Stache, who waved it off.

"Beer?" he extended to Sweet Pea, where it was promptly intercepted by Mindy.

"Thanks man, we're good for now," she said, taking a drink and staking her claim.

"Okay, so — three cool people and two dorks," said JP as the Camaro did a u-turn and sped down the driveway. Sweet Pea sent Mindy a silent *thank you* when JP wasn't looking, as everyone in the car basically ignored him.

Cruising along the asphalt en route to the barn, they were a good twenty minutes outside Culver now, chucking empties out the window every couple miles. Rosie timed one perfectly, dinging it off a speed limit sign, which was pretty impressive considering they were going at least seventy.

Sweet Pea took it all in from the back seat. Everything was so new to her — the people, the places, the drinking, the swearing, the sneaking, the fighting — it all felt like Christmas morning, where you keep opening present after present and your brain just keeps piling one new thing on top of the other. At some point, you have too much or they don't feel new any more, and you realize that most of them didn't live up to the anticipation or expectations that made you even want them in the first place. But in the moment, there's nothing else like it.

Minutes away from her first party ever, she couldn't stop thinking about all the little speeches her parents had given her about drinking, drugs and what older boys want. She pictured JP and twenty other guys just like him, dancing on hay bales with their shirts off, chugging beer, pounding their chests and howling up at the night sky.

She didn't even know how old Stache, Rosie and Mindy were, but she had a feeling they were just a grade or two ahead of her. And even though her new friends were doing things that she, herself, wouldn't do, Sweet Pea was able to separate the two: *I don't like all the things they do, but I like hanging out with them.* She felt accepted. And included. And a sense of belonging. And right now, all of those superpowers were stronger than the scary black monster in the sky.

"Here we go, people," said Stache, making a slow left turn into a cornfield, barely fitting his Camaro into a narrow opening flanked by ceiling-high stalks on either side.

"The corn just swallowed us," commented Rosie, awestruck by the walls of greenish yellow in every direction as they rolled forward. Between the dark sky overhead and the lack of lateral visibility, it felt like they were driving in a coal mine, waiting for any sign of daylight at the end of the shaft.

After a few minutes of navigating, a small flickering light appeared way up ahead and got bigger and clearer as they drove. Driving out of the corn tunnel, they entered a clearing with cars and trucks strewn all over the place, parked wherever their drivers felt like leaving them.

"Over there," Mindy motioned to Stache, leaning up into the front seat, directing him to a place to park. JP finished off another beer and belched his heart out, sending the girls scurrying out the door.

The group gathered near the front bumper as JP readied his cooler, finally catching their first glimpse of the barn at the end of the field. Glowing torches flanked the east side of the old wooden relic, highlighting a mass of people spilling outside where its big doors once hung. Music wafted through the airwaves, layered with the occasional *Woooo!* and *Yeaahhh!* from the crowd. As they made their way up the path, the lyrics materialized, reminding them that everyone and everything will eventually be dust in the wind.

"Kansas," Mindy nodded in approval.

"Never been there," replied Sweet Pea with more of her classic rock ignorance.

"Where'd you find this girl?" laughed Rosie, giving Mindy a playful shove.

"C'mon, Pea Brain," Mindy said as they reached the barn, "I think you need a drink."

# 24

L IZ WOULD HAVE ENJOYED cruising the streets of Culver in a yellow top-down Jeep a lot more if the circumstances had been different. But as it was, she squirmed in the back seat and gnawed on her fingernails, thinking every vehicle they passed was a Camaro with her daughter in it.

"If they were anywhere in a five-mile radius we would have seen them by now," said Gus after their tenth lap around town. "Let's just head home and wait for her."

"How do you two not know whose car that was?" replied Liz.

Austin weighed in. "I'm tellin' you, nobody at school has a Camaro like that. One of my dad's lawyer friends has a sweet sixty-eight that's black, but that thing Pea was in was like an eighty-five. Probably some Piedmont loser."

"I vote we go home, she'll show up," Gus restated. "Her little rebellion is probably running on fumes."

"I have a better idea," his mom said. "Austin, can you stay out a little longer?"

"Actually, Matlock comes on in twenty minutes, so I have to get home … *Psych!*" Nobody laughed except Austin. "Rough crowd, just kidding. I'm good for whatever."

"Okay, head out past the bus station, up where the old drive-in used to be."

"Uh oh, she has a plan," Gus marveled as they pulled a u-turn.

Austin drove north out of town, following more directions from Liz as they reached what was left of the drive-in. Veering left where the road split, they drove a few miles without seeing any houses, driving parallel to power lines that eventually fed a substation on their right.

"Keep going, almost there," she said.

"Okay, I'll ask," said Gus. "Almost where?"

"Mandy Jo's."

"Mandy who's?"

"Mindy's mother, and I use that term loosely. I'm sure you heard me this morning."

"The Dipettos are nuts," added Austin.

"And how do you know where she lives?" Gus asked. "Never mind, I don't wanna know."

"Turn up there, it goes to her lane."

The road curved down a hill along a rocky outcropping, through an underpass and eventually a few houses appeared in their headlights. They pulled into the driveway of a small two-story with a narrow front porch. A few lights were on inside, and a spotlight hung from a telephone pole shedding light on the half-collapsed porch roof. The house was sided in what looked like roofing shingles, but most of the asphalt had crumbled off, matching the rest of the property that was littered with rusty lawn mowers, a dilapidated shed and weeds that were taller than Gus.

"Wait here, this should be quick," said Liz, exiting the vehicle. "Don't worry, no hair-pulling, just talking on the porch."

"Assuming you don't fall through it," quipped Gus.

Walking up the driveway, she noticed a figure in the window, quickening her pulse as she reached the first step. A small black animal shot out from under the porch, startled by the creaking board, as she hurried up to the front door.

"Nice kitty," she said, before realizing it had a white stripe down its back. "Why am I not surprised."

Raising her hand to knock on the screen door, Liz froze — Mandy Jo was ready and waiting, staring her up and down through the mesh. A small hole was ripped in the screen, framing her left eye like a cyclops.

"Well it must be the end of the world, 'cause Lizzie Pendleton's on my front porch."

"Hello, Mandy Jo," she uttered, swimming in the cloud of smoke that was just exhaled in her direction.

"I dropped the Jo. Just Mandy now." Her eyes wandered, studying Liz's shoes, clothes and hair. "You don't look a day older than high school. What's it been, twenty years? Hell, I don't even know," she trailed off.

Liz skipped the small talk. "So look, I know we went out on a low note, but —"

"Low note, huh." Mandy shook her head, taking a few seconds to think. "I know what y'all say about me, so unless you're comin' here to my beautiful estate to apologize for —"

"Um, you owe me the apology."

"For what?"

"Are you gonna pretend it didn't happen?"

"If you're still moaning about your boyfriend —"

"Boyfriends. Plural," said Liz, drawing a guilty-as-charged

smile from Mandy.

"All the good boys liked Lizzie, didn't they. I was just tryin' to see which ones might wanna be a little bad, too." The devious look on her face left no doubt where Mindy got it from. She took a long drag on her cigarette and stared right through Liz. "Especially Mr. Prom King."

"What about him?"

"You two were so over the damn moon, sickening sweet on each other all the time. I just wanted to see what he was really thinkin'. You know, like is he *in love* or just waitin' for somethin' better to come along." She opened the screen door and stood opposite Liz on the porch. "He was definitely lookin' for somethin' better."

Liz realized the conversation was going sideways, as her hand curled into a fist and a vein pulsed on her temple. Sweet Pea's search and rescue mission was officially on hold.

"Nothing happened," huffed Liz, "he told me everything you tried to do."

"Well he musta left out the parts about everything he did to me —"

"This is ridiculous, I can't believe I'm actually talking about high school." Liz retreated a few steps and held up a just-a-minute finger to Gus.

"You and him still married? Got yourself some nice kids, nice house, I hear. See, it all worked out, doesn't even matter what happened that night —"

"Okay, that's enough —" she growled, pulling the plug on the video feed that her brain was starting to play. "Look, I came here to ask you —"

"Yeah, what *did* you come here for? I can't wait to hear this one."

"Apparently, my daughter is hanging out with your daughter, and I was wondering if —"

Mandy howled in amusement at whatever stroke of fate pitted their kids together. She threw her arms straight up like a touchdown, taunting Liz with a gleeful smirk.

"Go ahead, rub it in, I don't care," scoffed Liz, "I just need to know where they're at. Sweet Pea ran off and she's with your Mindy somewhere."

Mandy finished her cigarette and flicked it off the porch, landing on the hood of the Jeep with a splash of angry embers in the dark.

"First of all, I have no idea where my kid is at any hour of the day, any day of the week. And second, what the hell kind of name is Sweet Pea?"

Liz pushed past her and thumped down the steps, splitting the cracked bottom stair in two, regretting her plan to the utmost degree. She turned to Mandy before climbing into the back seat.

"Well it's better than Mindy — you just changed one letter!" she screamed with a slamming of her door. She definitely would have pulled her hair if she hadn't walked away. Mandy raised a middle finger, not the just-a-minute finger, gloating in victory as Austin backed the Jeep down the driveway. He stopped in the middle of a three-point turn, giving Liz a clear shot.

"Go to hell you piece of shit!"

As the Banana Split peeled out, Gus and Austin high-fived Liz and roared at the middle-aged moms' war of words. She threw her head back and closed her eyes as they gained speed, letting the air rush across her face and through her hair in a blast of wind therapy.

"Oh my God, I can't believe I said that. I'm so sorry, she just made me so mad."

"No apology required," assured Austin, seconded by Gus's proud smile. "Felt good, didn't it?"

Under the mounting weight of her missing daughter, her jailed husband and his now more questionable past, and the absence of sunshine that seemed never-ending, Liz forced a grin and laughed at herself as they drove back to Culver. It was the only thing she could do to keep from crying.

JP LED THE GROUP INTO THE BARNYARD, dishing out fist bumps to more than a few partygoers as they made their approach to what would be the head table if it were a wedding reception. Stache helped him carry the cooler, while the three girls kept close together, getting the sense that they were younger than most of the people surrounding them.

"Yo Todd!" boomed JP, landing a bro hug on a guy who looked like he was in charge.

"Jasper Patrick, you sonuvabitch." They punched each other a few times as if they enjoyed it. "Park your cooler over there, good sir. I hope that's Capri Sun?"

"You know it."

Now they took wrestling stances with each other, lunging a few times before connecting on another bro hug. Sweet Pea and Mindy looked at each other, mouthing *Jasper Patrick* at the same time.

"I always just called him JP. Never knew he was a Jasper," said Mindy.

"More like Jerk President," Sweet Pea cringed. "As in, the President of all the Jerks."

"Jello Pecker," said Rosie.

They laughed off some of their nerves and took in more of

their surroundings. Torches lit the grounds as groups of people were scattered everywhere, huddled in small circles, some bobbing their heads to the music, but most were just standing around holding cans or bottles. They could see inside the barn, where another hoard of people were gathered around an old tractor, and even more sat on hay bales near the doorway.

"There's probably a hundred people here," gawked Sweet Pea.

"Easily," replied Mindy. "I see like three dudes I know, but they're weirdos. Let's take a lap."

After making a few rounds and trying to not look like a soon-to-be freshman at a senior party, Sweet Pea realized she didn't know anyone. She recognized a few kids that were older siblings of kids in her grade, but that was it. Having Mindy, Rosie and Stache there helped, but most fourteen-year-olds were probably out with their parents or home playing Nintendo, not crushing beers in a barn.

"Pit stop," said Rosie, pulling up to the cooler and grabbing three silver cans. Sweet Pea knew what was coming next, as one was stuffed into her hand. "C'mon Pea, it's not gonna kill you."

Mindy and Rosie popped their tabs and held them up, dripping condensation and reflecting fire light, waiting to toast.

"Don't leave me hangin' here," Mindy said in a non-threatening way that still counted as peer pressure. Sweet Pea felt like she could tell them no, but part of her wanted to try it and be fully vested in their group, not just Mindy's little tagalong friend from Pet Depot.

"To beer!" said Sweet Pea, hoisting her can to theirs as the butterflies in her stomach prepared to be drenched.

*Woooooo!* Mindy and Rosie clanged their cans together and started chugging. Sweet Pea put the cold can to her lips, going all in on her first beer ever — but nothing happened. A puzzled look swept across her face as the girls lost it.

"Oh my God, she forgot to open it!" blurted Mindy, almost falling down and spilling her drink. Rosie was laughing so hard she didn't open her eyes for a full minute. Mindy reached over and gave the assist — *crack-fizzzz* — removing the last barrier between Sweet Pea and their liquid friendship.

*Sip-sip-gulp*

The rush of her first beer wasn't enough to overpower the disgusting taste that just trampled her tongue. She didn't try to hide it, scrunching her face like she just smelled a skunk, or drank one for that matter.

*Blechk!* she sputtered, almost spitting it out while barely managing to force it down. Mindy and Rosie celebrated her Coors Light coronation with all the high-fives, hugs and reassurances you would expect from teenage drinkers welcoming a first-timer to the club. *Burppp!* The bubbles came back up, tickling her nose and giving her another taste of the grossity in its gaseous form.

"I'm good til twenty-one, now," she said, rubbing her eyes. "Seriously, that was sick."

"So proud," beamed Mindy. "It gets better, don't pour it out."

The girls wandered around with their beers in hand, and even though she didn't like the taste of it, Sweet Pea liked the look and feel of it, the instant credibility it gave her to be at a party like this. Mindy led them around the side of the barn to the edge of the cornfield, where another dozen kids formed a circle around a bonfire and a boombox, a pretty even mix of guys and girls, screaming along with Axl Rose.

Without any warning, Mindy darted straight for one of the guys at the back, almost tackling him to the ground. Sweet Pea looked at Rosie, who mirrored her cluelessness, not sure if they should help her or run for cover. Her pulse barely had time to elevate, as she saw Mindy laughing in his arms, being lifted into a bear hug.

"Welp, I guess they know each other." Sweet Pea and Rosie loitered for a few minutes, trying to signal Mindy to hurry up. It felt like forever, but she eventually said her goodbyes and rejoined their trio.

"Who was that?" asked Sweet Pea, trying to keep up as they circled back around to the main party.

"My loser ex," Mindy said, grabbing another beer. "He still wants me," she bragged to Rosie, who also went for barn beer number two. She turned her Phillies hat backwards and kept drinking.

"We should probably see if Stache needs rescued from JP. I kinda forgot about him."

"Is he your boyfriend or what?" Sweet Pea asked Rosie.

"Sometimes," she laughed, "sometimes not."

As they searched for Stache, they talked about boyfriends and girlfriends, which wasn't a subject that Sweet Pea had much experience with. She mentioned a guy she liked who was a little older, but she wasn't ready to put a name to him. Their search went into the barn, thinking Stache was the kind that would be perched in the seat of the tractor, looking down on all the drunken fools, but he wasn't there either.

"I see him," said Sweet Pea, pointing across the barnyard to a shape sitting alone on a stone wall, smoke wafting above his head. "Stache!" she yelled as they approached, drawing a nod to their group.

Settling into their new space, Stache told them how he ditched "that asshole JP" half an hour ago. They traded more stories, and were able to people-watch for a while without having to actually interact with anyone. Sweet Pea would have been fine just staying right there for another hour and then leaving, but as the music played and the beer cans emptied, time seemed to stop for everyone but her.

As the night wore on, she kept checking her watch, wondering when they were going to leave. Maybe it's because she wasn't drinking, but their hourly routine of sit on the wall, walk a lap, grab a beer, and sit on a wall, wasn't nearly as fun as it was the first time around. And when she asked them when they were leaving, she lost count of the times she heard "not much longer," "we're almost ready," and "one more beer."

"Mindy, I have to use the bathroom. Come with."

"Sweet Pea has to *peeeeee!*" slurred Mindy, as the evening was catching up with her. "Okay, let's go — I'm going to go pee pee with Sweet Pea Pea — be right back."

"We're going for a walk," said Rosie, her hand wrapped in Stache's, "we'll catch you guys later on."

The pairs walked in opposite directions, as Sweet Pea and Mindy made the short trek to an outhouse that smelled bad but was better than nothing. Mindy tripped and stumbled forward, grabbing onto Sweet Pea for balance.

"Um, I think you're drunk," she said, faking a laugh that was mostly drowned out by the gigantic stack of speakers nearby. "Can we please go after this?" she said over Don Henley's words about never being able to leave a certain hotel in California.

"Yeah, I'm about partied out," replied Mindy without an argument. "But this is such a lovely place. You go in and do your thing, then we'll track down the lovebirds."

Sweet Pea opened the door of what was basically an old shed over a hole in the ground, while Mindy waited outside. It was pitch black inside, but she managed to find her way around without falling in. She thought about how nice it would be to have access to an actual toilet, but these were the sacrifices you made to attend barn parties. Her left hand bumped something beside her, which turned out to be a roll of paper towels. "Well, thank you to whoever put these here," she said to herself.

After a minute, she emerged from the outhouse, surprised to see three kids waiting to go next, but none of them were Mindy. She excused herself past them and glanced around and behind the structure, but didn't see her. *Great, where the heck is she.*

"If you're looking for that girl that was here, she left with some guy," said one of the other girls. "He picked her up and carried her off — not like kidnapped her — they were laughing, or we like totally would have said something."

"Oh, thanks," she said in a blur, feeling her heart pump a little faster. She walked in a hurry back to the wall where they had been sitting. *That's it, we are so outta here. It'll be three against one, Miss Mindy.* Arriving at the wall, Rosie and Stache weren't back from their walk yet. She looked back in the direction she had just come from, scanning for signs of Mindy, but it was just more faces she didn't know.

Trying to ignore it, she noticed her breathing was getting faster, and her face felt warm. She had felt like this before. *Okay, you're fine, they're coming right back. Just stay here and everything will be alright.* Sitting on the wall, alone in the darkness, her right leg fluttered in place like a hummingbird, as she tried to sing along to whatever song blared. One played, then another, and another, and another, and still nobody showed.

As she zoned out into a blank stare, a voice surprised her from behind. "Where'd your friends go?" JP slithered in front of her, looking even more drunk than Mindy was. Sweet Pea's head flared, putting her on high alert, while a rush of adrenaline armed her for whatever came next.

"They're coming right back."

*"Mmm-hmmm."*

He finished off his drink, chucked the can and sat beside her on the wall.

"You know what I think? I think they're all off havin' some fun. That's what people do at parties like this, ya know."

She smelled the beer on his breath and felt him looking at her body, but she kept her head down. A shiver jumped up her back, telling her to get further away.

"Stache wants me to meet him at the tractor," she lied, standing up and eying the barn, literally shaking in her shoes. JP quickly blocked her path, his face inches from hers and leaning in closer.

"Stache said that, huh? How 'bout you and me head somewhere else instead?" He reached out to touch her hair, but she pushed his hand away and bolted back over the wall. He yelled something as she ran away, but the pounding of her heart deafened everything.

Sweet Pea kept running in full-on fight or flight, looking back to make sure he wasn't following. She bounced through the party like a pinball machine, bumping into a few kids, spilling someone's beer, frantically trying to find her friends. *Deep breaths,* she told herself, but the panic was taking over. Finally, she saw the familiar white "P" on a backward-facing maroon hat, just a few people up in front of her.

"Rosie!" she yelped, bounding to her side and grabbing her arm. A startled girl, who wasn't Rosie, looked at her like she was crazy, as Sweet Pea apologized and wobbled away. In a dizzy state, she had made two laps and still didn't see them.

*Oh my God, what if they left?*

Pushing through more drunks, she sprinted to the field where they parked, but the Camaro was right where they left it. *I'll just wait in the car. I'll be safe there.*

Checking her back again for JP, she tried the doors but they were locked. "Shit!" A tingle of fear crept into her head when she realized there was nobody else in the parking area, and it was pretty far from where all the people were. What if he came down the path right now? She had nowhere to run and nobody would even hear her if she yelled for help.

Almost hyperventilating, she managed to rush back up to the party as her brain fired off distress signals and tried to protect her. *Just get me to the barn ... almost there.* Her eyes checked the crowd for JP, forgetting for the moment that she still needed to find Mindy. She saw a safe pathway to the barn and went for it, sneaking inside and around a corner to a small room with an open doorway at the end. Her head on a swivel, she went through the door, past rows of stalls that used to house cattle, and came to a set of narrow ladder rungs that disappeared into a hole in the ceiling.

Up she went, sending strands of hay flying with each step, reaching the top and crawling into a loft that followed the pitch of the barn roof. Two mice dropped what they were doing and scurried at the sight of a human. Sweet Pea looked around to make sure nobody else was up there, aided by some light pouring up through an opening at one end where farmers could throw hay down below. All seemed safe and sound in her second-floor refuge.

As her heart and lungs and mind gradually returned to normal, she found a tiny area sectioned off by two walls, piled high with hay, that had a small window cut into the wall. She climbed onto the scratchy bedding and curled up in a ball, silent and motionless, listening to the sound of her heartbeat.

In the still of the night, with her eyes closed and defenses down, everything started coming to her in tiny shockwaves. Her friends leaving her. Her dad's lies. The fight with her mom. The climb up the tower. The man at the swamp. And the darkness blanketing all of it. She had finally found something that felt so real, somewhere that she belonged, but now she was more alone than ever.

She just wanted to have a funnel cake with her dad, squinting at the sun as they waited in line. He would be teasing her mom about the powdered sugar on her chin, and Gus would be telling all of them to hurry up, while Austin kicked a hacky sack. How did she get so far away from everything she used to think was good and right? And with everything she'd done in the past twenty-four hours, how could she ever go back.

She felt a tremor coming up from her chest, but she bit her lip and closed her eyes as tightly as she could to hold it off. Erupting all at once, she released a cry so sad and painful that the barn swallows felt it from their perch on the rafter above. Sobbing and heaving, trying to catch her breath, she couldn't stop what her body was doing to her, giving in to all of it until she had nothing left to give.

Two of the worried birds strutted closer, almost directly above her now, moving their heads with every sound that she made. As the sobs trickled off and she settled into a deep breathing pattern, they gave each other a nod and flew back to their beam. Alighting onto the walls of their mud nest, they took solace in the silence, as Sweet Pea cried herself to sleep.

# 25

THE CLAMP-ON HEADLIGHT barely lit the road five feet in front of the Huffy's twenty-six-inch front wheel, but its rider plowed ahead, determined to complete his route. Balancing a shoulder bag filled with a few dozen rolled and banded *Culver Daily Heralds*, he pedaled along the road approaching the Beverly residence, straining to see the house number of his next target. A winter hat topped his head on the chilly summer morning, as planet Earth was starting to notice the sun's two-day sabbatical.

Taking one hand off the handlebar, he pulled a paper from the bag, holding it in the ready position, locked and loaded to launch when the geometry was right. Coasting in the darkness, simultaneously calculating speed, distance and arc with the skill of a NASA flight trajectory engineer, a flash of red darted in front of him, followed by a puffy white-tipped tail. In one motion, he jerked the bars to avoid the fox — that was trying to avoid the bike — and fired the paper over the Beverly's front yard without looking.

The fox dashed to safety as the bike wobbled but recovered, both of them avoiding a collision and continuing on their way. Flipping end over end, the oblong projectile followed a near-perfect path, landing with a smack against an empty wicker chair and falling at the feet of the next chair over. That chair was not empty, as its sleeping occupant jolted awake, flinching her hands in front of her face.

Liz looked up, down, left and right, trying to figure out where she was, what just happened, and why there was a newspaper lying on her left foot. Once she realized she had fallen asleep on her front porch, and she was not under attack, she removed the rubber band and unfurled Saturday's headline:

LAST DAY OF DARKNESS?

Some light from the kitchen spilled through the front window, just enough so she could read the cover story.

*Officials tracking the cloud's path are hopeful that original projections of a seventy-two-hour disturbance remain accurate, but remind the public that an event of this nature is unprecedented and difficult to predict...*

*Blah blah blah.* Liz folded the paper and tossed it back on the porch. Right now, she didn't care if it stayed dark for thirty more days — she just needed to know where her daughter was. Following their Mandy encounter, she had taken Gus's advice to wait for her at home, but that didn't pan out. Sitting on her porch at midnight, she told herself Sweet Pea would be home by one. Then at one, she talked herself into believing that it couldn't possibly be later than two. And by the time two o'clock rolled around, she was half asleep and a little delirious from the weight of it all, as her body threw in the towel and she conked out.

Now that the paperboy woke her up with his impressive throw under the duress of a blitzing fox, she was back in full worried-mom mode within seconds.

"Wow, I really slept," she said, checking her watch. It was late Saturday morning, almost a full twenty-four hours since her war of words with Sweet Pea. Did she really say anything that bad to make her run away? There was the whole *can't make good decisions* thing, and telling her she's not allowed to see her friend, and that her friend's mother is a loser — but whatever happened to just thinking *ew, I hate my mom*, then crying in your room for an hour, apologizing later on and going for pizza?

Liz went inside to see if Gus was up, racking her brain for what to do next. Seven years ago she didn't hesitate to call the police, but this was different. Sweet Pea was just out with her friends, finding herself, coming of age, yelling her rebel yell — whatever you call it, she probably wasn't in real danger, and this would all fix itself soon enough.

*But what if she's not? What if they got into trouble somewhere, or their car crashed and they're not even with her, and she's hurt or terrified and wondering why I haven't found her yet? Why we haven't found her yet. Oh my God, I forgot about Phil.*

Realizing that her jailed husband had slipped her mind, Liz put her Sweet Pea thoughts on hold and revisited his and her plight. Maybe his couple days in the slammer were enough of a punishment — she taught him a lesson and now it was time to get over it. But then she bristled.

*Wait a second — what did Mandy Jo mean by "everything he did to me"? He looked me in the eyes and swore on the Bible that nothing happened. And of course, I believed him, just like I did about everything else. So maybe it's not okay — who knows what else he's hiding.*

Plopping down at the kitchen table, a dull pounding started at the base of her skull, warning her that a migraine was on its way.

Gus appeared from the living room, sensing at a glance that his mom wasn't okay.

"Rough night?" he said, heading to the coffee maker and adding a scoop of Folgers. She raised her brow and nodded, barely making eye contact before putting her hand to her forehead with a yawn. He measured water into the pot and within a few minutes the aroma floated over to Liz and started massaging her temples.

"I thought she'd be home by now," admitted Gus. "What do you think we should do?"

"I don't know," she said with her eyes closed. "I had two thoughts and now I don't know about either of them."

"Okay, shoot."

"Well, I was going to call the police, but then I wasn't, because she's probably just sleeping at a friend's house or something." She paused.

"But what if she's not," Gus said. "I mean, what if — we don't know anything about the people in that car."

"Great, now you're scaring me," said Liz.

"What was your other thought?"

"Well, I was thinking about your dad."

"What about him?"

"That maybe he could help ... but I don't know if I can even deal with that right —"

"Mom —" Gus said with a more sincere look than he was usually capable of, delivering it with a hot cup of coffee.

"I know, you're right." She sipped the coffee, which tasted like it was made by someone who had never made coffee before, but it was, at the same time, as good a cup of coffee as she'd ever had.

"I think we can kill two birds with one stone," she said, taking a big swig and grabbing her car keys.

SWEET PEA'S SUBCONSCIOUS was receiving messages from the other side.

"Dude, wake up."

"I think there's a piece of hay up her nose."

"Should we kick her?"

In a reversal of fortunes, the dream she was having took place in her own boring back yard, while the reality she was awaking to was a hay-filled loft in an old barn the morning after a wild party. Peeking through crusty eyelids that weren't yet convinced it was time to open, a dull barn light filled in for the sun, shining on the familiar faces of her three friends, or at least that's what she thought they were.

"Rise and shine, Sweetums," Mindy said with all the charm of someone who hadn't just left her for dead the night before. "You're lucky you snore like a bear."

She rubbed her eyes and plucked hay from some places it didn't belong.

Rosie filled in some details. "We couldn't find you anywhere this morning, like maybe you left last night, or someone came to pick you up, or —"

"Or what?" challenged Sweet Pea, blocking out a horrific image of JP. Nobody said a word. "Not like any of you cared."

"No, no, listen," begged Mindy, "I'm so sorry, I totally left you alone, that's on me, I know. But I thought these two," punching their shoulders in succession, "were coming right back."

"Yeah, and we wouldn't have been gone so long if we knew Mindy was gonna run off with what's his name — Daryl? Darren?"

"Damon."

"Yeah, Damon."

Sweet Pea processed the trail of excuses, contemplating her next move while still trying to recover from her latest entry in the worst-night-of-your-life contest. She stretched and yawned, feeling the pinch of muscular pain around her ribcage and a burning in her throat.

"So if I was up here all night, where were you guys?"

"Umm, let's just say you weren't the only one who had a roll in the hay," said Rosie.

"I didn't roll in it, I just slept up here. That would be so itchy, why would —"

"How 'bout those Phillies," interrupted Mindy, stirring a laugh from Rosie and Stache.

"Anyway," Rosie continued, "we woke up a little bit ago and didn't see you, so we started looking everywhere. Mindy was gonna look down at the car, but then Stache heard someone snoring up in the loft. He found that hole in the ceiling, and there you were."

"I tracked you down like a Terminator," said Stache.

"Nerd," uttered Mindy.

*"He's from the fyu-chah,"* Sweet Pea said in Schwarzenegg-ar-ese, extending an olive branch and garnering a high-five from Stache.

An awkward silence floated above the hay, signaling the moment when two opposed groups might have found common ground, but neither wants to risk declaring everything to be okay until they're sure.

"So what are we doing today?" said Mindy. "Are you guys hanging out or going home or what?"

Sweet Pea shrugged her shoulders. The looming punishment tied to going home and facing her mother was competing against her slipping trust in the group that she felt so connected to yesterday. She felt a little better hearing the apology, but it didn't change the fact that Mindy knew she wanted to leave last night and ignored it. Her little whirl wasn't going to last forever — she knew that — but how and when it ended were still up for grabs.

"I'm good for whatever," said Rosie, "my parents don't give a shit."

"Last day of darkness. Or is it?" Stache said, his right brow raised to a peak.

"Pea?" prompted Mindy. "You need to go home or you ridin' out the darkness with us?"

"I'm good for whatever."

She wished she could have felt more excited about her words, but it was better than the alternative. The group made their way down the ladder and back to the room where the tractor was stored, loitering there for a few minutes as they surveyed the scene. Most of the partiers had left last night, and the few that pulled all-nighters were cleaning up and heading out. They saw Todd, but Sweet Pea was quick to notice that JP was nowhere in sight.

"Where's JP?"

"Gone," said Stache.

"Are you sure?" she asked, drawing a look from Mindy.

"Yeah, I'm sure," he laughed.

"Tell them your story, tough guy," said Rosie, causing him to politely shake his head.

"Fine, I'll tell it," Rosie volunteered. "A few hours after you and Mindy went to the bathroom, we were over by that big tree, way over there. We found a little place that was quiet, and after a while, we heard something." Sweet Pea and Mindy nodded along. "Like at first we thought it was people screwin' around or whatever, but then we could tell it wasn't okay. Like this girl was screaming for help, then we heard the guy tellin' her to shut up ... you know, gettin' rough with her."

"I knew it was Jello Pecker," Stache chimed in, impressing

Rosie that he remembered her moniker.

Sweet Pea's cheeks flushed and her stomach started churning as Rosie continued.

"So Stache gets up, goes over and grabs JP by the back of the neck, I'm standin' right there too, I could see everything. That chick was totally freaked out, her eyes were like — i don't know, she was terrified."

Mindy noticed Sweet Pea looking away, hiding her face from the group.

"So he has him by the neck with his left hand, and JP's trying to make up some bullshit excuse, and Stache just pounds him in the face with his right. Two shots, hon?"

"Two shots."

"*Bam! Bam!* Dropped him to the ground, then he ran off like a wuss. That girl was lucky, ya know?"

Mindy put her arm around Sweet Pea, who was fidgeting in the shadow of the tractor, waiting for the story to be over. She looked up, hoping Mindy wasn't staring at her, but their eyes met and shared an unspoken understanding.

"You okay?" she said low so they couldn't hear. Sweet Pea nodded, barely letting her chin quiver and holding off the urge to cry. Mindy initiated a subject change.

"Not that I don't love a good fight story, but I'm starving."

"I have some food in the car," he said, "plenty for everyone if you like grapes and deer jerky."

The lingering effects of last night's beer can bonanza lowered their breakfast standards, as Stache went to fetch the food. He must have sprinted down and back, because they were devouring venison within minutes of his offer. With half their group nursing headaches and dry-mouth, they were all content to lay around and do nothing for a while.

The morning dragged along as conversations ranged from Pink Floyd and The Breakfast Club to tampons and birth control. Sweet Pea's mind wandered a few times, staring off into the sky, looking for any sign of the moon's goodbye or the sun's hello. But it was just more darkness, as far as she could see.

"So if the sun does come up tomorrow — and we do have our doubts, am I right, Stache — are you guys just going back to the way everything was?"

"What do you mean?" asked Mindy.

"Like all this stuff we did yesterday, it's been crazy, but once it's over and the world's back to normal, what are you gonna do?"

Nobody said anything, trading a few glances before Mindy spoke for the group.

"This *is* what we do. This is our normal."

Sweet Pea shrunk back, not expecting it.

"We don't have another life to go back to. No offense, but none of us snuck out a window and have parents wondering where we are right now."

The air thickened, as nobody really knew what to say next. The harmony Sweet Pea had felt was starting to rattle and clang inside her head.

"Okay, okay, let's not get all serious," Mindy said, reading the room and climbing into the driver's seat on the big farm tractor. "Today is today, that's all that matters. And if it actually is the last day of darkness, I only have one thing left on my to-do list."

All eyes were on Mindy, waiting for any indication of her plan. Rosie nodded with a longing gaze, sending telepathic messages, waiting for Mindy to acknowledge. She did, slowly forming a dastardly smile paired with a scheming squint.

"Yes!" Rosie came alive, throwing her arms up in celebration. Even Stache looked thrilled, as if they knew what she was talking about but couldn't believe it was happening. Sweet Pea was afraid to ask, trying to pick up on any clue that she had missed.

Mindy stood in the seat now, high above her audience. "I told you guys when the time was right, we'd do it. Well my friends — it's time to execute Operation Krylon."

Sweet Pea raised her hand like a schoolgirl needing help from the teacher.

"Sorry class, no questions," Mindy laughed. "If we told ya, we'd have to kill ya."

# 26

"JUST BECAUSE I'M BAILING OUT YOUR FATHER, it doesn't mean things are back to normal between us," Liz told Gus as their Camry approached the Sheriff's office.

"You mean last week normal, or seven years ago normal?" asked Gus, cranking up the tension on their forthcoming family reunion.

She kept her high beams on to find parking, as this was her first trip to the courthouse complex since she was called for jury duty about ten years ago. She drifted back to that day, as yellow sunlight washed over the black and white scene playing on her windshield. She saw her jury group walking to the pizza place on the corner, her younger self tagging along at the back of the pack. She remembered feeling so excited to be somewhere new, on her own — even if it was just fifteen minutes up the road — armed with a meal voucher that meant she didn't need her packed lunch. The area looked different now in the Saturday afternoon darkness, but her headlights lit up a familiar bench in front of the restaurant.

"I sat on that bench right there and ate pizza when I was here for jury duty. You were just little."

"Yeah, it was the summer before first grade."

"There's no way you remember that."

"I remember everything since the day I was born. Try me."

"What color were the binkies in your crib?"

"Blue one with the little bear on it, and the other one was green with a dinosaur."

"Okay, that's not weird or anything," she said, mostly impressed but a little scared of his mental database.

"I remember thinking you were never coming home that first day," said Gus.

"Aw, you missed me," she said, finally finding a space that didn't require parallel parking. As she maneuvered the vehicle, she realized those were her stay-at-home mom years, and probably the first time she was ever away from Gus for more than an hour or two.

Gus revisited the past. "I just remember Sweet Pea crying the whole time, and Dad couldn't get her to nap, so he would take us on these really long drives on weird mountain roads. He said they were top-secret government roads that weren't even on the map."

Liz turned off the car. "Funny, he never mentioned any of that. I remember being so worried to leave you guys. All day in court, I just sat there picturing you and your sister screaming and crying and fighting, and then felt guilty that I was actually enjoying a little break. But every day when I got home, he just said you guys were great and asked me how my day was."

"No, we were definitely screaming, crying and fighting. I guess some of his lies were good."

Liz started to smile but her brain cut in to remind her why

they were here.

"Hmmm, I wonder where we go in?" At the far end of the huge building, a man exited a door and got into a waiting cab, and there were a few more doors facing the street, none of which looked more important than the others.

"That one looks like a main entrance," Gus said, pointing at stairs to their left, leading to an arched doorway with a dim light above it.

Mother and son got out and walked the short distance down the poorly lit sidewalk, climbing the steps, not sure of what to expect when they entered the building. She was hoping for an army of police officers waiting to launch a massive search party the instant she told them about Sweet Pea. And then somebody in a uniform would unlock Phil's jail cell and he'd run to her in his orange jumpsuit, holding her like they were eighteen again and begging for forgiveness. And she would have to think about it, make him sweat it out, then probably give in. Maybe.

"Ma'am, do you have any weapons on your person?" A deputy inside the doorway crashed her daydream, reaching out to pat her down.

"Me?" she flinched backwards, avoiding his hand. "Oh my God, you mean like a gun?" She quickly realized he was just doing his job. "No sir, no weapons on my person. Or my son's person."

He took her word and nodded to Gus, motioning them along to a desk at the far wall. Liz didn't see a single police officer in the place, other than the guy at the door, and the only holding cell in the back corner was empty. Maybe all the deputies and detainees were in another part of the building, or over in the courthouse.

They waited in silence at the desk for a while, wondering if anyone was actually on duty. After a few minutes, Gus slammed his hand down on the service bell.

*Bing-bing-bing!*

"Gus!" hushed Liz.

"That's what it's there for," he shrugged.

An older woman emerged from the bowels of the building, straightening her blazer and adjusting her glasses.

"Can I help you?"

"Yes, ma'am, I'm here for two things today. I'm not sure which one to start with."

"Let's start with your name," she said in a groggy voice, grabbing a form and licking the tip of her pen.

"Elizabeth Beverly, I need to —"

"Beverly," the woman repeated, looking like something was trying to register in between her ears. "I know that name."

"Oh, you might remember us from seven years ago when our kids were missing — well actually that's kind of why I'm here now, because one of them's missing again."

The woman removed her glasses.

Gus piped in. "She didn't lose us both this time, just my sister."

She put her glasses back on. "No, I don't remember anything about missing kids. There was a Beverly in here the last couple days. Nice fella who tore up that motel, tried to kill a few people because his wife was having an affair."

Liz tried to be polite. "Well, okay, I don't think that's entirely true. You can't believe everything you hear, Lois," she said, reading her nameplate. "That's actually the other thing I'm here about. … That Beverly is my husband."

Her glasses came back off again.

"Well, I'll be," she said with a disapproving tone, shuffling through a pile of file folders. "Let's get this paperwork started on your daughter —"

"Wait, did you say he *was* here, as in, he's not here any more?"

"You just missed him. Magistrate Robinson finally showed up, she was out of town, but she got through all her arraignments here already."

"Which prison did she send him to?" Liz was talking faster now. "He didn't even do anything, I was just mad at him for lying to me, well, to all of us, but I can explain everything to whoever I need to talk to. Where's the officer who —"

"Ma'am, calm down, you don't have to explain anything to anybody. Your husband was released." Lois pointed down a long hallway behind her. "Walked right out that door not but ten minutes ago. Said he was going home to see his wife and kids, and thanked us all for keeping him company."

Liz looked at Gus with eyes like saucers.

"The man in the cab," Gus murmured, "we can still catch up to him." He took a few steps toward the door, as Liz began to follow.

"Mrs. Beverly!" Lois cleared her voice, stopping both of them in their tracks. "Your daughter?"

Her face went blank, realizing she came to report her missing child and forgot to do it, as she scurried back to the desk.

"Oh my God, thank you, I don't know what I was thinking."

"Maybe you should be thinking more about your kids," jabbed Lois, turning around to grab more papers.

"I tell her that all the time," said Gus, not quite keeping the smirk off his face.

"*Hussy,*" she said under her breath, louder than her hearing aid told her she'd said it.

Rolling her eyes, Liz took her lumps and worked with Lois to finish the intake on Sweet Pea. She eventually spoke to a deputy, handing him a picture, describing her outfit, telling him all about their argument Friday morning, and the Camaro sighting and Mandy encounter Friday night. But a sinking feeling settled in — there really wasn't much for them to go on. And to make matters worse, he admitted they were stretched thin handling "darkness-related incidents," but they'd see what they could do "if time allowed."

Nearly an hour ticked by before they finished the report. Leaving the building with heavy steps, they retreated back to the car, empty handed, realizing that the cavalry wasn't coming.

"Well that was probably a waste of time," she uttered, pulling away from the curb and heading back toward Culver.

Liz hummed along to a song on the radio about a big yellow taxi, the bouncing melody brightening her mood just a smidge.

"Let's go find your sister … and your father."

PHIL'S CAB RIDE HOME was an emotional roller coaster. The rush of being released — turns out the magistrate had a soft spot for math teachers with no priors — was quickly tempered by the bleak, black skies hovering over him. And all his thoughts of Liz, Gus and Sweet Pea that got him through his stay at the crowbar hotel were colliding with the fear that they changed the locks and wanted nothing to do with him now.

He tried telling himself it would be okay, they could work things out, but a louder voice reminded him that his wife hung him out to dry at the Thunderbird, ignored all his phone calls from jail, and his only visitor in almost three days was Lois.

Gazing into the passing night, he drifted back to 1985 and the double-or-nothing bet he called in to chase his losses. He'd only been gambling a few months, a doomed-from-the-start savings plan to surprise Liz and the kids with a trip to Disney. At the end of a particularly bad week of wagers, he had one last chance to make it up before settlement day: $6,600 on the Lakers, minus four-and-a-half, at the Nuggets. If they covered he would break even, get the monkey off his back, and never gamble again (as was sworn on his grandmother's grave right before the opening tip). If they didn't cover the spread, he was in big trouble.

So when the Lakers won — but only by four points — his debt doubled and, unbeknownst to him, put a target on the family Suburban. He didn't know what a bookie would do to a guy who owed thirteen grand and couldn't pay up — kneecaps? — but he was naive to the business of chop shops and "calling in the collateral." If he possessed any streetsmarts, maybe he could have prevented "Covered Wagon Day" from ever happening.

But whatever guilt he felt for his own role in this mess, it was just as easy to blame it all on Hicks: the mob repo man who extorted him, set him up and sold him down the river. As the taxi approached Culver, Phil seesawed back and forth on a full range of highs and lows, hope and despair, love and hate, guilt and revenge.

So when he finally arrived at his house and tried the front door, the relief that his key still worked was replaced with a slap of disappointment that nobody was home. His big redemption speech and moment of truth would have to wait, which was good because he was still working out the kinks.

Hubbard greeted him, sitting pretty at his feet, raising a paw. "Hey boy, where's everyone at?"

His head tilted.

"Yes, I know I showed up unannounced," he conceded, stroking his fur, "but it's not like she would have taken my call." Phil wandered the rooms looking for clues to their whereabouts, venturing upstairs, taking it all in like he'd been gone for years. "This is weird — why do I feel like I'm trespassing in my own home?"

Hubbard laid down on their bedroom floor with a thud, as

Phil crashed on the bed like a sack of potatoes, releasing a deep breath that he'd held for hours, if not days.

"You know what, Hub?" he said to his silent companion after a few minutes of rest. "I know I should go look for your mother and sister and brother, but —" he eyed the bathroom door, "I really need a shower." Phil waited for Hubbard to approve or object. "Bark twice if that's a dumb idea."

A long, rumbling snore vibrated from the Retriever's ribcage, as Phil chuckled and stepped into the bathroom. He cranked the faucet handle, welcoming the blast of heat on his head and shoulders, washing away the top layer of the last three days of his life. He stayed like that for a while, water cascading, drumming on the tile as the faint sound of snores echoed from the other room. By the time his fingers had turned to prunes, his stay at the county jail was a distant memory.

"Clean as a whistle," he declared to Hubbard's closed eyelids, drying off and getting dressed in some stray light from the hallway. He stared out his bedroom window, scanning for a hidden moon, still marveling at the darkness and coming to grips with the sun's vanishing act.

"You keep sleeping, buddy, I'm heading downtown."

Phil's mind buzzed with a mental to-do list in order to right some wrongs and set things straight. Somewhere near the top was buying Sweet Pea a funnel cake.


"Let's check home first." Liz laid out her plan to Gus as the return trip to Culver was almost at their doorstep.

"So is this a Dad check or a Sweet Pea check?"

"Both, I guess, but if I know your father, he probably couldn't go anywhere without getting a shower first."

"True," said Gus, "probably had to have a bowl of cereal, too."

Liz turned into their driveway, replaying her thoughts for a tenth time on how the conversation might go. She was in the precarious position of not knowing which one of them would be, or should be, more angry than the other. In second grade playground terms, he started it, but she got him back pretty good.

So maybe they were even? Three nights in jail for seven years of family dysfunction — it didn't sound even when she put it that way, but the image of Phil being cuffed and stuffed with his kids watching was burned into her eyelids.

And then there was the gambling — who was she to punish him for an addiction, if that's what it was. Maybe he wanted to stop but couldn't, and if she would have seen the signs, paid more attention, she could have helped him before he got in too deep.

"Earth to Mom," said Gus, waving his hand at her scrunched face, snapping her out of it. "Are we going inside or staring at the garage door?"

"Whatever," she said, drifting to the front porch. "His car's not here, so he probably went —"

"His car's still at the motel," Gus blurted, "in Piedmont."

"Oh yeah, you're right. Didn't think of that."

Gus zipped past her and whipped open the front door, where a yellow blur with a wagging tail was the only Beverly waiting to greet them.

"Hey boy, where's everyone at?"

Hubbard's brown eyes stared, dripping with déjá vu, wishing he could speak English for thirty seconds to connect the dots for the humans.

Gus grabbed a drink in the kitchen while Liz made a quick look around the house before heading upstairs.

"Shower's wet!" she called down, staking claim to her on-the-money prediction.

That's when it hit Gus — his dad knew nothing about Sweet Pea's great escape and M.I.A. status. The poor guy probably came home and got all cleaned up so he could make his best pitch at being forgiven and forging the family back together. He pictured his oblivious father walking the streets of the Palooza, checking his hair in a storefront window reflection, hoping to see his family at every turn.

"Hey, come up here," his mom called again, "I'm in Pea's room."

Gus finished a slice of cold pizza that had been hibernating in the fridge, then went upstairs to join her.

Liz pored over her room like a crime scene detective. "Let's look for clues. Anything we're missing."

"Like what?"

"Like clues, I don't know, Gus. We can't just wander the streets and hope we bump into her."

Gus rustled through the drawers of her desk and flipped over a few things on her dresser, not really expecting to find anything. Liz did the same, seeing nothing of note before coming across a brown paper package.

"What the hell's this?"

Unwrapping it feverishly, her visions of drug paraphernalia and mini-bottles of booze were kindly replaced by the scent of handmade soaps.

"Oh yeah, her dumb soaps she got the other night," said Gus.

Liz vaguely remembered, but grew enchanted by the real-life aroma, crafty rough-cut edges and the rushing, swirling colors. Her hackles raised when she saw *Sweet Pea* printed across the paper band.

"Remind me why you guys were at a soapery?"

"We weren't. Me and Austin got tacos at La Choza, I mean, Choza Del Tacos, and she disappeared behind the stand somewhere. I guess that's where she got it, I didn't ask."

"The taco stand sells soap?" Liz questioned.

"No, she was snooping around that old flea market, maybe someone was back there selling it."

"So — a few days ago she meets a stranger who gives her soap with her name on it, and now she's missing. There's our clue. Was there a Camaro parked there?"

Gus tried not to laugh. "Now that I think of it, the guy who bagged our groceries last weekend said 'have a nice day' when we left. Let's grab our pitchforks and march over there."

"This is serious," she vented.

"I know — let's just go, this is a waste of time."

As mother and son left the room, Gus took one more look around, pausing at the old drawings taped to her desk hutch. He remembered lying on the floor beside her with a tub of crayons, coloring scenes from the swamp, since that was easier than talking about it. The slim chance that she wasn't okay snuck past his big-brother bravado and filled a tear duct, but he doused it before his mom noticed.

Walking downstairs, they stepped over Hubbard at the landing, who barely moved as they gathered their things to leave.

"You keep sleeping, buddy, we're heading downtown."

He squinted one eye open, thought more about learning English, then resigned to a long, satisfying sigh and more sleep.

# 27

—

SWEET PEA STARED OUT THE BACK WINDOW of the Camaro as they meandered along yet another country road, seeing what little she could from the glow of the tail lights. The most exciting thing to happen since they left the barn was watching the dials turn on the old-fashioned gas pump when Stache filled up at a little country store. Other than that, it was just cows and cornfields as they drove nervous laps in preparation for Operation Krylon. She was still in the dark, literally and figuratively, and not liking it.

"For the tenth time, can someone please tell me what we're doing."

"That was only seven," laughed Mindy. "I'll tell you when we get there, Pea Pod, it's a surprise, I don't want you to flake out."

"Which means it must be something dangerous or illegal."

The dashboard sent just enough light to the back seat for Mindy to catch a shimmer of Sweet Pea's glaring eye.

"Dude, you don't have to worry, it's —"

"C'mon, I mean it," bristled Sweet Pea. The morning apologies that she had accepted were already fizzling out, as the sour taste of the barn party abandonment didn't stay gone for long. Mindy felt a little threatened by the furrowed brow that was bearing down on her.

"Okay, okay. Let me think of the best way to say this." Mindy looked out her side window, then up at the cigarette-stained ceiling above her head. "We're not stealing anything … we're not breaking anything … we're not hurting anyone." Rosie looked at Stache, both nodding in agreement.

"Then what's the big secret, I don't get it."

"I'm just trying to keep life interesting," downplayed Mindy. "Remind me to never throw you a surprise party, though. Hey everyone, Sweet Pea doesn't like surprises."

Stache floored it on a straight stretch, pushing the speedometer just over ninety, interrupting some of the tension between the backseat passengers. Approaching a wall of cornstalks, he eased off the gas pedal and glided into a left turn, coasting back to their original cruising speed.

Sweet Pea's brow barely unfurled, but she felt a little better knowing they weren't going to be murdering anyone.

Mindy attempted to tie a ribbon on it. "Stache, Rosie — last time, are we committing any of the aforementioned crimes tonight?"

"Negative," Stache said.

"Nope," echoed Rosie, taking a pinch of Big League Chew from a pouch on her lap.

The car was quiet for a while, except for the low hum of the engine and an occasional crack of bubble gum from the passenger seat. The smell of artificial grape flavoring filled the cabin, as Mindy started worrying that she hurt Sweet Pea's feelings more than she thought she did. Not just here in the car, but the night before, too. She found her trusty flask and eased her mind.

Nobody spoke as they circled the valley again, like an airplane waiting for clearance to land. Breaking the silence, Mindy struck a serious chord out of nowhere.

"So there's this judge," she started, triggering Sweet Pea's chin to whip, eager for more. "Like, a real douchebag judge." She pulled at the end of her skirt and scratched a bug bite on her arm. "And he does what they all do, sitting up there playing God…"

Sweet Pea didn't know what to say, but she was relieved to finally get an origin story to whatever their mission was. Mindy kept going, throwing back another swig of encouragement.

"Do they even give a shit, or is it just like factory work, clocking their hours, sending the next one down the line. Like, 'Hey, I know I'm ruining your life, you piece of shit, and I don't really care. Wife and kid? Not my problem.'"

Nobody joked or tried to change the subject, as they were all pretty sure that Mindy was the kid in her story.

Sweet Pea put her hand on Mindy's hand. "I'm sorry."

"It's okay, I'm okay," she murmured. "It's just — he's the one who put my dad where he is now — so I owe him a little payback."

In the flickering darkness, Sweet Pea thought she saw her friend's eyes welling up. She knew her dad was in prison, but she had no idea what he did or how long he was in for. The gut-punch she felt for Mindy quickly transformed into her own worries: specifically, when would she see her own father again?

Since she climbed off her porch roof two nights ago, her little escapades masked over so many things that normally would have consumed her. And now that she had welcomed some trouble into her life, she had no idea how to get out of it. But she convinced herself that being trapped in a well was okay as long as she wasn't alone down there.

"Alright, we're getting close again," Stache announced. "You want me to make another lap or are we ready?"

Mindy sniffled. "Let's do this."

Sweet Pea stared out her side window, noticing more lights now as the winding valley road gradually brought them back to town. She recognized some of the areas they passed, but they were on the opposite side of town from her house, and it was pitch black beyond their headlights. More houses lined the right side of the road as they approached an intersection and took a slow left turn into a development.

The Camaro passed a pair of large stone pillars, perfect landscaping and a ritzy sign made from stacked stone — the kind of neighborhood where a judge would live. She squinted as they drove by, barely making out the name THISTLEWOOD ESTATES in the surrounding nightfall.

PHIL WAS ALMOST THREE DAYS LATE to the Pitch-Black Palooza, he wasn't with his family, and he didn't get to buy his daughter a funnel cake like he promised. On top of all that, his t-shirt was drenched in sweat and he was doubled over trying to catch his breath, sporting a skinned knee and bloody elbow. He looked like he had just run a full-contact marathon, but actually it was the result of riding — and wrecking — Gus's bike when he realized his Subaru wasn't in the garage. At the time, it seemed like a good alternative to jogging, but he underestimated the importance of daylight.

Roaming through the crowd, more than a few people stared at his tattered appearance as he looked for his family. *So much for that shower.* One gray-haired woman in particular fixed her eyes longer than most, shaking her head as she passed by, as if he were some kind of ex-con ruffian.

"Pot holes are hard to see in the dark!" he barked, chasing her off like a bad dog. *I really am an ex-con ruffian.* Phil's redemption tour was off to a rocky start.

With his eyes peeled for Liz, Gus and Sweet Pea, he noticed a sign board displaying the last remaining events of the last day of the Palooza:

7 PM THE HEMLOCKS

9 PM FIREWORKS

The scale of the downtown spectacle over-delivered on his expectations, as did the cool-factor of the missing sun. From his tiny holding cell window, or skylight basically, he got a taste of what the rest of the world was experiencing, but now that he was out in it, he couldn't stop craning his neck, looking at the vacant sky.

His stomach growled as he turned corner after corner with no sign of the Beverlys, before finally arriving at food truck row. *Man, I'm hungry, I should've poured a quick bowl of cereal before I left.* Wandering to the funnel cake line, he thought back to the last time he saw Sweet Pea, how he basically pushed her out the door so he could run the money to Hicks on time. And poor Gus, who tried to be his accomplice but got caught in the crossfire of Mom versus Dad. His last memory of Liz sent a jolt of heartburn up his throat, picturing her face in the motel parking lot, the look in her eyes when he knew that she knew.

A voice startled him from behind. "Wow, didn't expect to see you here."

He turned and faced Julia, who didn't like him and he knew it, but he didn't like her either.

"Oh, hey Julia," he uttered half-heartedly. "Why, what do you mean?"

"Little birdy told me you were in jail."

"You talked to Liz? When?"

Julia was enjoying his desperation. "Let me think, that was, uh, yesterday, pretty sure."

"Have you seen her today at all?"

"Nope. She was with some guy here, we all had a few drinks, it was fun. Maybe she's over at his place?"

Phil's fake smile melted off his face. "What guy."

"Don't get all jealous, she told me you two were separated or whatever." She played each card with a passive aggressive poker face. "Doc Antonelli. Or as she calls him … *Sebastian*." Julia added a cat sound for dramatic effect. "He's a good looking man."

"She told you we were separated?" His voice trailed off like his words had been sucked into a black hole.

"Good seein' ya, I gotta run." With a flick of her hair she strutted away from Phil's steamrolled soul.

Frozen in place and staring in the direction of the funnel cake worker, his inner self was processing the update on their marital status. Maybe everything was worse than he thought, and he was a sucker for thinking it wasn't.

Julia hadn't been gone more than two minutes when another voice startled him, this time from the opposite direction.

"Phil?"

Turning slowly to the familiar sound of his wife's voice, his blank eyes found hers, zapping his heart back to the world of the living.

"Liz," he said, still coming out of a fog. She formed half a smile, but he could tell something was going on. If this was the part where she told him there was someone else, he wanted her to just do it and get it over with.

"Hey Dad," said Gus, "how was jail?"

Phil rubbed his son's head like a puppy, but otherwise ignored him as he tried to garner any clue from Liz's pursed lips and widening eyes. His talk with Julia pulled the rug from the conversation he had rehearsed, leaving him speechless.

Liz looked as serious as ever. "Before you say anything, there's something I have to tell you."

His brain registered her words, but at the same moment he noticed that Sweet Pea wasn't with them. *She must be off with a friend ... or in line at the restroom ... or hiding somewhere to scare me.* He looked off in every direction, trying to catch a glimpse of her to know that they were all back together — even if it was just for a second before it fell apart again.

"Phil —" The lump in Liz's throat grew bigger. "Sweet Pea's missing."


STACHE FOLLOWED MINDY'S ORDERS as they moved into position for Operation Krylon, parking their car on a half-empty cul-de-sac at the far end of the development. Sweet Pea knew where she was now, just a few streets away from their dog walk a couple days ago. Apparently, Thistlewood wasn't just for doctors, as it was also home to the sinister judge from Mindy's nightmares. Maybe the kid that Stache pummeled on Friday was the judge's son, which would explain Rosie's "Thistlewood prick" comment.

Stache popped the trunk as they all got out and gathered around Mindy at the back of the Camaro. She pulled out a backpack and unzipped it, handing out supplies and objectives like a commanding officer. Sweet Pea was last to get hers, trying to make out what exactly she had just been handed in the dark. *Feels like a winter hat and some kind of bee spray,* she thought, waiting for someone to shine a light on the subject.

"Here," said Rosie, passing out tiny flashlights to each of them, impressing Sweet Pea with a level of planning and preparation she hadn't seen before from this group. *Maybe if they cared this much about school they'd be straight-A students.* As she fiddled with the items in her hands, Stache flipped on his beam, revealing the ski mask over his face and the can of Krylon spray paint in his hand. Her heart sank a little when she finally realized what they were doing, and she kicked herself for not knowing paint brands better.

Mindy gave her no time to dwell on it. "Masks on, follow me."

Sweet Pea was still trying to get the eye holes straight when she noticed the other three had taken off down the street. She scurried after them, unable to hit full stride because she was still fussing with the mouth hole.

Even though Mindy had beef with the judge, Sweet Pea had doubts about her own role as a graffiti artist. Maybe she could just pretend she did it, making fake hissing sounds with her mouth to really sell it. She practiced a few times before she reached the group. *Pffft-pffft!*

Jogging along with the pack now, they left the street and cut through a back yard, skinnying between fences and avoiding porch lights as they went, before shooting back onto another street. They ducked into a big yard with tall landscaping, following a right-of-way along the back of more dark properties. Sweet Pea had no idea where they were now, as their hurried in-and-out path had her internal compass spinning.

Mindy held up her fist at the front of the line, stopping her troops and crouching down behind a row of hedges where they took temporary cover. Four sets of lungs worked overtime, while four sets of eyes looked at each other through their masks.

"Target's in range, get your cans ready," Mindy whispered. All four mixing balls clanged in the dark like rattlesnakes ready to strike. "Stache, you hit the front of the house, Rosie, take the driveway, I'll do the garage door. Pea, just spray big red Xs on whatever the hell you want to."

Sweet Pea nodded, knowing she was about to be a part of something very wrong, but the thrill of yard-hopping in ski masks was overpowering the tiny voice of reason inside her head. Checking her spray nozzle like the others were doing, her shaky hands could barely keep a finger on it.

"Which house is it," Sweet Pea asked from their backyard position, eying the homes to their left and right.

"Neither, it's next row over," Mindy replied, before addressing them all. "We get in, we get out. If we get split up, meet back at the car." She stood up and gave her can one more shake for good luck, determined to complete Operation Krylon. Scanning their covered faces, she found the ski mask with Sweet Pea's eyes and mouth on it and gave her a nod.

"Here we go. Stay close."

Mindy led the charge around a landscaping bed, dodging a small pond and hugging the ground as she ran, with Stache, Rosie and Sweet Pea right on her heels. Shooting between the two houses, they emptied onto a street at the bottom of a hill, bringing the judge's house into full view on the opposite side for the first time.

Sweet Pea stopped breathing as the black canvas in front of her started to color itself with details she didn't want to see. Her brain filled in more and more familiar parts, completing the picture that hadn't fully appeared yet in the dark.

*Oh my God, it's Austin's house.*

Her stride fell apart, slowing her pace to a staggered walk, as she tried to stamp out all the fires in her brain. Stopping just short of the curb in front of his house, she stared helplessly at a blur of masked vandals cutting blood red lines into the brick exterior, across the front bay window, and down the white concrete drive-way. She wanted to run away or tell them to stop, but there she was again in her mental straightjacket. Her fuzzy eyes watched Mindy's silhouette spray a life-size crimson message across the garage doors in a silent act of vengeance.

Barely entering the side of her vision, Sweet Pea saw a light flip on inside the house. Her heart thumped even harder as she tried to warn them of the person moving quickly behind the curtains en route to the front door.

Her mouth formed the word *run* but it left as an empty gasp that fell short of their masked ears. Forcing herself forward, one step, then two, then three, she tried managing a full breath, ignoring the vice grip on her throat. She closed her eyes and focused on a long, slow exhale, but it was interrupted by the slamming of a door.

An angry voice on the front porch claimed the moment. "HEY!"

Mindy, Rosie and Stache took off like rockets, as a blast of adrenaline knocked Sweet Pea out of her trance. She finally found her legs, rushing after her friends, who had a good lead but were still in sight. A few seconds ahead of her, they left the street and disappeared behind a house on the left. A new panic kicked in, realizing she had no idea how to get back to the car if she lost them.

Running like a prison break, her heart felt like it was going to beat right out of her chest. Each footstep pounded in her ears, as she veered into the yard where Mindy had just gone. Her mask was somehow twisted now so she could barely see, and her nose was almost sticking through the left eye-hole. Slowing down half a step to straighten it out, her body suddenly jolted forward with a crushing blow from behind, spilling her sideways and down to the ground under the force of a flying tackle.

Once the echo of the thud left her ears, and the spots stopped dancing in her eyes, she found herself flat on her back, pinned down by the strong arms of her pursuer. The smell of fresh cut grass and the view of the starry sky refilled her senses, lying face to face in a very awkward position with her brother's unsuspecting best friend. Still heaving from the chase, she hoped to God the ski mask would do its job, but it was too late — Austin knew those eyes anywhere.

"Sweet Pea?"

Without thinking, she delivered a swift knee upwards — *oomph!* — landing a direct hit that sent him rolling over. Lying flat on his back, he winced up at the stars, watching out of one eye as Sweet Pea's shadowy figure jumped over him and fled into the darkness.

# 28

Gus and Liz caught Phil up to speed on Sweet Pea's mis-adventures — at least the ones they knew about. He wasn't surprised to learn that she climbed off the front porch roof, based on her performance at the Turret of Terror, but flying the middle finger from a powersliding Camaro was impressive. He asked a dozen follow-up questions and floated a few theories on where she could be, but nothing he said was new to their search efforts.

Liz was getting agitated. "I told you, we don't know who else was in the car, just the Mindy girl."

"And what's her last name, maybe I know the dad?"

"You don't, we already checked her house."

"But who is it, maybe I know them from work or somewhere." He wanted to grill Liz on her own whereabouts the last three days, but he bit his tongue.

"Phil, move on, it's a dead end."

"Gus, since your mom won't tell me —"

"God, you two are like toddlers," Gus reprimanded. "Dipetto. Mindy and Mandy, like it matters."

Phil stopped blathering when he realized why Liz was dodging the subject.

"Oh," he said, traveling to prom week and back in his mind.

"Yeah ... *Oh*..." replied Liz.

"Did you call them or go over there or anything?"

"Yes, I told you, dead end. Nothing there." Her squinted eyes questioned his intentions.

"So she didn't say anything?"

"Oh, she said plenty."

"What's that supposed to mean?"

Gus intervened again. "I swear if you two don't stop, I'm running away, too."

Phil and Liz suspended their argument, heeding the sixteen-year-old's threat and agreeing to a ceasefire.

Leading his beleaguered parents through the Palooza, Gus checked the last street they hadn't been to yet, completing their rounds unsuccessfully. Before any of them could say *now what*, Austin jogged around the corner, the look on his face hinting at big news.

"Yo, I tried calling your house —" he approached quickly, trying to catch his breath. "I just saw her."

"Where?!" the Beverlys erupted in one voice.

Austin took a seat on a nearby bench and told them about the four masked marauders outside his house, the ensuing chase, and his brief yet painful encounter with Sweet Pea.

Liz's eyes widened in more shock, as Phil chose to focus on the knee-to-groin part of the story, even more impressed than before.

"And how long ago was all that?" asked Gus.

"Like fifteen minutes? I ran back to my house, my dad was asking me who they were, calling the cops and everything." Liz offered him a drink of lemonade that Phil had bought her before their fight.

"Did you rat?" Gus scowled.

"Hell to the no. I told him they got away, had masks on, I didn't see faces. Left out the part where she nailed me down there." He motioned, as if there was any doubt to where *down there* was. "Mr. and Mrs. B, you should be proud — she's a feisty one."

Liz conjured half a smile, as Phil completed the other half.

"So, I don't know where they went, but she looked scared … I'm tellin' you guys, it was different. She was like … desperate … I've never seen her that way."

"Desperate how?" asked Phil.

"I don't know, she just had a look … like she needed help … or wanted to say something."

"Thanks, Austin, but they're probably just bored and feeling rebellious, garden variety mischief, I'm sure this will all blow over," Phil said, drawing a questioning glance from Liz.

"We don't know anything about the kids she's with," she sternly reminded him, "or what they're capable of."

"Actually," said Austin, "one thing I forgot to mention … I don't know who did what, but you should see our garage door." Everyone waited while he drank more of Liz's lemonade. "Gigantic word sprayed across the whole thing — KILLER — in big red letters. Like huge, bloody letters —"

"Okay, we get it," Liz said, fending off a flush to her temple.

*"Killer?"* asked Gus. "Your dad never killed anyone."

"I know, but lots of people hate him, he's made some enemies over the years. Inmates and ex cons are a lovely bunch."

Liz felt her temperature rising along with the stakes, trying to keep all the what-ifs at bay, as her worries tried to trample her sensibilities. She looked at Phil, expecting a dismissive smirk, but now he looked just as concerned as she was.

"Let's get out there and find her before she does anything stupid," said Phil.

"You're one to talk," jeered Gus. "Jailbird."

Phil had no words.

"They can't be very far," said Liz, "let's split up to cover more ground."

Austin was ready. "Me and Gus will head over to Thistlewood in case they doubled back." He was still coming down from the rush of his flying tackle. "Then we'll hit the valley, check some back roads."

"Okay, we'll swing by our neighborhood again, in case she's trying to come home," Phil said unconvincingly.

Liz added her hunch to the mix. "I want to check that old flea market, too, I don't trust the weirdo that gave her those soaps."

"Okay," Phil agreed. "Are we taking your car or my bike?"

She didn't laugh. "Everyone meet back here in an hour. Main stage."

"Alright Gus, *let's split*," said Austin, waiting for anyone to get his license plate reference. He laughed to himself. *Sweet Pea would've loved that one.*

SWEET PEA STOPPED RUNNING after a few minutes and stood alone in the middle of a quiet intersection at the heart of Thistlewood. Slowly spinning a full three-sixty under the stars, she looked down empty streets in each direction, with no signs of her partners in crime. Unfortunately, the minute she had spent on the ground, courtesy of Austin's chase-down tackle, made all the difference between catching up and being left behind. She tried to navigate her way back, but each wrong turn fed the creeping sensation of being lost.

Pulling off her ski mask, she sagged her shoulders and wiped a sweaty strand of hair from her forehead. Everything looked the same in the cookie-cutter development, as she passed a few cul-de-sacs during her escape but none of them had a Camaro waiting to whisk her away. Their plan to meet at the car would have worked better if she actually knew where they parked.

"MINDYYY!" she screamed at the sky, louder than she should have. There was no answer, but a few dogs engaged in a barking contest off in the distance.

Sweet Pea now had the misfortune of being abandoned twice in the last twenty-four hours — by the same group of friends. She wondered why none of them waited for her, or looked back to see if she made it out once Operation Krylon fell apart. They just kept running, saving their own butts — no different from her dad's self-serving, seven-year omission of the truth. Her hands made fists at her sides, as her jaw tightened at the growing thoughts of betrayal.

If the top of her tower climb was crippling fear, and the bottom of her barn party was all-consuming sadness, the humiliation of tonight's run-in with Austin was fueling an anger that she was unfamiliar with. It wasn't just another dose of bad decision making or random mischief — this time her little stunt hurt someone that she cared about.

She flashed back a few minutes ago to his face, the moment he realized it was her behind the mask. *Did that really just happen? I kneed him pretty hard, why did I do that? And his poor house, they're gonna be so pissed.*

She trudged along a curb, no idea where she was going, expecting any second to hear sirens and see red and blue lights bouncing off the dark mansions. Surely they called the cops by now, probably gave them her name. If they turned the corner right now, the thought of throwing her hands up and being taken away didn't sound so bad. She deserved to be caught. Or maybe it was time to head home and surrender to the other authorities — the ones that she probably put through hell the past few days. She wasn't sure which punishment would be worse.

As Sweet Pea ran her fingers through her hair, the dull hum of an engine got louder, and the glow of approaching headlights brightened her street. She thought about running, but figured she'd done enough of that. Walking to the middle of the street with no regard for the oncoming vehicle, she was ready for whatever happened next.

"Come and get me," she said to herself.

The blinding high beams outlined her silhouette, speeding to her position, weaving around her and skidding to a stop. Half of Mindy's body hung out the window of the Camaro, beckoning Sweet Pea for one more ride in the getaway car.

"Get in!"

Readjusting her eyes to the darkness, Sweet Pea blinked and stared into the car, barely making out the passengers, some still hiding behind their ski masks.

"C'mon, we gotta go, they made my car," Stache huffed from the driver's seat, as a few nosy families had stepped onto their porches.

Sweet Pea turned and walked ahead of them, still without a word having left her mouth. The wheels slowly rolled forward, following her steps and crunching tiny pieces of stray gravel as Mindy tried again from her window seat.

"Pea, get in, cops will be here any minute —"

She kept walking, wondering if this new offer was any better than the other two options that she had already resigned to: Cops, angry parents, or horrible friends?

The Camaro accelerated just enough to turn in front and cut her off. Mindy opened the door and jumped out, grabbing her by the wrist and making her mind up for her. Sweet Pea went along with it, indifferent to all her prospects, climbing into the front seat with a helping hand from Mindy.

Speeding away from Thistlewood and the far-off sound of sirens, there were no screeching tires or screaming speakers this time. Almost getting caught put a damper on their post-vandalism party, as they rode in silence for a few miles, soaking in the cool night air that blew through the cabin.

Heading up the on-ramp to the highway, a conversation finally ensued with Mindy and Rosie debating whether the judge, Austin's dad, was an "asshole" or a "douche." Stache tried to point out that they weren't mutually exclusive characteristics, but the girls insisted he had to be one or the other.

"Whatever, either way he deserved that shit tonight," declared Mindy.

Sweet Pea's blood was already on a low simmer before she got in, but the words in the car were pushing it towards a boil. Staring out her open window at the passing guardrails and road signs, she tried using the steady blast of wind to cool her jets.

Stache offered up his graffiti story. "Did you guys see my work on the big front window? I think I emptied the whole can on it." Mindy and Rosie celebrated, adding a few tales of their own before piling on Austin's family with more hate mail.

"Sweet Pea, what did you hit? I don't think I saw you in action," Rosie said from the backseat.

"Nothing," she murmured without turning around.

"Huh? Can't hear you back here," she pressed. "Speak up."

"Hey Stache," Mindy interrupted, "take the next exit, we probably shouldn't be up on the highway."

The Camaro rolled down Exit 32 and came to a stop sign before continuing onto a less traveled road. Sweet Pea stared at the Exxon station sign, trying to distract herself.

"So who yelled at us," asked Rosie, "was that the judge? I didn't really see."

Mindy answered. "No, that was his douchebag son. There, it's settled — son is the douche, dad is the asshole."

Sweet Pea's foot tapped on the floor, over and over, trying to suppress the urge she was having to blow her stack. She pushed out a long exhale as she thought about defending him, but she was outnumbered and knew they would just do what they always do.

"Pea, what's his name? He's your brother's friend, right?"

Her heart dropped. *She knew.* Sweet Pea had convinced herself that the hit on Austin's house was a coincidence, that if Mindy had known the judge was his dad, she would have said something or never dragged her along in the first place.

Mindy tried again. "C'mon, you know him … who's the douchebag?"

"Wow, so you *did* know." Her first words of the night accused Mindy of treason.

"Know what?"

"You knew that was Austin's house."

"Yeah, so —"

"And you know I'm friends with him, you saw us at mini-golf."

Mindy rolled her eyes. "Chill, dude, I thought he was just your brother's friend."

"YOU KNEW!" It was the first time Sweet Pea raised her voice since they'd met, stopping time as they all held their breath.

"Whatever, sorry, I didn't think it —"

"You're not sorry," Sweet Pea blurted with a quivery voice.

Stache and Rosie stayed quiet, letting them duke it out as the car sped along another dark road, keeping their eyes peeled for police. For the next few miles, nobody said anything, as Round One appeared to have ended. Mindy didn't seem all that bothered, nonchalantly fiddling with the ski mask in her hands while Sweet Pea brooded in the front seat.

"You know," Sweet Pea opened Round Two, "it's always someone else's fault. Everything you guys do." She thought about the kid Stache punched, the money stolen from the petting zoo, the vendetta against Austin's dad.

"You're seriously killing the buzz here, Pea," said Mindy.

"So your dad, I guess he's innocent and it's the judge's fault, right?"

Mindy sat up straight. "Leave it alone."

"He deserves whatever he got. You don't hear me whinin' about my dad."

More silence radiated, as Mindy wanted to cut her new friend some slack, but the subject of her father was striking a nerve.

"Shut your goddamn mouth, I mean it," she growled like a wounded dog.

"Guys, c'mon, let it go," said Stache.

"Yeah, God," Rosie muttered as the Camaro approached a T in the road.

Sweet Pea felt her head spinning as she squeezed the life out of the door handle. Everything started catching up to her, as her brain flashed picture after picture, replaying all the damage they caused, laws they broke, and people they hurt. Whether they were her ideas or not, she went along with it all. But she couldn't do it any more.

With the car slowing to a stop, she flung open her door and jumped out, slamming it shut before anyone blinked.

"Hey!" yelled Rosie.

"Let her go," Mindy said, "she doesn't need us, we don't need her."

"I'm not leaving her here," argued Stache, "we're middle of nowhere."

All four of them paused their predicament to figure out if the far-off sirens were getting louder, as they seemed to be. In the blackness of the rear and side mirrors, streaks of red and blue crept into their view.

"Get back in the car — now!" demanded Stache, but Sweet Pea planted her feet along the side of the road. The sirens wailed louder and the lights flashed brighter as a police car crested the distant hill, approaching fast.

"Go-go-go!" yelled Rosie and Mindy, as Stache reluctantly floored the gas and fled the scene, with one less passenger in his Camaro.

Sweet Pea darted away from the road, going further back and deeper into the tall brush until it swallowed her body. She threw herself down, feeling the sharp teeth of a thornbush on her forearm and the lumpy ground an inch from her nose. She covered her ears as the siren screamed and her eyes filled with the dancing shadows of red and blue strobes.

In a matter of seconds, it was gone, gradually returning the roadside to silent darkness. Lying in the brush, a calm washed over Sweet Pea as she rested her cheek on the ground, relaxing every muscle in her body. Like fleeing an inferno and being hit with a downpour that soaked her to the bone. She felt safe there, even though "there" was alone in the middle of nowhere.

She took her time standing up, waiting for her nervous system to recover, taking in her starlit surroundings. Walking along the road, she thought about the past hour of her life, trying to make sense of the whirlwind. Back at Thistlewood, she was ready for the cops to take her in, but here she just eluded them like a savvy fugitive. Breaking the chains from Mindy and gang made her feel new, like she was bigger than giving up and going home. Whatever made her climb out her bedroom window was still there, even though her troublemaking friends were not.

Sweet Pea spent most of the past seven years pining for Gus — or anyone — to brighten her world. So maybe she read too much into Miss Aurora's voodoo-soap prophecy, thinking Mindy was some kind of chosen one to save her soul. Turns out, she was just a nice old lady who made pretty soaps with cool names.

None of this changed the question dangling in front of her: Now what? She couldn't run forever, but she couldn't look her mother in the eye, either. Not yet. And if her dad was home, which was a big if, she needed time to prepare for his apologies and the next set of broken promises. A scary thought crept in: What if home wasn't really home any more?

After walking for what felt like a mile, she noticed a large shadowy structure across the road to her left. The shape of the stacked stones instantly fired a memory that grew clearer as she got closer. Looming in the dark and towering over her was an old iron furnace, like it had floated in front of her face from a dream.

"Pyramid with its top chopped off," she whispered.

Her spine tingled as she realized where she was, fixing her eyes on the dirt road just beyond the remnants. She was back to where it all started seven years ago. Sweet Pea stared at the furnace — it was still holding its shape, but missing some pieces that had broken off over the years.

"*Hmph*, kinda like me," she said. "Wait a minute —"

Something else that Miss Aurora said just dawned on her. Her brain replayed the last thing she told her that day: *"To fix up somethin' right, you gotta go back where it got broke."*

What if coming back here was what she meant? The Mindy thing was a miss, but maybe the universe or God or voodoo brought her here for some fateful reason. She walked to the entrance of the dirt road, looking right down its mouth, barely seeing anything in the black of night.

*My flashlight!* She remembered the only good thing to come out of Operation Krylon. Pulling it from her pocket and flipping the switch, she got a better look at the infamous path that Hicks took that day, flooding her mind with fragments of memories — the Suburban, the swamp, the tree, his words, the heron.

None of it really made sense, but on the last day of darkness, Sweet Pea found herself walking down a dirt road, without a friend, to the darkest place she'd ever known.

# 29

G US AND AUSTIN MADE A QUICK LOOP through Thistlewood, knowing they were at least fifteen minutes behind the flight of the graffiti artists. But they wanted to rule out the right-under-our-noses scenario where Mindy and crew came back to admire their work — or finish what they started — once the police cleared the scene.

"Damn, they got you guys good," said Gus as they cruised by Austin's house.

"Painted the town red," he replied, "or at least the part where I live."

The yellow Jeep slowed to a crawl as the search party plotted their next move.

"So let's think — where would you go if you were four punk kids running from the cops?" asked Gus.

"I dunno — probably just head to the valley and lay low. Or hide my car behind a billboard and cover it up with branches."

"Okay, McFly."

"For real, there's like a thousand places to hide out there. Camaro in a haystack." Austin turned left out of the development and picked up the road leading out of town. "All that's assuming she's still with them."

"Why wouldn't she be?"

"She was in panic mode, so maybe she ditched them, or they had a falling out. Maybe she never got in the car."

Gus bristled. "While we're doing maybes, maybe the person you tackled wasn't even her. Are you sure?"

"Yeah, I'm positive."

"You said she had a mask on her face and didn't say anything, so how do you know?"

Austin thought about describing how her ocean blue eyes caught a glint of starlight, and he recognized the coconutty smell of her shampoo, and it all made his heart flutter.

"I just know, trust me. She was done, she wanted out, I saw it in her eyes."

Gus thought about it. "So maybe the question is: Where would *Sweet Pea* go to get away from everything? Like, if she had nowhere else to run?"

As the Jeep sped through the darkness, a small billboard caught their headlights. Gus whipped his head as they passed by, taking in an advertisement for the *Blue Heron Café* at seventy miles per hour. Something was trying to click, but his brain kept sputtering on the connection. *Had they eaten there when they were little? Does someone they know work there? Do they have a good BLT?* Finally, a flare ignited from the center of his head.

"I have an idea — turn around, let's get on the highway."

THE DRIVE TO THE TACO STAND provided Liz and Phil with all the potential for a knock-down-drag-out of epic proportions. After three days of falling apart, here they were, close enough to breathe on each other in the family Camry.

She couldn't stop thinking about Mandy's new assertion that prom week was more eventful than Phil had admitted to. Oddly enough, that he-said-she-said from twenty years ago was bothering her more than the gambling cover up that put them in this situation to begin with. But she white-knuckled the steering wheel until her mind cleared, forcing herself to focus on finding their daughter.

In the passenger seat, Phil stewed over Julia's newsflash about their separation and Liz downing drinks with the hot doctor. He glared at her a few times while she drove, ready to read her the riot act, but the words died on his tongue. The here and now was finding Sweet Pea, and they couldn't do that from opposite sides of a gladiator pit. Part of him was still in shock that she was even speaking to him after gouging his heart at the Thunderbird.

Liz pulled into the parking lot and turned off the engine. "This is where she got the soaps, the night they all went golfing."

"Not sure how this is relevant, but okay," he said, getting out of the car.

"It's probably nothing, but someone here gave her a bar of soap with her name on it, right before all this started. Gus said she came running around the corner, right behind the taco stand. It's a little weird."

Phil agreed. "Okay, let's check with the taco guys first, they can point us in the right direction."

"Welcome to Taco Hut," said the worker as they reached the counter.

"Oh great, you speak English," said Liz, talking louder and

slower than necessary. "Where … are … the … soap people?"

"Sopapilla…" he called back to his cook. "Two dollars."

Phil whispered to Liz, "You just ordered dessert."

"No-no-no! We don't want —"

An order of sopapillas slid in front of them as the man waited to be paid. Phil dug into his wallet and put two ones on the counter, before taking a piece of the fried dough and popping it in his mouth.

"Mmmm, try one," he said, offering a piece to Liz. He finished chewing then practiced his three years of high school Spanish on the workers. "Dónde está el … jabón?"

Liz was impressed by the taste of the New Mexican specialty and the skills of her somewhat bilingual husband, as the men engaged in a back and forth, nodding their heads and motioning past the wall at the back of their stand.

"Gracias," he replied before turning to Liz. "I think I understood about half of what they said. There used to be a lady back there who made soaps — Miss Aurora — but they haven't seen her in years. This whole place is vació."

She side-eyed him.

"Empty."

"Well, she must be back in business," said Liz, scarfing down the rest of the sopapillas. They walked along the face of the flea market, shining their flashlight on the mess of long-forgotten tables, racks, displays and other relics in various states of disrepair. Behind them, one of the men called out, *"Diosa del sol!"* catching Phil's attention.

"What's that mean?" asked Liz, leading them around the corner.

"Beats me," he said with a raised brow, hoping she wouldn't push the envelope. "Let's just see if she's here, but then we need to get back to town."

Walking to the third row of booths, their eyes were peeled for signs of the soap lady. It was dark and nothing at all looked open, but someone like that in a place like this, could be sleeping on the floor, for all they knew.

"Some of them never took their signs down when it closed," said Phil, "I remember coming here with my grandparents when I was little. Most of it was old junk, but some people made stuff and sold it here, too."

"There it is," said Liz, shining her light on the sign for MISS AURORA'S SOAPERY & APOTHECARY, just a few steps ahead. Approaching the stand, it wasn't just dark — there were no soaps, no soap lady, no anything. Just empty tables and old shelving covered in dust and dirt, looking like no one had set foot here in decades.

"Vació," said Liz, puzzled by their discovery, or lack thereof. She noticed Phil staring at the sign, appearing to do mental math.

"*Since 1905,* it says ... that would put Miss Aurora around a hundred years old if she started in her teens."

Liz had already drifted behind the counter to look for more clues. The flea market sat on a gravel lot, so most of the booths just had dirt floors now. Phil stood with his hands on his hips, waiting for enough time to pass that he could suggest leaving without rushing her.

"Okay, let's get going," Phil said, "we should —"

"Wait —" said Liz, shining her light on a patch of color in the back corner that didn't belong. A cluster of red, pink, purple and white wildflowers were growing right up through the ground, glowing like a torch. The sight of the delicate, ruffled petals sent a shiver through her body, as she knew in a heartbeat what she was looking at.

"Do you realize what this is," she said, bending down to trace the flower with her finger, awestruck by its beauty and the strange place it had chosen to bloom.

"Umm —"

"Why do you think we call her Sweet Pea?"

"For the soup? I always thought it was for that pea soup your grandmother used to make."

"Oh my God, Phil, no. The flowers, these right here, they're Sweet Pea flowers. They were my favorite."

Husband and wife stared at them for another minute, dumbfounded by the coincidence of soaps, flowers, and missing daughters.

"Should we pick one or leave them here?" asked Phil.

Plucking one from the earth, Liz held it to her nose and took a long drag of the sweet, airy fragrance. "I think Miss Aurora wanted us to have it."

SWEET PEA COVERED GROUND QUICKLY behind the beam of her flashlight, walking the same dirt road that she did seven years ago — this time in the opposite direction. To ward off any shadow monsters, she talked out loud as she went, taking in the gloom and comparing notes with her memory banks.

"I can't believe I'm here, this is so weird." She thought about what awaited her. "Little Miss Heron, I hope you're not napping, 'cause we have some catchin' up to do."

Her fourteen-year-old stride kept marching along, catching the occasional glimpse of a tree cluster or a bend in the road that sent her back in time. Fuzzy visions of Gus holding her hand materialized, his muddled voice comforting her as they walked. Up ahead, her beam caught a patch of tall reeds, outlining the edge of a pond. Her stomach started percolating, smelling the gassy odor that she never forgot, realizing that the backdrop of her nightmares was only fifty yards out.

"Okay, almost there," she said, distracting any practical voice in her head that tried to question her. Her quest to fix what was broken had almost reached its destination, as the road widened into an opening and the swamp took shape to her right. Shining her light on the ground, her ears replayed the sound of spinning tires throwing gravel, as she ran her hand along the back of her leg, remembering each stone that hit her that day.

"So much for the little pink houses," she said, walking closer to the water's edge, fascinated that it was all still here, preserved in time like she had walked into a dream. Aiming her beam left and right, she found the big dead tree, still lying in the water awaiting a proper burial. Walking past its upended roots, she stepped onto the trunk and shuffled out as far as she could go until it got too narrow. Carefully taking a few playful bounces, she watched the still water send ripples towards shore.

From her perch on the very tree branch that was burned into her mind and drawn onto her pictures, she looked back at the bank where she stood seven years ago. Squinting her eyes, young Sweet Pea stared back at her — it was just the two of them, no Gus, no Hicks. She sighed at the sight of her tiny frame, vulnerable and powerless to what she became after that day.

Wiping her eyes, she turned her attention back to the reeds, shining her light around the perimeter looking for the long legs of her feathered friend.

"Come out, come out, wherever you are," she announced to the swamp, knowing that it was probably long gone, but hoping nonetheless. A sound from the trees to her left startled her.

"That you, girl?" She walked back down the tree, around the

roots, and made her way along the bank for a better view. It just now hit her that any number of woodland creatures could be lurking in the dark, some not as friendly and graceful as a blue heron. Treading more cautiously, she stayed out of the taller grass and stood still, listening for the sound.

There it was again. Turning off her flashlight, everything went pitch black as Sweet Pea focused her senses on a faint light across the swamp. Glowing at the base of a tree cluster, it flickered like a soft white fire — too fuzzy to be a flashlight, too big to be a firefly. Staring harder, her stomach lurched as the blurry dot moved quickly right to left, disappearing into the trees.

*Oh my God, someone's over there.*

Just when she was close to retaking control of this place, of maybe her life, her brain snagged a thread and started unraveling. Who in their right mind would be out here at this hour? Of all places. It didn't make sense. The safest, smartest thing to do right now was to leave — fast — go back to the road and flag down a car just like they did last time.

With her light still off, she snuck a few steps back toward the dirt road. Here she was, leaving unceremoniously without thanking the heron, letting fear win again. After a few more paces, her feet stopped moving and she felt her legs freeze up on her. So many times her body had paralyzed her with fear, stopping her from saving herself, but now it had reversed its engines. Her pounding heart wanted her to stop running, to stay and face whatever this was, to find any kind of closure that might be hiding in the dark.

Feet still planted, she turned at her waist, flipping on her flashlight and aiming it back where she saw the light. Her legs followed, easing her toward the water's edge.

She whispered to herself. "As long as this pond's between us, I'm safe." Training her beam across the water one more time, she caught a face peeking out from between two trees. It jerked back into its hiding place before she got a good look.

"Looks like you're just as scared of me," she said, trying to comfort herself. "Kinda like Dad always said about spiders."

Sweet Pea turned off her light and crept around for a better angle, feeling the slightest bit less likely to be murdered than she did a few minutes ago. Pushing the boundaries of her own personal safety net — again — she snuck further along the bank, cutting the distance in half. Blasting her beam back on the tree line, she tried to catch her target in the act of repositioning, but nothing was there. She scanned left and right along the trees, up one and down another, but whoever was there must have taken cover.

Her pulse spiked. "Unless they're on the move, too — *shit!*"

Breathing heavier, she fumbled with her flashlight, firing it in every direction, desperately trying to locate the figure. She side-stepped her way back toward the fallen tree, head on a swivel, checking her back, then her front, then her back. Leaning against the upended clump of earth and mangled roots, she killed the light again and listened for any sound that wasn't made by her own self.

After a full minute of begging her lungs to relax, a splash broke the tension on the other side of the pond, drawing Sweet Pea to peek around from her hiding place. A second splash dotted the silence, followed by the loud croaking of a bullfrog.

"Dumb frogs," she whispered, turning back around — but she wasn't alone any more.

*AAAAAAAAAGH!*

Two screams erupted simultaneously, triggering a family of muskrats to run from their nest and dive into the pond. The first scream came from Sweet Pea, startled by the dark figure in front of her. The second belonged to the dark figure, who mirrored her surprise with a matching howl.

Scrambling from the scare, they collided and went down, climbing over each other in the darkness. Sweet Pea's flashlight never left her trembling hand, as she struggled to find the switch, finally lighting the chaos with a *click*.

She gasped. "What are *you* doing here?"

"I came over to ask you the same thing."

The beam of light illuminated the girl's eyebrow piercings, casting eerie reflections on the ground.

"Light down, you little shit —" she huffed.

Sweet Pea lowered the beam, unblinding her, then repositioned it like a table lamp to light up the immediate area.

"Feral Dawn?"

"You don't have to stare, Tower Girl."

Sweet Pea didn't know she had earned a nickname, but she instantly wore it with pride. The girls eyeballed each other, doubly dumbstruck by the presence of someone else in this godforsaken place, on the same night, at the same time, under the same mysterious circumstances.

Nervous, she bantered. "I'm not staring, you are."

It was Saturday night and the sun hadn't shown its face since Wednesday evening when it dipped behind the ridge for a three-day vacation. The pesky electromagnetic cloud had its fun, dousing Earth's daylight and freaking out half the population who thought this could be the end. Now it just needed to complete its slow crawl past the sun and be on its merry way so things could get back to normal.

The dormant star hung where it always had, idling its nuclear engine, waiting for its dimmer switch to crank all the way back to full steam ahead. It only needed eight-and-a-half minutes to deliver its first batch of rays, so it was burning for the chance to light the skies, warm the oceans, and restore hope to any lost souls who had spiraled through three days of darkness.

Two of those souls stood face to face at the edge of the swamp, dusting themselves off, gathering their wits and studying the person across from them. Sweet Pea noticed Dawn's backpack had spilled some of its contents — old envelopes, folded papers, a length of rope and a book of matches — causing her to frantically stuff everything back in and close the zipper. She looked bothered that her things were spotted, clutching her backpack tight with a death grip that made Sweet Pea back up a step.

"Don't worry, I don't care about your stuff." Sweet Pea had heard all the stories — legends — of Feral Dawn, but she hadn't physically seen her in years, not since she transferred schools. For all the talk of her "feral" ways, Sweet Pea sensed something about her tonight that was far from the scary figure people made her out to be. Something was hiding in her eyes.

"Okay, I'll start," said Sweet Pea. "What am I doing here? Good question, I don't really know." She walked to the downed tree and sat on its trunk. "I was ridin' around with my friends — well, they're not really my friends any more — actually one of them might still be, but the other one never really was. And the one who was my best friend, we just had a fight so I jumped out of the car. I started walkin' and found this road and — well that's another story — but I came over here to look for a heron that used to live here."

Dawn didn't say anything, but she nodded along to Sweet Pea's tale.

"I need to find Miss Heron, actually she could be Mrs. Heron now, I don't know. I just want to tell her thank you, I never got to say thank you." She knew she was starting to sound like a freak, so she shifted gears. "So how do you know I'm the 'Tower Girl', is that like a thing that people talk about now? Am I famous like you?"

"We're infamous. Big difference." Dawn spoke with an intellect that went beyond her skull-crushing reputation. "I was at the park the other day when you went up. Saw the whole thing after some little squid ran into me. Spilled my fries, I was pissed."

Dawn joined her on the log. "So you're just here by yourself looking for a bird?"

"Yep, that's about it," she said with a shrug. "Your turn — why are you here?"

Dawn stared across the water, hesitating to answer, but finally gave in to Sweet Pea's request.

"I was actually sitting over there, reading some old letters with my lantern. This is kind of my place." Dawn stood up and walked further out on the tree, thinking about telling her more but not sure yet.

"No fair, this is *my* place," joked Sweet Pea. "Guarantee you I was here first. What letters were you reading, if you don't mind me asking?"

"They're from my dad," she sniffed, hiding her face in the dark.

Sweet Pea could tell it was a touchy subject, and she didn't want to say the wrong thing.

"That's cool … does he live somewhere else, or is he like in the Army or something?"

Dawn didn't answer.

"Never mind, none of my business. So what do you mean, this is *'your place'*? Do you come here a lot?"

"Yeah, when I need to think about stuff. It's kinda like a graveyard."

The word "graveyard" made Sweet Pea's eyes go wide, as she

had thought the same thing a hundred times about the swamp. It was the place where her childhood died, and short of having a tombstone with her name on it, she was grieving what she lost here, too.

Dawn saw her reaction. "Don't worry, nobody actually died here. Just me."

Sweet Pea should have been more puzzled by her words.

"Me too," she added, shocked by how much she understood her.

The girls turned their eyes to the reeds for any sign of the heron, trying to make sounds that would attract her, without knowing the first thing about heron calls.

Dawn broke the silence. "These letters from my dad … they're all from when I was younger." A bullfrog splashed again as she chose her words. "But he hasn't written in years."

Sweet Pea wanted to put her hand on her shoulder, or comfort her somehow, but her brain had been conditioned to never make physical contact with Feral Dawn.

"Maybe you could write to him now?" she said. "Not like right now, obviously, but tomorrow?"

"No, he doesn't give two shits about me."

"Aw, I doubt that's true … he's your dad."

Dawn pulled the matchbook from her backpack and struck a match, lighting up their corner of the swamp.

"It's my fault, anyway. That he doesn't write." The flame burned all the way down to her finger and thumb but she didn't flinch. She flicked the dead match into the pond, making a quick hiss as it hit the surface. "Back when he went away, he wrote the nicest things in the world. I checked the mailbox every single day that first summer."

"Hey, I'm sure it's not your fault —"

"So he kept writing, and writing, and writing, and I read every single word, over and over. Kept them all under my bed. I would just pull out the shoebox whenever I missed him." She struck another match and flung its burning head out over the water, fizzling out like a shooting star.

"How's that your fault, you —"

"I never wrote back," her voice trembled. "Ever..." she trailed off, her eyes filling with tears.

Sweet Pea put her arm around Dawn's heaving shoulders, not caring if she wanted to be touched or not. She stared down, pretending to not see her crying, when something caught her eye on the backpack. It must have happened when she got her matches, but the rope was hanging out of the opening now.

Sweet Pea's face went ghost white as she tried to hide the sound of her gasp — the end of the rope was tied in a loop with a couple big knots above it, the kind she had seen in movies or TV shows that she wasn't allowed to watch.

"Hey," she tried changing the subject, "wanna know why I climbed up the Turret of Terror? First, give me one of those matches, I wanna flick one."

Dawn passed the matchbook and showed Sweet Pea how to take a match, press it against the striker, and fling it in one quick motion. She fired one a couple feet above their heads, but it missed the water and landed on the log. Dawn snuffed it out with her thumb.

"So, the tower," Sweet Pea continued, "I was trying to show off for my brother, because he never really pays attention to me any more. But he used to be an awesome brother when we were little. So I thought, you know, if I climb up there and scream for help, he would come to the rescue and save me again. ... He already saved me once when I was little, right here actually when we got kidnapped, but that's a whole nother story." She teed up another match and launched it. "So, obviously, my stupid plan didn't work. But my dad's the one who actually climbed up and saved me, which was cool, because he always felt guilty for not saving me back then. Sorry, I know this makes no sense, but it's all kind of why I'm here tonight."

Dawn appeared less puzzled than she should have looked.

"So 'back then,' that was what — seven years ago?"

Sweet Pea sat up straight. "Yeah. How'd you know that?"

Dawn took her time. "I think I know the person who took you."

Sweet Pea's eyebrows shot up. "Well it's no secret, he was in the papers and everything."

Dawn's voice was barely a whisper. "I know. He's my dad."

# 30

PITCH-BLACK PALOOZA'S MAIN STAGE finally welcomed The Hemlocks, a group of high school kids obsessed with the popular new band, Nirvana. Liz and Phil barely noticed the spot-on grunge covers belting out behind them as they stood at the edge of the crowd, waiting impatiently for Gus and Austin to honor their one-hour rendezvous time. But it had already been an hour and fifteen minutes.

"The fact that they're late could be good," said Phil. "Maybe they had better luck than we did," he lamented at their own empty stops at the flea market and Beverly house.

Liz didn't say anything, as her brain was still processing the mystery of Miss Aurora, on top of her already-there worries about Sweet Pea and Phil. She even had a tinge of guilt over her own little jaunt with Sebastian.

Phil noticed her fidgeting. "Hey — she'll be okay. I promise."

She looked up, making real eye contact with him for the first

time all day. Years ago, that kind of statement came with a reassuring hug, but the unassuming glance was enough for both of
them right now.

A five second silence between songs was crashed by an opening bass riff that the audience seemed to have been waiting for.
The entire roundabout was shoulder to shoulder, bouncing in
unison as Lincoln Square was in the midst of a proper alternative rock concert. As the throng of people screamed along to the
first verse, one face in particular was uninterested, trying to make
his way through the sea of Hemlocks fans. He was a good stone's
throw away from Phil and Liz, with a hundred people between
them, but he caught Phil's attention as he tried parting the crowd,
drawing a few angry reactions in the process.

Phil's blood ran cold as he spotted the familiar beady eyes and
whiskered face. His jaw clamped shut and a hushed "Oh my God"
slipped out as Liz strained to see what he was reacting to.

Pointing to the moving target, he put his mouth to her ear.
"Hicks."

She quickly honed in on his path, realizing her one and only
job right now was to prevent another ride in a police car for Phil.
It was just three days ago that he whipped a chunk of concrete in
Hicks' general direction, so the last thing they needed was Round
Two.

Phil watched him walk away from a safe distance, craning his
neck as he plotted his next move. *Bastard took my kids ... wrecked
my marriage ... sent me to jail.* He liked having someone to blame.

"C'mon, we're following him," he said over the sound of
crunchy guitars. Phil grabbed Liz's hand, pulling her through the
crowd before she had time to object. She was already failing at her
job, distracted by his firm grip. Once they left the crowded square,
keeping their cover was more difficult in the open, as they ducked

into booths and hid behind groups of people while they kept him in sight.

"Where's he going?" asked Liz. "He's either looking for someone or trying to get away from someone."

"Yeah, he's not here for the funnel cakes."

Following their adversary down one street and over to the next, they watched him navigate like a man on a mission. He finally slowed down when he reached the carnival games, eying up each one like a toddler, fascinated with the colorful prizes hanging behind each challenge.

Phil backtracked half a block to a table selling big striped hats, oversized sunglasses, fake pink beards and other makeshift disguises.

"Take your pick," he said to Liz, grabbing the hat and glasses for himself.

"Ooh, we're playing dress up," she said, strapping a beard over her ears without needing an explanation.

"You look good in pink," he joked.

With a hidden smile, she paid the worker and they hurried back to the games, now in full incognito mode.

Hicks hadn't gone far, waiting his turn behind a family at the water gun race. Gigantic stuffed animals hung from a wall — polka dotted piglets, sparkly unicorns, rainbow dolphins, neon monkeys — which made no sense for a guy like him to be playing for.

Phil's mind went from rational to ridiculous. "That sonuvabitch," he muttered.

"What?"

He wasn't ready to say it out loud yet, but he was thinking through a theory that just popped into his head.

"Nothing."

They found a nearby booth where they could lean against its

sidewall with decent cover and a good line of sight. For the most part, Hicks looked like any other guy playing a carnival game. Slamming his hand on the counter when he lost by a hair, then forking over more money to play again. And again, until he finally won. The worker handed him a unicorn, which typically is then handed to a child, or a date, but he just took it and walked away.

"What the heck," said Liz. "If he's trying to impress a girl-friend, it would help if she were actually here."

"Or actually existed." Phil went silent, keeping their distance as they continued trailing him. After a few blocks, he tried sharing his theory again.

"Okay, I hope I'm wrong, but —" he cut himself off.

"What, just say it —"

"Well — Sweet Pea's missing — and he's out here acting weird." Liz wasn't there yet. "So?"

"So what if the unicorn's for her? Like he has her in his base-ment and it's to shut her up."

"Then that means you watch too much television," she said with an eye roll.

He slumped his shoulders, realizing it was a little far-fetched.

"Yeah, you're probably right," said Phil as they approached the high decibel levels of the main stage again. "But so help me God, I'll kill him if you're wrong."


By the soft, flickering glow of the kerosene lantern, Sweet Pea and Dawn filled in the gaps about how their dads ended up on opposite ends of their current vendetta. Sweet Pea had no idea that Hicks even had a daughter, so when Dawn explained that her parents weren't married and she was given her mother's name, it made sense. And it was news to Dawn that her dad was out of prison — she'd bounced from house to house and great-aunt to great-uncle so many times throughout the past seven years, he would've needed a private investigator to track her down. Dawn also never knew that Sweet Pea was one of the "names withheld to protect identity" in the news reports about the kids in the Suburban. But the more she saw her now in the full light of the lamp, Dawn started registering Sweet Pea's face from further back in grade school.

"I think I remember you from school," she realized. "You look older now, but I know your face."

"What do you mean?"

*"Yeahhh,"* she marveled, "now I see it."

Sweet Pea shrugged her shoulders, welcoming the story.

"A couple years after my dad went to jail, right before I got shipped off to Remington, fourth grade I think. It was recess, I'm there on the playground looking for someone to mess with. That's just how I was." The lantern hissed as she spoke, layering in some white noise over the bullfrogs. "Jeremy Barr — remember him? He comes up, asking me something about geography class, and I fell for it. One of his dickhead buddies was kneeling down behind me, so when he shoved me up high on my shoulders, I went down hard right over him. Landed on my back and hit my head."

Sweet Pea nodded along, starting to remember the same event.

"I think I was out for a couple seconds, but when I realized what happened, I'm sitting up, trying to figure out if my head's bleeding … a circle had formed around me. Barr was pointing right at me, laughing his head off. I can see that prick right now. Then someone behind me took a cheap shot, shoved me when I tried to stand up, and I went down again. Everyone was laughing, staring at me like I was King Kong. I saw every single face around that circle."

Tears started welling up in Sweet Pea's eyes as she revisited that day.

Dawn continued. "Half of 'em I didn't care, I knew they hated me, whatever, but some of the kids who laughed and said shit actually used to be my friends. Holly and Christie? I used to play at their houses when we were little — Jesus." She took a deep breath and let it out slowly.

"But there was this one kid," she said, trying not to let her voice break, "one face in that whole crowd wasn't laughing or joining in. She just stared at me like *she* was gonna cry."

Sweet Pea's heart ached for Dawn, always wishing she had done more that day, stood up for her somehow or gone to her side at least.

"That was you, wasn't it?"

Sweet Pea nodded, never realizing that Dawn had even seen her. Neither girl said anything for a while, staring off at the pond again.

Dawn's gaze landed on Sweet Pea's sheepish face, then down at the ground, taking a heavy breath. "When the world hates you … like everyone just wants you gone … then one little thing happens that keeps you going … never mind … this is stupid."

"Oh my gosh, no, that's not stupid," said Sweet Pea. "I'm so sorry that happened to you. And I should have done something, I just stood there."

"I was a bully," Dawn said with an edge to her voice. "I deserved what I got. How could you even feel bad for me?"

"I don't know, I just saw you and you looked sad, and you were hurt, and I wouldn't want people to treat me that way if I were hurt."

Dawn shook her head in disbelief, agitated by her kindness.

"And what about now? Why are you being nice to me? My dad kidnapped you for God's sake. You know I'm *Feral Dawn,* right? Aren't you afraid I'll rip your face off?"

Sweet Pea was stoic for a few seconds, staring down the pain in her eyes with serious intentions, before tiptoeing into a quiet laugh.

"Well everyone thinks *I'm* feral — maybe not like a wild animal, but I climbed the freakin' drop tower ... my own brother called me psycho." Dawn's pierced brow raised. "I probably *should* be afraid of you. I mean, you could've thrown me in the pond by now if you wanted to." Sweet Pea was being honest, but she was also very aware of what was hiding in Dawn's backpack. Every word mattered.

"You know what," she said, standing up with a burst of energy. "Let's see if we can find my feathered friend. She's gotta be here somewhere."

Dawn grabbed her lantern and the girls started walking around the pond, avoiding the deep rushes and staying where the ground was passable. Sweet Pea picked up a small stick and tossed it near the edge of the water, careful not to hit the reeds where she might be sleeping. A splash rippled out, but nothing stirred in the darkness.

"So what's up with your dad," asked Dawn. "He went superhero mode for you at the park, and now a week later you're out here by yourself? That makes no sense, what are you, like thirteen?"

"Almost fifteen."

"Still — a girl like you should be watching fireworks with her family right now."

"Why does everyone say that — *a girl like me* — what's so special about being me?"

"Oh please ... live one day as me and ask yourself again."

They kept walking, almost halfway around the water now, still no signs of wildlife.

"Yeah, but you don't understand," argued Sweet Pea. "Everything changed a few days ago. Right before the darkness. All the stuff that went down when I was younger, my dad never told us why any of it happened. He basically lied to us for seven years, blamed it all on Hicks. Sorry, I mean your dad."

"Well if my dad was sent to take your car, your dad must've been messed up in something bad."

"That's what I mean, he was, but he covered it all up. Then, he got in a fight and thrown in jail, we found out he was lying, then I had a big fight with my mom and ran away. Hello swamp."

Something rustled in the tall grass up ahead, too far away for the lamp to shed enough light on it.

"You wanna know what I think?" asked Dawn.

Sweet Pea nodded as they approached the clump of trees where she had been hiding earlier.

"The world has an endless supply of shit to dish out. We're all just waitin' in line."

Sweet Pea thought about the past seven years, month after month, day after day.

Dawn backpedalled a little, not wanting to douse all the light in her eyes. "But I bet your dad's trying to make things right. Right?"

"I guess. I mean, I haven't seen him since then. I don't know what he's doing, or where he's at. He might still be in jail. I don't even know."

"Well I haven't seen my dad in seven years. At least you still have a chance."

"What if we both still have a chance?"

Dawn didn't answer.

"You know? We could try to find your dad, too, and he'd probably —"

"Nope, don't go there, I can't —"

"How come? I'll go with you."

"It's not that easy … I'm dead to him, he's dead to me."

Lantern light painted the pond as if the moon itself was back, their eyes fixed on the water's shimmering surface.

"Wanna know what I think?" said Sweet Pea, building up courage but not waiting for a reply. "Maybe we could get in a different line."

The girls were almost back to the fallen tree, having walked a full lap. Dawn picked at her eyebrow piercing, flipping it up and down with her pointer finger.

"Can't."

"Yuh-huh."

Dawn looked at Sweet Pea, half scared of her relentlessness, not used to someone standing up to her like this.

"But I never wrote back — I never even went to visit him," she sniffled.

"We don't have to just keep waiting for more bad stuff to happen," Sweet Pea said, climbing onto the tree trunk where their conversation first started. "Let's just go find our dads — together. Oh my God, that was so lame," she laughed. "Speech over, I promise."

"It doesn't work like that," shot Dawn, joining her on the tree. "It all sounds great, until you try and you try and you try but nothing ever changes. Nothing ever makes it feel better." Sweet Pea felt the momentum shifting as Dawn continued. "It's just gonna be more of the same. Then I'm back here tomorrow night with —"

"With what — your rope?" The words just came out, stopping everything. She looked at Dawn, scared of her for the first time tonight. Caught red-handed, Dawn closed her eyes and stood motionless.

"Sorry," Sweet Pea retreated, "I shouldn't have said that." It was as ghostly quiet as it was dark. "But I saw it earlier, and I just keep thinking about you trying to —" she stopped short of saying it out loud, scrambling to recover. "I keep thinking about how awesome it's been meeting you tonight, talking about our crazy lives."

Dawn's eyes slowly opened after what felt like minutes, sensing for the first time that Sweet Pea's words were ringing hollow. "It's fine, don't worry about me. I'm not your problem to fix."

"Dawn, I meant everything I said, I swear, I'm not just —"

"Give me one good reason why I should care about a single part of this bullshit life." Her voice raised at the end, challenging all the good that Sweet Pea had rallied around. She had one chance to say the right thing, to grant a saving grace, but she was at a loss. They stood like statues, waiting for the perfect words to materialize, but they never came.

Breaking the silence, a loud sound erupted from the darkness, startling Sweet Pea so badly that she grabbed Dawn's arm to avoid falling in. With a frenzied flapping of wings, the heron surged from her hiding place, parting the reeds and bursting from the water. Once she was airborne, the clamoring stopped and the stillness returned as quickly as it had been shattered.

Sweet Pea held her breath, watching in slow motion as the beautiful bird sailed over their heads, gliding from one end of the pond to the other. Her sweeping turn disappeared into the shadows, but she came back into the light for another pass. Dawn's mouth had dropped open and her head started feeling lighter, like she might float above the ground. The heron approached, lower this time, her outstretched legs skimming the water, cutting a line right down the middle of the swamp.

Splashing down across from them, she tucked herself back into the reeds, with just enough light catching her beak to show that she was still facing them. Sweet Pea balanced on the narrowest part of the tree trunk, inching closer to the heron. Her hands at her sides, she offered a graceful bow across the water, a silent expression of her gratitude.

Dawn shimmied out to Sweet Pea's position, drawn to the moment, matching her bow with a respectful curtsy of her own. Nature had never spoken to her like it did right now, as their previous conversation faded into oblivion.

Before either girl could say a word, the dull sound of an approaching vehicle stole their attention. Scurrying back down the trunk toward land, the engine grew louder and the glow of headlights started to fill in through the trees along the access road.

"Anyone know you're here?" asked Dawn.

"No — you?"

She shook her head as they exchanged panicked glances.

"Hide!"

# 31

———

THE ROUND HEADLIGHTS OF AUSTIN'S JEEP peeked into the clearing, following Gus's hunch on his sister's last-ditch hideout destination. It was his first time back here, too, since their parents never cruised to the swamp for a family picnic, and up until now, none of his friends could drive. He took in the dismal visuals and caught a whiff of the swampy odors, poignant reminders of what happened here that day. But his flashbacks weren't of blue herons, whiskered men or waiting to catch a tire iron to the head — his mind was burned with images of Sweet Pea's eyes, the fear he couldn't make go away.

"Cut the engine," he said to Austin.

Austin parked the Jeep, keeping the headlights aimed towards the pond.

"Man, it's been a while. See that tree —" Gus pointed, "that's right where we stood that day. This is crazy, it all looks the same. Grown up and creepy, but the same."

"You haven't been here since?"

"Nope."

"And you think she's gonna be here," said Austin, "doing what — sacrificing a goat?"

"I know my sister," Gus doubled down, scanning the landscape in front of them. "High beams would help."

Austin complied, lighting up more of the scene in front of them, followed by his best Obi Wan Kenobi voice, *"You will go to the Dagobah system…"*

Gus would have laughed but something caught his eye. The upended tree root was about three car-lengths in front of them, a little bit in the shadows but mostly illuminated by the headlights. An odd shape was casting a shadow near the ground on the left side.

"Watch this —" he said, standing up in his seat, looking over the windshield and clearing his throat. "Show yourself, Pea Brain!"

Sweet Pea's butt inadvertently waved hello from her hiding place.

At the sound of her brother's voice, she slowly stood up and stared into the headlights. *What? How?* She tried to piece together Gus's unexpected arrival, fumbling over her thoughts as she scrunched her face at Dawn. "It's my freaking brother."

Austin turned off the headlights, keeping his fog lights on so they could see each other without going blind. Reaching into the back seat, he grabbed her prize giraffe and hoisted it above his head.

"C'mon, it's okay … just get in the Jeep, I have your giraffe right here," he coaxed her, drawing a glare from Gus.

"Bait? Seriously?" he sneered.

"Your mom said she might not come willingly."

Gus grabbed the giraffe and tried pulling it down, but Austin resisted, as they wasted precious time grunting and wrestling over the stuffed animal.

"Hey taxi!" blurted Sweet Pea from two feet away, right at Gus's door, giving both of them a jump. "What's your rate to Culver?"

"Let's see," Gus played along, "that's a good fifteen miles, I'd say — five hundred twenty-nine dollars."

"Hold on, there," added Austin from behind the steering wheel, as Sweet Pea held back a smile. "Tonight only, we have a coupon for five hundred twenty-eight dollars off, so if you —"

"Cool, I'll owe you a dollar." Sweet Pea jumped in the back seat, triggering a wave of laughter around the vehicle, before cutting in quickly with a serious tone.

"Okay, listen up and don't freak out — someone's here with me, I'll be right back." She jumped out as quickly as she got in.

"What?!" yelled Gus, watching her bound back to the tree, disappearing once again behind the clump of earth.

Sweet Pea sidled up to Dawn, who was still in hiding — literally and from herself — keeping one eye on the pond, hoping to catch another glimpse of the heron.

"So … we're heading to town," Sweet Pea started, remembering Dawn's position on the matter. "And I really want you to come." She had more words planned, but only the important ones came out.

Dawn looked in her eyes for a split second, then back down at her feet.

"What if we find him and he doesn't want me?"

Sweet Pea thought about all the what-ifs that plagued her lost childhood, and what she would give to have any of them back. She never had a friend to push her into — or pull her out of — life's little decisions that needed a nudge or a helping hand. There was

nobody to challenge her no's or bend them into maybe's or en-
courage more yes's.

She turned to Dawn. "But what if he does?"

Time was running out on the last day of darkness, and the
spell it had cast over the skies was soon to wear off. It was already
losing its grip.

Dawn stood up, slinging her backpack over her shoulder as
she shot past Sweet Pea.

"Let's go, we can still catch the fireworks if we hurry."

A LOW-LYING MIST HAD CREPT FROM THE MARSHES, covering the
ground where the Jeep was parked. So when Austin started his
engine, the entire area glowed red, dispersing his brake lights in
every direction. Having made their slightly awkward introductions — including a brief sidebar that Hicks was her dad — they
circled the clearing for one last hurrah before leaving the swamp
behind them.

"Wait, pull over there before we go," said Sweet Pea, "I just
need a minute."

The topless vehicle pointed toward the dirt road exit now, as
Austin threw it into park along the water's edge. Sweet Pea's driver-side back seat gave her a front-row view to the pond on their
left. It was the same hair-raising setting from her nightmares, but
as she stared at it now, it almost looked fake, like a movie set. She
pictured young Sweet Pea as a character in the film, like Gus and
Hicks were, all along just reading lines and playing their parts. She
was ready for a new role.

She whispered across the seat to Dawn, "Pass me your matches — I wanna flick one on the water to say goodbye."

Dawn opened her bag and rooted for the matchbook. "Here

you go — fire away."

Sweet Pea readied her finger, striking a match and sending it like a flaming arrow over the pond, drawing *oohs* and *aahs* from the front seat.

"You do one," she told Dawn, passing them back, "then we're both done with this place."

Dawn prepared her match from the passenger side, standing up so she could fire over the driver-side occupants. With a magician's sleight of hand, Sweet Pea snatched the rope from her backpack and held it close to the other side of her body, as the boys cheered on another fiery flight and splashdown.

"Alright fellas, let's get outta here," Sweet Pea said, bundling the rope in her hands as the Jeep pulled forward.

When the coast was clear and Dawn wasn't looking, Sweet Pea ejected her stolen goods from the vehicle. Half-arming her throw, she got some good distance on it without drawing attention to herself.

*Splash!*

Three heads whipped to the sound on the surface of the dark pond.

"Those frogs are havin' fun tonight," said Sweet Pea, satisfying Gus, Austin and Dawn's curiosity with her white lie. They kept driving, more interested in the road ahead than what they left behind.

Floating on the inky water, the rope grew heavier and heavier, slowly sinking to the bottom where it couldn't hurt anyone. The hum of the engine faded into the distance, and the last glint of light disappeared, leaving the swamp as dark and empty as they had found it.

Speeding down the highway, halfway back to Culver, Austin finally paused his blaring music to change CDs. Nobody had said much of anything since leaving the swamp, content to numb their senses with Metallica in their ears and wind on their faces.

"Taking requests," Austin announced, turning on a light as Gus flipped through the sleeves in his case. He had secretly played Metallica for Feral Dawn, thinking it was the closest thing in his collection to match her piercings and heavy-metal persona, but he was hoping Sweet Pea would ask for something else.

"Got any John Denver?" yelled Dawn from the back seat, drawing side-eye stares from the group.

"Umm, no …" he called back, realizing his assumption had missed badly. "Guster, play her some Croce, close enough."

Thrash metal was replaced with folk songs, and the exit ramp emptied onto a quiet two-lane road, giving the group their first chance at conversation. Austin made eyes at Sweet Pea in the rear-view mirror.

"Barely recognized you without your ski mask on." It was his way of saying he was happy to see her and glad she was okay.

She formed half a smile, having already forgotten about the knee-jerk ending to their last encounter, but nobody could tell she was blushing in the dark.

"Speaking of…" Austin continued, "I must say, Gus, your sister is a total badass. You could learn from this girl."

Gus shook his head, amused by Austin's need to entertain.

"I mean it — first she's friends with Mindy Dipetto, and now Feral Dawn. That's some serious shit right there."

"You can drop the *Feral* part," corrected Sweet Pea. "Her name's just Dawn."

In Dawn's whole lifetime, nobody had stood up for her before, so it was a new sensation to know that someone had her back. But something Austin said was distracting her from fully enjoying the warmth of the moment.

Dawn spoke up. "Dipetto? I know that name —"

"Yeah, she goes to Piedmont," said Sweet Pea.

"No, wait … oh my God…"

Dawn unzipped the front pouch of her backpack and grabbed a handful of her dad's letters. Sweet Pea handed over her flashlight as she sorted through the envelopes, scanning pages and paragraphs like a dog who had picked up a scent.

"Here," she said, pointing to a section, reading to herself while everyone else waited. Sweet Pea could tell this was important to her.

"Okay, this is from one of my dad's prison letters," she announced before reading aloud to Sweet Pea, Gus and Austin.

> … *Missing you more than ever this morning. My friend Eddie went to heaven last night. You would have liked him a lot, he even had a little girl at home, same age as you. We talked about getting the two of you together sometime after we got out. Can't believe he's gone. R.I.P. Eddie Dipetto…*

She had Sweet Pea's full attention now.

"Damn, that's messed up," said Austin. "*Hi honey, my friend just died.* Kinda dark."

"I don't think he had anyone else to tell," said Dawn, "so his letters were like, I dunno, his way to get things off his chest."

"What was his daughter's name?" asked Sweet Pea, her stomach on the verge of plummeting.

"He never said, but there's more," said Dawn. "A couple years later when I was in juvie, I heard some guards talking about him, so I got closer and listened, because that was my dad's friend. I mean, I didn't know the guy, and I barely knew my dad at that point, but that part of his letter stuck with me."

Culver was just a few miles ahead now, as they passed a development on the outskirts. Austin turned the music all the way down. "What'd they say?"

"The one guard was talking about 'that Dipetto guy that got shanked,' said he knew the whole story. Basically, there was a hit out on Eddie — may he rest in peace — and a bunch of guards and inmates knew about it and went to the warden, 'cause everyone liked him. And it wasn't the first time, either, so warden put in for a transfer. They were sending him to another prison, you know, for protection."

"So how did he end up dead?" asked Gus.

"Judge denied it. Last minute. The whole thing was set but the judge had final say because it crossed counties. Later that night, they stuck him, right in his bed."

Sweet Pea's pulse ramped up with each piece of the puzzle that her brain completed.

"Which judge?" asked Austin, more serious than usual.

"Don't know, they didn't say."

They didn't have to.

Dawn looked to Sweet Pea. "I always wondered how that little girl from the letter made out. Do you think that's your friend?"

Sweet Pea didn't answer, desperately replaying every word Mindy had said about her dad, wondering why she wouldn't have told her he was dead. But it had to be her. Then she pictured Austin's garage door, and it made even more sense. *Oh God.* Her throat tightened as her last words to Mindy repeated in her head: *He deserves whatever he got. You don't hear me whinin' about my dad.*

Her stomach churned as she took a few deep breaths, trying to reset her system as her head flooded with guilt. For all the trouble that came along with Mindy and crew, and as righteous as Sweet Pea felt jumping out of their car, now *she* was the terrible friend. If Mindy spray-painted her house next, she would understand why.

"Pitch-Black Palooza in two minutes," Austin said with a scratch in his voice, breaking a silence that had put a damper on their drive.

"We were supposed to meet Mom and Dad half an hour ago," said Gus. "Main stage, let's hope they're still there." He turned to his sister. "You good, Pea?"

She nodded, wiping tears from her eyes.

"I'm good."


DISGUISED IN GLASSES, HAT AND BEARD, Phil and Liz had been tailing Hicks long enough to know he liked unicorns, blue cotton candy, and apple cider. They also knew it took him eleven minutes to conduct his business in the porta-potty, as they watched and waited for the door to open from across the street. But none of these details gave them a clue to what he was up to, which was making Phil angry.

"Let's go see what he knows. Just talk to him. Simple as that." Phil was tired, and the longer they followed him, the more he was forced to look at him. And the more he looked at him, the longer he thought about their exchanges at the Thunderbird. Hicks had played him like a fiddle and he knew it — from the ridiculous demand for three thousand dollars, to his damning lies to the police, to the hidden truth he revealed to Liz.

"I don't think that's a good idea," she replied, talking louder now as they were on the move once again, almost back to the main stage. "The boys should be here, let's just worry about finding them. Forget Hicks, maybe they found Pea."

The crowd had almost doubled since the band started, sprawling further out so there was no beginning or end to the audience. It seemed like everyone in a full block radius was a Hemlocks fan, taking over the streets with Nirvana t-shirts, air guitars and pop-up mosh pits. Phil and Liz were getting swallowed by the scene, along with Hicks, as the throng of people funneled them all towards the same area near the street clock.

They were close enough now that the speaker stack vibrated their chest cavities. A wall of people formed ahead of them, forcing Hicks to change direction, slowly migrating back toward their position. Phil put both hands on Liz's shoulders, steering her around bodies, trying to shift left or right, but they were pinned in by a few groups that had no intention of moving.

"*Stop* — you're pushing me into them," she grunted.

"We need to get over there," he vented, eying an open pocket to their right, but they weren't going anywhere. A small cluster of people were all that separated them now.

"*Thank you, Culver! We are the Hemlocks!*"

The wild reaction sounded more like a Three Rivers Stadium concert than a local music festival. Phil stared hard at the back of Hicks, a mere ten feet in front of him, who was scanning the other direction for a way out. A smooth riff hit the air, repeating and building tension as it plunged the group into their next song.

"*...Come ... as you are ... as you were...*"

The people in between them launched a moshing session, throwing their bodies, colliding, falling down, getting up, then doing it again.

Phil stared into the mosh pit, thinking they were idiots, but at the same time wishing he was ten years younger and right in the middle of it. Taking in the chaos, a gap in the action allowed him to see straight through to the other side of the circle that had formed. Hicks stood right across from them, the twelve o'clock to their six, looking through the same gap, glowering towards Phil. A few moshers criss-crossed in front of them, but when it was clear again, Hicks' eyes had shifted to Liz. Was he randomly staring at people in stupid disguises, or had he seen right through them?

Phil and Liz exchanged words, almost shouting in each other's ears, debating the effectiveness of their hidden identities and what to do next. Phil's tolerance level bottomed out.

"I'm done," he said, tossing his hat and glasses to the ground in the same motion as his decisive step forward. A random shoulder caught him the instant he entered the pit, but he kept his feet, throwing a forearm into the ribs of another shape flying at him from the right. Driving his legs like a halfback, Phil planted a hand to avoid going down as the mosh pit spit him out the other side. A few kids steadied him as he stood up straight, instantly stepping to Hicks with an adrenaline-fueled glare that he held like a psychopath. He leaned in, their foreheads nearly touching, reading every line on his enemy's face.

"Where is she?"

Hicks took his time, still not intimidated by Phil's best shot. "Get outta my face," he said over screaming guitars. If he was amused by Phil back at the Thunderbird, this time around he was just annoyed.

Phil stood firm, his mind clouded by the delusions of his Sweet Pea theory, convincing himself every second that he had his man. Three days of self-induced torment had pushed him to the brink.

He gestured toward the unicorn. "Who's it for?" he demanded without breaking eye contact.

"None of your goddamn business."

A long, distorted note hung in the air as the frontman addressed the crowd.

*"Alright everyone, we're gonna play one more ...*
*Give us a minute here..."*

A hand yanked the tail of Phil's shirt, pulling him backwards just enough to break up the standoff. Liz let go and wedged herself in the middle, prying them apart as she leaned into Phil.

"Hey!" she barked at her husband, trying to catch her breath. "Let's go — NOW."

Phil regained his position, facing Hicks in the same battle stance as before they were interrupted, but his eyes couldn't get past Liz. She spoke to him without saying a word, slowly talking him down with a blink of her lashes. His temperature dropped, suddenly forgetting why he was here, surrendering to her spell like he did when they met in tenth grade.

Hicks took a parting shot. "Yeah Suburban, do what the bitch says..."

Liz fired a pointer finger that landed an inch from his nose, ready for war, but Hicks was in no mood to be lectured. Swiping his big right paw at the finger in his face, he made more contact than he meant to, with more force than he realized, catching Liz with an open hand to the chin. She stumbled to her right, catching her foot on someone or something, falling sideways and gaining momentum as she tried not to go down. With all eyes in the crowd fixed on the stage, waiting for the encore, nobody caught her fall or slowed her headfirst plummet into the base of the cast iron clock. A heavy, metallic *thump* put Liz on her side.

The entire block wailed as The Hemlocks erupted from their short break with a raw, powerful hook, joined by four thundering hits of percussion, before launching their final assault on the Pitch-Black Palooza. Phil ignored the sonic melee, paralyzed with fear at the sight of Liz's motionless body. He could go to her side … or go after Hicks.

A second wave of adrenaline powered up his fists like an arcade game street fighter. Teeth clenched, he lunged with the first right hook he'd ever thrown in his life.

# 32

———

LETTING LOOSE A BATTLE CRY, Phil struck a brutal blow to the side of Hicks' head as angst-ridden lyrics poured kerosene on his white-hot rage.

> *"... With the lights out ... it's less dangerous ...*
> *here we are now ... entertain us..."*

The oblivious crowd sang along while Phil reloaded and fired a hard cross to his jaw, then another, unleashing years of pent-up anger.

He'd always wondered what it would feel like to hit someone, if he could really go through with it and hurt somebody if he needed to. But now that it was happening, it didn't feel real — like his body was doing things while his brain looked the other way.

This wasn't Hicks' first fight, stumbling backwards but mostly absorbing the punishment. Phil admired his own handiwork half a second too long, as a counterpunch smashed the bridge of his nose, buckling his knees and flooding his senses with stars and the taste of blood. Phil tried to steady himself, but a driving shoulder stood him up straight. He tried to guard his face, but Hicks had already swung, connecting bare knuckles to his left eye socket with a *crunch*. A sharp pain rattled through his teeth and skull, and before he could figure it out, a left uppercut buried into his abdomen, doubling him over and down to one knee.

Phil's eyes blurred over and ringing filled his ears as he struggled for air. He felt like his lungs were already at the bottom of a deep breath, ready to inhale, but nothing happened when he tried. Gasping to breathe, he put his hand to his chest as Hicks lurked.

"You know, Suburban, I was probably done with you," he said, hovering over him with his fist cocked and monologue ready. "When you didn't pay up the other day, and we had our little encounter with the law, I actually moved on. But thank yourself," he sniffled, wiping a streak of blood from his cheek. "I'm back."

Phil looked up, trying to convince himself he wasn't in pain, fending off the panic in his throat as he waited to get his wind back.

Hicks leaned down closer. "I'm gonna make your life hell, and there's nothin' you can do about it."

LIZ KNEW SHE WASN'T IN HEAVEN, because everything was pitch black, but she didn't think it was hell either, since she felt calm and peaceful, wherever she was. The muffled sound of electric guitars buzzed around her head like flies trapped in a jar. Wrapped in darkness, she touched her fingers together and wiggled her toes, making sure she was still in one piece. Voices passed in and out, softer, then louder, stuck in a fog that was slowly peeling away.

The smell of a nearby cigarette pulled her closer to consciousness. *"Mom,"* said a voice, more clear than the others, *"wake up."*

She felt a hand holding hers now, squeezing it, tapping on her palm, repeating her name a few more times. *"Time to rise and shine, Mrs. B,"* floated another familiar tone. *"Nice beard, by the way."*

*Gus ... Austin...* Liz slowly opened her eyes, turning on the rest of her senses, as a tidal wave of pain gushed from the top of her head. She slammed her eyelids shut, wincing out loud and scrambling back to her semiconscious state. Still on the ground, lying just how she had landed, she reached for where it hurt, touching wet strands of hair.

"Dude, she's bleeding," said Austin. Gus looked to Sweet Pea, who aimed her flashlight on their mother's wound, sharing a moment of shock at the sight of red.

"Get a rag or towel or something," he blurted to Austin, sending him sprinting to the backpack hanging from Dawn's shoulders.

An angry, unpolished guitar solo blared from the speaker stacks, bending and squelching like it came from Kurt Cobain himself.

As the boys were occupied with Liz, a scary thought entered Sweet Pea's head: *If Mom's here and Dad's not helping her, he must be in trouble, too.* She turned her eyes to the sea of people around them, still bobbing and swaying in unison to The Hemlocks. To her left, she saw a group of people pushing and shoving each other, so she shined her beam into the mosh pit looking for her dad.

Something behind them caught her eye, as she shuffled her feet around the circle for a better view. A shadowy scene made her stare harder: one man down on a knee, another man standing over him in a threatening position. Her blood surged as she got closer, realizing with squinting eyes that the man with the high ground was Hicks. She didn't need to see the other face to know she'd found her father.

Hicks raised his fist, poised to deliver a knockout blow, but before he could swing, a blinding flash of light forced him to shield his eyes. Seizing the opportunity, Phil sprang up, planting his shoulder into Hicks' gut and sweeping his legs out from under him, driving him to the ground with a swift *thud*. Flat on his back, he scrambled to defend himself but Phil lunged on top, pinning his arms.

He wanted to say something cool before he hit him, like a movie fight, but he just hit him — hard — driving his fist with a bone-on-bone crack. Bloodied and defenseless, Hicks sputtered curse words when he was silenced by Phil's hands around his throat.

Locking eyes with his opponent, Phil was consumed by a torrent of shattered memories as he tightened his grip. His mind drifted back to Gus and Sweet Pea playing squirt guns, hearing her laugh, feeling Liz at his side and the warmth of the sun — but they faded to black. This was the revenge he thought he wanted, the darkness he hoped he was capable of. Funneling more anger through his fingertips, he held his breath as a wave of guilt blindsided his conscience.

All around them, the crowd pulsed in unison, still throbbing to the driving chords, swaying as the last words of the song repeated.

"...*A denial ... a denial ... a denial...*"

Phil's mind went numb, dissonance firing in every direction, when a gentle touch landed on his hands. Calming every nerve under his skin, he loosened his stranglehold on Hicks and turned his gaze to the shape of a girl kneeling in front of him. Her hands slowly pulled his from Hicks' throat as he succumbed to whatever power she was wielding.

The last guitar note disintegrated as a voice bellowed across the P.A. system:

*"Are you ready for some fireworks?! Three … Two … One!"*

The first shells exploded high over Lincoln Square, showering the night with neon trails of red, pink and purple, followed by crackling white light.

Phil managed a disoriented glance through his one good eye that wasn't swelling shut, making out Sweet Pea's face in the flickering glow of fireworks. A mixture of emotions bounced between father and daughter as they slowly stood up, still holding hands.

"Hey," she said.

"Hey," he hesitated.

Sweet Pea started to say more, but Phil pulled her in tight, hugging her like he'd been gone a lot longer than three days. More fireworks exploded over their embrace, providing all the makings of a picture-perfect moment, except for the fact that Hicks was still lying at their feet.

Beaten and wheezing, he crawled out from under them and gathered himself a few feet away. His neck felt like it had been hit with a sledgehammer, as a cough sent him clutching at his throat. Catching his breath and seething in pain, his eyes landed on Phil, who was still buried in a hug. Hicks stood and slowly approached from behind, eying up a clean suckerpunch or a chokehold of his own.

Before he could do either, he froze at the sight of another girl who had approached, stopping right in front of him, staring like she knew him. Normally he would have yelled "get the hell outta here" or "mind your own damn business" but something was different.

His heart pounded like a drumbeat, staring into the same eyes he'd memorized from the photos he kept in his prison cell. He saw every detail now, reflecting the colorful explosions overhead, realizing with a gasp that his daughter was all grown up. Abandoning his plan of attack, Hicks turned to Dawn, mouth agape in a dumbfounded trance.

She had come this far, but the last step between them loomed as a bittersweet reminder of the years they'd spent apart. Dawn fought back tears as her bottom lip quivered. Seeing the emotions on his daughter's face, his eyes welled up, too, instantly scared of what was next. *What if she doesn't want me.*

Without warning, Hicks took a few steps back, hanging his head before turning away, then disappearing into a thicket of people whose eyes were glued to the sky.

Dawn's heart sank as tears spilled out, tiny sobs erupting as she watched Sweet Pea and her father sharing the moment she almost had. *This whole thing was a mistake,* she cursed herself for believing she deserved anything close to a normal life.

Before another tear hit the ground, Hicks pushed back into the clearing, leading the way with the biggest stuffed unicorn that Dawn had ever seen. Sweet Pea looked up, cheering on her friend from the swamp.

"*Whoa,* somebody won you a prize!" she called out, which was all the encouragement they needed. Dawn's tiny sobs turned into full heaves, changing over to laughter, then back to sobs, as she ran to her father's open arms. Sweet Pea gawked at Hicks in full girl-dad mode, holding his daughter, wondering how the Beverlys spent the last seven years being afraid of him.

More artillery shook the ground as the Pitch-Black Palooza's grand finale boomed, blanketing Culver in a million tiny stars. Phil and Sweet Pea stared at the sky, basking in their reunion, when both their internal alarms sounded.

"Mom!" she gasped, shooting a worried look at Phil, who was already a step ahead of her. The mosh pit had dispersed, clearing a direct path to the base of the clock, and a clear view of Liz, Gus and Austin. Phil hobbled over to where she was, clutching at his ribcage, feeling each breath leave his lungs as he knelt by her side.

Liz sat with her back against the same iron base she'd head-butted, as Gus and Austin stabilized her on each side. Blood smeared her forehead and cheek, but she still smiled at the sight of her husband's arrival.

"She's okay," announced Gus, addressing Phil's worried look.

"Gonna have a killer headache, but she's good," added Austin, speaking through the pink beard he commandeered.

Phil was stunned to see his wife injured and bloodied, forgetting what he must have looked like to her. She winced back at his closed eye, the open gash across his nose, and the blood caked on his lips and nostrils.

"Hey," she spoke softly, extending her hand, "I saw you over there." Their fingers intertwined, the first time in years. "Pretty sure you kicked his ass."

Phil pushed a smile through his swollen face. "Sure doesn't feel like it," he said, applying pressure to his nose. "But when I saw him hit you, I just lost it, I don't know…"

*"Oh, Phillip,"* she purred.

Gus noticed their intimate exchange. "Good Lord, she's calling him Phillip. Mom definitely has a concussion, right Pea?"

In her semi-concussed state, Liz almost forgot about Sweet Pea. They finally shared a glance as she stepped out from behind Phil, waving her fingers with a sheepish smile, not sure if she should be happy, or scared, or sorry, or sad. It all mixed together somewhere behind her eyes as she crumbled at her mother's side, gently curling into her arms.

"Excuse me, folks," interrupted a voice from behind them. "Ma'am, are you okay?" asked a police officer, noticing her injury. Liz nodded her head slowly, trying to keep the pain level from worsening. He looked at the rest of the group, stopping when he got to Phil.

"Sir, what happened to your face?"

"Oh, nothing," said Phil.

Turning back to Liz, the officer was concerned. "Ma'am, did this man hurt you?"

She looked at Phil, sending him a wink as they recalled their last Q&A with the police. "Oh my God, no, he's my husband. I just fell, he's helping me." He squeezed her hand and winked back.

Hicks had been watching intently from a few feet away, waiting to see if Phil was going to point the finger or not. The officer noticed his bloodied face as well.

"Hey you, come over here," he yelled at Hicks.

Hicks trudged onto the scene, flanked by Dawn, both carrying nervous looks as the officer looked him up and down.

"And what happened to you?"

Hicks looked at Phil, telegraphing a reminder that neither of them could handle assault and battery charges in their current states of release.

"Moshing, officer," he deadpanned. "Me and my friend here were moshing."

Phil chimed in. "Got a little rough in there."

Sweet Pea looked at Dawn, stifling a giggle.

Whether or not the officer believed either of them, he seemed content with the situation, advising all three of them to visit the paramedic before they went home. With a raised brow, he wished them all a good night, leaving the group in their own awkward company.

Smoke lingered as The Hemlocks packed up their gear and vendors hung around, hoping for one last sale. People filed out in all directions, while Hicks, Dawn, Austin and the Beverly crew stayed and chatted, still coming down from their adventurous evening. Most of the conversation took place between the teenagers, as the adults pretended they hadn't just tried to kill each other.

Dawn and her dad stepped away for a private talk, giving the Beverlys some family time, as well. Nobody pushed too hard on Sweet Pea or asked about her escapades. None of them were all the way innocent, anyway, so they were all content just being together. Hicks returned with a serious look on his face.

"Hey Suburban —" he started before Dawn elbowed him. "Mr. Beverly," he corrected himself. "My daughter tells me that your daughter…" he paused, choking up, "…saved her life tonight." Everyone turned their eyes to Sweet Pea. "Said she almost drowned in a swamp, and your girl pulled her out." Sweet Pea found Dawn's eyes welling up, same as hers, acknowledging the hidden truth between them. "So," he stepped toward Phil, "I don't usually do this with guys like you … but you and me are square."

Phil's first incredulous look went to Sweet Pea, followed by a second incredulous look back at Hicks.

"Shake my damn hand before I change my mind."

"Square," said Phil, applying a firm grip to the delight of their families. "And this way — bonus — you don't have to worry about getting your ass kicked again." Nobody knew if Phil was kidding at first, but Hicks' sly grin triggered a wave of laughter as he delivered a playful — but painful — slap on his back.

"One more thing," Hicks continued, giving his full attention to Liz. "Back there, I didn't mean to — I was just trying to push your finger out of my face — you know, I would never hit a —"

"Apology accepted," Liz smiled, never imagining in her lifetime that she would hear Bruce Hicks apologize.

As the adults engaged in more smalltalk and compared battle scars, Sweet Pea spotted a familiar face walking across the street, making eye contact with Claire as they were leaving.

"Mom, Dad — look," she said, pointing to the Wexlers halfway across the street. Claire had alerted her parents to the Beverlys, too, as both groups saw each other now. Phil and Liz smiled and waved with bloody faces while Sweet Pea stood next to Dawn, the same person who three days ago called Claire a "dumb piece of shit" and growled at her father. Tom and Bonnie's eyes popped, and without reciprocating a hello, they grabbed their daughter and whisked her away from the dysfunctional Beverly family. Again.

"I don't think I'll be invited to Claire's house anytime soon," laughed Sweet Pea. After a few snide comments and Wexler jokes, everyone realized at almost the same time that they were exhausted and ready to go home. The group said their goodbyes, as Dawn and her dad left on a new path together.

"Call me," she said over her shoulder to Sweet Pea, who held her hand to her head like a telephone. Watching her friend disappear around the corner, she finally allowed herself to relax and let everything start to sink in. So many things that could have gone horribly wrong, finally went wonderfully right.

Walking toward the street where they parked, Phil put out his arms to stop the group in its tracks.

"Wait!" he yelled. "Stay right here, I'll be back in two minutes."

"Phil —" Liz whined.

Already running away, he called back. "Two minutes!"

"I swear, that man's bowels aren't right," mused Gus, shaking his head as they plopped down on a bench.

*"C'monnn, Dad,"* Sweet Pea sighed, realizing she was minutes away from completing her journey home. She started thinking

about her bedroom, her pillow that smelled like her head, her giraffe she slept with since she was five, her other *new* giraffe and where he would sleep. Even Hubbard's wagging tail crossed her mind.

Breaking the silence, two vehicles screeched around the corner, jerking to a stop across the street from their bench. The group whipped their heads to see a police car block in a black Camaro, as doors flew open and three figures fled the scene. Sweet Pea held her breath as she watched the officer chase down and catch one of them from behind, grabbing a handful of backpack that hung from the girl's shoulders, as the other two got away.

*Please be Rosie,* she wished, but as the officer turned her around, his headlights framed Mindy's anguished face. They all stood and stared, realizing this was *the* Camaro, and that was Sweet Pea's crew, but nobody said a word as it played out in front of them.

Sweet Pea, Mindy's graffiti accomplice, should have walked away or hid her face, but she couldn't stop thinking about the god-awful way their last conversation ended. She never would have said that about her dad if she knew he was dead, but words have consequences. Seeing Mindy this way — the wild cheetah finally held in captivity — sent an ache to her stomach.

"Young lady, hands behind your back, please," the officer said politely, reading her rights and rattling off a slew of charges that had finally caught up with her. His words faded out, waking Sweet Pea's conscience, reminding her that she wasn't innocent, either.

He continued. "Mind if I take a look inside your backpack?"

Mindy slouched against the police car. "Knock yourself out, amigo."

"Yes or no, Miss," he clarified.

"Sure, why the hell not."

He opened her backpack, pulling out a ski mask, spray paint and a bottle of whiskey. Mindy's gaze wandered to her surroundings, ignoring the evidence, scanning the small crowd that had gathered across the street. She passed over all the gawking faces until she met Sweet Pea's blank stare. The girls locked eyes. Sweet Pea expected Mindy to flash angry, bitter, blaming looks at her — but her eyes were just sad and forlorn.

"Who else was with you tonight?" the officer questioned her. "We know there were four of you, and two of your buddies already left you here. Where's your other helper?"

Sweet Pea's heart pounded, realizing she could be next. Mindy said nothing, still holding her gaze.

"Look, give me some names and we'll see what we can do for you," he tried again.

Mindy looked down, replaying her three-day whirl with Sweet Pea, and the crushing words that ended it.

"It was just me. I did it all."

The officer shook his head. "Last chance…"

Mindy paused under the flashing lights, faintly squinting as she stared back across the crowd. Sweet Pea waited, eyes wide, blinking back tears as the corner of Mindy's mouth lifted into a soft smile. On the verge of caving in, Sweet Pea returned the same smile, a beautiful exchange of subtlety, undetected by anyone who might have seen it.

"Have it your way," he said, opening the rear door and motioning for her to get in.

Mindy looked deep into Sweet Pea's eyes, gave her a nod, then ducked her head into the patrol car and disappeared.

Sweet Pea went weak, not knowing which of her emotions to listen to, but she noticed that the pressure in her head was gone, and her shoulders relaxed a little more. Before anyone could say a word, Phil sprinted into sight from behind them, blaring like a foghorn.

"Who wants funnel cake?!"

Sweet Pea had forgotten — who could blame her — but seeing her dad with paper plate in hand and powdered sugar flying, brought his promise rushing back.

"Sorry, that was longer than two minutes, but they were closing and —"

"Gus thought you were taking a dump," said Austin, forcing smiles from Phil and Gus.

"Why are boys so disgusting," muttered Liz.

"Funnel cake, please," Sweet Pea beamed, stepping first in line and tearing off a chunk of golden-brown delight. In between bites, she glanced up at her dad's gracious eyes, or eye, as the rift between them felt smaller and smaller. Liz went next, enjoying the waffle-like treat as it melted on her tongue.

"Oops," said Phil, wiping powdered sugar from his wife's chin and smearing it on her nose. Gus and Sweet Pea exchanged quick glances of shock and amusement, as their parents leaned in for a kiss. Liz's cheeks flushed pink and she closed her eyes, tilting her head as Phil followed suit until their lips met in a gentle kiss. Still going, the smooch lingered to the warm disgust of their children.

"Okay, this is gross," prodded Gus, imploring them to stop.

When they finally pulled back and opened their eyes, they were standing alone.

"Hey!" yelled Phil, catching a glimpse of three shapes running to the Jeep.

Liz took his hand. "Ah, let 'em go, what's the rush," she said, leaning in for another kiss.

"*Ouch ... nose...*" Phil readjusted, reaching to stroke her hair.

"*Mmph ... not there...*" flinched Liz, pulling his hand away from her banged up head.

As the last of the crowd shuffled around them, smiling at their bodies pressed together, the Pitch-Black Palooza was over, and the only thing missing was a romantic sunset behind the silhouette of the happy couple.

# 33

——

AFTER THREE DAYS OF CONTINUOUS DARKNESS, every living thing was ready and waiting for what used to be the most certain of happenings: a sunrise. The Earth and her ocean's had dipped a few degrees, the animal kingdom was all out of sorts, and mankind — especially the Beverly family — was ready for a redeeming dose of Vitamin D.

When they got home, Phil, Liz, Gus and Sweet Pea were so exhausted they couldn't sleep. Physically, mentally and emotionally flattened, they just laid in their beds staring at their ceilings. So, at some point in the middle of the night, they all migrated outside to the back porch, occupying a pair of rockers and two cheap folding chairs, commiserating in the dark.

"What time's the sun supposed to come up," asked Sweet Pea.

Phil pressed a button on his watch, putting off a green glow. "We still have a little while, but we should be getting some twilight any minute now."

"With everything we've been through, it better be coming," said Liz.

Sweet Pea stared across their yard, over the swingset at the hovering sky, waiting for the faintest change.

"Even if it doesn't, I'm good for a few more days. I kinda got used to it."

"Yeah right," said Gus, quickly realizing he didn't know much about his sister's recent whereabouts. "So what *were* you doing the last couple days? Like, where did you sleep last night? Night before last, actually."

Liz interjected. "Gus, let's not —"

"That's okay, Mom," she said, "I got nothin' to hide from you guys. Whatever happened, happened." She looked right at Gus. "Slept in a barn."

Phil changed the subject, trying to prevent family time from becoming a confessional. "Let's just watch for the sunrise. We all need this."

"Okay," Sweet Pea gave in, "but while we're waiting, you each get one question. Ask me anything."

Phil and Liz shrugged at each other.

"Mom, you first."

Liz hesitated, going over her multitude of worries from the past seventy-two hours. "Alright, I'll play. Did you do anything dangerous or illegal?"

"That's two questions," said Gus.

"One question, two parts," Liz argued.

"Dangerous … *hmmm* … well, Stache drove pretty fast sometimes. That Camaro was wicked."

"Stache?" asked Liz. "You were riding with someone named Stache?"

"Yeah, he was pretty cool. I don't even know his real name, but he had a thin little mustache. Like black licorice."

Liz raised her brow at Phil.

"Anyway," Sweet Pea continued, "there was that, and then this weirdo JP who was creeping on me at the big party when I got abandoned. He was nineteen." She reflected with a long pause. "That was actually pretty scary."

Liz gulped. "Maybe we should talk about this tomorrow," she said, not wanting to know more until she was mentally prepared.

"Nah, it's fine Mom, that's about it for danger. For illegal stuff … let me think… "

Gus was loving this game, realizing with each admission that he was racking up get-out-of-jail-free cards for the rest of his years at home.

"I did take some of the money that Mindy stole from the petting zoo, so I guess that was illegal. And Operation Krylon was illegal, but I didn't really do — "

"*Shhhhhh* … it's starting," said Phil, halting her self-incrimination and gazing into the distance.

Everyone stopped talking and looked to the sky.

"It's still black," said Gus, not seeing it.

"No, close your eyes for a few seconds, then open them."

They complied, going black behind their eyelids, then opening them to the slightest hint of color.

"That's dark blue," Liz bubbled, more excited than she expected to be.

Sweet Pea saw it, too, her eyes widening. "Yep, that's definitely lighter than it was a minute ago."

Gus finally nodded along, somewhat slightly stupefied. "Deep, dark, blue."

They kept staring, knowing that the faintest hint of light signaled the beginning of an unstoppable crescendo, like a flame finding its fuel.

Purples and lavenders gradually materialized from behind the horizon, mixing and folding into the blues, reminding them of the artistry they'd taken for granted.

"Dad, your question," continued Sweet Pea, basking in the realization that the darkness was on its last breath. Their eyes were still locked on the eastern ridge line, anticipating the first slice of sun, as they slumped back in their chairs.

"Okay," he said, steering away from any dangerous and illegal subject matter. "When you ran away, who did you miss more — me or your mother?"

"Hey!" Liz blurted. "Objection!"

Sweet Pea laughed. "Umm, I'd have to say … Mom." Liz pumped her fist. "Dad, you're disqualified since you were in jail."

The family that not so long ago was hanging on by a thread, was thoroughly enjoying their own company as the sky blossomed. Pinks and oranges snuck onto the canvas, filling in beneath the low-level clouds, giving vivid clues to the spot where the sun would soon be arriving. The longer they watched, the more the clouds came to light, stretching for miles in swirling hues, a stunning contrast to the corners of sky that hadn't yet awakened.

"My turn," said Gus.

"You already went," replied Liz, still in damage control mode. "She slept in a barn?"

"Nuh-uh, that was before she said we each get one."

"He's right," admitted Phil. "Ask her something Gus, then we're done."

He nodded at Sweet Pea, who nodded back. "You said ask you anything…"

"Yep, give it to me."

"On a scale of one to ten…" Gus paused to heighten the drama. "How big is your crush on Austin?"

"I knew it!" burst Sweet Pea, an ear-to-ear grin taking over. "You're so predictable."

"Did we miss something?" Liz asked Phil. "I mean, Austin and Pea — I guess so — that would be better than the Stache boy."

Gus sent his sister a look of approval, even if he would never say it out loud.

Sweet Pea cut their moment short, whipping a finger straight out. "Guys, there it is!"

A sliver of pure light broke over the horizon, led by the deepest orange glow they'd ever seen — maybe because their eyes had been focusing too long on darkness, or maybe the sun had saved its energy for a dazzling return while its dimmer switch was turned down. The Beverlys squinted as the sun rose, inch by inch, deliberately taking its time, bathing Culver in golden yellow that was worth the wait.

"Hello, dawn," said Phil, wiping a tear as he put his arm around Liz, beaming at his kids, silently vowing to never screw up his second chance. It was hard to tell who teared up or who stared too long at the sun, but they all rubbed their eyes for one reason or another.

"Dawn..." repeated Sweet Pea, staring at the colors of the sky like she had just solved a riddle. "Be right back." Jumping up from her chair, she disappeared into the house as the screen door slammed behind her.

"I'm afraid to ask," said Liz, closing her eyes and resting her head on Phil's chest. The sun had only been up for a few minutes, but the warmth on her face felt better than anything in the universe. She had almost drifted off to sleep, when the screen door slammed again.

"Okay, back to the sunrise," sighed Sweet Pea, plunking down in her chair, excited about the brown package in her hands. Opening the paper, she grasped her soaps, studying their colors, their textures, taking in their scents all at once. She knew there was something special about Miss Aurora's gift, but she had been trying too hard to find it. The Mindy connection turned out to be wrong — sure, the gold and purple soap seemed like a meaningful match to her cheetah skirt and eyeliner — but she had missed what was right under her nose.

Turning the bars over so the banded labels faced front, there they were, side by side: *Sweet Pea and Dawn*. An electric rush pinged from her toes to her fingertips. With a shudder, Sweet Pea realized that she might not have gone back to the swamp if it weren't for Miss Aurora. Which meant Dawn's evening could have ended very differently. Which meant both their dads' nights could have as well. Maybe it all happened for a reason, the way it was supposed to, like someone or something was working them with invisible strings.

"Thanks, Miss Aurora," Sweet Pea said quietly to herself. But she couldn't help wondering — did she find Miss Aurora or did Miss Aurora find her?

Liz had gone into the house to fetch her own memento from the day. Stepping back outside, she crouched down in front of Sweet Pea.

"Hey, we have something for you," whispered Liz, as she and Phil presented their flea market treasure to their daughter.

"Aww, that's so pretty," she said, not recognizing anything special, but appreciating it all the same.

"Honey, this is a Sweet Pea flower," her mom explained. "We found it when we were looking for you. At the old flea market, of all places, growing in the dark."

Sweet Pea wrinkled her brow, connecting dots.

"Straight from Miss Aurora's Soapery," added Phil. "And Apothecary, whatever that is."

She took the flower, holding it up, studying its delicate beauty like a jeweler, completely in love with its gentle fragrance. The velvety soft petals seemed to dance in the air, fragile yet confident as they opened ever so slightly toward the sunbeam shining on their shoulders. Sweet Pea smiled, respecting the darkness it had survived and appreciating the sunlight that traveled ninety-three million miles to get here.

It was the perfect beginning to a new day for the Beverly family. Daylight chased away the night, laughs and smiles replaced lies and tears, and a warm hopefulness soaked their skin that they hadn't felt in seven long years. Like it was the sun's way of saying, *thanks for not giving up on me.*

Mother, father, sister, and brother slouched back in their chairs, drifting off to sleep with morning sunshine — finally — resting on their eyelids.

# EPILOGUE

*One year later*

---

GREASE DRIPPINGS FLARED UP FROM THE GRILL, searing the hamburgers as Phil watched over them, spatula in hand. He couldn't decide if he should move them out of the center to a safer space on the grates, or try and let the flames lick them to perfection. As he toiled over the burgers, indecision riddling his forehead, Liz approached in her signature summer tank top — today's color was somewhere between melon and coral.

"Need help?" she asked, applying a soothing hand to his back.

"Maybe," he said, still studying the ground beef. "Play it safe or perfect sear?"

"Skip the grease fire. Nobody cares what they look like."

"Good call, babe." He shuffled the patties to safety.

She pecked him on the cheek and walked away, continuing to prep the yard for company. Fetching extra chairs from the garage, she caught a glimpse of yellow pulling into the driveway, as booming bass announced Austin's arrival. Liz waved through the open garage door and took the folding chairs back to the picnic area.

"Burgers done?" she asked, rushing past Phil.

"Cheese going on now. Sounds like Austin's here."

"Ya think?"

Coming through the garage and into the back yard, Austin greeted Liz and Phil with a container of brownies.

"What's up, Mr. and Mrs. B," he said from behind his aviator sunglasses. "Fresh out the oven, baked 'em myself."

"Wow, thanks Austin, you didn't have to do that," said Liz.

"Tricked you. I bought 'em on the way over."

"Wow, some trick," uttered Phil.

"I'll let Gus know you're here," she said, instantly realizing her mistake and shaking her head. "Sorry, I keep forgetting." Austin laughed it off as Liz walked to the porch and called through the screen door. "Sweet Pea … Austin's here…"

As if she'd been waiting backstage to hear her name announced, the back door opened and Sweet Pea flew out, swooping right over to Austin, happy as a lark. They paused their hello kiss before it started, side-eying Liz instead who had infiltrated their space.

"Go ahead, you two. Don't be shy."

"Oh my God, Mom, stop."

The moment passed, so they settled for awkward nods, followed by a twelve-step handshake that Austin taught her last fall on their third date.

Phil closed the lid on the grill. "I put cheese on all the burgers, so I hope everyone's okay with that."

"Mine's pepper jack, right?" Gus yelled from the kitchen, eavesdropping through the open window above the sink.

"No, everyone's getting American."

"I asked you twice…" Gus vented, busting outside to scold his father. "If Sweet Pea asked, you would've." He turned to his sister. "No offense."

"None taken. I know I'm his favorite."

Phil went into self-defense mode. "That's not true, I don't play favorites."

Gus pounced on the softball. "Right, I forgot … you play the underdogs."

A collective *ooohhh* went up from the crowd.

"Gambling jokes, nice," Phil groaned. "That's okay, Gus, I deserve it, and I still love you — even though you're a dick sometimes."

Another *aaahhh* followed the counterpunch. Phil looked at Liz. "He's almost eighteen, I can say that now, right?"

She ignored the question with her hand stuck to her forehead.

"That's it," Gus said, fake anger filling his eyes. "I'm climbing the drop tower and running away."

*Ooohhh* they reacted to another jab.

Austin took Sweet Pea's hand, half expecting her to need comforting after Gus's dig, but then he remembered — this was Sweet Pea and these were the Beverlys. Seconds after slinging mud in every direction, they were all smiles and giggles, fully enjoying their verbal boxing match.

"Oh, Phil — better check those burgers," reminded Liz.

He opened the lid and tended to the grill, admiring his work. "Okay, they're ready — should we wait for everyone? Pea, she said they were coming, right?"

Before Sweet Pea could answer, a voice yelled from the garage.

"Said *who* was coming?" Dawn stepped through the doorway carrying a covered dish, followed by her dad, dressed in a collared shirt with Sears embroidered on the pocket.

"Dawn!" called Sweet Pea, running over and landing with a

hug. Phil looked almost as excited to see Hicks.

"*Bruuuuuuuce,*" he exclaimed, greeting his former rival with a forearm bash like they'd just hit back-to-back homers. "Glad you guys could make it. How was work — sell any refrigerators?"

"No, but I tackled a shoplifter on my lunch break. I was walking by the Radio Shack and old Ralph, the security guard, was chasing some guy towards the arcade … what's it called…"

"Aladdin's Castle," chimed Austin.

"Yeah, well he didn't make it. Couple of those Walkmans went flying across the floor."

"Nice job," said Gus, extending a high five.

Hicks took his seat beside Dawn at the picnic table, passing her a napkin and plasticware that her place was missing. The summer sun beat down on them all as they filled their plates and fished cold drinks from a big red cooler. Pleases and thank yous were exchanged as dishes of food passed left and right.

Two bites into his burger, Hicks got Phil's attention across the table. "Suburban, forgot to tell you — I brought your miter saw, it's in my truck."

"Okay, you can keep it if you still need it."

"No, I'm finished, thanks. And another thing — you're gonna be Phillip from now on. No more Suburban. You know, it's kind of — I don't know…"

Dawn finished his sentence. "A constant reminder that you stole their vehicle and kidnapped their children?"

"Well, I suppose," shrugged Hicks.

"Darnit, I always loved Suburban," said Phil. "It makes me feel tough. How about something else, though, not just Phillip." He took a bite of potato salad, deep in thought. "I know — Thunderbird."

Liz wasted no time objecting. "So you want to be named after the place where our marriage almost ended and you got arrested?"

"Phillip sounds good!" he obliged, drawing a round of laughs and wiping sweat from his brow before planting a kiss on his wife's hand. As the chatter was dying down, Dawn stood up, nervously awaiting everyone's undivided attention.

"Guys, I have something I'd like to say." The afternoon had been anything but serious to this point, but Dawn's hands were shaking now as the tone suddenly shifted.

"Umm, this year was the best year of my life … Sweet Pea … I wouldn't be here without you, you know that." Tears formed around the table. "You and your family have been so kind to me, and, here we all are, so I just wanted to say thank you. For like the hundredth time."

Phil led a small round of applause, as Liz placed her hand on Dawn's shoulder.

"But there's something else," she continued. "Mr. Beverly, you're not the only one at this table with a name that doesn't really fit you any more." Dawn turned and looked down at her dad. Hicks sat up straight as his face went flush, not ready for what was happening.

"Dad —" she started but choked up, waiting until her voice worked again. She had rehearsed this part in her head for days. "I didn't know what to think about us a year ago, how it would work — or if it would work." A tear ran down Hicks' face, remembering their lives before he got sucked into the mob job. "But getting to know you again, and having a father again, just having you in my life has been the best thing ever." She heaved a deep breath of air to settle down but her heart was racing. "That's why I've decided…" she slowly exhaled, "I want to have your last name."

Hicks sat stunned, but his expression softened. "You want to change your name?"

Dawn nodded, waiting for him to catch up. "When I turn

eighteen or however that works. If that's okay with you."

"Dawn Hicks," he said with a crackly voice, two words he never thought would leave his mouth. "Honey, you don't have to do that for me. Are you sure?"

"Hundred percent. And I'm not doing it for you." A calm came over her. "It's for us."

He stood up and took her hand, pulling her in for a hug that almost pulled the vinyl tablecloth off the picnic table.

"*Whoooohooo!*" yelled Austin, breaking the tension as everyone joined in with a pile of hugs and congratulations for the Hicks family. Sweet Pea tried not to stare, but she couldn't take her eyes off of Dawn and her dad. She was happy for her friend.


As FAR AS SUMMER PICNICS GO, the Beverly's version checked all the boxes.

Everyone stuffed their faces with too much food, with Gus earning the crown for most food stains on his shirt. Brown bottles lined the table, not so coincidentally right where Phil and Hicks were sitting, emptied in part by a dozen or so bromance toasts to each other.

A game of two-hand touch football took place, that almost had to be four against three, but Rotty showed up just in time to make teams even. The Beverlys lost to the non-Beverlys, highlighted by Rotty's tight spirals to Austin, and Hicks' lead blocking on Dawn's four touchdowns. There was a close call on one play when Austin tackled Sweet Pea and he flashed back to Ski Mask Night (as it came to be known), covering his midsection with cat-like reflexes.

After the football game, a water battle royale materialized, pitting every man, woman and child against each other. Rotty's

A-shirt was drenched, Sweet Pea hid somewhere new where Gus couldn't find her, and Liz disappeared during the middle of the game to sneak an ice cream sandwich inside the house.

If they were looking for the perfect ending to a perfect day, it came in the form of Rotty's homemade blueberry lattice pies. Going around the table, he earned an average score of 9.85, with six perfect tens and a nine from Gus, who blamed the pie for falling off his fork and landing on his shorts.

As the grownups were saying their goodbyes, Sweet Pea and Austin snuck into the garage for a goodbye kiss where Liz couldn't stalk them.

"I'll call ya later," she said, pressing her lips to his one more time.

"Later, Paisley," he said, gently dropping her fingers and walking to his Jeep. She liked when he called her Paisley. And she liked kissing him in the garage.

The engine roared and the woofers came alive, as Austin stood up in his seat, looking at Sweet Pea over the windshield and drawing a heart in the air. She giggled and drew one back, then went to find Dawn, who was talking to Liz and Phil.

"Hey, you ready?"

"Yep, we can take my dad's truck," said Dawn. "He said he'll get a ride home with Rotty."

Phil held up a finger. "Pea, if you're going to Pet Depot, can you grab Hubbard's food?"

She nodded with an *ugh* and rushed off.

"Wait, here's the money," he chased after her, handing over the cash and telling her to be safe and not stay out too late.

"I know," she said in a hurry, before slowing down for two seconds to turn around. "Thanks ... love you."

Phil watched their truck back out and drive down the road

— not the first time that Sweet Pea left in a hurry with a Hicks at the wheel — laughing to himself at the funny way things work out sometimes.

SWEET PEA AND DAWN WALKED INTO PET DEPOT about five minutes before closing, so they rushed to the dog food aisle and found Hubbard's brand. Sweet Pea volunteered Dawn to carry the twenty-six pound bag, who obliged without making any jokes about upper body strength. On their way to the checkout, they passed the kittens, with barely enough time for a passing *meow*.

Dawn slammed the bag on the counter and startled the worker, who didn't see them coming.

"Dudes, you scared the shit outta me." Mindy caught her breath as Sweet Pea and Dawn cracked up. "I'm done in like two minutes, then we can roll."

"Nice shirt," Sweet Pea said, as Mindy rang up the dog food.

"You don't have to point that out every single time you come in here," she snickered. "I *love* my Pet Depot uniform," she fibbed, rolling her eyes. "Twenty-nine ninety-nine, please."

"Wow, she even says please," teased Dawn.

Mindy smiled at Dawn while Sweet Pea fished in her pockets. "Got your dad's truck again?"

"Yeah, he lets me drive it when he's not working. You still saving up?"

"Two more months, I think I should have enough by the end of October," said Mindy.

Sweet Pea chimed in. "Has your dream car changed or is it still the little white one?"

"Eighty-six Honda CRX, Greek White with sunroof. My mom knows the guy selling it, he said it's mine once I have the money."

Sweet Pea was thinking ahead. "That's nice, a two-seater. For the three of us."

"Who said you're riding in it?" Mindy fired back with a sly grin as she rushed off to the back room. "I'll meet you guys outside!"

Dawn and Sweet Pea lugged the dog food to the truck and waited in the cab for Mindy. Sweet Pea thought about the first time they met, at the kitten cages, and all that had happened since then.

"You know, I pick on her but maybe I'll apply here, too. Just like weekends or something."

"You and Mindy on the same shift would be fun," laughed Dawn. "And you'd have your own little petting zoo there if you got bored."

"Good point," she replied. "Here she comes."

Mindy climbed into the open bed of the truck, backpack over her shoulders, sliding the rear window open so they could talk.

"Hey, on the way to the park, can you swing by the cemetery real quick?"

Dawn gave a thumbs up as they left the parking lot, taking a slight detour from their evening plans, but nobody minded. Mindy's hair blew in the moving air as she tried to forget about cleaning reptile cages and focus on her next stop. It had been ten years since her dad died, and for nine of them she either avoided his gravesite altogether, or only went with a bottle in her hand. But now, each trip was a little easier than the one before.

After a few miles, they pulled off the road at the cemetery, as Mindy jumped over the tailgate before the truck had even stopped. Jogging up the green hillside, she followed the familiar path to her dad's stone, having learned it well over the past six months. She passed a big dead oak tree that scared her when she was younger, but now it just looked like arms reaching up to heaven.

Approaching a small, modest headstone engraved EDWARD J. DIPETTO, she sat cross-legged on the ground in front, looking eye-to-eye as if it were him. Sliding her backpack off her left shoulder, she unzipped the front pouch — her Jack Daniels pouch, as she used to know it — and pulled out a small bunch of plastic flowers.

"Hi, Daddy … these are for you."

She placed the flowers at the base where they wouldn't blow away, adjusting them a few times until they looked just right. Mindy looked up at the pale blue sky, still shedding daylight but the sun was on its downward path toward the horizon.

"Sorry, I don't have a lot of time tonight — Dawn and Sweet Pea are waiting, we're heading over to the park."

She inhaled the evening air, running her fingers over the smooth granite marker.

"Every time I see Dawn's dad, he says 'Eddie would be so happy' that we're friends. So … I really do hope you're happy up there."

Her lips pressed together as she tried not to cry.

"Sweet Pea's really nice, too, you would like her a lot. She's the one that wrote me all those letters last year when I was away. I read a couple to you here that one day. All those people I thought were my friends — not one of 'em wrote or visited me. She was the only one. I've never told her that."

Mindy's body shook with silent sobs, her eyes tightly shut.

"And the crazy part is that me and Sweet Pea only knew each other for like a week. I was basically nobody to her, I don't get why she even cared. But she did.

"I know you can't answer me, but you would be so proud of me, Daddy, I've been tryin' so hard. You know — to be good."

She waited for another wave to pass.

"I made honor roll last two marking periods ... regular honor roll, not the high one yet ... I'm saving money from my job, lookin' at a car ... I haven't had a drink all year long, I swear ... and I'm even being nice to Mom."

A tiny laugh broke through the tears, as she looked back at the oak tree, following the lines of its branches.

"Anyway ... we're gonna go ride some rides and eat some funnel cakes. I don't wanna keep them waiting too long."

Mindy stood up with a sniffle, running her fingers through her hair as she looked down, resting her hand on his stone, the only piece of her father she could touch.

"Love you and miss you," she whispered, taking a deep breath, then letting it out slowly, counting backwards from ten, before running down the hill to where her friends were waiting.

THE LINE AT THE FAMILY CASTLE funnel cake stand was longer than they expected it to be, but Dawn thought the guy working the register was hot, so they waited anyway. Sweet Pea stared across the midway, drifting off as the sky slowly darkened and the rides turned into spinning blurs of warm yellow light.

They'd already ridden the bumper cars on repeat, played a dozen games of Skee-Ball in the arcade, and talked to a few kids they knew to kill some time. Their summer routine only had a few more weeks left before it was back to school, and since they all went to different schools, they wanted to wring every drop. Their funnel cake was finally served, as three hands tore it apart like vultures.

"So what are doing tomorrow," said Dawn.

"Beats me," Sweet Pea replied.

"I don't care," said Mindy, noticing the time. "Hey, they're closing soon. One more ride?"

"Okay," said Dawn. "Pea, your turn to pick."

Sweet Pea shrugged. "Pirate ship again?"

"Something we haven't done yet," Dawn countered. "How about the tower?"

Mindy kicked her shin and elbowed her ribs.

"Shit … sorry, I'm an idiot, I didn't —"

"It's okay," laughed Sweet Pea, "yes, the Turret of Terror is right over there, we don't have to pretend it's invisible."

"But … you haven't gone up since, right?" asked Mindy.

"Actually, I rode a couple times with my cousins from Ohio. When you guys weren't here."

Dawn and Mindy stared down her lying eyes until she caved.

"Fine, no, I haven't. Big deal."

Dawn argued. "Must be if you're lying about it. Right to our faces, I might add."

"Cousins from Ohio," laughed Mindy. "It's cool Pea, let's just hit the bumper cars, no pressure."

Dawn apologized. "My bad for bringing it up. Slip of the tongue."

Sweet Pea had thought about it all summer long — every time she heard the screams of the falling riders, or walked in the shadow it cast across the park, she was right back there, hanging upside down a hundred feet up. As far as she'd come the past twelve months, the tower was the last dragon left for her to slay.

"Let's go, I'm doin' it."

Dawn and Mindy backpedaled again, insisting she didn't have to, feeling guilty for forcing her hand if she wasn't ready.

"Dude, seriously —" sputtered Mindy, but Sweet Pea was already running toward the tower.

"She's doing it," huffed Dawn, taking off after her in a full sprint. Halfway there, she almost ran over a kid eating a bucket of french fries, barely dodging him at the last second. Mindy brought up the rear, stealing a fry as she passed him. *That doesn't make me a bad person,* she thought, downing it in one bite without breaking stride.

When they finally caught up to Sweet Pea, she was standing at the base of the tower, gazing up at the mighty beast. Before anyone could say a word, a *crunch* of metal rang out above them as the ride plummeted to a screaming halt right in front of them.

As the riders exited, Sweet Pea faced her friends. "Now boarding the Turret of Terror … take your seats, ladies."

Dawn and Mindy had wondered all summer when it might happen, so they were in a happy shock that it finally was. Now *they* got to be there for Sweet Pea, to help her through something, like she had done so many times for them. They just hoped she didn't have a panic attack halfway up.

Moving toward the first row of three-across seats, the girls climbed in and pulled down their harnesses. Sweet Pea studied the apparatus above her head, trying to figure out how she even got up there last year. *Maybe they Pea-proofed it,* she wondered.

"You good?" asked Dawn.

Sweet Pea was a picture of confidence.

"No, really," said Mindy, "don't be puking on me or anything."

The worker made his rounds, checking their buckles and pulling up on their harnesses to make sure they were secured. When he got to Sweet Pea, he stared hard like he'd seen a ghost. She stared back, realizing with a rush of embarrassment that it was the same guy from last year.

"Hi — remember me?" she chuckled, scaring him off with a half-crazy look. "I promise I'll stay in my seat this time!" she called out as he completed his checks on the other side.

The girls laughed and made faces at him as he gathered himself at the control panel and started the ride. A loud *clang* echoed as the platform began its hundred-and-forty foot climb, instantly putting a serious face on Sweet Pea. She reached out in both directions as Dawn and Mindy read her mind, locking arms for the journey upwards.

"Not to get all mushy," Sweet Pea said, kicking her feet, "but I really love you guys."

"More than Austin?" teased Mindy, prompting their locked arms into a playful nudge.

They were higher than the treetops now, offering a front-row view to the unfolding sunset, a majestic display befitting their castle surroundings.

Sweet Pea elaborated. "For real, I know everyone says it, but let's always be friends. No matter what."

"Nah," said Dawn, "this is it for me. I hate you both." Their locked arms nudged in Dawn's direction this time.

Staring at the burning sky as they crossed the midpoint, Sweet Pea used the bird's eye view to find her house across town. She knew their black roof and the shape of their long back yard from the dozens of times she rode as a kid. She wondered what her parents were doing — probably kissing, they did that a lot now. And Gus was probably playing Nintendo or practicing new ways to insult their dad, while Hubbard slept in the hallway, waiting for her to get home.

Her daydream popped as she realized they had reached the height she climbed to last year, about forty feet from the top. Other parts of that day were foggy, but the aerial images in her mind were perfect matches to her current view.

"This is where I was," she murmured.

"You shoulda carved SWEET PEA WUZ HERE on the ladder," said Mindy, slapping a smile across Sweet Pea's serious face.

As they kept ascending, Sweet Pea was so high and the sun was so low, that she wasn't staring up and it wasn't shining down — they were finally on the same level. Squinting straight across at the last slice of the deep orange ball, remembering the three incredible days of darkness, Sweet Pea silently thanked the sun for coming back and painting more beautiful pictures for her.

"Almost there," said Dawn.

The platform came to a stop with a deep *clang* signaling the end of the climb. Every second at the top was precious, knowing it wouldn't last very long, that the bottom would drop out at any second. Savoring the moment with her friends at her side, Sweet Pea stared out across the Culver landscape, her heart pounding for what lied ahead.

"Guys, when we get to the bottom —"

*Crunch!*

*A*

 *A*

 *A*

  *A*

  *A*

   *A*

   *A*

   *G*

   *H!*

They disappeared from the sky, screaming all the way down to a whiplashed landing. Sweet Pea caught her breath and finished her sentence.

"Let's do it again."

# NOTES AND ACKNOWLEDGMENTS

Sweet Pea's story almost didn't happen. Like so many aspiring authors, I hit a wall near the second act and convinced myself that I sucked at writing. That voice was so loud that I abandoned my manuscript for TEN YEARS, thinking about it every now and then, but never finding the courage to pick it back up. Then I turned fifty.

Call it a midlife crisis or just a palpable fear of dying before my characters' fates were told, but something clicked and I found my groove again. A year later, I discovered how good it feels to actually finish writing a book. Like, really good. I think I smiled for three days straight, gushing to people whether they cared or not, "Hey — I finished my book!" So ... apologies to everybody around me who endured that giddy phase while resisting the urge to roll your eyes or tell me to get lost.

I want to thank all the people that contributed, in big ways or small, to help me reach the finish line:

My beta readers, Megan and Emily, for their plot checks and character discussions when we were supposed to be working.

My CMO (Chief Motivation Officer), Darren, who made me trust the creative process again, even the parts of it that make you feel like crap on a regular basis. Additional thanks for the fancy headshot on the last page!

My cover illustrator, Kate, for taking my AI comp and turning it into something only a living, breathing, human being could do. And a wonderfully talented one, at that.

My original cover illustrator, Irine, whose beautiful work graced the first edition and continues to live on the shelves of my earliest readers. Thank you so much for being part of this book's initial journey.

My older brother, Roland, for providing the science behind the sun's weak-force hiccup. (Check out his own books, the *Lincoln, Fox and the Bad Dog* series.)

My younger brother and former Sheriff's Lieutenant, Ben, for his expertise on police procedure and criminal charges. (Retired State Trooper, Pat, thanks for your help in this area as well.)

My parents, for our thirty-three phone calls discussing each new chapter the next day during my dog walks.

My son, Ethan, for inspiring the ~~rude insulting~~ playful father-son banter where Gus always wins.

My daughter, Olivia, for binge-reading the final manuscript in a weekend and writing a *New York Times* level analysis, pointing out cool things I did that I didn't realize I was doing.

And my wife, Shannon, who listened to me read each new chapter out loud, usually when she was already in bed, but graciously paused Netflix every time.

Last but certainly not least, my deepest thanks to every single reader who picked up this book and followed Sweet Pea's story all the way to these final words. I truly hope you enjoyed the ride and found some characters to root for along with way. Remember to be kind to one another, even the people who might not seem to deserve it — you never know who you might bump into at a dark, spooky swamp someday.

DUSTIN M HESS is an accomplished Brand Manager and Marketing Copywriter in the plotless, characterless world of industrial absorbents. He's written thousands of mundane product descriptions and sleepy corporate pitches to pay the bills, but *Sweet Pea and the Three Days of Darkness* is his first book. It earned critical acclaim from his teenage daughter, who sent him a detailed five-page analysis and a selfie of her crying at the ending.

## CONNECT

dustinmhess.com
dustinmhess
contact@dustinmhess.com